THE SERAPH'S COAL

Pamela Gordon Hoad

Also by in the Harry Somers series

The Devil's Stain
The Angel's Wing
The Cherub's Smile
The Martyr's Scorn
The Prophet's Grief
*****

First published 2020 by Silver Quill Publishing

www.silverquillpublishing.com

A CIP catalogue entry of this publication is available from the British
Library

Cover photograph copyright © Pamela Gordon;

Artwork copyright © Fiona Ruiz

Typeset in Georgia

ISBN: 978-1-912513-63-5

Silver Quill Publishing

With love,

in memory of Harry Gordon

and for Peter Hoad

Acknowledgements

I should like to record thanks to the friends who have supported me during the process of writing and preparing *The Seraph's Coal* for publication. As with my previous books, I owe a particular debt of gratitude to my son, James, who raised many useful points on the draft, both as proof-reader and historian, and to Oliver Eade, who advised on innumerable matters, technical and literary.

In the course of my topographical researches for this book Peter and I visited Bordeaux and the surrounding area. I should like to record thanks to those we met there who assisted me with information and ideas. In particular the staff at the Office de Tourisme in Cadillac were immensely knowledgeable and helpful. I must also record my sincere gratitude to Juliette who returned my camera to me in Scotland after I left it in the bistro at Castillon!

I am very grateful to readers of my earlier books in this series – *The Devil's Stain, The Angel's Wing, The Cherub's Smile, The Martyr's Scorn* and *The Prophet's Grief* – who have expressed their enjoyment of those stories and encouraged me to continue the tale of Harry Somers.

Any errors are of course my own.

CONTENTS

Prologue

Part 1 Aquitaine 1453

Part 2 Westminster, Windsor, London and East Anglia 1453-4

Part 3 Windsor, Westminster, Saint Albans, London and Hertford 1455-6

Part 4 London and across the Narrow Sea 1456-8

Epilogue

Principal characters in order of appearance or when reference is first made to them

Harry Somers, *physician, investigator and chronicler*

Piers Ford, *wheelwright, acting as Harry's assistant in Aquitaine*

*John Talbot, Earl of Shrewsbury, *leader of the English forces in Aquitaine*

*King Henry VI of England

Andy Armstrong *English soldier in Aquitaine*

Lord Richard Palgreve, *leader of a troop in Talbot's army*

Ned Bartley, *sergeant in Lord Palgreve's troop*

*King Charles of France

Monsieur Guillaume Coustances, *farmer from near Aquitaine*

Madame Marie Coustances, *his wife*

Rendell Tonks, *sergeant in Lord de Lisle's troop*

Bess Willoughby, *widow of Robin Willoughby, in attendance on Lady Maud Chamberlayne in England*

*Richard Plantagenet, 3rd Duke of York, *rival to Duke Edmund of Somerset, in England*

*Lord de Lisle, *son to Lord Talbot, with him in Aquitaine*

Sir John Baldwin, *leader of a troop in Talbot's army*

Sir Guy Binwood, *English governor in Cadillac*

Jasper Coote, *officer in Lord Hanwell's troop*

Lord Hanwell, *leader of a troop in Talbot's army*

The marquise de la Baule, *French noblewoman living near Cadillac*

The late Mathilde de Crézé, *companion to the marquise*

Perkin, *steward at Harry's manor of Worthwaite, Suffolk*

Thomas Chope, *master carpenter in the City of London*

Dame Elizabeth, *Perkin's wife, at Worthwaite*

Georgie Antey, *Perkin's assistant at Worthwaite*

Mistress Ursula Bateby, *lodging at Harry's manor*

The late Kate Somers, *Harry's dead wife*

The late Stephen Boice, *uncle to Kate Somers and Ursula Bateby's lover*

The late Roger Egremont, Earl of Stanwick, *relative of Lady Eleanor Fitzvaughan*

Gaston de la Tour, Lord Fitzvaughan of Hartham Manor, Norfolk

Mistress Judith, *formerly attendant to Harry's late wife, Kate*

*Queen Margaret, wife to King *Henry*

Gilbert Iffley, Baron Glasbury, *adherent of Richard of York*

Steward at the chateau of the marquise de la Baule

Johnny Tate, *English soldier in Lord Hanwell's troop*

Madame Claude, *resident of Cadillac*

Fishermen on the River Garonne between Bordeaux and Cadillac

Yolande, comtesse de Saint Etienne, formerly the dowager comtesse de Langeais, *French noblewoman*

Minette Coustances, *daughter of Guillaume Coustances*

Sir Nicholas Chamberlayne, *courtier at the English court*

*Edmund Beaufort, 2nd Duke of Somerset, *King Henry's chief adviser*

Madame Claude's 'protector'

*Jean Bureau, *French master gunner*

*Philip, Duke of Burgundy, Duke of Brabant, Limburg and Lothier, Duke of Luxembourg, Count of Artois and Flanders, Count of Hainault, Holland and Zeeland, and Margrave of Namur

*Lord Clinton, *Lord Talbot's deputy in command of Bordeaux*

Grizel Chope, *wife to Thomas Chope, Rendell's sister*

*Duchess Cecily, *Richard of York's wife*

Lady Eleanor Fitzvaughan, *wife to Gaston de la Tour*

Michael Radford, *herbalist at Windsor Castle*

Lady Maud Chamberlayne, *Sir Nicholas's wife, mother of Lady Eleanor Fitzvaughan*

*The late Humphrey, Duke of Gloucester, *King Henry's uncle, Harry's first patron*

*Richard Neville, Earl of Warwick, *son to the Earl of Salisbury and nephew of the Duke of York*

Mary, *maidservant to Ursula*

Hal, Dickon, Tom and Margery Chope, *Thomas and Grizel's children*

Nicky Chamberlayne, son to Sir Nicholas and his first wife

Roger of Ravensmoor, *natural born son of the late Roger Egremont, Earl of Stanwick*

Leone, *physician at Wingfield Castle, Suffolk, at one time Harry's assistant*

Father Wilfred, *Chaplain at Wingfield Castle, Suffolk*

Robert de Beaune, *Burgundian emissary*

Alys Somers

*Abbot John Whethamstede of St. Albans Abbey

Master John Webber, *apothecary by Newgate in the City of London*

Betsy, *maidservant*

*The Dauphin, Louis, *son to King Charles, heir to the French throne*

Jane, *nursemaid*

Gregory, *a mutilated man*

*Isabelle and Anne Neville, *daughters of the Earl and Countess of Warwick*

Norbert, *late servant of the Earl of Warwick*

*Historical characters recorded in the annals

Isaiah, Chapter 6, verses 5 – 7

5 And Y seide, Wo to me, for Y was stille; for Y am a man defoulid in lippis, and Y dwelle in the myddis of the puple hauynge defoulid lippis, and Y siy with myn iyen the kyng Lord of oostis.

6 And oon of serafyn flei to me, and a brennynge cole was in his hond, which cole he hadde take with a tonge fro the auter.

7 And he touchide my mouth, and seide, Lo! Y haue touchid thi lippis with this cole, and thi wickidnesse schal be don awei, and thi synne schal be clensid.

Wycliffe Bible 1382 - 1395

5 Then said I, Woe is me for I am undone; because I am a man of unclean lips, and I dwell in the midst of a people of unclean lips; for mine eyes have seen the King, the Lord of hosts.

6 Then flew one of the seraphims unto me, having a live coal in his hand, which he had taken with the tongs from off the altar;

7 And he laid it upon my mouth, and said, Lo, this hath touched thy lips; and thine iniquity is taken away, and thy sin purged.

King James Bible 1611

Prologue 1459

The summer haze blurs my view across the river. The sharp outlines of the boats plying their way downstream are softened and I imagine myself cocooned in a veil of warm and comforting silk. The sensation complements the enchantment of my sanctuary, captivating me, while in so many other places I have known, disharmony, rancour and violence persist. I cannot believe that I am here. Nor can I have confidence that this respite will continue.

Eighteen years ago I was confined within the stone walls of the Tower of London, awaiting probable execution. In my windowless cell I began to write an account of my short life and the circumstances which had brought me so close to its premature termination. When, through lucky chance and the intervention of friends, I was rescued from imprisonment, I had with me an incomplete manuscript which I never expected to finish. So much has happened to me since then that I am now resolved to compose a full description of the events which preceded my arrival in this peaceful riverside haven. My work as a physician limits the time I shall have for writing so my task may occupy me for many years. It is a commitment I readily accept and hope I shall be free to complete it.

I must not allow myself to be distracted by the movement of the water washing against the riverbank. The sight and sound bring to mind a miscellany of recollections. Many watercourses, broad and narrow, feature in my history. I have lived beside them, crossed and re-crossed them by ferryboat and bridge and on occasion I have been plunged into their depths. It will be painful to record incidents of grief and cruelty, bitter losses and disappointments: but all must be recounted.

Where I am now is not where I ever thought to find myself until the wheel of fortune directed me to my destiny. This haven offers me the opportunity to turn chronicler. May honesty guide my hand and fluency grace my words.

Addendum to Prologue 1463

Fortune has been gracious to me since I began my account four years ago so I have made good progress with my story. I have now reached the final volume of my memoirs. It still grieves me to look back at some elements of the history it must record and how they changed my life. Yet there was much that was joyful and satisfying in the years it covers. There was humour, affection and companionship as well as sadness and hurt. No human life, outside the cloister perhaps, is lived without its complement of good and evil, happiness and melancholy; and I suspect, for all we are enjoined to reverence the sainted lives of those sequestered from the world, even holy anchorites experience the confusion of seething emotions familiar to us all. I must brace myself to give a full and truthful description of a particularly perplexing time which led me at length to my refuge beside this restless river.

Part 1 Aquitaine 1453

Chapter 1

This was not the first time the man had been flogged. I looked at the whipping post as I entered the square in front of the ducal palace, carrying a handful of clean rags and a pot of salve, and I identified recent weals visible among the newly weeping wounds on the fellow's back. I noted with a professional eye that these slightly older scars had not received a physician's attention.

Long-bowmen returning to the garrison from archery practice outside the city walls stopped to glance at the scene of punishment. A few jeered half-heartedly at their colleague and a liveried servant spat in the general direction of the prisoner. Most passers-by ignored the all too familiar sight, doubtless accepting that it was their good fortune to have escaped comparable retribution for their misdeeds. The victim had begun to squirm but there must be six or seven more lashes to come. The sergeant took his time, pausing majestically between each stroke, jerking his wrist to and fro as if to improve his aim.

While I waited to play my part in the distasteful proceedings, it occurred to me that it was unusual for a man to be flogged more than once within a short period. The harshness of the penalty dissuaded casual recreants from repeating whatever misdemeanour they had committed, while those guilty of recurrent offences could expect to be hanged.

There was no opportunity for further abstract reflection. Piers Ford had joined me, his expression one of fury. He carried a flask of wine to dull the man's senses while I staunched the bleeding with astringent lotion. He was a skilled wheelwright but he had travelled to Aquitaine as my assistant. Each of us had his own reasons for leaving England hurriedly. Neither of us relished involvement in warfare but we were ready to minister to the wounded.

Reading my thoughts, Piers swore. 'Christ in Heaven, this isn't what we came here for. The army thrashing its own.' He unrolled a horse blanket.

'A dedicated physician is bound to treat anyone in need, whatever the circumstances.' I sounded pompous but was sincere.

They had loosened the ropes and were hauling the fellow away from the post, dragging him towards me, ready to fling him at my feet.

'Lay him face-down on the blanket – and gently. He's had his punishment.'

'I'd have his tongue cut out and his ears lopped off if I was Lord Talbot,' one of the soldiers said.

'Better still: string him up on the gibbet. Be done with his mischief once and for all.' The second soldier had a cast in his eye which enhanced his look of malevolence when he glared.

I ignored their comments, sent them on their way and set about my business. My patient was a slight, wiry man with ginger hair. He was already only semiconscious when I dabbed his wounds with vinegar before applying the salve and after Piers poured some of the wine into his mouth he became senseless. We carried him to my quarters in an outhouse built against the side wall of the palace. Since the English force garrisoned Bordeaux, all the subsidiary buildings round the fortified palace had been taken over by King Henry's army. The square in front of its entrance served them as marshalling point, occasional parade ground and the site for punishments and public humiliation.

'Cutting out a tongue and lopping off ears would be a fit sentence for a spy,' Piers said as he sponged the cloth where the man's blood had run down and soiled his hose.

'If he was reputed to be a spy for the French, he'd have been executed. Even if it couldn't be proved, I suspect. He can't have been accused of spying.'

'That sergeant's a vicious type. I saw the look on his face as he landed a blow. He was enjoying it.'

'Ned Bartley's his name. He came to tell me there'd be a patient ready for my attention when he'd done his duty. He's one of Lord Palgreve's principal henchmen.'

'That swine of a noble! He's known for harsh discipline. I've heard from his men how he treats them. It's a pity Jack Cade didn't have him beheaded along with Palgreve's mate, Lord Saye and Sele.'

I grunted at my friend. We had first met, nearly three years previously, at the camp on Blackheath outside London, where Jack Cade rallied disaffected men and submitted their grievances to King Henry, Sixth of that name. The rebels' demands for the law to be upheld by all men and corruption rooted out were reasonable but, when they were ignored, Cade resorted to force of arms. Later he was tricked by senior clerics sent by the King to negotiate a settlement. He died a traitor's death although most of his followers were pardoned.

'I thought you disliked violence. Isn't that why you're helping me rather than fighting alongside Rendell?'

Piers tapped his nose in imitation of the young soldier I had known since he was a boy, who had come to Aquitaine with us. 'I can't deny warriors like Rendell Tonks have their uses while we live in this misguided world. When we achieve the state of grace John Ball proclaimed, with justice and liberties for all men, there'll be no more need for fighting – and no scope for nobles like Palgreve to behave as if his followers were serfs.'

After the mischances Piers and I had both suffered since Jack Cade's rebellion, it was remarkable that he retained his belief in the pronouncements of an idealistic monk who had met his demise in another fruitless uprising some seventy years earlier. I was about to say so when my patient twitched and tried to scramble onto all fours.

'Quietly now,' I said, putting my hand on his arm. 'I'm a physician and you must rest. It'll be best if you stay here tonight so I can treat your back. You've got some nasty gashes.'

Suspicion narrowed his eyes. 'Who are you?'

'My name's Harry Somers, Doctor Somers.'

'Ah!' He subsided onto his stomach. 'The saints be praised for bringing me to you. But I must send word to the farm that I'm still living.' He had an accent I could not place although I had heard something like it years previously when I spent some time in the north of England.

'The farm?'

'The Coustances farm, just beyond the city gate to the south from here, near the convent of the Clares. I've been helping them out with some fencing. Madame Coustances needs to know I wasn't executed.' Again he tried to struggle onto his knees but groaned with the effort.

'I know the farm outside that gate,' Piers said. 'I bought eggs there. I'll take your message. I can be back before curfew.'

'God bless you, if you will, sir. Tell Madame Coustances I'll see her tomorrow: Andy Armstrong's the name. Give her the message direct. Monsieur Coustances is away from home and the daughter is a flibbertigibbet.'

Piers curled his lip in distaste at being addressed as 'sir', which he associated with those of a status he disparaged. Nevertheless he accepted his commission and set off with long lolloping strides.

My patient turned his head to look at me and I knelt beside him. 'I think you recognised my name. Had you heard of me?'

'Nothing but praise, Doctor Somers. They say you know your trade, not like most quacks with the army. Sergeant Tonks says you're an honest man, too. That's rare.'

I laughed. 'Rendell Tonks is an old friend. He spins a good tale. You'd best be wary of putting reliance on his plaudits.'

'There you are – honest, like he said.'

I brought him a stool and helped him to sit on it while I applied extra salve to the worst contusions. 'Some of your old wounds have opened up afresh with the force of

6

this new whipping. You'd best take care not to face the lash again.'

He was more alert now and looked at me sideways. 'You've not asked what crime I committed.'

'Not my concern. My task is to treat the wounds.'

'Ned Bartley claimed I'd stolen a chicken.'

Conversation seemed to brighten his mood so I humoured him. 'And you had?'

'Only in a manner of speaking: taking back what another had stolen and returning it to its rightful owner.'

This was hardly convincing. 'Couldn't the rightful owner have vouched for you if you did such a good turn?'

'There were circumstances made that difficult. Sod Ned Bartley. He bore witness against me. All lies. He's a lousy bastard.'

'How long have you been in Aquitaine?'

'Arrived with the first troop last autumn. Lord Palgreve and his men were with us and that's when I first came up against self-important Sergeant bloody Bartley.'

I had no wish to hear details of the words or blows Andy Armstrong had exchanged with Ned Bartley over the past few months.

'You must excuse me for a few minutes. I have to check on the fellows who were injured in yesterday's skirmish with the French raiding party across the river. I shouldn't be long. They weren't badly hurt. If you slump forward gently over your knees it'll take the pressure off your back.'

My patients were lodged in another outhouse further along the side-street. They were making satisfactory progress and, after I examined them, I pronounced two fit to re-join their comrades in the morning. I promised to check on the others before noon next day and opened the door to return to my quarters.

Ned Bartley was only a few yards away and when he saw me his heavy features assumed an expression which was neither a scowl nor a smile but managed to suggest both. His presence there seemed an unlikely coincidence.

'God give you good day, Doctor Somers. I've come to enquire after the wretched rogue I was compelled to flog. Is he inside there with your patients?'

Instinct made me cautious. 'No, he's not here. I treated his wounds but I didn't bring him here.'

Bartley nodded. 'Thought as much. He's as wily as a fox. Pretends to be hurt worse than he is. I should have thrashed him harder. Too soft-hearted I am when I wield the lash.'

I sensed vindictiveness in his words. 'Who sentenced him to be whipped?'

'Lord Talbot himself, no less. Some say he's a strict commander but many another would have strung the villain up on the gallows. Lord Palgreve recommended execution. Armstrong had stolen from the peasants we're here to defend – in direct defiance of Lord Talbot's orders. Thorough-going bad lot, he is. Be warned, Doctor, don't get taken in by his japes.'

There was an edge to the sergeant's final words which caused me to shudder, reminding me of those who had threatened me in the past. I was pleased to see Ned Bartley stride away towards the side entrance to the palace where Lord Palgreve was accommodated: two of a kind, it seemed, master and man.

After what his lordship's sergeant had suggested, I half-expected Master Armstrong to have vanished from my quarters with anything of value he could find, but my misgivings were unjustified. He was still crouched forward on the stool, as if he had not moved, although I could see that the documents and flasks on my shelves had been disarranged. There was nothing among them to interest an opportunist thief.

'Sergeant Bartley asked after you,' I said. 'He made out he'd been restrained with the beating he gave you.'

8

'Christ damn him! Did you tell him I was here?' He looked up nervously and flinched with the pain of the movement.

'No. He thinks you've bunked off. He's gone into the palace. Lie down on the blanket, on your stomach, and try to get some sleep. You can join your troop in the morning. Which lord's contingent is it?'

'I'm part of Lord Talbot's own retinue.' He sounded sheepish but lowered himself obediently onto the blanket and drank the cordial I gave him. 'God bless you, Doctor Somers,' he said and crossed himself.

I left him and went to sit on a bench outside the building, welcoming a few minutes in the May sunshine after weeks of rain, albeit little enough sunlight penetrated the narrow street between high walls. I had arrived in Bordeaux at the beginning of a dismal winter, travelling with reinforcements for Lord Talbot's invasion force led by his son, Lord de Lisle. King Henry had sent the army in response to an invitation from the provincial authorities who resented the taxes imposed by the French after they took control of Aquitaine two years earlier.

For generations the Kings of England had held the dukedom of Aquitaine, as they then also held much land further north, in Anjou, Maine and Normandy. The great victory at Agincourt, won by our King's redoubtable father before I was born, had consolidated this territory but, in the years since then, all had been lost, except Calais, a toehold on the coast of the Narrow Sea. Within the French King's expanded realm, only the inhabitants of Aquitaine seemed to regret the enforced change of allegiance. They were concerned about taxation but also wanted to protect the wine trade with England which was highly valuable to them.

England and France had been at war, on and off, for as long as anyone could remember. Fortunes had favoured one and then the other but the loss of Normandy three years previously was regarded as shameful by many of King Henry's subjects. This meant that the expedition

9

led by John Talbot, Earl of Shrewsbury, was charged with nothing less than the restoration of England's pride, by regaining for our King at least some of the lost lands. The Earl had made a good start, taking the French by surprise and speedily winning back the city of Bordeaux. Now he held much of Aquitaine for King Henry and had garrisoned various castles in the duchy.

Yet the situation was not secure. During the winter there had been several skirmishes with the French, as territory was won and reprisals were mounted. These encounters were likely to increase because it was reported that the French intended to lay siege to towns and strongholds which the English held. It was said Lord Talbot was confident of driving off such assaults, but sooner or later we could expect a major counter-attack. King Charles had apparently mustered his troops in Normandy, the more obvious place for an invasion by the English, but as the weather improved they would be moving south and a serious confrontation would take place. Our troops needed to be battle-sharp in readiness for the inevitable onslaught.

The outcome would be in God's hands but, whatever transpired, after any combat I would be kept busy dressing wounds which might be healed and giving what relief I could to those with injuries beyond my skill to remedy. It was not for this that I had trained as a physician, benefitting from my first patron's support to rise above my humble origins. Nevertheless, I welcomed absorption in my gory tasks, for the sake of the poor wretches I treated and because I considered that only my work helping others justified my continued existence.

I was far away from my homeland, where I had suffered almost insupportable grief, and I bore responsibility for actions there which troubled my conscience. I could not come to terms with all that had happened to me but I strove to fill my mind with immediate concerns, to drive away what could not be undone.

It helped that the setting in which I found myself was unfamiliar. For years most of my time had been spent in households, large and small, where there were families. My patients usually included women and children and their presence benignly influenced the atmosphere of my workplace and living quarters. Unlike most men, I had limited experience of entirely male-dominated establishments, except for the abbey where I had lodged once for some months. Apart from brief association with Jack Cade's assembly of the discontented, I knew little of military encampments and the hostilities they engendered. In Bordeaux, barely suppressed aggression ran like an undercurrent of menace through the garrisoned town. Intimidated citizens did their best to avoid notice and bored soldiers whiled away the hours of waiting with eruptions of bad temper and violence. I would never be at ease in such a situation, which upset me more than the Spartan nature of my accommodation, but the effort of concentrating on its challenges did at least distract me from other painful reflections.

The sun had sunk beyond the palace walls when Piers Ford reappeared. I stood up to accompany him into our quarters but he motioned me to stay where I was while he spoke to me.

'Did you manage to see the farmer's wife, as our patient requested?'

'Yes, she was mightily relieved to hear Master Armstrong wasn't dangling from the nearest tree. It seems he had permission from his captain to help at the farm while Monsieur Coustances is away. Something a bit odd there, if you ask me, more than meets the eye. We don't send soldiers to help on every farm that's short-handed.'

'Did she know what crime he was supposed to have committed?'

'Yes. That's a bit bizarre too. She claimed one of her chickens was taken by the servant of an English lord but Andy Armstrong chased after him and took it back. He'd no sooner done so when Ned Bartley jumps out from behind a hedge and takes him in charge as if he was the thief.'

'Didn't Madame Coustances vouch for him?'

'She mumbled some gobbledegook about reasons why she couldn't.'

'That's consistent with what Armstrong told me – certainly odd but not up to us to resolve.'

'I was propositioned too, at least I think so.' Piers spoke softly and rolled his eyes.

'By Madame Coustances?'

'No, the daughter: a pretty little thing of about fifteen who's apparently learned soldiers from the garrison will pay well for services she might be prepared to give. Diabolical shame! War makes beasts of honest working men and debauches virtuous women.'

'You didn't succumb, I take it?'

Piers punched my shoulder in mock outrage. 'Certainly not: I hope you know me better than that.'

I nodded, not disposed to pursue the subject. Piers had been a widower for much longer than I had and he nurtured hopes of remarrying when he returned to England, if Bess Willoughby was willing to accept him. She had declined his offer when he courted her within months of her husband's death but I believed she might relent with the passage of time. With entire justification, Bess held me responsible for Robin Willoughby's violent demise and this was one burden of guilt I would never lose.

A shout from along the street, towards the square, caught my attention. Young Rendell Tonks, now known as Sergeant Tonks of Lord de Lisle's troop, was approaching with an authoritative air.

'Can you come, Doctor Somers? One of Palgreve's servants has been stabbed in a brawl over by the inn opposite the palace. Christ knows why but Ned Bartley's asking for you to see to the fellow.'

'Of course: I'll fetch my bag.' The instinctive reply but I paused. Within the English garrison quarrels all too often resulted in blood-letting but my services were

12

seldom invoked as a result. 'Can you stay here with Piers while I'm gone? On sentry duty, as a precaution, but without making it obvious. Piers will explain.'

Rendell could sense mystery and drama at a hundred yards. He rubbed his nose with glee. 'Got someone inside needs protection? What are you up to, Doctor?'

I wish I knew, I thought, as I hurried towards the palace square.

It only heightened my unease when I realised that the servant's injuries were slight, hardly requiring a physician's attention. I formed the impression the fellow was humouring me, perhaps following instructions, and I treated him swiftly. There was no sign of Ned Bartley. I returned to my quarters along the darkened street, walking with care, and was amused to see Rendell sitting on the threshold, beneath a lit torch, sharpening on a whetstone some of the instruments I used for minor surgery.

'Thought you might like a keener edge on your knives. I borrowed the stone from the armourer across the road.' He grinned. 'Mind you, I might have used one of the blades myself if that arrogant bastard had come any nearer.'

'What happened?'

'Ned Bartley chose to stroll this way not long after you left. He said he'd seen you set off across the square and knew the injured servant would be in good hands. Nasty bit of work, he is, one of Lord Palgreve's jumped-up parasites. Wouldn't trust him an inch. He was annoyed to see me here.'

'But you explained your charitable purpose in sharpening my instruments?' I could not hide my smile.

'Yeah. I'm not sure he believed me but he didn't challenge it. Have you got old Andy Armstrong in there?'

I nodded. 'You know him?'

'Not well. We've chatted. It's generally reckoned Bartley hates him. He'd have liked to flay the life out of Armstrong but there were too many people watching the

13

flogging. We'll all know where to put the blame if Armstrong's found with a dagger in his guts one day. Can I go now?'

'Of course. Piers and I can manage overnight. We'll barricade the door to be on the safe side. Thanks for your help. I hope I haven't made you late if you've got an assignation in the town.'

For an instant Rendell looked uncomfortable. 'No, I ain't exploring the local talent. Not at the moment.' He stood, straight-backed, and saluted me.

I bit back the banal and ironic rejoinder that he was doubtless saving himself for someone special, realising with a jolt of astonishment that this could possibly be true. It was not a situation I should probe. He marched off with martial aplomb.

Common sense told me there was no reason for me to be further involved with Andy Armstrong but I had a nagging feeling that this would not be the case. At least I could ensure that, while he remained in my care, his well-being would be protected. Despite what I said to Rendell I half-expected the door of my quarters to be rammed open during the night so Piers and I took turns to stay awake and I kept one of my newly honed blades ready to hand. My mildly sedated patient snored with vigour while we watched over him.

Chapter 2

My instinctive reservations about Andy Armstrong appeared to be unjustified. He left, unhindered, at first light and over the next two weeks I heard nothing of him, dismissing him from my mind. Indeed, I had far more immediate concerns when I prepared to answer a summons to wait on Lord Talbot, Earl of Shrewsbury, in person. I had met our commander briefly when he welcomed me formally to the garrison on my arrival. I could think of no reason why he should send for me now. He had his own physician so I could not imagine he wished to call on my medical experience but I took my bag of instruments with me when I presented myself at the entrance to the palace.

Lord Talbot had chosen not to lodge in the rambling old palace where some of his senior colleagues took rooms. He was accommodated in a fine building half a mile away, in the Rue des Ayres, but he maintained offices in the ducal residence for conducting military business and it was there I was to attend him. I was duly escorted from the gatehouse through a warren of passages and small antechambers, some of which were in a shabby state with windows and ceilings in need of repair. Servitors, litigants and clerks scurried along passages and emerged from doorways looking harassed, self-important or bemused, as their concerns dictated. I wondered whether I would be able to find my way out if left without a guide.

The English did not have sole occupation of the palace. The provincial authorities responsible for the administration of justice, under the Sénéchal, Louis de Thiers, were also based in the ramshackle building. They had been established there before the invasion force arrived and it would have sent an unfortunate message to men who invited King Henry to retrieve his duchy, if they had been ejected from their headquarters. Showing admirable respect for their sensitivities, Lord Talbot had

15

selected a humble corner tower for his own use, where he was protected from the bustle of lawyers and agitated claimants demanding attention to their cases.

I expected to be kept waiting outside his audience room but was ushered into the veteran's presence without delay. He had a formidable reputation going back decades, for he fought the French in a score of battles including the famous encounters at Agincourt and Orleans. More recently he was taken prisoner during the fighting in Normandy and had been released under parole in exchange for a high-ranking French captive. I had heard he was now about seventy but some claimed he was even older. Whatever the truth about his age, he was upright and dapper, sharp in understanding, known as a master of tactics and a severe disciplinarian. With few exceptions, his men esteemed him and would follow his lead with confidence.

I bowed on entering the room, trying not to appear ill at ease. He waved me to a stool and I was surprised that he dismissed his attendants, except for the slightly-built and delicately featured young nobleman, in whose company I had travelled from England. For a moment Talbot sat quietly in his high-backed chair, appraising me, and I wished I had worn my better gown for the occasion.

'I've heard a good deal about you, Doctor Somers, from both nobility and men at arms. You have an enviable reputation, except perhaps among some who serve Richard, Duke of York. They will be known to you.'

Richard of York was a scion of the royal house who some considered had a stronger claim to wear the crown than our gentle King Henry. I had encountered him in person only briefly but formed a favourable impression of his ability and integrity. Yet, to my cost, I knew he had attracted the support of unscrupulous men who sought to advantage themselves and harm others by promoting his cause. I inclined my head in confirmation of Talbot's words, worried where this conversation would take us, hoping I need make no response at this stage.

'There may be erstwhile adherents of Duke Richard present here among our soldiery,' the Earl continued, 'but so long as they fight loyally for King Henry I have no quarrel with them. It's the French and their intentions which are my concern and I resent any diversion from this issue. I need my captains in robust health to take the field and with ability to thwart intrigues on behalf of the enemy. I believe you can assist in achieving both objectives. Have you treated those troubled with the stone?'

I drew breath at the sudden question, welcoming the focus on my professional knowledge. 'Yes, my Lord. It can be a pernicious condition but there are remedies which may assist.'

The Earl nodded but his next words were disturbing. 'You are not merely a physician, I understand, but a practised investigator. Is that so?'

'I have undertaken various enquiries, my Lord. Not always successfully.'

'Good, you don't dissemble. What I am about to tell you is known only to myself and this gentleman here.' He beckoned the young nobleman forward. 'I think you are acquainted with this son of mine, Lord de Lisle. With his elegant frame, some may think him more fit for dalliance in the court rather than mortal conflict on the battlefield, but he will prove his mettle.'

I noted the affectionate grins father and son exchanged and was charmed by the easy relationship between them despite their evident differences in temperament. Nevertheless I waited nervously for the next disclosure to come.

Talbot leaned forward in his chair and lowered his voice. 'It won't surprise you that at this cat and mouse stage of warfare, before we reach the battlefield, each side has in hand arrangements to learn the intentions of the other. Fighting men, even their high-born officers, can be suborned with gold and among the local populace there will always be some whose true allegiance lies elsewhere or can be bought. These are risks we must live with and seek to circumvent. Nevertheless it's irksome to find that within our own ranks there may be those disposed to undermine their commander, for their own advantage.'

He paused without asking a question but it was incumbent on me to say something. 'What leads you to suspect that is the case?'

'This!' Lord Talbot drew a folded letter from his gown and handed it to me. I smoothed the scrap of parchment and read:

JB has much old JT lacks
Glory will come when he attacks.
England's great champion put to shame;
T'will be RP shall win the game.

I managed not to gulp. 'How do you interpret it, my Lord?'

'I think the reference to *JT* is both insulting and self-evident and among my foremost lieutenants are Lord Richard Palgreve and Sir John Baldwin. Both are men who do not enjoy my full confidence and both are ambitious. The initials in the rhyme coincide with theirs.'

'Can you make sense of what it says?'

'All I can think that Baldwin possesses and I do not is youthfulness. He is one of my youngest captains, full of tiresome energy and over-confidence, green, immature. I've sent him to join our forces at Fronsac where we recently accepted the surrender of the French garrison. I hoped that would keep him occupied with a useful task. Lord Palgreve is a different matter. He's experienced and capable. We've known each other for years, without mutual cordiality. I can well believe he envies me command of the army.

'Where did the note come from?'

Lord Talbot scowled but not, I thought, at me. 'A week ago, two leagues upstream from here, scouts from the army encountered a rider making towards the fortified town of Cadillac which we hold for King Henry. The fellow refused to answer their questions and they took him in charge, concluding he was a French spy. When he attempted to escape they slew him on the spot – which in the circumstances is inconvenient. This outrageous note was in his pouch. They delivered it to the English governor at Cadillac, Sir Guy Binwood, a good friend of mine – I've known him for years, we fought together at Orleans. With some misgivings Guy sent it on to me.'

The Earl sank back, clearly upset, and Lord de Lisle put his hand on his father's shoulder.

'Forgive me, my Lord,' I said, 'but if the rhyme refers to men under your command who aspire to displace you, why should a French spy be carrying a copy of it?'

'His masters might find evidence of dissension among the English interesting. Perhaps he had acquired the rhyme from a dissident soldier in my army.'

'Do we know who the dead man was? Did he have other documents in his possession?'

'These are matters I should like you to investigate, Doctor Somers. I wish you to go to Cadillac. Sir Guy suffers with belly pains so you may do him good while you're there: that will be the public reason for your mission. But you will also seek to identify the rider, where he was going and from whom he obtained that – scurrilous – note. I must ask for discretion in your enquiries, however: I shouldn't want to alert the miscreants prematurely to my suspicions. How do you propose to proceed?'

'I'd like to question the soldiers who encountered the rider, to understand what led them to kill him. Are they based in Bordeaux?'

'The officer in charge has returned to Bordeaux: one Jasper Coote. He's in Lord Hanwell's company. The soldier with him is still in Cadillac, I believe. You can see him there. What do you think of the note itself?'

'The writing is in a round hand. It's likely to be that of a reasonably educated man, but not a clerk. It's consistent with the sensitivity of the subject that the rhyme was not dictated to a scribe. That may narrow the field to those who are sufficiently literate: not exclusively the nobility and gentry but most probably among them. Unfortunately this kind of derogatory rhyme is likely to have been circulated more widely. There may be several copies passing from hand to hand, each copied by a different writer. It seems essential to identify the dead rider and trace where he was given the message.'

'Do that, Doctor Somers, do that. I'm satisfied you are the right man to investigate this wretched business. I shall write at once to Sir Guy Binwood and arrange your visit. Be ready to travel in three days' time.' He turned to his son 'What have you organised, John?

Lord de Lisle stepped forward. 'I know Doctor Somers finds long rides tiresome. One of the barges which bring stone to Bordeaux from the quarries upstream will take him most of the way. A horse and escort will be provided to convey him the last few miles to Cadillac after he has concluded his visit to the de la Baule estate.'

I stared blankly at the young man and then at his father who gave a bark of laughter. 'Well done, John, to remind me so courteously of what I have so far omitted. On your way to Cadillac, Doctor Somers, I'd be obliged if you would call at the marquise de la Baule's chateau to give her my condolences on the death of her friend. It's only a few miles from Cadillac and on your route.'

'Forgive me, my Lord, I do not know of the lady.'

'She's a French noblewoman but the widow of a marquis who was friendly towards King Henry in the past. She's lived quietly at the chateau since her widowhood with a companion, Mathilde de Crézé, herself a lady of noble birth. I've been informed this lady recently died and, in view of the marquise's status, it's appropriate for me to send a personal messenger with my commiserations. It won't delay you starting your main commission. John will furnish you with letters of authority.

'I'm at your service, my Lord.' There seemed nothing else to say.

'Good, Doctor Somers. I wish you well and look forward to receiving your report.'

He clamped his jaw shut and it was clear the interview was at an end. I was flattered he was prepared to put confidence in me and I warmed to him even with his formidable reputation. Nevertheless, the situation was totally unexpected and the task before me was preposterous, unwanted and wholly daunting.

*****

I sought out Rendell when he returned from a scouting exercise outside the city. It was disheartening that, despite his absence from the immediate neighbourhood, he already knew of my visit to Lord Talbot. Effective channels for disseminating rumours within the garrison were well developed – even if the substance of the gossip was not necessarily reliable.

'I thought you might be consulting me when I heard you'd been to see the old man.'

I sighed. 'Is that how the soldiers refer to their renowned commander? He's given me a task I could do without but you may be able to help. It's confidential of course.'

'Of course,' Rendell repeated, looking cherubic. 'I'm glad his lordship's discovered your real talents. How can I help?'

'Some days ago English soldiers intercepted and killed a horseman they believed was a spy, somewhere out towards a place called Cadillac. Have you heard anything about that?'

Rendell sniggered. 'I'll say: it's been the talk of the camp. They're two of Lord Hanwell's men. Can't make out what they were meant to be doing but they're crowing about their success, or rather one of them is.'

'You know these men?'

'Yeah, after a fashion. One of Hanwell's officers was in charge, name of Jasper Coote. He's a blabbermouth, full of himself. I've come across him a few times, more's the pity. He's back in the city now and he claims all the credit for identifying a spy and despatching him. The chap he had with him is called Johnny Tate. I don't know him. He's still in Cadillac but apparently he's keeping mum while Coote brags about their little escapade.'

I thought for a moment. There would be time for me to speak to Coote before I left for Cadillac and I could see Johnny Tate when I visited the town. 'That's interesting. Talbot wants me to find out more about what happened but it's to be done with discretion so I need to be careful. It could help if you keep your ears open to gossip about the incident.'

Rendell pinched his lip between thumb and forefinger – a new gesture for him. 'Leave it to me,' he said.

'One thing you may know. Have you come across a cheeky rhyme suggesting England's great champion will be put to shame?'

'Christ! No I haven't. It's not doing the rounds among the soldiers – and it would be if someone started quoting it.'

'Interesting. Thanks; don't mention it to any one.'

'What d'you take me for? Mind, I'll expect you to keep me in the picture about what happens. Nowadays I ain't just a little lad at your beck and call when it pleases you, Doctor Somers.'

Recognition of his maturity was overdue. 'It's a bargain, Sergeant Tonks, and my name's Harry when we're working together in future.'

'Blimey! Now I am admitted to the élite. Right you are, Doctor Harry. Leave it to me.'

Rendell gave me a wink and turned to go but he looked over his shoulder as he remembered what he needed to tell me. 'I've heard ships from England are expected at Blaye on the estuary and they'll sail on up the river to Bordeaux: might be here in a day or two. I wonder if they'll bring news from home.' He gave a shrug and ran off without waiting for a reaction.

I too wondered whether there would be letters for me from England, perhaps from Perkin, the steward at my little manor in Suffolk, or Thomas Chope, master carpenter in the City of London, my friend since boyhood. Both potential correspondents would be able to give me news of events since I left my homeland and the welfare of those for whom I felt responsibility. Such news might allay some of my persistent fears – or, just as easily, deepen my gloom.

*****

Jasper Coote had already regaled half the garrison in Bordeaux with his exploits while out on patrol, but he was happy to repeat his tale to anyone willing to listen. I stood at the back of a group in the tavern where Rendell told me he was holding court and heard his well-practised account. He was a good-looking man, fashionably dressed, and he was fully aware of his attributes, revelling in the admiration of his colleagues. I tried to repress my instinctive dislike of the fellow.

'The rogue was riding quite fast and when he saw us, with the English banner we were carrying, he pulled on the reins to change direction. I reckoned that suspicious. No honest man has cause to evade English soldiers about their lawful business, here to protect all the people of Aquitaine. I shouted to him to stop but he ignored my call and headed back the way he'd come. That reinforced my suspicions and I spurred after him. You'll know the turn of speed I can achieve on a good horse – I've won many a prize both in the lists, in front of nobility, and when we've held races between our companies. There's few can match me and this scoundrel certainly couldn't.

'I came alongside and reached out to seize his reins but he managed a burst of speed which pulled him clear for a moment. Luckily I'm observant and I'd spotted that

23

nearer the river the ground was heavy after all the rain we've had. I edged him towards the bog and his horse was soon wallowing. I grabbed his reins and dragged him from the saddle. He struggled and tried to draw the knife in his belt, under his heavy clothes, abusing me in French. I punched his face, meaning to subdue him and take him prisoner, because he could have information of value to our commander. But he was a cunning bastard. He whipped a dagger from his boot and made at me, shouting for the Frenchie King Charles as he did so. I had no choice but to drive my sword into his chest. He died cursing the English and wishing perdition to our souls.'

The audience shouted in acclamation, praising Coote's courage, skill and acuity, begging him to repeat some of his narrative. He was happy to humour them and for some time he enjoyed their applause, accepting offers to refill his glass with wine along with their plaudits, until at last most of his listeners drifted away. I came forward to sit beside him.

'That's a fine tale,' I said. 'Did you discover the fellow was carrying documents showing him as a spy?'

Coote gave me an unfriendly look. 'I took his pouch to the English governor in Cadillac, the nearest town where we have a garrison. I believe they found incriminating messages.'

'Were you alone on the road when this happened? You could have been in some peril.'

Coote smiled with satisfaction. 'I had no doubt I'd overcome the rogue, physician. I know my capabilities.'

'But were you actually alone?'

He frowned, possibly uncertain whether I was seeking to belittle his achievement or augment it. 'As good as,' he said. 'A soldier from Lord Hanwell's troop was with me when we saw the rider. He followed me to accost the wretch but was thrown from the saddle and received a nasty hoof-blow to his groin from his agitated horse. He could do nothing to assist me.'

'He helped you take the body into Cadillac, I suppose?'

Coote's temper flared. 'You ask too many questions, master leech. It's not for you to know details of military operations.' He stood, thumping his glass on the table. 'Watch yourself and curb your curiosity if you're to prosper in this town. I serve Lord Hanwell and I've a mind to report your nosiness to him. You could be a spy yourself for all I know.'

With reluctance I became obsequious. 'Forgive me, officer. As you see I'm no soldier and I'm filled with admiration for your exploits. I meant no harm.'

Coote grunted and strode across the room to join other drinkers while I gave a slight bow and left the inn. I found the man obnoxious and felt sure he was hiding something but I must do nothing to strengthen his distrust of me.

*****

I made arrangements to help Piers handle any medical cases which arose during my absence. He knew the remedies I used for straightforward cuts, bruises and bellyaches, which were the most common conditions referred to me, and he had established good relations with the apothecary who supplied us with herbs. A physician billeted near the cathedral and a barber-surgeon in Lord Talbot's entourage would deal with any more complicated ailments or injuries. Despite the difficulties of the task I had been given, I began to look forward to my expedition out of Bordeaux.

Piers had taken it on himself to pay a further visit to the farmer's wife, Marie Coustances, at the farm just outside the city. He told me her husband was often away from home and she missed the assistance Andy Armstrong had given her in recent months.

'I've been able to overhaul her carts, make sure the wheels are in good condition,' he told me. 'I feel sorry for her. Her biggest worry is her errant step-daughter. It seems the girl's father lets her run wild and now she's of an age to get into real trouble. Sergeant Ned Bartley's been sniffing round the girl and she's encouraging him.'

'That's bad news. Madame Coustances isn't the mother then?'

'No, the mother died some while ago and the daughter had already grown wayward when Monsieur Coustances remarried. I think you ought to go and visit Madame Coustances when you get back from Cadillac. You might be able to advise her.'

I laughed, although I feared he was serious. 'I'm not sure what useful advice I could offer the poor woman. We'll see how things are when I'm back.'

I was glad to see Rendell putting his head round the door, preventing further discussion, and he beckoned a servant into my quarters. 'Letter for you from England, Doctor Harry: come on the ship just in. Can I wait and hear the news?'

I took the letter and nodded to Rendell as the servant went on his way and Piers excused himself. Piers would not expect to hear anything of personal relevance to him in a communication to me and he might find reminders of those in England upsetting.

My letter was from Perkin, the steward at my manor of Worthwaite in Suffolk. It had been written two months previously. Because I knew some of its contents were likely to interest Rendell, I read it aloud.

'I am pleased to report, Doctor Somers, that all is well at the manor, both Dame Elizabeth and myself being in good spirits. The winter has not been uncommonly severe and our stores are adequate. Lambing will be starting soon and the ewes are in good shape. The lad you sent to help us, Georgie, is a great boon to me and the fact that he knows his letters and can figure is valuable as my sight is fading somewhat. He seems happy here and I like to think I might train him up to take my place when it pleases our Lord God to call me to Him.

'The young woman, Mistress Ursula Bateby, is not so biddable, but Dame Elizabeth finds her company agreeable. Mistress Bateby enquires regularly whether I have news of you. I am uncertain how long I should expect her to stay at Worthwaite and, if you are able to reply to this letter, I would welcome your guidance how to respond to her.'

At this point Rendell rocked with laughter. 'Poor old Perkin! He must guess she's sweet on you. Do you think he knows what's already gone on between you?'

'Nonsense. Nothing of significance has gone on between us. I owe her a home for the time being, as you very well know, after I eased the passing of her protector, my wife's foul uncle, Stephen Boice.' I did not wish to be led into further discussion about Ursula Bateby for what I had said was not the whole truth and I was not ready to decide what I really felt about her. I let my eye travel down the page and became serious. 'Listen, Perkin has other news.

'Lord Fitzvaughan's family are reunited at their home, Hartham Manor, after their dreadful ordeal. I understand they are all well. Mistress Judith is with them and helps care for the children. At the Feast of the Nativity she paid us a visit which we appreciated. I regret to say she is not in the best of health but she is resolute in facing her difficulty. She asked me to give you her good wishes and bid you tell your friend, Sergeant Rendell Tonks, that her gratitude towards him is undying. She hopes he will find companions worthy of his wit.

I remain your devoted servant, William Perkin.'

Rendell was white-faced and I misread the reason. 'I'm so sorry Judith is unwell. That's hard after she gave my wife years of faithful service, never thinking of her own wellbeing.'

'You fool!' Rendell leapt to his feet. 'Don't you see? She's pregnant – by that bastard, Roger Egremont, who raped her. She's having to carry his devilish seed, bear a

27

brat she must hate. Oh, God, if I'd only realised how I felt about her sooner, she'd never have been in his clutches.'

'I pray God you're wrong about her condition. But I think she's realised how she values you. Doesn't that give you hope?'

'Christ, Harry Somers, you're a bloody idiot! She's bright enough to know I could never take her with Egremont's sprog. She reads me like a book. You may think it unworthy, unmannerly, but I'm just a coarse soldier. I ain't got the finer feelings I'd need to foster that vile man's bastard.'

Rendell stormed out of my quarters while I sat shattered by the confidence he had shared with me. He and Judith had bantered with each other for years, exchanging clever barbs and sparking ingenious ripostes, and I realised there was depth beneath the veneer when he killed her abuser. Yet I had not thought beyond that until more recently when it occurred to me that he might seek to court her on his return to England. I had not even speculated that Egremont's assault might have left her with child, still less how Rendell would respond to such a situation. The inextricable misery I sought to escape by leaving my homeland had not ended and others must also endure its pain.

Chapter 3

I was well used to travelling short distances by river on the Thames in the heart of London and to seeing the variety of craft that brought produce and materials from suppliers upstream, as well as sea-going vessels putting in to dock at the City's quays. My first journey by barge on the Garonne was noticeably different: much longer than the familiar ferry crossings and the river was wider, unbridgeable, stretching through acres of vineyards on higher ground with occasional clusters of buildings well back from the water. Nearer the water's edge there was profuse vegetation, long grasses bending in the breeze between clumps of trees and shrubs. I found it relaxing to sit idly gazing at the quiet scene, leaving aside for the moment both cruel memories and present uncertainties.

One piece of general news had been reported in the correspondence from England and I hoped it augured well for peace in my homeland. After nearly eight years of marriage, Queen Margaret was with child. If a boy was born and survived the vicissitudes of infancy, Richard of York's bid to be named King Henry's heir would be undermined. The machinations of his unscrupulous supporters like Gilbert Iffley, Baron Glasbury, a man I feared, would attract fewer disciples. It was a happy prospect.

The rowers had a relatively easy task, with the barge emptied of the stone it had carried to Bordeaux and the in-coming tide vigorously in our favour. Only a scatter of miscellaneous bundles lay on the deck for delivery to the quarries where a new consignment of blocks and slabs would then be loaded. The workman who supervised transporting the cargo could rest on the return journey and he came to sit beside me.

'You'd not believe how high the river can rise,' he said in an accent which was difficult to follow. 'Only two weeks ago it reached the farm over there and all those bushes were in the water.'

29

'There's been a lot of rain recently. I expect that's made everything lush.'

'Nothing unusual here. But sometimes the tides are unpredictable. There's tales told by grandfathers of enormous floods there's been some years. Yet there are sandbanks and mudflats to catch out the unwary on the river. Quite a skill it is, to bring a barge along the Garonne.'

I nodded agreement and he continued to describe inundations spreading to the walls of Cadillac and boats with a deeper draught beached on the inside bends of the river. I did not wish to be impolite but I was glad when he pulled himself to his feet and shouted to some fishermen in a small rowing-boat we were passing. The exchange was in the local tongue which I did not understand but a fellow in the boat held up a boot, laughing as he emptied its murky contents into the river, and I surmised that it was not unusual for them to catch a variety of jetsam as well as fish.

I noticed the sun had reached its zenith and soon afterwards I observed that the higher ground to the east of the Garonne was shelving upwards several feet to form a rocky cliff. Further ahead the sunlight glimmered on the turrets of a castle situated on the ledge above the cliff and I presumed this must be the chateau of the marquise de la Baule. Sure enough, we pulled in to a point where the shore shelved into the water and a man in Lord Hanwell's colours was waiting with two horses. It was necessary to clamber out of the barge into ankle-deep water and splash my way to join him.

The soldier, who was skeletal-thin, stood stiffly to attention and saluted me, holding the horse I was to ride steady while I mounted. He hauled himself into the saddle on the other animal and led the way slowly to a track which wound uphill. He spoke only to warn me when there were obstructions on the ground and, with the wind becoming more noticeable as we climbed, I decided that if I tried to converse from behind him my words would be blown away. We proceeded in silence until we approached a gatehouse.

The estate of the marquise de la Baule covered a vast area, with mile upon mile of vineyards as well as forested enclosures reserved for the chase. At its heart stood the complex of buildings where the grapes were pressed, the precious liquid stored in barrels and sampled periodically, until it was judged to be ready for drinking, where also extensive documentation was prepared to attest the unique properties of the Baulois wine. In addition there were stables, kennels, barns and miscellaneous outhouses surrounding the chateau's defensive tower and newer hall, together with a chapel renowned for housing a venerable figure of the Madonna, darkened with age. Later on I was to be conducted on a tour of these noteworthy features but when I first arrived I was awed by the obvious affluence and importance of the proprietor and did not register particulars.

'I don't expect to be long inside the castle.' I said to my companion. 'Perhaps they'll find some refreshment for you in the kitchen.'

He turned his cadaverous face towards me. 'With respect, sir, they won't let you in. They'll take your message but the lady won't receive you. She lives like a recluse, they say. Here's the gatekeeper. I'll announce your business.'

My escort's conjecture was accurate. I was taken into the gatehouse and greeted most courteously by the marquise's steward, an upright, dignified man whose manners were exemplary. I gave him Lord Talbot's message which he repeated with grave precision.

'My lady will be deeply gratified,' he said. 'It is gallant of the Earl to send his condolences by a personal messenger, a man of peace and not a soldier. She will be most obliged to him and to you for coming. You will understand that the death of her dear friend has been a bitter blow and she has retired from the world until the pain has eased. I will acquaint her with the Earl's message

31

at the earliest opportunity. May I give her the name of the physician who kindly brought it?'

I was clear from his sonorous tones that I would gain nothing by protesting. I bowed my head. 'Thank you. Lord Talbot will be grateful to you. I know he esteems the marquise greatly. My name is Doctor Somers, Harry Somers.'

The steward bowed in turn and came with me to the outer door to see me on my way. He stood watching as I mounted and turned the horse to follow my guide down the hill. I sensed his eyes boring into my back.

When we reached flatter ground I pulled alongside my companion. He told me it could take two hours to reach Cadillac as the ground was waterlogged in places and he assumed I would not wish to hurry. This was correct and it gave me the opportunity to follow up his opening and encourage some conversation between us.

'You were right about my reception at the castle. I'm glad you prepared me.'

'I've heard about the lady from gossip in Cadillac. Seems she's lived quietly here since her husband died and now she's lost her friend too. They never ventured out in the neighbourhood much.'

'Have you been based in Cadillac for long? I didn't know Lord Hanwell had some of his men out here.'

The soldier inhaled. 'I should be in Bordeaux. I hope I can travel back with you, sir. I was injured ten days ago and the quack – begging you pardon, sir – the physician at Cadillac said I must rest there as I wasn't needed urgently in the city.'

A tremor passed through me as I wondered if this was mere coincidence. 'That was hard luck. What's your name?'

He did not look at me. 'Tate, sir: Johnny Tate.'

I gripped the reins tightly but kept my voice even. 'I've heard of you. You received a nasty blow to the groin, I believe. You did quite right to rest. I've listened to Jasper

Coote's account of the incident. He's told the tale all over Bordeaux.'

'I'll bet he has.' Johnny Tate spoke under his breath but with obvious annoyance and then looked at me anxiously. 'Sorry, sir. Bit out of turn, that was.'

'Don't worry about me. I'm not a soldier. I guessed his version was focussed on his own part in the business and might be exaggerated. I'd be interested to hear your story – to pass the time as we ride.'

My companion frowned. 'I'm not one for sticking my nose into what doesn't concern me. Wiser sometimes, that is.'

The implication of his reticence was intriguing. 'I can keep my mouth shut. There've been occasions when I've had a duty to speak out, as a physician, and I did so without disclosing where I obtained key information.'

Tate gave me a thin-lipped grin. 'I can't deny I'm tempted. I've not told a soul; not seen it as my place to contradict anything Coote's said, as I might. I reckon he'll have spread a packet of lies.'

'The truth's important. I'd be honoured to hear your story.'

We had come to a standstill and he regarded me closely, assessing my integrity, I imagined. I said nothing while he made up his mind and eventually he nodded. 'Be a pleasure, sir. Jasper Coote and me, we'd been sent to ride south to Cadillac. Coote had messages to take to the governor there. He'd been second in command in the town after the English took it over, until he moved to Bordeaux a month back. We crossed the river by ferry and then rode along the right bank. Coote said we should keep our eyes open for odd behaviour by anyone we met. There'd been rumours of toing and froing by some of the locals in the land between the two rivers – the Garonne and Dordogne. Coote said some of them were unreliable.'

I was impressed by Tate's lucid description and evident intelligence. 'So you were looking for ne'er-do-wells?'

'On the alert, sir. We hadn't seen anything to worry us when we got somewhere near where we are now. That was when this hooded horseman comes careering towards us, shouting. He started waving.'

'Did you know him?'

'I couldn't see his face except for a thin pointed nose under his hood. Quite prominent, it was. I don't think I'd ever set eyes on him. I'd have remembered that nose if I'd seen him.'

'Did your officer recognise him?'

'At first he acted as if he didn't, yelling at him to stop, but he got very angry when they spoke to each other.'

'Jasper Coote did?'

'Yes, sir. The man slowed down and let Coote hold his bridle. That's when I thought they must know each other. They talked for a bit, in French. I could only understand the odd word. Then they started shouting, obviously arguing. The man's voice became quite high-pitched. They sounded really vicious – as if they hated each other.'

'Do you have any idea what they were saying?'

'The rider sounded pleased with himself at first. He patted his pouch and grinned at Coote. "Vous savez," he said several times. I could get that though I didn't know what he was talking about. Coote was more and more furious and next he whips out his dagger and slashes the fellow's throat. That's when he told me the man was a French spy and we must deliver the packet he was carrying to Cadillac. I thought we'd want to take his horse with us too so I jumped down to grab the reins but that was when the bastard animal kicked me where it hurts and then careered off along the track.'

'What about the dead man?

'Coote lugged him off his horse, pulled the hood right over his face and tied a cord round it to keep his head covered. Then he got me to help sling the body into the river. Not that I could do much, nigh on screaming with pain, I was. Don't mind telling you as you're a doctor.

34

Coote pushed the corpse off the bank and it splashed in the water. The tide took it downstream. Coote said not to bother about the horse so we rode off. I hardly knew what was happening. I passed out when we got into the town. Coote said he hoped the body would be carried all the way out to sea.'

'Did Coote open the fellow's pouch?'

'I don't remember. Not that I saw. He dismissed me to quarters when we got back to town but the guards got a doctor to come and see to me. Mind you, Coote had already said that I'd know what was good for me and I understood I was to keep my mouth shut. So I have, so far.'

'It won't surprise you, Johnny, that Coote's account differs from yours in several ways. I'd like to see how it fits together. I know it's tricky remembering details, especially when you were in pain at the time, but are you sure the man said "vous savez" to Coote? Don't make anything up but I'd like you to think hard whether those were his actual words. Say nothing if you can't be sure.'

Johnny Tate looked me straight in the eye and I knew he realised my question was not a casual one. 'It sounded exactly like "vous savez", sir, and it was before I was kicked so I wasn't in pain. I thought it was odd: as if Coote understood what he was talking about.'

'And that's why you haven't mentioned this to anyone else?'

'Soldiers have to look out for themselves, don't they? It's not wise to show you know too much, most of all where officers are concerned. Coote doesn't think I can understand any French. But I don't like dirty tricks so I'm glad to have told you, Doctor. Provided you keep your word and don't snitch on me.' His fingers touched the hilt of his dagger.

'I'll keep my word, Johnny, but you're wise to be on your guard, particularly when you get back to Bordeaux. If Coote were to decide what you knew was inconvenient...'

'Exactly.' I fancied he winked at me but he turned his head to the side as we rode forward again.

35

'What was your occupation, back in England?' It was meant to sound like a genial afterthought.

'I'm a skinner, sir. I'd strip you a nice pelt to put fur on your gown or calfskin for your best boots. I'm handy with a knife.'

I was reassured that he knew how to look after himself but not wholly confident about his reliability. We rode on in silence while I reflected on the new dimension he had revealed to the incident of the dead spy.

*****

Sir Guy Binwood was John Talbot's representative at the fortified town, as well his long-standing friend, but command of the castle itself rested with the local leader, Captain Gaillardet. Both men received me with enthusiasm and I suspected the Earl had given me unwarranted praise in the letters he sent to advise them of my coming. They entertained me liberally at supper and when Gaillardet left us to speak to the watchmen Sir Guy invited me to join him in his chamber for a glass of wine. I presumed he might be creating an opportunity for a discreet medical consultation and so it proved.

He was a squat, solidly-built man, younger than the Earl but probably not so healthy. He did not disguise the reason for our meeting. 'Did Talbot tell you of my problem, Doctor Somers?'

'He mentioned you were troubled by bellyaches.'

'It's true and I'm content to use my ailment as the excuse for your visit. I do want to pick your physician's brains. The leech here says it's a stone in my bladder causing the trouble. He wants some surgeon fellow to cut into me.'

'Ah! I'm sorry, that's an unpleasant prospect. Did your doctor physically examine you to identify the location of the stone?'

'He did but I'd be glad of your opinion.'

He threw back his gown and undid his points so, with equal industriousness I put down my wineglass and set about pummelling the gentleman's nether parts. I confirmed the diagnosis without hesitation.

'So you agree I should go under the knife?'

'I didn't say that. It's a dangerous procedure, making a perineal incision to reach the stone with forceps without puncturing the bladder or any other vital organ.'

'Could you do it?'

'No, absolutely not. It's a task for a skilled surgeon. Most physicians find they need to carry out minor surgery in the course of their treatments, although there've been attempts to forbid us doing even that; but removing a stone is a different matter. It's hazardous. The finest surgeons have had successes but there are charlatans who offer to undertake the operation with dire consequences.'

'I appreciate your honesty, Somers. I was reluctant to offer my guts to this unknown fellow. Now it appears he could well be a mountebank. I'll have to carry on with the discomfort. The quack gives me potions to deaden the pain.'

'If you can manage, it would be wise to wait until you're able to consult one of the foremost surgeons with a good record of success. In the meantime you may be able to stop the stone getting bigger, if not dissolve it to a degree.'

'Ha! I've heard one of those remedies: blood and skin of hare burned to ash – I tried that. It gave me the runs.'

'A gentler prescription recommends saxifrage tempered with wine and pepper, drunk warm. It won't do you harm at any rate, though I can't guarantee improvement. Prunes and ginger morning and night may help too.'

Sir Guy slapped me on the back. 'The saints be praised for a sensible physician. I'll try following your advice.'

He poured wine into my goblet, spilling a little, and I realised he was understandably agitated. 'Now listen,' he went on, 'I know you're here to look into this spy business. There's something you should know. Jasper Coote was based at Cadillac throughout the winter. Lord Hanwell recommended him to be my second-in-command but I found he became a dubious asset: too full of himself and inventing exploits to show how good he was. Others noticed as well. Representations were made to have him moved and I took the chance to send him back to Bordeaux. Never wanted to see him again.'

'He brought you the pouch with the insulting rhyme after killing the spy?'

'Yes, he acted correctly there, I admit, but I packed him off, back to the city. There wasn't anything in the pouch except a few coins and that one scrap of parchment. Killing the rogue by the riverside seemed unnecessary. It could have caused difficulties with the locals if he was someone they knew. Might have been damned awkward. Fortunately nothing's happened so far. The fellow must have come from further afield and wasn't missed by anyone round here. No one's reported losing a horse either. There's a fair number of lawless men in the area so I suppose one of them commandeered the animal.' His words had come in a rush but then he paused and shrugged. 'I couldn't make head or tail of the silly rhyme. Not to my taste, poetry.'

I forbore from questioning the attribution of poetic status to the verse. 'Do you know anything about the soldier who was with Coote, Johnny Tate?'

'Got kicked in the balls, poor bastard. He's been no trouble, I understand, and he's well enough to return to Bordeaux. We've been lucky, Somers; it could have been a thorny problem if the dead man had been identified. My message to John Talbot is give the blessed Virgin thanks and leave well alone.'

I recognised I would learn no more from Sir Guy whom I took to be a bluff, down-to-earth soldier of limited intelligence. When I had finished my wine I wished him goodnight.

He held my arm for a moment giving me an unreadable look. 'You're a young chap, Somers. You might like a bit of company before the night's done. My man will get you in to Madame Claude's residence, if you've a mind for it. She's a high-class hussy, only entertains the best, not like your common whores in the brothel outside the gate.'

I pleaded weariness after my journey and made my escape. It seemed clear that I would discover little else of value in Cadillac but Johnny Tate's account was the pearl in the town's gritty shell and that had already justified my long exhausting day.

*****

It was polite to stay another day in Cadillac and I arranged for Johnny Tate to show me round the town beyond the castle bastion. The whole place was impressively fortified with four robust gates giving access to the countryside and three defensive corner towers. The townsfolk owned strips of land beyond the walls where they could keep beasts and grow produce and it lay around half a mile from the river, so shipping goods was no problem. Nevertheless, as the quarryman had told me, it was not secure from flooding when there were exceptional water levels and the river regularly seeped into the gatehouses, even along the lower streets. Otherwise Cadillac was impregnable to attack from enemies outside its encompassing walls.

Neither Tate nor I wanted to linger and I arranged for our departure on the second morning. We were provided with horses to ride the whole distance to Bordeaux as there was no convenient vessel going down river on that day and, although it would be a long ride, I welcomed the chance to think through all I had learned while in the saddle.

We had ridden fifteen or sixteen miles following the track which wound to and fro, following the Garonne but avoiding the waterside where it was marshy. We passed below the rocky cliff surmounted by the de la Baule castle and I thought fleetingly of the doubly bereaved widow mourning the loss of her friend. I was about to suggest taking a rest when I caught sight of a group of men on the riverbank ahead of us and I signalled to Tate to observe them. There was no mistake: they were hauling a body from their small fishing boat onto the grass. Within moments we had joined them and I was peering excitedly at the soggy corpse as they turned it onto its side. He had been a tall thin man but I exhaled with disappointment when I realised he could not have been in the water more than a few hours. His handsome features were still clearly visible and they did not include a thin pointed nose.

'I thought you might be retrieving the man the soldiers killed the other week,' I said, assuming they were the fishermen we had encountered when I was travelling by barge. 'I'd heard he was thrown in the river.' I spoke in French as I knew only a few words of the local patois and to my relief the response, also in French although heavily accented, was intelligible.

The oldest man eyed my physician's gown. 'Oh, you're behind the times, Doctor. We got him out days ago, soon after he was killed. We found him further downstream, caught on some branches under water. He'd had his throat cut. This one's been garrotted, I reckon. Look.'

The marks on the man's neck confirmed the diagnosis. 'Is the road dangerous? Does this happen regularly?' I remembered how the Thames in London was often the recipient of those meeting untimely deaths.

'Not uncommon. Like anywhere, those journeying alone put themselves in peril. There's a lonely stretch of road a few miles upstream from here where scoundrels can hide in the bushes. The bodies get carried down to the mudflats across the river. We bring them in if we find

40

them. It's near one of our fishing grounds. The Sénéchal knows he can rely on us to do things properly.'

I hoped my laconic informant would not think it odd if I showed greater curiosity about the alleged spy. 'What was the fellow you found before like? How did you know it was the man the soldiers killed?'

The fisherman humoured my stupidity. 'We knew to look out for him in case he was washed up on our patch. We'd been told. He'd had his throat cut and his hood had been tied over his head. It hadn't even worked loose by the time we found him. Besides, he hadn't been robbed. He still had money in a purse hidden under his clothes. Not like poor Guillaume Coustances here.'

I stared blankly while I made the connection. 'Is he related to the people who farm just outside Bordeaux?'

'He's the farmer himself: was. I imagine he was coming home from market at one of the little towns round here, with his purse full, and the robbers set on him. It happens.'

'He has a wife and a daughter, I believe. Poor Madame Coustances.'

'Don't worry: the Sénéchal will let her have the body, after we've reported to him at the ducal palace.'

Johnny Tate gave a sound of disapproval in his throat but I put my question before he could protest at the man's inhumanity. 'Was the spy's body taken to the Sénéchal?'

I was conscious that the fishermen were becoming restless and wondered if I had showed too much interest in the previous corpse. Their spokesman spat in the water. 'No, the English had sent word for us to look out for that villain and to let them know at once if we found him. A couple of men came, along with their leader, and collected the body.'

I was astonished. 'Lord Talbot came in person?'

'No, not the old Earl. He's got better things to do, I'm sure. They took the body off for Christian burial.'

'Where did they take it?'

41

'Nothing to do with us.' The man's patience was wearing thin.

I understood it would be imprudent to persist with my questioning. The fishermen did not consider the information they had given me to be confidential but doubtless they received payment for their pains and they might well feel it their duty to report my enquiries to their paymaster. I thanked them and put some small coins into the open hand extended in front of me.

Johnny Tate and I rode on towards Bordeaux in silence until I could contain my curiosity no longer. 'Did you know anything of this? How soldiers collected the body?'

'Not a scrap. I'm flummoxed. Why should Coote have asked the fishermen to look out for it?'

'I'd guess because he knew it might be washed up and he didn't want to risk the man being recognised – he'd taken the precaution of hiding the face. But is it likely Lord Hanwell was personally involved in removing the corpse? He's Coote's overlord, isn't he?'

'Yeah. He's known for his piety. He might have felt the fellow deserved Christian burial. But by the Rood, it's a bloody surprise!'

I murmured agreement with Tate's summary and continued to ponder the situation. Maybe Lord Hanwell shared his officer's concern to conceal the identity of the victim. Coote had gone to considerable lengths to achieve this. He must have feared the fellow might be recognised locally or perhaps the spy had notable features which might aid identification. I touched the dark stain which has marred my left cheek since birth and wondered whether something of the sort flanked the thin pointed nose Johnny Tate had noticed.

As we rode on and I formed no conclusion about the mysterious spy, my thoughts strayed to the dead farmer and the newly widowed Madame Coustances. Unsettling ideas came into my head which I did not care to pursue.

Chapter 4

I was weary when I arrived back in Bordeaux but could not allow myself to rest. I should have liked to report at once to Lord Talbot about the discrepancies between the accounts I received from Coote and Tate and the information given by the fishermen. Unfortunately he had left the city to visit Fronsac, now held by the English under Sir John Baldwin, and was not expected to return for at least a week. In his absence, I sought out Lord de Lisle and shared all I had gleaned with him. He clapped his hands with glee.

'By the saints, Harry, you've done well. Father will be pleased.'

'I don't know where the truth lies or who to trust. I'm reluctant to confront Coote with what Johnny Tate told me at this stage but I'll need to speak to Lord Hanwell. I don't know him. Is it plausible that he'd be involved in retrieving the dead man's body?'

Lord de Lisle gave me a boyish grin. 'Father's been known to refer to him as the Pope's representative with the army so it's in character for him to exude piety. It's all a bit odd though. You'll need to be careful how you approach him. He's prickly about rank. Quote Lord Talbot's authority and of course I'll vouch for you. As soon as my father gets back to Bordeaux I'll let you know.'

I was ready to return to my lodgings, relieved that the Earl of Shrewsbury's son was now aware of all I had discovered, but when I encountered Rendell in the guardroom below Lord de Lisle's quarters I persuaded him to walk with me. I provided him with an abbreviated account of my findings, anxious to learn any garrison gossip about the principal players I named.

Rendell gave a low chuckle and corroborated Lord de Lisle's view. 'Sanctimonious and opinionated ass, Lord Hanwell is,' he said. 'If I was Talbot I wouldn't have him on the battlefield anywhere near me. I reckon he wanted to share the glory of Jasper Coote's assertive action. And be seen as a pious Christian soldier.'

'There could be more to it. I've been thinking of Coote as the key figure but maybe he was acting on behalf of his lord. Anyway, if Coote knew the rider he called a spy he must have decided it was inconvenient to be recognised by him. Probably he didn't want Johnny Tate to realise they were acquainted.'

'If Coote and the spy were in cahoots together about something, why didn't they dispose of Tate?' Rendell answered his own query. 'It'd be more difficult to explain the death of an armed English soldier in a friendly area, wouldn't it? Coote must have made his decision on the spur of the moment but he knew what he was doing.'

'If Lord Hanwell was involved, I don't think Coote would have taken the fellow's pouch to Sir Guy at Cadillac. Surely he'd have brought it to his own lord?'

Rendell puffed out his cheeks. 'Double-bluff?'

'I can't follow the logic. Where do you think they buried the corpse?'

'Lord knows: somewhere unobtrusive. I can tell you one thing. They didn't bring it into the city. Word would have gone round. Why do you think they went to fetch it?'

I had been puzzling out an answer to this question ever since meeting the fishermen. 'If Jasper Coote knew the man, others might have recognised him so he wanted to make sure the body wouldn't be seen by anyone who might identify the fellow. He hadn't been able to dispose of it effectively after he killed the rider because he had Johnny Tate with him. He hoped it would be carried out to sea but that's a long way so as a precaution he arranged for the fishermen to look out for it.'

'You don't think Tate was in on whatever they were up to?'

'I don't believe he was.'

'What will you do next?'

'I fear I must make the acquaintance of a certain sanctimonious and opinionated ass. But I won't quote you, Sergeant Tonks.'

Rendell smirked, before clapping his hand to his head. 'Oh, I nearly forgot to tell you. Andy Armstrong's back in town and he had an almighty slanging match with Ned Bartley outside St. Michael's Church. Stopped at foul words this time, they did, though they nearly went for each other in the middle of the marketplace. They were dragged apart. One day cold steel will decide between them.'

Rendell returned to his duties and I did not mention to him the identity of the body the fishermen had just retrieved at the time I saw them. When I joined Piers, by contrast, it was that news I shared because he was acquainted with the Coustances family. I knew he was sensitive to the suffering of others and he was predictably upset. He marched up and down our small room beating a fist on the palm of his other hand.

'The poor woman, left on her own with the farm to run and having to cope with that silly young floosy lifting her skirts for Ned Bartley.'

'Andy Armstrong's back in Bordeaux, I hear, and ready to tear Bartley apart. Maybe the girl was the reason for their brawl.'

Piers was thinking along other lines. He came to a sudden halt. 'You don't think there's anything funny about the farmer's murder?'

'I can't see why there should be. What I heard from the fishermen about wayside assaults was all too credible.'

Silently but defiantly I resolved to myself that mystery surrounding one death was quite enough, without another.

*****

Next morning I received a curt message, in reply to my request, saying that Lord Hanwell was fully engaged for several days. He would grant me an audience on the following Monday, directly after the service of Sext had concluded in the palace chapel. I regretted the delay but hoped Lord Talbot would return before this appointment so I could consult him in person. Meanwhile I was occupied attending to my duties, bandaging slashed arms, administering balm for sore joints and in one case rectifying a dislocated thumb. It was what I was in Bordeaux to do until battle lines were engaged.

On the second day following my return to Bordeaux I had not seen Piers since daybreak. I could manage without his help while I was not too busy but I wondered where he had gone without telling me. Then, in mid-afternoon, he lumbered into the room wafting the aroma of freshly baked bread.

'Hope you didn't need me. I've been to see Madame Coustances. I guessed she'd know about her husband by now. I thought there might be something I could do to help her and as it happened a wheel on one of the farm carts had gone askew. I righted it. She insisted on giving us a loaf in payment.'

'How is she?'

'Sorrowful but resigned, I'd say. I hardly know her but she seems strong-minded. What's most upset her is her step-daughter taking off as soon as the girl heard about her father's death.'

I looked up from the labels I was writing for my newly mixed potions 'The girl's left home?'

'God knows where she's gone but it won't be for her good.' Piers paused, a knuckle pressed to his mouth. 'I sense the farmer's murder might not be what it appears.'

'Surely that's fanciful, Piers? Did she tell you something to give you that idea?'

He shook his head. 'Only that her husband hadn't been to market. She thought he'd been to meet someone out at Cadillac – where you went. She's sure he didn't have any money in his purse.'

'So the thieves would have been disappointed. They made a mistake, that's all. Frustration could have fuelled their violence.'

'Go to see her, Harry. I'll take you there, if you like.'

Before I could reply I heard angry shouting in the distance and Piers opened the door onto the street. 'Oh my word!' he said. 'It's Andy Armstrong and Ned Bartley, going for each other like tomcats up towards the square.'

Piers headed for the disturbance while I lingered on the threshold but he came back and grabbed my arm, pulling me along the road. 'I don't know who started it,' he said, 'but Armstrong's a fool if he provoked Lord Palgreve's sergeant. It'll be worse than a flogging if he's charged with affray.'

As we reached them, two guards appeared from the palace gate intent on separating the adversaries, but a group of onlookers had formed to cheer on the entertainment and they impeded the would-be peacemakers. Both antagonists grasped knives and looked murderous, stalking each other. There was a red streak on Armstrong's chin and his opponent's sleeve was ripped. The guards fell back confronted by the crowd's hostility, but an officer I recognised as one of Lord Talbot's personal entourage had followed them and immediately took charge. He roared at Ned Bartley to desist and seized Armstrong's collar dragging him clear of a threatening blade. The sergeant's expression was vicious but he acknowledged his superior and, notwithstanding his resentment, he complied with the order. He knew circumstances had turned against him and this would not be the occasion when he exacted retribution from his foe.

Armstrong stood stock-still under the officer's hand and Talbot's man spoke to him in a low voice. I thought they would move off together but when he saw me on the edge of the restive audience the officer beckoned me to join them.

'Doctor Somers, I believe you're acquainted with Master Armstrong. I'd be grateful if you'd accompany him to the Toscanan Gate. He has a horse waiting and is about to depart on important business. Make sure he leaves without impediment. You are authorised to use Lord Talbot's name if there are questions.'

Bewildered and alarmed, I did not demur but bowed. I estimated it would take no more than ten minutes at a brisk pace to reach the Toscanan Gate. I had no need to urge Andy Armstrong's co-operation, for he skipped along beside me grinning broadly.

'Bit of luck you coming then, Doctor,' he said when we were clear of the onlookers. 'Will you get a message to Madame Coustances that I've been sent off again before I could manage to see her? Tell her I'd have taught Ned Bartley a lesson he wouldn't forget if that nob hadn't come out to stop us. The bastard has brought Minette into the city, set her up as his whore, with the girl's father hardly cold in his grave.'

I accepted the inevitable. 'I'll take your message myself. Will you be away from Bordeaux for long?'

He gave me a hangdog look. 'Not in my hands. I've got a long ride once I'm across the Garonne. I'm sorry to be leaving when that poor woman needs help but I've no choice. If you'd check she's all right, I'd be grateful.'

At least Piers would approve of my undertaking, I thought with resignation as I watched Armstrong ride through the gate and spur his horse into a gallop. I turned on my heel to retrace my steps but I could not dismiss the episode and its implications from my mind.

After he was flogged, Armstrong had told me he was part of Lord Talbot's retinue but I now suspected he had some specific and perhaps confidential role, working directly for the Earl and under his protection. The intervention of Talbot's officer could have no other explanation. I told myself firmly it was not my concern. Subsequently, my errant thoughts wandered into speculation that the mysterious fellow might have some illicit liaison with Madame Coustances and I had no wish to explore that possibility. Yet, as I pondered the woman's sudden bereavement, I began to fear Andy Armstrong might have instigated her husband's demise. His rapid departure could be a matter of expedience until a decent period of time had elapsed and he could pay court openly to the widow. This was definitely not for me to pursue – unless I found evidence of criminality to put before the Sénéchal as well as Lord Talbot. Without any proof, I must dismiss these fancies and keep an open mind, but I hoped I had seen the back of Master Armstrong.

*****

My first surprise was that Madame Coustances was younger than I expected, not beautiful but pleasant to look at and clearly intelligent. Her eyes were red but she was composed and courteous, welcoming me as a guest and greeting Piers who accompanied me with decorous familiarity. My second surprise was that she spoke slightly accented but impeccable English. I accepted a glass of wine from the produce of the farm's own small vineyard and savoured its quality.

I gave her my commiserations and passed on the message from Andy Armstrong which she received with lowered eyes. A blush spread upwards to her cheeks. At this point Piers bustled to his feet and said he would go to check on the cart-wheel he had repaired earlier. Knowing how moralistic he was inclined to be on some subjects, I wondered if he shared my suspicions about the widow's relationship with Armstrong. He might well be embarrassed that, by acting as their go-between, I was complicit with impropriety.

Madame Coustances raised her head, looking towards the door. 'Master Ford is very kind but he should take proper payment. I am not impoverished and am capable of overseeing the farm.'

A doctor can sometimes presume upon his profession to put questions which might seem impertinent from a stranger. 'I can see you have a sizeable farm. Will you have adequate help without Monsieur Coustances?'

She spread her hands on her dark skirt. 'Guillaume had many calls on his time. We've always had workers to help look after our few animals, cut the hay and tend the vines but I am competent to play my part. The men know me and will be content to accept my directions.'

'It's a pity Master Armstrong has to be away from the area.'

She looked at me sharply, the flush colouring her throat once more. 'Master Armstrong was Guillaume's friend from years ago. He has assisted us on occasions since he returned to Bordeaux but we've never depended on him. He has many duties.'

She might be discouraging me from pursuing the subject of Andy Armstrong but it was interesting that he had been in Aquitaine previously. He would know the area and have contacts. I felt awkward. 'I'm glad you're not in practical difficulties to compound your loss. Master Ford tells me your husband was almost certainly the victim of a robbery, even though the thieves would not have benefitted greatly from their violence.'

Madame Coustances pursed her lips. 'You know as much as I do, it seems. It's always a risk to ride alone at dusk on lonelier stretches of road. There's no mystery about that.' Her words had a tone of finality as if she had no wish to prolong discussion of the subject.

'Forgive me. Master Ford meant no harm in speaking to me. He feared your bereavement might leave you with a host of problems.'

She gave a weary smile. 'My greatest difficulty lies in my own failure for I have been unable to safeguard Guillaume's child. I feel guilt for that.'

'I'm sure you're not to blame. Young people can be very headstrong.' I had no children or living siblings but I was thinking of Rendell who had become like a younger brother to me.

She stared into the distance. 'Guillaume took me to wife within months of Minette's mother dying. He particularly wanted me to care for her, to fill the gap left in her life, but I think it was too soon. She rebelled and would not listen to my guidance. Then when the English soldiers came last year she found a potent way to distress me. Modesty meant nothing to her and she mocked my prudishness.'

'Couldn't her father check her waywardness?'

Madame Coustances sprang to her feet and I began to apologise for my insolence but she fluttered her hand and shook her head. 'You don't need to apologise, Doctor Somers. In different circumstances Guillaume would have constrained her, I'm sure, but he had other responsibilities, other conflicting responsibilities. He relied on me to counsel Minette and I failed him.'

I had no right to persist with my questions on this subject. 'Have you other family in the neighbourhood, Madame?'

'No. My father died three years back. I had kept house for him but he was happy to see me married in his last months. He thought well of Guillaume, as did my brother.'

Her last words were spoken in a whisper.

'Your brother? Does he live in the neighbourhood?'

'My brother is no longer a...' She paused as if she could not bring herself to say the word 'alive'. 'He is no longer available,' she said firmly.

'Forgive me, I didn't mean to add to your sorrow. I shouldn't intrude. I can see Master Ford returning across the yard. We'll leave you, Madame, but if there's any help we can offer, please let us know.'

She was fully in control of herself once more and she thanked Piers courteously as we departed before she turned to me. 'It was a pleasure to speak to you, Doctor Somers. I am inevitably unsettled at present but I didn't find our conversation intrusive. If you were able to influence Minette towards a more fitting way of life, it would ease my heart from its greatest affliction.'

I took no pleasure from this request but Piers found it amusing. 'Madame Coustances sees you in the guise of a make-weight priest, it seems,' he said as we walked back on the way to Bordeaux, 'reclaiming a lost sheep from her sinfulness. Good luck to you, Harry! Mind you, you'll have to account to Ned Bartley if you succeed.'

It was only a short distance to the gate of the city by the convent of the Clares. During daylight hours there were normally few delays in securing access so, although dusk was falling, we were surprised to see a crowd milling round the gatehouse. Fortunately one of the keepers recognised me and beckoned us to the wicket gate at the side of the main entrance where men at arms were standing with pikes at the ready. He hustled us past the guards and did not answer my question as to the reason for this situation until we were inside the walls.

'No one's allowed to leave the city and we're only to admit those we're sure of. There's been a dastardly murder, not far from the ducal palace: an English soldier, would you believe? The body slung in a pile of shit.'

'Someone deemed important?' Piers, ever the advocate of the common man, sounded disapproving.

The gatekeeper missed the irony and nodded. 'One of Lord Palgreve's sergeants, no less,' he said 'A real trusty by all accounts. Name of Ned Bartley.'

'Oh, Christ!' Piers and I spoke in irreverent unison.

Chapter 5

Liveried servitors were waiting at the door to my quarters to request or, from their tone, more accurately to require my attendance on Lord Palgreve as soon as I returned. Puzzled and unenthusiastic, I brushed myself down and set off to accompany them to the palace, hoping I was not needed to examine a body recovered from a noxious sewer. Rendell came bounding across the square to join us as we approached the gatehouse. He was anxious to play a part in the forthcoming scene and I was happy to have him with me. Whatever the reason for my summons, I did not doubt it would prove testing.

I signalled silently to Rendell. 'Is there anything I should know?'

He shook his head and muttered, 'I've only just heard about it. My troop was practising sword play down by the river.'

We were escorted to a tower similar to the one Lord Talbot used and ushered at once into Palgreve's presence. The room was more lavishly furnished than the commander's office and I noted the fine turkey carpet on the table. Palgreve was a heavily built man of about fifty, bow-legged from many hours in the saddle, and I could not prevent myself hoping the horses he rode were robust creatures able to sustain his weight without injury. He oozed confidence and I could believe the implication in the crude rhyme that he coveted Lord Talbot's position as commander of the English army. He addressed me without preamble or courtesies.

'You have learned of the outrage which has occurred?'

'Your sergeant, Ned Bartley, has been killed. That's all I know. I've been out of the city since mid-afternoon.'

'During the morning you were seen at the Toscanan Gate talking to that reprobate, Armstrong, after he attacked Sergeant Bartley in full public view.'

'I didn't see how the disturbance began. I heard shouting and went over to find out what was happening. Lord Talbot's officer came to resolve the matter and asked me to conduct Armstrong to the gate as he had a journey to make on important business. I was authorised to use Lord Talbot's name if necessary but we encountered no problems. The last I saw of Armstrong, he was galloping away from the city downstream towards the river.'

'He was observed to speak to you as if in confidence. What did he say?'

I had no wish to become embroiled in this distasteful matter but I baulked at Palgreve's arrogance. 'It was merely something between patient and physician, my lord. I had treated Armstrong's wounds after he was flogged the other day.'

'Lawfully flogged by Sergeant Bartley in accordance with the sentence passed on him for his misdeeds.'

'Indeed, my lord. And in accordance with Lord Talbot's decree, when a man is flogged a physician is asked to be on hand to minister to the miscreant after he has had his punishment.'

'Pah!' Palgreve was not about to criticise his commander but his attitude was clear. 'When Armstrong has been apprehended this time he will be strung up on the gibbet. He is proclaimed as Bartley's murderer.'

'I know nothing of this, my lord. When I last saw Armstrong he had left the city.'

Palgreve swore under his breath and turned his attention to Rendell. 'Who is this soldier at your side, Doctor Somers?'

'An old friend, my lord: Rendell Tonks, sergeant with the troop of men sent by Sir Nicholas Chamberlayne to fight under Lord de Lisle's banner.' Sir Nicholas was a distinguished courtier, close to the Duke of Somerset, the King's chief adviser. Neither the Duke nor Sir Nicholas was with the army in Aquitaine but both had facilitated the expedition.

Palgreve's tongue moistened his lips. 'You are Somerset's man, Doctor Somers?'

I looked him full in the face. 'I served briefly as physician to the Duke's household but have had no position with him for more than a year. My allegiance is to King Henry, my lord.'

'I don't doubt it,' he said drily. 'Lord Talbot will be absent from Bordeaux for several more days – he's moved on from Fronsac but is visiting other towns we hold. While he's away I am the most senior noble here. Remember that. If Armstrong contacts you in any way you will notify me immediately and refrain from responding to him. That is my order and I hope it is clear.'

'Absolutely, my lord. I will comply: saving only any obligations on me as a physician to succour those in need of my medical services.'

'You may go.' Palgreve spoke between his teeth. 'I advise you not to trifle with me – and you, Sergeant Tonks, will be wise not to associate yourself with jumped-up hangers-on at the army camp, too clever for their own good. Remember that on the field of battle the good opinions of Somerset and Nicholas Chamberlayne will count for nothing.'

We were shown out of the palace by Palgreve's retainers and stayed silent until we regained my lodgings, whereupon Rendell erupted with indignation. 'Bloody swine! Was he threatening us? He'd got no time for Somerset. Is he one of Richard of York's faction?'

'I don't know. He's careful what he says. Don't do anything to antagonise him. He'd be dangerous to cross.'

'What'll you do if Andy Armstrong contacts you?'

'It'll depend on the circumstances.'

Rendell's laugh was cut short by Piers returning to our quarters with details we had not possessed when we saw Palgreve. He swallowed a draught of wine and then sat cross-legged on the floor, commanding our attention.

'I've pieced together what happened,' he said, reaching up for a hunk of bread on the table. 'Bartley's body was found while the chapel bell was ringing for Vespers. That couldn't have been long before we arrived back here. It was slung in an outlet from the latrines, a foul ditch running from the palace towards the little river Peugue before it joins the Garonne. He was gagged and his throat had been cut. He'd probably been there an hour or two. The crows were already at him.'

'So nobody saw how he got there?'

'No but the word's out that Andy Armstrong was responsible.'

'So we've gathered. Has Armstrong been seen round the palace since he left the city this morning? He was meant to be miles away by now.'

'I haven't been able to pin down anything. Various attendants think they may have seen him – or someone like him – but only because the idea's been put around that he was the murderer. Do you know where he was going when you last saw him?'

I shook my head. 'It was supposed to be a long journey. I imagined he was to cross the river somewhere, down towards the confluence with the Dordogne. There's nothing we can contribute that's going to help anyone. We'd better keep out of it.'

Piers wiped the back of his hand across his mouth. 'There's a consequential matter, Harry, which I think you should be involved with, as a physician and decent man.'

Rendell guffawed. 'Sounds ominous!'

I had a premonition of what my wheelwright friend was about to say and I shuddered.

'While you were with Palgreve, the Coustances girl was dragged from the garret in one of the houses near St. Michael's where Bartley had lodged her, a squalid place. She was in a deluge of tears, genuinely upset, I think. Bartley's mates thought it was open season to have her and she tried to run away. Luckily I'd been questioning a stallholder in the market square and I saw what was going on. I managed to get her into the palace gatehouse and the wife of the senior keeper is with her. She can't stay there though, the keeper won't have it. I begged her to return to her step-mother. I said I'd escort her there but she categorically refused. So... so I... I offered... that is, I suggested...'

'Oh God!' Rendell was in an ecstasy of mirth. 'They're bringing her here. You'll need to barricade the door if she stays here overnight.'

'She may need a physician's care,' Piers said, more in hope than certainty. 'One of the serving women from the palace will come with her.'

It was the moment for righteous pomposity. 'She needs protection,' I said. 'Piers and I will sleep across the threshold and I'll ask for an armed guard to be posted beside us. In the morning I'll try to persuade the girl to return to her stepmother. Let's hope this horrible business has brought her to her senses.'

'Amen,' Piers added as if I had uttered a prayer.

Perhaps I had.

*****

Minette Coustances was small, delicately built and very pretty. Her dark hair was loose, cascading over her shoulders in extravagant curls, and she had a habit of fixing her blue eyes on the person speaking to her as if enthralled. She tried to appear pert but I surmised she was in fact frightened, as well she might be.

'You'll be safe here overnight, Mademoiselle,' I said. 'I'm sorry you've suffered such distress with the loss of your protector.' She fluttered her eyelashes and gazed as if waiting for me to say more but what I added was probably not what she expected. 'I advise you to take off that gilded chain round your neck until you are with those who can offer you permanent security.'

Her fingers grasped the gaudy ornament. 'Ned Bartley gave it me. He was good to me, generous. Is it because of me, he was murdered? He wanted me for himself. The other men were jealous.'

57

I should not have been astonished by her self-regarding suggestion. For all her bravado, I reflected, she was a naïve country girl. 'I think it very unlikely that was the reason someone hated him enough to kill him. You mustn't worry that his fondness for you led to his death. There will have been other issues. Men say he had enemies. Now you must get some rest. You won't be disturbed and I'll talk to you in the morning.'

Before she could protest, I picked up a heavy cloak in which to wrap myself and hustled Piers out of doors. Rendell was squatting on the doorstep with a drawn sword across his knees.

'It's getting monotonous keeping guard outside your quarters, Doctor Somers, but with that hussy inside there's no other soldier I'd trust to stay at his post all night. Still, I don't think we'll be bothered. I've started a rumour that she's been brought to you because she's showing signs of having the pox. It's put the wind up one or two of Palgreve's men, I can tell you. Sweet dreams.'

*****

By the time I entered my lodgings after sluicing my face under the pump in the square, Minette was tidying her hair with her fingers and I noted with approval that the glittering chain was no longer visible about her person. The serving woman who had stayed with the girl during the night wanted to return to her duties but I asked her to remain while I spoke to her companion and she withdrew into the corner where Piers usually kept his pallet.

'Mademoiselle,' I began, 'we need to arrange for you future safety. I'm sure you realise you can't stay here.'

Minette had regained her poise and she pouted at me, leaning back against my table with her legs slightly apart. 'Why not, Doctor? I could look after your lodgings, sweep the floor, cook your meals, give you any comfort you wished for. You've need of a woman I'm thinking.' She rolled her eyes to give unnecessary emphasis to her words.

58

'No, Mademoiselle: that would not be appropriate. It's my duty to see you fittingly placed where you will not be in danger. The most suitable haven would be your own home, with your stepmother.'

She gave an angry screech. 'It's not my fucking home! I'd rather go on the streets.'

'You don't know what you're saying. Madame Coustances is concerned for you. She wants to help you.'

'She's a bloody tight-arsed English cow. My father only took her because she brought him the farm. I hate her. I'll never live with her.'

It was not the moment to pursue the interesting information she had just divulged. 'Then you should consider going as servant in some respectable household. I'm passing no judgement on you but life as a soldier's doxy is not an enviable one. You're young and you've suffered a cruel fate to lose both your father and your protector so quickly and so violently. You deserve a chance to think things through and make a decent life for yourself. It'll be up to you how you behave in the future but give yourself time to consider what might happen.'

Piers had arrived and was standing in the doorway so he heard our exchange. 'The inn by the south gate has need of a kitchen maid,' he said. 'It's not the most elegant of taverns but the landlord's a good sort. I could take you there.'

Minette moved forward, peering up at him, wiggling her hips. 'Do the soldiers go there to drink?'

'Some do but you could bide in the kitchen. You wouldn't need to serve at table.'

She giggled. 'I wouldn't mind. So long as I can make my own choices, like the Doctor says. I'm not going with any man just because he fancies me. It's worth a try; better than skivvying for that sour-faced bitch at the farm. Will you take me to the inn?' She pouted with practised charm.

Piers nodded and held out her shawl. She let him drape it over her shoulders and went with him to the door.

59

On the threshold she stopped, wriggled her bottom, turned and blew me a kiss. 'He's a beanpole, your friend, isn't he? Is his prick as long as his forearm? You'd know, I'm sure.'

*****

I was annoyed with myself for being irked by Minette's impudent mischief-making. She set out to provoke and shock, aiming to demonstrate her sophistication, but she was little more than a silly child in need of protection and likely to bring calamity on herself. I recollected the worried expression on Madame Coustances's face when she spoke of her stepdaughter and I could not help but conclude it would be best for her to be spared continuing responsibility for the headstrong girl.

Was I becoming prematurely crotchety? Were my own misfortunes making me unsympathetic to youthful wilfulness? I was now thirty years old, bereft and denied the blessings of a wife and family. Those I had loved, I had lost: my sorrow culminating in the death of the beautiful but afflicted woman I married. Meanwhile, the promising career I established in England had been exchanged for the thankless role of physician with an invading army across the sea. I shook myself in irritation. I must not indulge futile regrets.

Such was my malaise that I welcomed the appearance at my door of the grumpy servant in Lord Talbot's entourage who regularly sought to detail his imaginary ailments and seek my diagnoses. I was unusually tolerant with him, letting him ramble on about his aching joints without interrupting, murmuring sympathetically at his descriptions. When eventually I showed him out Piers had returned from escorting Minette to the inn and was clearly anxious to speak to me.

'I met that soldier you mentioned, Johnny Tate. He was lurking up the road, hoping to run into you. He guessed I was your assistant, he'd heard I was on the tall side, so he asked if I'd arrange for you to see him. He wants to come as if consulting you as a physician. He claims he's hurt himself. He's clutching his chest.' Piers gave a meaningful look and raised his eyebrows.

'Of course. Fetch him in. You'd best leave me alone with him.'

Johnny Tate staggered through the door and asked me in a loud voice to check whether he had broken a rib. 'Fell off a ladder while we were practising scaling a wall. Bloody painful.'

I told him in all seriousness to slip off his jerkin which he did, while retaining the sheathed dagger in his belt. I duly probed his chest and he gave an impressively realistic groan causing me to wonder for a moment whether he had actually injured himself. 'Piers will be watching outside,' I said in a whisper. 'No one will be eavesdropping.'

He was obviously nervous so I rubbed some vile smelling ointment onto his intact ribs and grinned encouragingly. 'Bruising inside your chest: that's what you can tell your mates. They'll smell you coming yards off. What else is it you want?'

He fumbled with his jerkin as he drew it over his head and shuddered. 'It came to me when I saw a messenger delivering letters to the gatekeeper, taking them out of his pouch. I'd clean forgotten but it all came back. You asked if Coote had opened the spy's pouch and I didn't think so. But he did, I've remembered. I was struggling with that devil of a horse but I had a glimpse of Coote taking a letter out of the packet. I'll swear I did.'

'A letter? Not simply one scrap of parchment?'

'No. He was holding a sealed document but I don't think he undid it. That's all I saw. I was crumpled up a moment later when the horse kicked me. I thought I should tell you.'

'I'm glad you did. It could be helpful.' It was important to sound convinced but I was doubtful about this convenient but belated recollection. 'Have you hurt yourself behind the ear?'

He clapped his hand over his left ear but I released his fingers gently and lifted his straggly hair from the swelling. 'How did this happen? Did someone thump you?'

He twitched and looked round the room cautiously. 'Last night. In the dark, coming from the tavern. Someone jumped from a doorway. Luckily I was alert and swerved. I think it was aimed at my temple, something hard like a mace. Whoever it was ran away. Other people were coming round the corner. Next time I'll be ready for the bastard.'

'Any idea who it was?

'Haven't a clue but he won't catch me off guard again. I didn't want to draw attention to it. That's why I didn't use that as my excuse for coming to see you. If the bastard guessed I'd told you about it, you could have been put in danger.'

'That was thoughtful. Take great care, Johnny. It could have been a casual thief but I suspect not. It's probable someone sees you as a threat.'

'I've worked that out and know where to look, don't I? Coote doesn't trust me – can't think why!'

I opened the door for him to leave and spoke loudly so passers-by could hear. 'Come to see me again if your ribs still hurt after a day or two. Don't risk injuring them further.'

What he had told me could be of key importance but I was amused by the zest with which he acted the role he adopted.

*****

When the appointed day came I was on edge as I waited for the chapel bell to ring for Sext and proceeded into the palace to find Lord Hanwell's lodgings. I rehearsed in my mind the story I had devised to engage his lordship's compassion, if he truly possessed such an attribute. I was taking a considerable risk to confront him with a mishmash of truth and invention but I prided myself it was designed to evoke his sympathy. I was reassured to know that Lord Talbot was expected back in Bordeaux by the end of the day.

From an antechamber I was taken up a spiralling stair into a small turret, nothing so grand as Lord Palgreve's accommodation but comfortably furnished and with a view towards the river. The soberly dressed young nobleman had positioned himself in front of the window so his face was shaded but his posture indicated that he was conferring a favour on me by agreeing to our meeting – and it would be short.

'My lord,' I said and bowed as obsequiously as I could manage. I was ready to deliver my prepared speech, which was at least partly true, in as mater-of-fact a manner as possible. 'I'm grateful for your time. I've been approached by a priest with a concern for the spy your officer killed the other day. He doesn't question what happened but says he's always troubled by those who die unshriven, with all their sins upon them. He would like to pray for the fellow's soul and its salvation at the place where he's been buried. I've learned that you supervised the removal of the corpse from the riverside, in order that the man could be given decent burial: a most Christian act, my lord, if I may say so. If you would let me know where the grave is, I'll inform the priest who will be most obliged. He'll say his prayers at the graveside and bless your act of charity while he docs so.'

While I was speaking I moved to the right so I could watch the colour drain from Lord Hanwell's cheeks and then begin to return as his anger rose. 'Who told you this farrago of lies? I've had nothing to do with the dead villain. Are you saying the body was retrieved from the river? Who told you his nonsense? Who is this interfering busybody, physician? Why has he come to you? He's most likely a counterfeit priest, another spy in disguise, and you should have him arrested. If you repeat this slander to anyone else, I'll have you imprisoned.'

I had expected a confused rebuttal of the story I fabricated, but not Hanwell's outraged denial of any

63

personal involvement. His surprise and indignation seemed genuine and this dangerously undermined my contrivance. Horribly aware of the treacherous ground more falsehoods could lead me onto, I needed to recover my position urgently.

'My lord, I believed the evidence of my eyes and ears that the man is a sincere priest although I have no proof. I knew you were renowned for your devoutness so it seemed credible that you'd be concerned to see the dead man suitably buried. Jasper Coote never mentioned the spy's body had been found but I knew the corpse of a local farmer was taken from the river by fishermen the other day. Because of that, I did not question an account of the deceased spy being recovered from the water. As I described, it involved soldiers sent to collect the body under the direction of their leader. Because of your reputation for piety, my lord, I assumed you were that leader. I thought only that it redounded to your credit and meant no offence.'

Hanwell glared at me but my sycophancy had mollified him. 'The so-called priest who told you this pack of lies is to be arrested, do you hear?'

I bowed my head. 'Yes, my lord. I'm due to report on other matters to Lord Talbot on his return. If you permit it, I'll notify him of the slander against you and ensure the man responsible is brought to justice.'

'Good. That will satisfy me. Otherwise you will refrain from repeating the allegation?'

'Of course, my lord.' I simpered and gave grovelling thanks as I retreated.

I was trembling as I left the palace, ashamed of my incompetence in the mishandled interview and fearful of its consequences.

*****

I needed a diversion to fill my mind during the afternoon, before I could hope to see Lord Talbot. Piers set off to visit an apothecary with a list of herbs I wanted to replenish my stocks and soon after he had gone I also left our lodgings and made my way on foot to the south gate of the city. I had a duty to fulfil and curiosity to allay.

Madame Coustances was working in the farmyard, forking hay into barrows which two labourers trundled away before returning for them to be refilled. She was sensibly dressed in fustian for this activity and a twist of dark auburn hair had escaped from her cap. I realised with a jolt that I found her surprisingly attractive.

There was a moment of embarrassment when she caught sight of me and tried to pull her cap straight but she abandoned the attempt and laughed.

'I told you, Doctor Somers, I was competent to run the farm.'

'I must apologise for intruding without warning. There are things I should tell you.'

She spoke to her workmen and led me into the house, once again offering a glass of her excellent wine. I sipped and sat rigidly on a wooden-backed settle to describe my conversation with Minette.

'I fear she will not remain at the tavern if one of the soldiers takes her fancy and offers her protection but she's resolute in refusing to return to her home.'

'You've been kind, Doctor Somers, and I'm grateful. Master Ford tells me the garrison may be reduced in size before long if Lord Talbot plans other sorties against the French. Minette may become disillusioned if only the less robust soldiery with few coins in their purses are left in Bordeaux.'

Her astuteness was striking and I felt at ease in her company. She reminded me of someone I had known in the past although I could not identify who it was. There was no opportunity to daydream about this as her next statement prompted me to broach the questions I wanted to put to her.

'I expect Minette was foul-mouthed and rude about me.' She looked down at her lap, as if embarrassed to be inviting further confidences.

'I'm afraid she was disrespectful. One thing intrigued me: she referred to you as English.'

'English cow is one of her favourite descriptions for me. Leaving aside the offensive second word, the first is not entirely accurate. My father was English; my mother French. My father fought in the wars with King Henry's men for many years. He met my mother in Orleans and decided not to return to England. They came south to Aquitaine, acquired the farm and I was born here, where they made their home. He died before the French king captured Bordeaux two years ago. He would be glad Lord Talbot has come to reclaim King Henry's duchy.'

'So the farm came to your husband through your marriage?'

'Guillaume farmed a smallholding adjoining my father's land. It was sensible to amalgamate the two areas and my union with Guillaume brought this about. There now, you know my history.'

'My father also fought in northern France. He was killed there while I was a small boy.'

'That was hard. I have been fortunate. Until the French king's men arrived, Aquitaine was spared the horrors of armies marching across our lands. Now our countryside may become a battlefield like those in the north and meanwhile there are divisions closer at hand between men who favour the return of King Henry's rule and those who believe our future should be with France.'

I did not hide the interest I had in her comment. 'I've heard rumours of spies. Are some local people seeking to undermine Lord Talbot's mission?'

She stared at me as if astonished by my query before shifting position uncomfortably on her stool. 'Of course,' she said. 'It is inevitable.'

There was a pause and I decided it was time for me to leave so, after draining my glass, I stood. Madame

Coustances also rose to her feet but she had one more thing to say. 'Doctor Somers, I owe you an apology for my curtness when you called before. I think you were puzzled by Guillaume's visit to Cadillac, when he had not been to market and was carrying little money.'

'No, no, please don't...'

'You have been kind and I should like to give you the explanation I shunned previously. The reason for Guillaume's journeys to Cadillac is simple. A woman he visited from time to time lives there. Any money he took with him would have been left with Claude. I was squeamish and avoided the subject but there it is – no mystery.'

'There was no need for you to indulge my curiosity,' I said, suppressing my dismay at her words. 'I'm humbled you trusted me enough.' I was too embarrassed to question her further.

I walked back slowly to the city gate, ruminating on our conversation. I was touched by Madame Coustances's willingness to confide in me, yet in both our meetings she had been at pains to insist there was no mystery about the circumstances of her husband's death. Was that really because her husband had a mistress in Cadillac? Could the Claude she named be the "high-class hussy" Sir Guy had mentioned to me? Was it likely such a woman would have a continuing liaison with a mere farmer from miles downstream? Somehow it worried me even more acutely, whether Guillaume Coustances's behaviour complemented, or perhaps encouraged, Marie's own ambiguous relationship with Andy Armstrong?

Armstrong's name had not been mentioned in our latest conversation and I did not know if she was aware of the allegations against him. It was possible to fabricate a theory whereby he had killed Ned Bartley on her account, in order to please her by freeing Minette from the sergeant's pernicious influence. Just as it was possible that Armstrong had murdered Guillaume Coustances – for more heinous and personal reasons! Idle speculation could be seriously misleading but I was unable to rid myself of the suspicion that Madame Coustances was trying to conceal something.

My visit to the farm had only enhanced my sense of melancholy and added to my mushrooming uncertainties.

On the other hand, Piers was maintaining contact with the woman and she seemed to trust him. That was for the best. He was a generous-hearted man, anxious to help those in distress. He deserved reciprocal friendship. I hoped concern for Marie Coustances's plight and his practical attempts to assist her would divert his thoughts from the fear that Bess Willoughby might reject his suit a second time when he returned to England. The preoccupations which absorbed us in our homeland hundreds of miles away continued to trouble us, while simultaneously they seemed to belong to a different world.

Chapter 6

I was summoned to see Lord Talbot early next morning, not in his office within the palace but at his lodgings in the rue des Ayres. Despite the hour, soon after dawn, he had clearly been at his desk for some while, with correspondence piled in front of him and a clerk at his side. This fellow was dismissed as I entered and I proceeded to summarise all I had discovered about the spy's death and the suggestion Lord Hanwell had been involved in the recovery of the body, which he vigorously denied.

'He claims he's been slandered and wants the culprit brought to justice.'

'Do you believe him?'

'His reaction seemed genuine. When I think back, the fishermen spoke of a couple of men with their leader. I assumed this was someone more senior but perhaps they simply meant Coote. He's an officer and he may have seemed important to them. He'd have acted as if he was, I'm sure. He must have arranged for them to tell him about finding the body while he was still in Cadillac and collected it on his way back to Bordeaux.'

'How long did he stay in Cadillac?'

'I don't know. It didn't seem significant before. I could ask him straight out, or Johnny Tate might know.'

'Better still, Doctor Somers, go back to Cadillac and explain our concerns to Sir Guy. He can make enquiries; find out if anyone knows about a body or a rough grave. As it happens, it fits in well with another expedition I want you to undertake. I'll see Lord Hanwell and soothe his ruffled feathers. Don't fret about him.'

That reassurance was welcome but I was unnerved by his mention of another expedition. I waited in suspense to learn what the Earl had in mind, hoping it would involve a physician's professional duties.

'I need this matter cleared up quickly, Harry,' he said, compounding my anxiety with use of my familiar

69

name. 'The French are advancing from the north and our attention must be concentrated on military affairs. We have a little time and must use it wisely. I'm reinforcing the garrisons at several towns. If there are traitors in our midst, they must be prised out. I've left a reliable man to keep an eye on Sir John Baldwin at Fronsac in case he's part of a conspiracy as that vulgar rhyme suggests. I expect the French to invest the towns we hold one by one and I'm confident we can drive them off, eroding their strength. But we cannot risk collaborators in our garrisons opening the gates to our foes.'

Lord Talbot took up a letter lying in front of him.

'I've heard from the marquise de la Baule. She's gracious enough to apologise for not receiving you as my emissary on the previous occasion. But she's seeking my permission to leave Aquitaine and return to her family lands in the north. Since the death of her friend she has no wish to stay here where she's suffered great unhappiness. I shall grant my permission and provide an armed escort to see her safely out of the duchy. Her departure represents no threat to the English army and it would be churlish to deny her request. I'd like you to take my letter of authority and give it to her in person.'

'She may not wish to receive me in person, my lord. She'll still be in deep mourning.'

Lord Talbot gave a gruff chuckle. 'Oh, I think she will. She discovered who you were after your last futile visit and she's asked particularly that Doctor Somers might bring my reply to her. I suppose she wants to express regrets for her impoliteness to a physician: a person of standing, worthy of respect. I think you know how capricious noble ladies can be. We'd better humour her.'

'If you wish it, my lord.' This unexpected journey would permit me to make enquiries in Cadillac which might throw light on the other strange business that troubled me. 'I'm at your service. You'd wish me to see Sir Guy as well?'

'Indeed. Be ready to leave tomorrow. My clerk will prepare authority for the marquise to leave Aquitaine. Do you have a preference as to the sergeant to lead the lady's escort?'

'Sergeant Rendell Tonks of Lord de Lisle's troop is utterly reliable.'

'Good. So be it. Tonks can choose his men.'

I thought quickly. 'My lord, it would be useful if Johnny Tate could be with me, given that he knows the background. He could accompany me to Cadillac while Sergeant Tonks escorts the marquise in another direction. However he's one of Lord Hanwell's men and his lordship may not wish to release him.'

The Earl snorted. 'He will when I've spoken to him. Proceed as you see fit.' I bowed, ready to leave but he beckoned me forward and spoke confidentially, with a disconcerting wink. 'I entreat you to be restrained in your conduct, Doctor Somers. You have a certain reputation, you know, where noble ladies are concerned, but there are times and places. Indeed, yes: times and places.'

I cringed as a faint smile of reminiscence played on his lips.

*****

I had not seen Rendell for several days and suspected he had been irritated that his contingent was not chosen to accompany Lord Talbot's expedition to Fronsac and the other fortified towns. He had a formidable capacity to sulk. Accordingly, I found it pleasing that he was cheered by the opportunity to lead the bodyguard on my visit to the marquise and conduct her to the border of Aquitaine.

'I don't think you'd have found the Earl's trek to Fronsac very interesting,' I said. 'There wasn't any fighting. There may be soon, when you get back from this mission. The French army are expected to arrive in force to lay siege to towns and castles.'

71

'How come you know so much?'

It gave me immodest pleasure to tease my young friend. 'Lord Talbot told me.'

'My, oh my, ain't we in with the nobs! What's this marquise like then?'

'I'll tell you when I've met her. She lives reclusively and is in mourning.'

'By the way, Doctor Harry, I still ain't heard a whisper of that rhyme you mentioned. Private joke, it must have been.'

Private among whom, I wondered. The answer would be revealing.

I prepared myself to face a grieving but probably arrogant French noblewoman and felt irrationally nervous at the prospect. It would be a formal occasion. I would give her Lord Talbot's safe conduct for her to travel, explain about Rendell's escort and exchange courtesies with her when she expressed regrets for failing to receive me on my previous visit. That was all there was to it, except that I should like to ask her questions which she might consider impertinent.

She was sitting against the light when I entered the room, a small figure dressed in an established widow's plain gown and headdress. Her face was in shadow and I could not tell her age but her voice was melodious.

'I am obliged that you have come, Doctor Somers, after the ill-mannered treatment you were afforded before.'

'There was no lack of manners, my lady. Your steward was impeccably polite and I entirely understood your wish not to be disturbed in such circumstances. I'm privileged to meet you now and can only repeat the commiserations I was ready to give you then.'

She stood and moved forward so I could see her more clearly: a delicate featured lady, possibly in her late-thirties. It was natural that her manner would be solemn but she gave me a searching look.

'It has been a most difficult time but that does not excuse discourtesy. Since your previous visit I have learned you were making enquiries in the district about the killing of the spy near here, on behalf of Lord Talbot I assume.'

I was surprised that she mentioned the subject but saw it as a positive step if she could show interest in something unrelated to her grief. Her next words were even more surprising.

'The officer who is said to have despatched the spy used to call at the chateau when he was based in Cadillac during the past winter. He saw it as his role to maintain contact with noble households in the neighbourhood. I found him unpleasant, offensive in his self-conceit. I thought I should tell you this, although I cannot add anything of relevance to the death of the spy. I have not seen the officer for some months and recently I have been totally consumed by the agony of my own bereavement.'

'I understand, my lady.' It crossed my mind that the marquise might have sought Coote's removal from Cadillac. Sir Guy would certainly have heeded representations from such a person. 'Was your friend's death sudden, my lady? That would mean enduring shock as well as grief.'

'How well you understand, Doctor Somers. Your experience as a physician must have guided you. Mathilde suffered a scizure some days before this adventure with the spy. She was breathing for a day afterwards but never opened her eyes again.'

'I have suffered my own losses, my lady. My wife died a violent death less than a year ago.'

'Ah! Is it the suddenness of loss that provokes strange fancies? I was bereaved of my husband whom I sincerely esteemed but he had lain sick for months and I accepted God had taken him to his rest. Yet, with Mathilde, I feel as if I bear some responsibility, perhaps because I still live while she has gone.' The marquise sank back on her chair and her next words were spoken so softly they could have been addressed only to herself. 'I must live for the rest of my life, bereft of the one person I have truly loved, and I feel guilt.'

'The human heart is unfathomable but I know too well how painful it is to carry guilt in one's heart and to wish the past undone.'

She stared at me, dry-eyed. 'I think you do, Doctor Somers. I think you do. I hope to find some semblance of peace away from the scene of this abrupt tragedy, leaving my dear Mathilde in the vault of the chapel where we worshipped together, which is now her shrine. This estate is the property of my son. He is a squire in my cousin's household but when he comes of age he will take up his inheritance here. I shall not encumber him with my presence but live quietly on my family's lands in the north until I am called to join my beloved friend.'

I warmed towards this consciously desolated, self-lacerating woman. I did not question the sincerity of her grief, although I judged she was in full control of her emotions, and the strange notion came to me that she would be capable of weaving a web of half-truths to mislead a man, if it suited her. I smiled and was disturbed when she responded with pursed lips and a coy look which seemed out of place. It was time for me to leave.

'My lady, I shall not intrude on you any longer. I must continue my journey to Cadillac but my colleague and his men will conduct you to the edge of Aquitaine. Here is Lord Talbot's letter of authority to enable you to cross into King Charles's lands without hindrance.'

'That is thoughtful. I shall leave at first light tomorrow.'

The marquise seemed weary but she held up her hand to prevent me ending our encounter. 'When I heard who it was I had declined to meet, after you called here, I was mortified, Doctor Harry Somers. You see, some time ago, when I was at King Charles's court, I heard of you from a friend who is dear to me, not as Mathilde was, but nevertheless very dear. Do you understand?'

I thought she was merely explaining the nature of her friendship and I nodded.

'The comtesse de Saint Etienne has a high regard for you. I was privileged to receive her confidences which she has given to no one else. I know she holds you in her heart and always will.'

My mouth was dry. I had not heard the title but it could only be one person.

'You knew her years ago when she was the dowager comtesse de Langeais, a widowed noblewoman who served your Queen Margaret at the English court.'

I bowed my head. 'Madame Yolande,' I whispered. 'She was content for those she trusted to call her Madame Yolande.'

The marquise held my eyes with hers and she gave an equivocal smile. 'She has a daughter now, an infant who has brought her joy. But she remembers you and I was intrigued to meet this English physician who had caused her to behave with uncharacteristic abandon. My curiosity has been rewarded and I know you will respect her confidences – and mine. God keep you, Doctor Somers. Continue on your way in the pursuit of truth and justice but, if you will accept advice from a forsaken woman, trust no one in this cruel world.'

As I rode on to Cadillac, with Johnny Tate at my side, I was lost in thought. I had fulfilled my duty to the marquise, completed that part of my remit which required me to meet her, but I could not set aside the memories her words evoked. More than six years previously I had longed to marry the cultured, alluring woman she mentioned, although in the end we bowed reluctantly to the knowledge that such a mésalliance would ruin us both. Yolande returned to France to wed a distinguished count and I had gleaned no certain news of her since then. Yet only weeks before I left England for Bordeaux, my enemy Stephen Boice told me he had ferreted out our secret: the birth and brief life of our baby son. He threatened to disclose our doomed liaison to Yolande's new husband, to bring about

75

her public disgrace for consorting with a mere physician. He used this threat to secure my compliance with his demands and I had known he would hold it over me so I would remain obedient to his will forever after. Only his death had removed the danger.

I viewed Boice's death as due recompense for his villainy in tormenting his niece, Kate, my wife, whom I had married years after Yolande left England. Now it pleased me to reflect that his quittance also safeguarded the Countess and I rejoiced for her happiness with a living, healthy child, after so many years of disappointment.

Some instinct told me the marquise de la Baule could be manipulative but she had conferred a blessing on me by giving me that joyful news about Yolande. Unequivocally I thanked Heaven for her agency.

*****

Sir Guy Binwood was obviously very busy, sitting at a desk stacked with maps and letters, when I was shown into his chamber in the castle at Cadillac the following morning. Perhaps for this reason he was far less affable than at our first meeting. He did not conceal his irritation at my arrival while preserving a veneer of civility. Neither of us mentioned his affliction with the bladder-stone.

'Didn't expect to see you again, physician. I have dispositions to arrange in case of attack. The French army's on the move.'

'Lord Talbot told me and I've no wish to impede your preparations but the Earl wished me to visit you again. Just to check some points in the light of other information relevant to the spy's death.'

'What other information?' he barked. 'I told you all I know.'

I concluded my approach was too brash and I should soften it. 'A suggestion rather than firm information, I should say. Perhaps I've misremembered. I wanted to be sure what you found in the spy's pouch.'

He glared at me and spoke with deliberation between gritted teeth. 'Coins and a foolish rhyme. Nothing else. Why should you think otherwise? Now is that quite clear?'

I had the impression he was challenging me to dispute his statement but I was not about to divulge what Johnny Tate had told me.

'Entirely, Sir Guy. Thank you. I have two other questions. First, do you know how long Jasper Coote stayed in Cadillac after he brought you the pouch?'

'How should I know? You can ask him.'

I hurried on with my next enquiry. 'Did you hear that the body was recovered from the river and presumably buried somewhere in the neighbourhood?'

He tried to master his exasperation. 'What nonsense is this? I've never heard such rubbish. John Talbot sent you all this way to check something I'd already told you and ask absurd questions?'

'Not exactly. It was convenient to call at Cadillac after a mission to the marquise de la Baule.'

His eyes narrowed. 'I heard she was to leave the district.'

'That's true. I brought her a safe conduct and an escort to take her to the edge of Aquitaine.'

He seemed to relax slightly. 'Good, a woman like that is best out of the way if there's to be fighting. Apart from her own safety she could be troublesome. High and mighty, full of herself, liable to interfere. It was due to her I had to send Jasper Coote back to Bordeaux.'

'She complained about him?'

'What did she tell you?'

'Only that she found him conceited and unpleasant.' I noted the apparent inconsistency between Sir Guy's attitude towards Coote on this occasion and his hostility when I saw him on my first visit. 'You were reluctant to send him away?'

'He could be difficult but he's a damned good officer. Bloody woman should have kept her nose out of military matters. Still, all in the past now.'

He rose from his seat, his hand disturbing a pile of documents in front of him, and I reached out to steady them. Seals hanging from the letters knocked against each other and I jolted myself upright, trying to keep my face blank and show no reaction.

'Sorry to be so brusque, Somers. Imperatives of the time, you know. It's a damned pity you've come all this way with nothing to show for it. I do urge you to get some entertainment from your expedition this time. I mentioned the incomparable Madame Claude when you came before. Go to see her this evening. I'll arrange an introduction. She'll give you an appointment if I request it.'

This was not the method I would have chosen to contact Madame Claude in order to question her about Guillaume Coustances, but it was fortuitous and more certain of success than casually calling at her door. I gave a sheepish grin. 'I'd be obliged, Sir Guy.'

'Good man. I'll send my body-servant to take you to her after dark. You'll find her an expert in conferring pleasure on her callers. I've heard her ministrations described as a ride to paradise.'

He laughed and made vulgar thrusting movements while I vainly attempted to stop my cheeks burning.

When I was outside the door it was not Sir Guy's antics which worried me but the sight of a particular broken seal hanging from parchment: the seal of a man I feared, Gilbert Iffley, Baron Glasbury, a cultivated, clever, ruthless man who could display great charm but who, when he chose, commissioned torture and murder. Iffley had plagued me for years with blandishments and threats, urging that I throw in my lot with Richard of York, whom he served. Now he had cause to hold me responsible for the death of his wife's brother, Stephen Boice, and his animosity would be unremitting.

York had shown himself to be effective as a military leader and in upholding law and order in a troubled kingdom – when he was given the opportunity. Despite his accomplishments, however, or perhaps because of them, he had lost King Henry's trust and was mortal foe to the Duke of Somerset, the King's closest adviser. I remembered Lord Talbot had indicated that there might be adherents of Duke Richard with the army but he was not concerned by this if they were willing to fight loyally for King Henry. That was reasonable, as was the likelihood of such men remaining in touch with friends among York's followers in England. Yet, was it possible Sir Guy, Talbot's friend, was of that persuasion – or was he, like me, a recipient of Gilbert Iffley's baleful hostility?

*****

I spoke to Johnny Tate who grinned at hearing of my appointment with Madame Claude, although he understood I had questions to put to her.

'Would you object if I indulged in a minor escapade of my own while you're engaged elsewhere? There's a girl at the whorehouse by the gate I'd be pleased to see again. I visited her when I was in Cadillac after my injury – just to check things were in working order after the horse's hoof had done its worst. It was enjoyable.'

I sent him off to his assignation and shortly afterwards Sir Guy's servant arrived to take me to Madame Claude's house in a network of lanes behind the church of St Blaise. My companion rapped on the grille in the door, the hatch opened and a rugged, unshaven face appeared, glaring at us. Sir Guy's man offered a brief introduction and I was admitted to pay my due. I was told to wait in the vestibule while Claude's huge and intimidating protector lumbered up the rickety staircase to speak to her. He soon reappeared and indicated I should follow him to a room above the entrance where the door stood open.

The woman who beckoned me into the poorly lit chamber was fully dressed, sitting on a stool beside her bed. Heavy perfume filled the air and almost choked me as I drew breath. I gave a nod of acknowledgement and she rose, dropping the wrap from her shoulders to reveal a low-cut stomacher barely constraining her ample breasts.

'You wish for my services, physician? I have only a little time. What is your preference?'

I welcomed my feeling of nausea provoked by the oppressive scent, which moderated any lustful instinct. 'Madame, forgive me. I should like to speak with you.'

Claude glanced at the ledge behind her where a small handbell stood alongside a statuette of the Virgin. If the Holy Mother could not protect her, presumably she would summon the ruffian downstairs to eject a distasteful client. Perhaps her experience was that those who wished to talk were unreliable, perverted in their tastes, prone to be violent.

'I mean no harm. I happened to be in Cadillac and was interested to encounter you...'

'Ah!' Her exclamation surprised me, suggesting relief, even pleasure. I hurried on with my account.

'I've met the family of the late Guillaume Coustances. I understand the poor man had been visiting you before he was...'

'Did Marie Coustances send you here?' Her voice had acquired a new sharpness.

'No. She knows nothing of my visit but I learned that her husband was acquainted with you. It seemed likely he'd seen you the night before his death.'

'You say you happened to be in Cadillac. How did you come to be here?'

'I had business in the neighbourhood.'

She frowned and it occurred to me that I had given the wrong answer. Was it possible her interrogation was in some way coded and required a pre-ordained reply?

She held out a ready-poured beaker of wine and took a second for herself. I lifted the vessel to my nose and breathed in the aroma. The wine was strongly spiced. I smiled at her.

'You say you met Guillaume's family – who else?'

'His daughter.'

'Minette? A forward little minx, he called her.'

'A garrison town offers a variety of amusements and temptations to a young girl.'

'Indeed. But it is not unique to towns with garrisons, physician. I was thirteen when the bailiff of the river took me by force. I learned after my initiation that I possessed favours men would pay for. Minette will do likewise.'

'Perhaps.' I told myself not to be diverted from my purpose by her provocation. We would exchange question for question. 'How long had you known Farmer Coustances?'

'Five or six years, I suppose: since his first wife's illness. His visits were occasional of late – I think you know why. Who else have you met who knew him?'

'No one, except the fishermen who found his body and recognised him.'

She seemed satisfied with my reply and swallowed some wine. 'Drink up, physician. Where did your business take you, in the neighbourhood?'

'I called on the marquise de la Baule,' I said and raised the beaker towards my lips, while watching her expression change from controlled curiosity, to a hint of alarm, to seductiveness.

She sidled forward and sank onto the floor beside me, putting her hand over mine so that I did not drink. Closer at hand, I noted how pretty she was beneath the touches of paint and practised manner.

'Are you sure you are not toying with me, physician? It was clever to secure an introduction from Sir Guy but you do not deceive me. You expect to trick me into disclosing what you want to know.' She opened her hand as if to offer something; then clenched it shut.

I shivered but tried to hide how unsettled I was. 'I wanted to ask you about Guillaume Coustances.'

She giggled and wagged a reproving finger at me. 'You think me naïve? You came to me after calling on the marquise? She would tell you nothing. You've been sent in place of Guillaume, haven't you?'

She slipped her arms round my neck, drawing me towards her, and as desire seized me I let my hands stray to her bosom while we kissed. Then she pulled me to the floor with a decisive thump which rattled the shelf and caused the bell to tinkle. She threw up her skirt, spreading her legs. 'Take what you've paid for, what Guillaume always had when he came, despite our differences.'

To my shame, heedless of my misgivings, I began to loosen my points, ready to couple with her before seeking to discover what her provoking words meant. Only the creak of the stair outside the room brought me to my senses and I rolled away from her as the door flew open.

The massive form of Claude's protector filled the doorway, a dagger glistening in his hand, but I judged his girth might make it difficult for him to move quickly. I tried to scuttle past him on hands and knees but he gripped my shoulder, twisting me round with agility, and pummelled my chin with his fist. I crumpled in his grasp but was conscious of Madame Claude's instruction.

'He's come to betray us. Sent by Talbot. Get rid of him.'

She took the dagger and held it to my throat while the monster extracted cord from his jerkin and tied my hands behind my back. 'He drank no wine,' she said.

'Don't worry: I can deal with this weakling without drugging him.' His deep growl froze my blood.

With justifiable contempt for my physique, he hurled me to the floor and strapped my ankles together before gagging me with a filthy cloth. He did not bother to remove the small knife which I always carried in my belt but flung me over his shoulder and clumped down the narrow stairs with my head swinging from side to side.

Battered and befuddled, I remained sufficiently sentient to appreciate what was happening but my thought-processes were laboured.

We left the building by a side door where a horse was tethered: the conclusion to my visit had been carefully prepared. My captor tossed me across the saddle, clambering up behind, and as we rode off his bulk nearly squeezed the breath from my chest. I knew it was useless to hope we would be halted at the town gate and indeed the portcullis was raised immediately we approached. Within moments we were galloping towards the river.

Misty moonlight showed the scatter of houses and barns outside Cadillac and then we were hurtling along the deserted roadway beside the Garonne. The only certain sounds were those of the horse's hooves and my erratic breathing. Once I fancied I heard a distant whinny and listened for a faint jingle but I knew I must not allow myself the indulgence of hope. There would be horses roaming freely in a nearby field disturbed by our frantic passage. Anyway, even if a benighted farm-hand glimpsed us, no one would attempt to interfere with that mountain of a man who held me captive.

When we came to a halt and I was dragged to the ground I saw we were on a grassy bank jutting out into the water. Below us the river narrowed slightly and the current, flowing downstream, quickened. My mind was now unexpectedly clear. I understood that Guillaume Coustances had not met his death on the lonely track from Cadillac at the hands of thieves, but at those of Madame Claude's thuggish defender, probably at this exact spot. Guillaume's killer hauled me to my feet, smirked, spat in my face and took out knotted twine twisted round a short stick, instruments for the garrotte. He span me round, forced me to my knees and threw the cord over my head, tightening it slowly with excruciating deliberation.

Chapter 7

My mouth was still constrained by the gag and extraordinary noises came from my throat while my body twitched, out of my control. When the spurt of blood poured onto my face and shoulders I thought, fantastically and against all I knew of anatomy, that the top of my head had split open. I was incoherent with pain and shortness of breath as the rope slackened and I subsided to the ground but it was not my voice screaming in agony. Hands wrenched me sideways as the colossal frame of my captor fell forward while he pawed at the air trying to recover his grip on me. I stared uncomprehending at his back, jerkin and flesh apparently slit down the spine, and saw the blood bubbling all along the incision. He was not yet dead and he attempted to seize the foot of my rescuer but the fellow was ready for him. With unerring precision the man drove his blade into the side of the giant's thick neck and wrenched it round, through skin and gristle, to sever the vital blood vessels in the throat.

I choked and spluttered as my gag was removed, unable to speak while I struggled to breathe normally. I thought I might lose consciousness but an arm enfolded me and a voice I knew spoke gently at my ear.

'We need to get away from here. I can't heave that huge carcase into the river. We'll have to leave him. His horse has run off, probably back to Cadillac, so we'll both need to mount mine. We must hurry. They'll send a search party. Can you stand?'

Johnny Tate's face swam in front of my eyes as I attempted to get to my feet and he had to lift me onto the saddle. He slashed my wrists and ankles free from their bonds and held me firmly as we rode from the horrific scene. 'It's a long ride to Bordeaux,' he said after we had covered a mile or so. 'Can you manage?'

My palpitations had calmed and my mind was beginning to clear. I made rumbling sounds in my throat and eventually succeeded in croaking a reply.

'Go to the chateau,' I said, lifting my arm feebly to point uphill.

'The marquise was due to leave the chateau yesterday morning.'

'I know. But we'll go there. I can rest.' I shut my eyes as we started to climb the ridge, gathering my strength for a difficult encounter.

The marquise's steward was dismayed to see us: not, I suspected, solely because of my condition. Nonetheless I begged for shelter overnight. When he demurred, Johnny came to my aid, threatening retaliation if Lord Talbot's personal emissary was turned away and came to harm.

'If you refuse to help, the men who've taken your mistress to safety will return and raze the chateau to the ground. Will the young marquis de la Baule thank you for that? Will you keep your position, do you think? Or shall I use my blade on you as I did on the colossus who tried to kill Doctor Somers?'

Which threat proved effective, I do not know, but the steward complied and I slept that night, exhausted and aching, between soft bed-sheets.

When I woke in the morning I felt weak but fully cognisant and I lay for some while going over events and conclusions that might be drawn from them, outlandish though they were. I was startlingly sure of explanations which had previously eluded me and what I must now do. First, however, I pressed Johnny for a description of his remarkable exploit in rescuing me. He gave a wicked grin.

'From what you told me I thought you might be in danger. I heard rumours about Sir Guy Binwood when I stayed in Cadillac: suggestions he was a devious bugger, not to be trusted. It could have been soldiers' usual rudeness about their leader. I didn't like to mention it before, him being a friend of Lord Talbot and you sent to see him – but I decided I'd keep an eye on you. That's why I went to the brothel outside the gate. Well, one reason. When the horse came clattering down the street after curfew and the portcullis was raised, I was out of the door fast as an arrow. I knew there were horses waiting for their owners who were occupied in the whorehouse so I just borrowed one and set off after you. I had an inkling where you might be going and took quick cuts off the track to gain on you. Thank God I managed it.'

'Amen. I owe you my life. But how were you so silent?'

He put a finger to his lips. 'I told you I'm a skinner and that's true. But sometimes I catch my prey before slicing the pelt. Best tracker in Hertfordshire, I am. All the same I was afraid the horse would give me away when I was coming up behind you. I managed to quieten him and when you stopped I slid out of the saddle and crawled on my belly to reach you. Tough as leather that bastard's hide was. Half blunted my knife, it did.'

I gave Johnny all the praise he deserved and left him to negotiate with a groom for us to borrow two of the horses remaining in the stables at the chateau. The weary creature Johnny had ridden the previous night was to be returned to Cadillac after we were securely back in Bordeaux. I went in search of the steward, whose name was René, and, despite his obvious reluctance, prevailed on him to accompany me into the chapel.

'The marquise told me her companion, Mathilde de Crézé, is buried in front of the altar,' I said as we entered the nave. My voice was still hoarse and my throat sore.

The steward was sickly pale but he nodded. 'Beneath the paving, in the vault. Some of the old marquis's relatives were buried there years ago but it hadn't been used in my time until the lady, Mathilde, was put there.'

A single candle burned on the altar by the blackened figure of Our Lady, its glow reflected in the silver edging to the Madonna's dark robe. I knelt to say a brief prayer and then rose to speak again with the steward.

'I should like you to lift the stone so I can see the coffin. I intend no disrespect and all will be returned to its present state.' He looked horrified and I took his arm. 'I know what we shall find, René, but I need to see with my own eyes. I think you understand. Your mistress is safe, away from Aquitaine. Don't be afraid to tell what you know.'

He coughed and I thought he was about to refuse but he bowed his head. 'We all loved the lady, Mathilde,' he said. 'For all she was unusual, we loved her.'

He fetched a heavy chisel-like tool from a box standing beneath the piscina and prised the stone upwards. It moved easily and he set it to the side of the opening. He lit a taper from the candle on the altar and held it aloft to reveal some shallow steps into the vault which we descended. Without a word he used the tool to dislodge the slab which covered the stone coffin nearest us. The distinctive stench, moderated by the scent of sweet herbs, wafted to our nostrils.

'I can't remove the cover entirely on my own, Doctor Somers, but I think you will see what you wish to.'

I took as deep a breath as my windpipe could manage and peered into the coffin. The body had been respectfully laid out and was not unsightly. Nevertheless there were signs it had been in the river and washed up on the bank where vermin and maggots claimed due tribute. Moreover I could discern that the head had been almost severed from the trunk by the ferocity of Coote's attack. The corpse was richly dressed in a brocade gown and the lady's dark hair cascaded over her shoulders. Her ravaged features had been restored by the embalmer's art. I could not tell how realistic was the effigy created but the bone structure of a narrow pointed nose was unmistakeable. Between the stiff, gloved hands there was a folded bundle of heavy cloth, still veined with remnants of slime which the laundress had been unable to remove from the saturated woollen material.

I lifted my head to face the steward, catching my breath 'Those are her man's clothes?'

'Yes, sir. Normally she wore them only in the chateau or when riding nearby but on that dreadful day she told the marquise she would have to go, disguised, to Cadillac. It was the only reliable way to deliver something.'

'She went to see Sir Guy Binwood?'

'Yes, sir. During the winter there were irregular communications passed to and from him. While he remained at Cadillac the officer, Coote I think is his name, was the go-between. But he had returned to Bordeaux so when something urgent came from France, the marquise agreed her friend should make the journey.'

'And by cruel misadventure Mathilde encountered Coote himself. I can construct a narrative to explain what happened then. Your mistress spun me a web of lies to deceive me about the timing of her friend's death and its circumstances.' I faced René squarely. 'Who sent the communications to the marquise which were passed on to Sir Guy?'

The steward looked down as he heaved the slab into position on the tomb. 'I couldn't say for sure, sir. But the marquise received letters from her brother and her young son. I would never betray my lady while she remained in English-held lands but I am a man of Aquitaine and I could not condone what was happening, what she allowed herself to be involved in.'

I asked the question which had been puzzling me. 'How was the marquise able to recover her friend's body after it was taken from the river?'

'The fishermen recognised Mathilde and brought word to the chateau. I accompanied the marquise with two labourers to bring the lady to her proper place of rest.'

'And the fishermen kept your secret?'

'We agreed a story for use if anyone made enquiry. The marquise is respected in the neighbourhood. The fishermen are her tenants. And she pays well.'

I reflected how easy it was to be misled, to jump to an erroneous conclusion. I had taken it for granted that the men who collected the body were soldiers, that their 'leader' mentioned by the fishermen was either Lord Hanwell or Jasper Coote, and of course no one had sought to disabuse me of my convenient misapprehension. The marquise knew all about her friend's true nature but was intent on drawing a veil over secrets which would have dishonoured Mathilde's memory. I could not find it in my heart to condemn her deception but was bound to acknowledge her guile.

We climbed the steps from the vault and René replaced the stone over its entrance. 'I'm not here to blame you in any way, but to build a picture of the truth. Would it be true to say that Coote attempted to play on the marquise's affections, flirted with her a little maybe?'

The steward sighed. 'How conceited some men are, to consider they are irresistible. Clever women see right through them and find amusement in teasing them. After he realised the truth, Coote and Mathilde quarrelled bitterly and the marquise requested his removal from Cadillac. It was a woeful chance that he met Mathilde again by the riverside.'

'I'm deeply grateful to you, René', I said. 'I have no wish to harm your mistress or Mathilde's reputation. It is Sir Guy Binwood I must expose but I will protect the marquise's secrets and those of her dear companion. I have reason to be grateful to her too.'

'God bless you, sir,' the steward closed the chapel door behind us. 'My mind is soothed to have told what troubled me. Now I can pray with a clear conscience for Lord Talbot's success.'

Later that day, escorted by three burly labourers wielding cudgels, Johnny Tate and I took horse and rode north to Bordeaux. I pleaded discomfort in my throat to explain my silence but I had much to contemplate.

*****

I went directly to the castle, asking to see Lord Talbot, but discovered he was not in Bordeaux. Instead I

89

reported to his son and felt more comfortable telling him, rather than his father, about Sir Guy Binwood's perfidy and lies.

'A network existed for passing messages to and from the French, using the marquise's family contacts and linking them to Sir Guy. I presume he supplied them with information about the strength of the English army and where it was deployed.'

Lord de Lisle whistled as I concluded my account.

'Back in England Sir Guy was an acolyte of Richard Plantagenet, Duke of York, during his quarrels with the Duke of Somerset. But he came willingly to fight for King Henry and I'm sure my father's never doubted his loyalty.'

I remembered Gilbert Iffley's seal hanging from a letter on Sir Guy's desk; it had gained new significance. 'Lord Talbot must know what's been discovered.'

'It may be best if I tell him, Harry. He'll rant and rave a bit but I can cope with that. Was Coote suborned to play a part in Sir Guy's treachery? He's been sent, along with Lord Hanwell and his whole troop to augment the defences at a place called Castillon on the River Dordogne.'

'It isn't clear how much he knew. He may have had his own motives for becoming involved. He needs to be questioned but I think we can leave him for the moment. Is the news about the French army's advance confirmed?'

Lord de Lisle stretched languidly. 'They're coming, no doubt of that. Father's confident we can pick them off if they spread their forces, laying siege to several different fortresses at the same time. They're heavily armed with artillery, presumably for battering town walls. We've not found cannon of much use otherwise. They seem to be putting trust in a master gunner, Jean Bureau, a fellow of base birth elevated to command as if he was a nobleman. Our archers and knights will put them all to flight.'

'Do you expect Lord Talbot to return to Bordeaux before the fighting starts?' Something niggled in my mind from what Lord de Lisle had said but it was rapidly dismissed from my thoughts by new speculations.

'Oh yes, it'll be a week or two before we find out where the French intend to attack. I'll let you know when I've prepared him; then you can make your report. Have you heard the news from the east? That's giving pause to all the loyal sons of Christendom.' I looked blank and he continued. 'A ship came in yesterday. The infidels have taken Constantinople. How far will they ravage now?'

It was known the Turks had been camped outside its walls since earlier in the year but the fall of that renowned city would be considered a devastating blow by many devout Christians. It was seen as a last bastion before the Mohammedans swept once more into western lands they had captured in the past. Meanwhile, Christian rulers were at war with each other.

This news might prompt renewed talk of a crusade, I thought as I returned to my lodgings. The possibility had already been mooted by some enthusiasts but it was said Pope Nicolas had not favoured it. Our own gentle and pious King Henry would surely never go to war in person but he was likely to grieve deeply for the loss of a holy city. A frisson of sadness passed through me but by the time I joined Piers it had gone.

*****

Piers flung his arms round me but was quick to comment that I did not look well, so I was forced to give him a summary of recent occurrences. He was solicitous but I brushed his concern aside and asked him if anything of note had happened in Bordeaux during my absence.

'There've been soldiers deploying all over the place: boatloads crossing the Garonne. Rendell and his band of men got back yesterday and they were sent straight off to Libourne, where the two rivers meet I'm told. Even so, there's still a big garrison here. Lord Palgreve and his men remain in the city and he continues to demand Andy Armstrong be brought to justice.'

'There's no sign of Armstrong?'

'No. But I'm concerned about Madame Coustances. I'm doing all I can but I'm glad you're back because you may be able to help. She's worried about something and hinted she'd like to see you. She seems to find you trustworthy.' There was an odd note in his voice but whether it signified he was sceptical or simply crestfallen, I could not tell.

I laughed awkwardly. 'I'm honoured. Just don't tell Rendell. I'll go in the morning.'

I did not say so to Piers but I welcomed the opportunity to see Madame Coustances, not only because I had a responsibility towards her which must be discharged. I had remembered who it was she reminded me of when I first met her. Margherita Fratta was the sister of a friend when I spent twelve months in northern Italy ten years earlier. She was a charming and intelligent widow whom I had greatly admired but, although she liked me, she was far too wise to engage in an amour. Madame Coustances, by contrast, was probably Andy Armstrong's paramour, yet I thought of her as a prudent, capable woman cast in the same mould as Margherita. It was perhaps a mark of my heart's slow healing after my wife's death that I could find the prospect of this woman's undemanding company pleasing.

She greeted me courteously but she was agitated, spilling a little of the wine she poured for me. Then she sat facing me across the empty hearth and puckered her brow reproachfully.

'You did not tell me of Master Armstrong's predicament, Doctor Somers. I'm disappointed you left me ignorant of the charge levelled against him. He was my husband's friend – and mine too – I'm most concerned for his safety.'

'I'm sorry, Madame, at the time I didn't want to add to your distress. We spoke of Minette and your husband's death... it seemed too much to refer to Master Armstrong's difficulties as well. I didn't know if the accusations against him would persist. I hoped they might be dropped, that he could be vouched for with an alibi.'

She sighed. 'You considered my feelings. That was kind. I feared your failure to tell me was callousness, lack of concern.'

'On the contrary: I was embarrassed. I recognised your attachment to Master Armstrong and didn't want to cause you pain.'

She leapt to her feet, twisting her hands, white-faced and trembling. 'Attachment? You don't... you can't... it isn't possible...' She subsided as quickly as she had risen and a slow smile spread across her face. 'You believed Master Armstrong was my lover! Oh, Doctor Somers, I did not realise. I can assure you it isn't true.'

I sighed in turn but was not quite sure of the reason. 'Forgive me, Madame. It was reprehensible of me.'

'It was a natural error for a man to make, judging as the world customarily judges. Master Armstrong was here when I was a girl. My father knew him, as did Guillaume. There has been no impropriety.'

I stood and bowed. 'I am rightly reproved. I will leave you.'

'No, please.' She was on her feet again. 'As an honest woman, I beg you to tell me: is there any way to help Master Armstrong? They say that when he returns to Bordeaux he will be charged with murder and almost certainly found guilty. It will be circumstantial but I know he will be convicted. You don't believe him guilty, do you?'

'I saw him leave the city before Sergeant Bartley was killed but I can't swear he didn't return. The animosity between the pair was widely known. We must hope someone Master Armstrong met miles away from the city can vouch for his presence elsewhere.'

She held her hands in front of her face. 'They will not. They cannot. His mission was confidential. Even Lord Talbot would not be able to intervene to save him. It would risk the whole enterprise.'

I stared at her as I grasped her meaning which confirmed the suspicion I had entertained about Andy Armstrong's covert role. 'Master Armstrong carries out secret missions for the Earl?'

She nodded sadly and a wave of sympathy swept over me. I took her hands in mine. 'I can make no promises but I will do all I can to ensure he is protected. As soon as the Earl returns to Bordeaux, I will speak to him. If you hear from Master Armstrong in the meantime, contact me immediately.'

Her eyes were brimming with unshed tears as she looked at me and raised my hand to her lips. 'God bless you, Doctor Somers. God bless you.'

I kept her hand in mine while I told her what I must. 'I've discovered the circumstances of your husband's death. As I think you always knew, it was not an act of casual violence at the hand of robbers. He was ensnared, as I was, because his enemies thought him dangerous. I nearly shared his fate. His murderer is now dead – at the hand of my rescuer.'

She gasped but did not speak, clutching my fingers tightly.

'Forgive my intrusiveness, Madame, but I surmise that your husband had a purpose in visiting Cadillac, not just to call on the woman, Claude. Was he trying to obtain information?'

She bit her lip and did not reply immediately. 'He was asked to go. It was a dreadful misjudgement. His liaison with Claude was no secret and someone believed she knew about treachery in the town.'

The sequence of events was all too clear. 'Andy Armstrong asked him to go?'

She withdrew her hands from mine to wipe her tears. 'Andy has connections in France. He gathers material which may be useful to Lord Talbot. He had deduced that the French were receiving confidential details from Cadillac. He wanted to see what could be confirmed by enquiries in the town but Lord Talbot required him to go elsewhere. Andy knew Guillaume favoured the English so he invited him to take on the mission. It was dangerous and Guillaume was not accustomed to such underhand activities. Andy will never forgive himself for involving my husband and bringing about his death.'

'You knew what had been arranged?'

'I had forebodings it would not end well but Guillaume was insistent he would play his part. You and your rescuer have avenged his death and that has eased some of the pain in my heart: the pain of uselessness in the face of loss and grief.'

I was touched by her gratitude and her brave composure but I was not fully persuaded by her protestations of innocent friendship with Andy Armstrong. His well-being seemed so important to her. My doubts were troubling for I found her attractive and instinctively wished to pursue our acquaintance. Yet, from more than one point of view, I must not risk engaging in dalliance with someone who might hoodwink me. The encounter with Madame Claude was too fresh and searing.

'Has there been news of Minette's whereabouts?' I asked, jolted by the memory of Claude's heartless words about the girl. Madame Coustances shook her head and pressed her lips together tightly.

'Soon I shall go with the army to wherever there is serious fighting. When I return to Bordeaux, when the fighting is over, may I visit you again?'

She looked surprised and turned away before answering. 'If you wish it, Doctor Somers, I shall be honoured to receive you. If God blesses the English cause and King Henry's servants are spared, perhaps Andy and Master Ford will be able to join us.'

My parting from Marie Coustances was entirely decorous.

Chapter 8

Events moved quickly over the next ten days and although I saw Lord Talbot briefly on two occasions he had no time, or perhaps, inclination, to pursue the issue of Sir Guy Binwood's treachery.

'I will confront him when we have beaten the French,' he said at our second meeting. 'He can do little harm in Cadillac when our armies are in the field. Cadillac will be a backwater. The main action looks set to be around the fortresses along the Dordogne. I expect it within days and as soon as I hear which towns are under siege, I shall lead our march to relieve them. Lords Clinton and Palgreve will remain here to hold Bordeaux. Each of our bastions has adequate defences to hold the enemy at bay until reinforcements arrive to support them.'

'Lord de Lisle told me the French are well supplied with artillery.'

'Pah!' The old warrior was not impressed. 'Heavy cannon can pound walls but they're an encumbrance on the battlefield. They're slow and cumbersome and their aim is unreliable. I put my trust in the skill of our archers and horsemen. They've brought us the victory over many years.'

I had no intention of venturing an opinion on military matters.

'Warfare on the battlefield is an art, Somers, with its own conventions of chivalry and honour. You know, I suppose, I was taken prisoner by the French years ago? When I was ransomed I gave my pledge never to come again in arms against them and I shall keep my word.'

'You won't take the field in person?' This seemed eminently sensible in view of the veteran's advanced years.

'We shall see.' The Earl laughed. 'If the need arises, there are ways and means. Now listen, I'm concerned about this Jasper Coote fellow – and possibly Lord Hanwell too if he's part of the conspiracy. They are in Castillon which is more exposed than Cadillac. I've no time to interrogate them so I'd like you to go there and question them on my behalf. I'll furnish you with letters of authority. Take an escort. It's probable our main army will need to move before you've finished in Castillon so you can join us directly when the call comes. Knowledge that a good physician is at hand to patch up their wounds is a great encouragement to soldiers facing the enemy. You'll be attached to my own troop and can set up your station in my field headquarters, wherever that happens to be. Get your man to prepare your potions and roll up your dressings.'

With a lifetime's experience, he sounded cheerful, eagerly expectant. My first-hand encounters with combat had been limited and I viewed my imminent exposure to serious warfare with deep apprehension and revulsion. The prelude with Lord Hanwell and Jasper Coote was hardly more enticing. I had made a fool of myself when I last saw his lordship and Coote had every reason to want me dead.

*****

I left Piers to prepare my supplies which he would bring to me when the main army moved to the expected site of battle. Johnny Tate had been detailed to join the muster at Libourne so he was able to accompany me part of the way and we set off together to cross the Garonne and strike north-east. After saving my life Johnny was enthusiastic about my investigation but he was relieved he need not encounter Coote in person

The fortress at Castillon was situated in the highest part of a small town, the walls of which sloped down towards the River Dordogne. This watercourse was not quite so wide as the Garonne but it was still impressive. To the north of the town fields and vineyards spread across to a low ridge roughly parallel to the river. I presented my credentials, asked to see Lord Hanwell and was admitted to the castle without equivocation.

My reception by his lordship was inevitably less cordial. 'I remember you, physician,' he said. 'Have you come to accuse me of body-snatching once more? Why does the Earl take heed of your outrageous allegations?'

I had already decided an honest admission of fault would be wise. 'I owe you an apology for my wild assertions previously. I know now you had no role in the recovery of the body or its burial. I had imagined that because your officer, Jasper Coote, was responsible for the death, you as his overlord might have sanctioned his action. I'm pleased to tell you that the body was given Christian burial.'

He grunted and I hoped the fawning implications of my words might have placated him. 'You said something of the sort before and I accept it would have been proper for Coote to confide in me as his lord. He hasn't done so and I know nothing whatsoever about the killing, the body or what has happened to it.'

'I accept that, my lord. I have the Earl of Shrewsbury's authority to investigate the death further and I propose to interrogate Coote. It would be fitting to do so in your presence. Would you agree to that?'

He stared at me coldly as he considered the position; rapid decision-making was obviously not one of his talents. 'It would be fitting. I shall send for Coote forthwith.'

While we waited I outlined what I had discovered about the 'spy' and Lord Hanwell's eyes bulged with indignation. To pass the time I then referred to the fall of Constantinople and the misfortune this represented to Christendom by giving the infidels a symbolic prize. My comment proved judiciously chosen.

'That's discerning, Doctor Somers. Alas, my comrades are blind to the dangers it represents. I pray the rulers of Christian countries will assemble their forces for a crusade to retrieve the Holy City. Since Jerusalem was lost, Constantinople has been precious to us all. Yet only

Duke Philip of Burgundy seems committed to take the cross for such a mission.'

Duke Philip's intentions were not a subject on which I could comment but I was saved from the attempt by the arrival of Jasper Coote. At least I had won Lord Hanwell's trust sufficiently for him to allow me to proceed with questioning.

'Doctor Somers will conduct this interrogation in my presence on Lord Talbot's behalf,' he said to his officer. 'You will answer him fully and truthfully. If we are dissatisfied at the end of our meeting, there remains the possibility of putting you to the instruments. Is that clear?'

Coote looked startled, as well he might, and I was rattled by Hanwell's new-found enthusiasm. I was nervous as a field-mouse under the eye of a swooping hawk.

'Jasper Coote, a good deal of information has come our way since we last spoke. I should like you to tell us first how it was that you knew Mathilde de Crézé before the encounter which led to her death.'

He gulped and glared at me, horrified and uncertain how much to admit. 'I never said I knew her. What has this to do with me?'

'I suggest that you don't waste our time. We've established the identity of the so-called spy you killed and we have a sworn statement from the marquise de la Baule. Nonetheless, we wish to hear your own account.'

'Cunts, both of them. Unnatural bitches.'

Lord Hanwell rapped the table angrily, murmuring, 'instruments'.

Coote glanced at his lord, then at me, and shrugged. 'I was second in command of Cadillac after we took the town before Yule. The marquise has a manor-house nearby and I was sent to give her assurances of King Henry's goodwill to his subjects in Aquitaine. She was gracious towards me and welcomed the arrival of the English army. At her invitation I visited her house several times. It was an amiable exchange of courtesies.'

'And Mathilde de Crézé was present on these occasions?'

He grimaced. 'The de Crézé woman scarcely left the marquise's side: a hoyden who wore breeches and hose beneath a robe.'

'She customarily dressed as a man?'

'Only in the house, I thought: when the fancy took her. Perverted jade!'

'So when you saw her riding towards you by the riverbank, while you were scouting with Johnny Tate, you quickly recognised her?'

He did not answer at once. 'She shrieked at me. She was abusive and threatened me with death at the hands of the French when they came to reclaim Aquitaine.'

I could hear Lord Hanwell harrumphing behind me and determinedly ignored him. 'Were you surprised to hear her express those sentiments?'

'I'd always suspected she hated the English. I guessed that was why she was offhand when I visited them.'

'Does the marquise share those views?'

Coote flushed with annoyance. 'The marquise was invariably gracious and showed no prejudice.'

'You know very well that Mathilde de Crézé was part of a chain passing messages between contacts in France and Sir Guy Binwood in Cadillac. You were employed as go-between for these treasonable communications, were you not?'

Coote had been attempting to brazen out the situation concerning Mathilde's identity but he believed his own role was not in question. Suddenly he saw the gulf opening beneath his feet. 'I... I know nothing of this...the woman invented this insult to my honour.'

'I have reason to believe you were a fully cognisant and willing player in a conspiracy.'

'No! It was only when the woman accused me of complicity in their plot, I learned there was malfeasance.

That was why I slit her foul throat before she spoke more lies. I gave the pouch to Sir Guy, as was my duty.'

'Why did you kill her?'

'I was in a rage with the two-faced cow. I see now I should have kept control and denounced her to Lord Hanwell but I was in a frenzy. She was trying to involve me in treachery. I admit my fault, in losing my temper and failing to think straight. I accept the punishment that is due to me for this dereliction.' Ostentatiously he dropped to his knees in front of his overlord but Hanwell ignored him.

I did not comment on his contrition. 'How did the lady Mathilde refer to the papers she carried?'

Coote looked puzzled. 'We spoke in French.'

'I imagine you did as the soldier with you would overhear what you said. I suggest she spoke to you on the basis that you had prior knowledge of similar communications. Did you?'

'Of course not! What rubbish is this?' For all his bluster, he appeared ruffled.

'Did Mathilde de Crézé tell you what the letter said?'

'How? Why? No. Letter?'

'You seem uncertain. There was a letter, sealed but possibly not addressed to anyone. How did you know it was appropriate to pass it to Sir Guy?'

'He is the senior English officer in Cadillac. The bitch was disloyal, a French catspaw. It was obvious the letter would be incriminating.'

'And you thought she was trying to incriminate you?'

'Why? What? Yes, I've said so.' Coote was having difficulty keeping up with the implications of my questions and trying to avoid inconsistencies in his replies.

'Why would she want to incriminate you?'

'To disgrace me – perhaps get me hanged. She hated me.'

101

'Why, Jasper Coote, why did Mathilde de Crézé hate you?'

'I...she... she was a cantankerous woman. She knew I would expose treachery as a loyal Englishman. She saw me as a danger to their plots.'

'Why should she do that when you'd worked with her previously? Had she come to see you as a rival for the affections of the marquise de la Baule?'

Lord Hanwell coughed but his attention and mine focussed on Coote. The officer's face was puce and he was quivering. He waggled his arms and opened his mouth but did not speak while he mastered his alarm. There was no immediate denial so I added a more specific query.

'Were you, have you in fact been the marquise de la Baule's lover or was this merely an unachievable aspiration?'

He gulped twice and found his voice. 'You impugn a lady's honour to say such a thing,' he said with an attempt at grandeur.

'I suggest you succeeded in winning some show of affection from the marquise, perhaps no more than innocent flirtation, and this offended her companion. I don't imagine you succeeded in seducing the noble lady. It was you who saw Mathilde as your rival. Isn't that so?'

Coote spluttered. 'You've no grounds to accuse me. And no right to impugn my manhood. Do you really think a hot-bloodied noblewoman would prefer a woman's tinkering to a lusty fellow's cock? If there's been an offence of the flesh, it'll be one for Holy Church...' His voice faded as he realised what he had implied.

'I suggest that you killed Mathilde de Crézé because she thwarted your access to the marquise and used her influence to have you moved from Cadillac to Bordeaux. I conjecture that, despite this redeployment, you maintained contact with the marquise, thus infuriating her companion still further. Was it possible she sought to bring about your disgrace when she accosted you by the riverside? I have an open mind on that but Mathilde may well have hated you as much as you hated her. You were rivals to share the lady's bed, weren't you?'

I had been aware of Lord Hanwell's simmering outrage but he could no longer stay silent. 'It's obscene. Vile. Disgusting.'

The interruption gave Coote a moment to recover himself and he spoke with bitter calm. 'Mathilde de Crézé was a traitor. That's all there is to it.'

'What was the purpose of the impertinent rhyme in Mathilde's pouch, apparently making fun of Lord Talbot? Who wrote it?'

'It was a nonsense rhyme. It was simply there to verify that the message accompanying it was genuine.'

He gaped at me as I grinned. 'So there was an accompanying message? What did it say?'

'I didn't look at it. I took it to Sir Guy Binwood.'

'So you delivered it to the person who was meant to receive it? Just as Mathilde de Crézé asked, just as you'd always done in the past when you collected messages for Sir Guy at the chateau.'

Only then did Coote realise that Sir Guy's guilt had been established as well as his own and he showed himself the consummate opportunist. 'Oh Holy Mother, I've been tricked,' he said, 'inveigled into passing treasonable messages between traitors. I knew nothing. I obeyed orders. I'm appalled. My honesty has been abused. I'd no idea Sir Guy had ulterior motives in sending me to the chateau. I'm devastated. Lord Talbot's lieutenant in Cadillac a villain!' He put his face in his hands.

Lord Hanwell wished to hear no more. He called for the guards and ordered that Jasper Coote be confined while considered what action should be taken. He came to my side after the officer had gone and peered at me searchingly. 'How on earth did you work all that out?' he asked.

'Experience may have taught me to make perverse connections but several threads needed to come together to give me warp and woof. Something the soldier who was present said about the way Coote and Mathilde spoke to each other at the riverside provided me the first clue. Later, after I made some deductions about her death, I was conducted to the lady's tomb at the chateau and saw the body. When I met the marquise I formed the impression she might have indulged in mild flirtation with Coote during his visits to the chateau: a meaningless diversion for her but it risked boosting his self-esteem before puncturing his pride. As for Sir Guy Binwood, he arranged to have me murdered. I found that convincing evidence of his guilt. It was chancy putting my conjectures to Coote so baldly, but interrogators need to take chances sometimes.'

His lordship nodded. 'As do Christian soldiers. We all have our campaign techniques. I confess I'm uncertain how much Coote knew about the conspiracy. He could have been duped into doing Binwood's dirty work. But to involve himself with that filthy household... to aspire to share the marquise's favours...! I'm speechless.' Almost immediately he gave the lie to his last pronouncement as his curiosity overcame his scruples. 'One thing surprised me. You hadn't mentioned to me that you obtained a sworn statement from the marquise.'

I lowered my eyes. 'An omission which would speedily be rectified, my lord, if ever I were to see the lady again.'

'By all the saints,' he said with a hint of admiration in his voice, 'you are a cunning bastard!' He turned to his table with this ungodly exclamation and I bowed. I had developed a sneaking regard for this dour and censorious nobleman.

*****

I stayed the night at Castillon and when I awoke next morning I breathed in the warmth of a southern summer along with the scent of rosemary swatches hanging from a beam above my pallet. I stretched in a leisurely fashion, eased of tension now Lord Hanwell was fully aware of the situation and Coote was incarcerated in a cell. I heard distant shouting but life in a small garrisoned castle is often noisy and I thought nothing of it. After a moment, through bleary eyes I noted that the two other men accommodated in the guest chamber had already risen so the hour must be later than I imagined.

I put on my outer garments as the shouting increased in volume and no sooner was I fully dressed than a servant arrived with the request that I attend Lord Hanwell immediately in his room. Half a dozen other men were already present when I arrived and I was hustled to join them, peering through a window looking east from the town. Across the fields in the distance I could see a dark line and a thin column of smoke drifting upwards.

'The French,' a soldier told me. 'Maybe just an advance party. Our scouts are assessing numbers.'

Lord Hanwell called for order and repeated what my informant had just said. 'I've sent messengers to alert Lord Talbot in Bordeaux and our comrades in Libourne and other towns along the Dordogne. We can expect to be put under siege but if the French army is divided into sections, this will not be the only town invested. The Captain of Castillon has called all men to action so take your stations. Go!'

Lord Hanwell beckoned me. 'Doctor Somers, you should leave at once while you can still evade the French by riding west. The Captain can spare one retainer to guide you. With good fortune you should encounter English reinforcements on their way here. The blessed saints protect you. Go!'

I hurried obediently on my way, collecting my bundle of possessions and taking to horse alongside a portly cellarer who wheezed alarmingly as we picked up speed. We called at the town of St. Emilion, where we confirmed that the councillors had already been advised of the impending danger. Then we rode on to Libourne which was swarming with soldiers sent ahead by Lord Talbot in the expectation that a French attack was most likely to come on the Dordogne. When I learned that Lord de Lisle was in charge there, I asked to see him and advised my purple-faced companion to rest.

Lord de Lisle was inevitably occupied with military matters but he greeted me genially and made time for a brief conversation. He approved my suggestion that I might as well remain in the town until we knew the Earl's intentions for deployment of the main army. This would depend on moves by the French but Lord Talbot would certainly bring his forces across the Dordogne at some point and Piers would be with them. I could meet up with my assistant and my medical supplies when I was sure of their whereabouts. If I tried to continue towards Bordeaux I might well miss them.

I was free then to wander round the town, taking care not to impede soldiers assembling and dispersing, collecting arms and sharpening weapons. I hoped I might encounter Rendell but the first person I recognised was one I had temporarily forgotten. The sight of Andy Armstrong filled me with conflicting sentiments.

He bounded forward with alacrity. 'Didn't expect to find you here so soon, Doctor Somers. I thought the physicians would arrive later.'

'I had a commission to undertake in Castillon and spent the night there. I was sent away before the French besiege the place.'

'Sensible. They've got some powerful ordnance with them, heavy and light guns. Jean Bureau has entrenched his cannon and it'll be no easy task for the English to engage with them. He's a master gunner, Bureau, knows how to use artillery. If he decided the cannon should let fly against the town, the walls of Castillon would rupture, but I fancy he may have other plans to thwart our advance.'

There seemed no need for pretence. 'This is intelligence you've been gathering?'

He inclined his head with mock admiration. 'You've fathomed my role. I've been reconnoitring along the ridge above Castillon. There's a priory which would serve Lord Talbot well as his headquarters. The French have occupied it but it's a weak garrison. We'll soon get them out.' He beamed with satisfaction. 'It's a pleasure to get on with my work without hindrance, since that bastard Bartley isn't around any longer.'

It was clear Armstrong did not consider himself to be in imminent danger of arrest and I certainly did not intend to ask if it was he who removed the hindrance. I was relieved to see Rendell running towards us, waving enthusiastically.

'You learned to fly, Doctor Harry? How've you managed to get here before anyone else?'

I repeated my explanation and Rendell was impressed that I had actually seen the French army, albeit obscurely and at a distance. 'Could you make out those great guns they're supposed to have?'

I shook my head as Andy Armstrong protested. 'Nothing supposed about it. There are six hundred French gunners with culverins and ribauldequins to keep them occupied. Jean Bureau's got what Lord Talbot lacks.'

I froze. 'Jean Bureau's got what Lord Talbot lacks. Oh my God, we're idiots!'

Rendell grasped my meaning at once: 'The rhyme!'

Armstrong was bemused as we drew him aside into a quiet corner where passers-by were unlikely to catch much of our conversation.

'Have you ever heard this before, Andy? I asked.
JB has much old JT lacks
Glory will come when he attacks.
England's great champion put to shame;
T'will be RP shall win the game.
'No, never, but it's clear enough what the first bit means.'

'The rhyme was in the pouch of the French spy killed by Jasper Coote, who we now know was part of a

107

chain passing messages to and from the enemy. Coote claims it simply verified that the message accompanying it was genuine but I think it might possess a meaning of its own.'

'Who's RP then?' Rendell asked.

'We thought it might refer to Lord Richard Palgreve. He might hope to become commander if Talbot was discredited.'

Neither Rendell nor Andy Armstrong was impressed and I was ready to discard the theory. I racked my brains, searching for something Lord de Lisle had said but I could not call to mind. Armstrong was quicker.

'I've heard gossip among dissidents with little respect for King Henry, naming one person who could gain from England's defeat in Aquitaine. In England, I mean.'

'Richard of York but...'Rendell began. I cut across his words as at last I recalled the elusive clue.

'I should have remembered. Lord de Lisle spoke of him as Richard Plantagenet. He uses the name to stress his royal blood. It all fits. We know there are followers of York in the army and some of them must have turned traitor, working for Lord Talbot's defeat and King Henry's humiliation.'

I did not refer to Sir Guy Binwood or his correspondence with Gilbert Iffley. I would tell Rendell privately about my discoveries but was not sufficiently at ease with Armstrong to share sensitive information with him. I regretted this made me think of Marie Coustances and wonder anew about her relationship with a man who customarily played a clandestine role. Deception came naturally to him. Might it do so to her also?

Chapter 9

Two days later Lord Talbot crossed the Dordogne with around eight hundred mounted knights and other horsemen, to be followed twenty-four hours later by some five thousand foot-soldiers. He came directly to Libourne to spend the night, giving time for reinforcements to join the main army. I thought it a daunting task to find Piers in the throng milling about in the town but he came looking for me and he had brought all the supplies and equipment I requested. My wheelwright friend was pale, his manner tense, and I knew attendance on the battlefield would be a terrible ordeal for a man who hated violence and longed for harmony between people everywhere.

At dawn Lord Talbot moved forward into the woods on the ridge overlooking Castillón and duly captured the Priory of St. Florent from the French. He kept the resident monks corralled in one corner of their enclosure and sent a party to pursue the remnants of the enemy garrison who had taken flight. Through a servant, the Earl invited me to establish my base within the precincts of the priory and I was glad to draw breath there, although I knew my proper business would lie nearer the field of battle. In the meantime I was well positioned to pick up the latest intelligence brought to the commander.

I learned that during the last three days the French had constructed a defensive enclosure where I first glimpsed their camp, a mile or so to the east of Castillon. It was said to be surrounded by ditches and embankments reinforced by tree trunks, flanked by the River Dordogne to the south and its steep-banked tributary, the Lidoire, to the north below the ridge. Numbers were difficult to estimate but it was clear the enemy's strength was considerable. This was no isolated raiding party, rather the main might of King Charles's army. A full-scale confrontation was in prospect which Lord Talbot had hoped to avoid. Its outcome could be momentous and its enactment would be bloody.

Very quickly reports spread of the first hand-to-hand fighting when Lord Talbot's troops, chasing the French fugitives bundled out of the priory, encountered resistance. They returned to the Earl claiming success because they had trapped a band of French foot-archers and killed five or six score of these unfortunates. Shortly afterwards, a messenger from Lord Hanwell in Castillon reached the priory. He urged his commander to follow up this initial achievement by marching speedily to the town's relief. He gave assurances that when the size of Talbot's forces became clear, the French would flee. I am no military man but, in view of what we had now learned about their defences, this optimism seemed to me unwarranted.

While he waited for the last of the English foot-soldiers to arrive, the Earl ordered that a cask of the local wine be broached for his men and it was during this period for refreshment that I held a hurried conversation with him. He greeted me jovially, telling me to quench my thirst while I could, and he expressed the hope that I would not be overburdened when battle was engaged.

'We shall make straight for their enclosure,' he said. 'I don't doubt that, once we break into their field, they'll take to their heels. Hanwell thinks so and I've seen it before. It'll be a delight for this old warrior to put the French to flight again. I shall be there to rally my men and it will be a joyful day for me.'

'You mean to take the field yourself, my lord?' I remembered he had told me of his pledge never to come again in arms against King Charles. It would be quite normal for a venerable commander to direct manoeuvres from a position above the battlefield and this is what I had expected him to do.

'I shall be there, Somers, where my duty lies and my heart insists. But I shall not break my sacred oath. I shall ride a small hackney, not a war horse, and I shall wear no armour. I shall not be in arms.'

'My lord, that is...' One could not tell King Henry's commander it was foolhardy, indeed downright absurd, to put himself in peril. 'That is scrupulously honourable.'

He smiled. 'Exactly, Somers. It is the honourable way to behave. I hope these young gallants beside me and those crude gunners whom the French employ will recognise the importance of acting honourably – on the battlefield as much as in the royal court.'

'Indeed, my lord. I pray all will go well. I have matters on which to consult you when the fighting is over, arising from my enquiries.'

'Certainly. When the French have been sent packing and the banner of St George flies freely throughout Aquitaine, I shall attend to all you have to tell me. I know from my son that you've done well and I thank you. Now you must excuse me. Scouts have just returned from reconnoitring the enemy encampment and I must see them before I hear Mass.'

I bowed as he strode away. I was filled with admiration for his noble spirit and resilience but a spasm of fear gripped me: fear that the old man was holding to values younger warriors might no longer recognise or see as relevant. I hoped I was wrong.

Within minutes there was a flurry of activity throughout the priory. The scouts had reported clouds of dust rising in the distance above the location of the French camp and it was confidently assumed that the foe had taken flight. It fitted so well with what Talbot and his officers believed likely and wanted to hear. The supposition was not questioned and no further patrols were sent out to confirm the enemy's departure. The order was given for an immediate advance. The objective was concisely stated: the utter rout of King Charles's army.

*****

As the heat of that July day intensified, the English army moved forward from their quarters. Horsemen in full armour gleamed in the rays of the sun, preparing to ride downhill from the priory, plumes waving from their helmets, visors for the moment raised. In the fields at the foot of the slope, where the majority of soldiers had camped, the famous English long-bowmen, most wearing quilted leather jerkins, took up their weapons and marched proudly, in close formation, to form the front rank in the usual order of battle. Behind them a more motley collection of foot-soldiers lifted spears, pikes and halberds, swung maces and brandished a miscellany of blades, ready to take up their intended positions in the second rank. The cavalry would be drawn up behind them, equipped to charge into action when the archers and spearmen had depleted the lines of the enemy. I watched and was impressed by the assembly, exuding discipline, control and determination.

I counted eight banners under which the army advanced, recognising those of England, St. George, the Trinity and Talbot's own crest. The others would belong to noblemen who had brought their own contingents of fighting men from their demesnes at home. The area where battle would be engaged was obvious: the flood plain of the Dordogne lying between that river and the Lidoire, below the higher ground of the ridge, and extending eastwards from the town of Castillon towards the French enclosure.

It was time for me to move closer to where the fighting would take place. Other English physicians were in attendance but most of them chose to stay in the vicinity of the priory. Some of their patients would be carried or might limp to reach them once the fighting had ceased. Many would not be identified as in need of treatment until the desolate battlefield was searched, when living bodies would be distinguished from the corpses of their comrades. The longer the injured lay untended, the more probable became their demise.

I thought it might be helpful to have a forward station where some of the wounded could be treated with greater immediacy. So, with Piers at my elbow, both of us carrying bundles of instruments, potions, ointments and bandages, I set off along the ridge to identify the best place to position ourselves. Under the feeble shade of a wizened tree at the lower edge of a copse on the slope, we laid out our tackle and prepared to offer physic and makeshift surgery to the combatants. We were both trembling with expectation of the horrors to come.

Piers hauled his long frame up into the tree and balanced on the most substantial branch to see better what was happening ahead. He reported that the English vanguard was fording a sizeable stream, which must be the Lidoire, and they had to narrow their formation to pick a way across this obstacle. He could discern no sign of movement in the distant French camp but, like me, he was sceptical about the assumption it had been deserted. Neither Piers nor I had any real knowledge of military strategy but months in the company of soldiers gave us some jargon with which to appear more informed than we were. He commented on the heavy carts bringing up the rear of the English column, conveying ponderous and unwieldy cannon.

'If the French are relying on the power of their artillery, as Andy Armstrong suggests, they must have found a way to make the things more manageable. The weight on our wagons means they're liable to get stuck in muddy ground. Even when the cannon are stationary, they can only fire in one direction.'

I laughed. 'Skilled wheelwright, you are, but you sound like a martial sage. I'm afraid this bids to be infinitely worse than the so-called battle of London Bridge.'

We held each other's eyes, remembering the occasion when we had worked together giving succour to those injured in the bitter night-long encounter between rebels led by Jack Cade and the citizens of London. That had been three years earlier but the barbarity of the event remained fresh in our memories.

'May the saints help those about to fight,' Piers said, 'and whatever the outcome, may it not lead to brutality beyond the battlefield. God protect the innocents who rest at home while their menfolk exchange blows. May they be safe from the mad bloodlust savagery creates.'

His entreaty was well judged. There were women and children in the town of Castillon, so near across the narrow plain, who could easily become the prey of a victorious army – whichever sovereign lord it served.

For some time we could not make out what was happening and it was not until after the battle that we learned the true sequence of events from those who survived. The first indication we received that our misgivings about a French retreat were justified came with the boom of their cannon: three hundred guns, we were told, all firing simultaneously. From a mile away we heard the thunderous noise and shuddered.

Explanations were given subsequently by men who had been in the thick of the battle to clarify what they had experienced and understood. The French camp had not been abandoned: far from it. The misleading dust had been raised when servants moved baggage away from the area cleared for combat while ranks of soldiers waited silently, under orders, in their positions behind impregnable defences. As soon as the gunners fired, the impact on the English attackers was appalling. One cannonball could take down five or six men and the culverins were speedily reloaded. Severed limbs shot into the air as salvo after salvo ripped, in turn, through the English archers, the foot-soldiers and the mounted men-at-arms. The ground acquired a slimy, slippery overlay of guts and gore. Again and again the shattered battle lines regrouped but the attackers struggled to breach the barriers around the enclosure and some began to pull back. Then, with victory already in their sights, the French flung open their barricade and horsemen debouched ferociously into the fray.

At the time we knew little of this narrative but we could see indistinctly when French soldiers erupted from their encampment and the English rout began in earnest. Extra mounted men held in reserve by the French, who we later learned were Bretons, charged from the shadow of trees to the north of the enclosure and joined the mêlée as the attempt at an orderly English retreat became a stampede for survival. When the French attempted to block possible escape routes, the fighting surged across the plain until bitter hand-to-hand tussles were taking place only a few feet away, below us. We watched in revulsion as running men were slashed and heads bludgeoned, knowing there was no role for us while this frenzy continued. Haze obscured the scale of the slaughter but the stink of blood, urine and faeces wafted to our nostrils and made me retch.

At last the fiercest fighting swirled away from our position, in the direction of the town, and two wounded foot-soldiers dragged themselves upright and staggered towards the ridge. Piers ran forward to assist them up the incline so I could stitch a slashed arm and try to staunch the bleeding from a crushed shoulder. The cries and groans of men, the squeals of injured horses and the clash of metal were deafening while we forced ourselves to concentrate on our acts of compassion. Despite my trembling hand I managed reasonable stitches to clamp together the ripped flesh of a forearm and, to my disbelief, my patient then ran down the slope to re-join the battle. I applied unguent to the other fellow's wound to encourage clotting of the blood but he needed more attention than I could give on an exposed hillside.

'Can you get yourself along the ridge to the priory? There are physicians there who could dress your shoulder better than I can.'

'Oh, Christ in Heaven, no!'

I span round at Piers's scream to look where he was pointing. The soldier whose arm I had just patched together lay immobile at the feet of a war horse, while his adversary withdrew a sword-tip from his throat.

'What's the use? Why are we here? Mankind are monsters. Oh, God! Oh, God!'

Piers was distraught, sobbing in anguish. I understood how profoundly the gruesome scene we were witnessing tormented his peaceful nature. I had been wrong to expose him to such suffering. I grasped his arm.

'Take this man to the priory as quickly as you can. There's a chance you can save a life. Stay there to help the other physicians. We'll meet up later.'

Piers stared down at me, relief and distress competing in his expression. 'God bless you, Harry Somers. I pray we'll find each other.'

He scooped the injured soldier into his arms and set off along the crest of the ridge, striding as quickly as he could with his burden.

Soon afterwards I moved down the slope to be nearer the twitching bodies scattered across the plain, but I dared not run out to tend them while armed men were still rampaging in their midst. I helped half a dozen fellows, who were hobbling or on all fours, to climb the ridge and slapped balm on gashes and abrasions. I urged them all to hurry on their way to seek refuge from the carnage.

I was about to descend to the plain once more when I felt the ground vibrate beneath my feet and looked round to see a posse of French riders pounding towards me along the ridge. I flung myself to the ground and rolled down the blood-spattered grass to avoid thundering hooves and flourished maces, but my little store of salves and dressings was smashed and scattered. Worse than that, I knew that the fugitives I had assisted and directed to the priory were to be pursued and pitilessly hunted down.

I sat with my head in my hands at the foot of the incline, hopeless and numbed, expecting at any moment to be slashed in pieces regardless of my physician's garb. I was aware of a horse wheeling about beside me and waited for the blow which must follow but an arm stretched out and a hand gripped my shoulder.

'Quickly, get up onto the saddle. There's a chance we can get to the town.'

I took the gauntleted hand offered and was hauled in front of the rider. Despite his plate armour, of a quality above his station, I knew him to be Andy Armstrong but my wits were blunted as we wove a circuitous path across the battlefield and round by the walls of Castillon. He used his sword to good effect to secure our passage while I crumpled forward, shielding my head as best I could. By the time we reached the river gate I was sufficiently alert to realise the portcullis was raised and a thin line of battered Englishmen was trailing into the town. Once inside the walls, we climbed the steep road to the castle and were helped to dismount. It was then I observed that Armstrong's face was fretted with streaks of blood issuing from beneath the brim of his helmet.

'You're hurt. Let me see what I can do. I've lost my supplies.'

'The Captain of the castle will have a physician and you can help him. My cut's not deep. The helmet's strong and saved me from the worst of a slanting mace blow. It rammed the rim into my forehead. But listen, Doctor Somers. I think you won't know the worst.'

I must have looked blank and puckered my brow trying to think what he meant.

'Lord Talbot is dead; Lord de Lisle too and scores of other nobles, hundreds of foot-soldiers, maybe thousands.'

'Lord Talbot? He went unarmed.'

'He did, more fool him. His hackney was shot from under him and an axe finished him off as he lay on the ground, his red velvet surcoat stained a deeper scarlet. I saw it all. My place was always near him. We'd tried to plant his banner at the French enclosure but were driven back.'

117

'And Lord de Lisle too? He was a friend to me.'

'It's a disastrous day for England. The poor old commander wouldn't listen. He had no time for our advice, rubbished the French cannon, scorned Jean Bureau. Our army's destroyed. There'll be more skirmishes but Aquitaine is all but lost to King Henry. There'll be consequences in England as well as this side of the Narrow Sea.'

I blinked, trying to concentrate, sure he was telling me something beyond the literal meaning of his words, conscious that he sounded more authoritative than I had ever heard him.

'Richard of York will exploit this disaster?'

He nodded. 'You guessed, Doctor Somers. We can speak freely now. But first there are things which must be done. You'll want to tend the injured and I must see what can be arranged to get us away from Castillon after nightfall. Come morning, the French cannon will move into position to bring down the town walls. I shouldn't wonder if the Captain of Castillon surrenders as soon as they're aligned. I can't be here then, no more can you. There's work for us to do away from here.'

My mind was working slowly and it latched on to random issues. 'The cannon can be moved without difficulty?'

Armstrong grinned. 'We'll make a soldier of you yet. The French cannon are on low platforms with wheels, simple to haul about and switch direction. Brilliant, Jean Bureau is. We've no one to match him. Now get about your physician's work and I'll find you after dark.'

*****

As I worked alongside an elderly physician from Libourne, my mind cleared and I learned more of our situation. Not only had the slaughter of Englishmen on the battlefield been immense, but the chances of escape for survivors were limited. I heard of a fearsome pursuit along

118

the ridge as far as the town of St Emilion and hundreds drowned trying to flounder their way across the Dordogne. I feared for Piers, probably struck down when the French recovered the priory, and wondered whether I would ever learn the fates of Rendell and Johnny Tate whose broken bodies might now be lying on the plain beyond the walls of Castillon. There would be untold numbers of wounded prostrate among the dead but I could not help them. I must put my efforts into tending those who had reached temporary sanctuary in the castle and there were more than enough of them to occupy me fully.

The Captain of Castillon was much in evidence, inspecting his guards, visiting our patients, encouraging the townsfolk not to panic; he seemed an exemplary leader. It occurred to me, by contrast, that I had seen or heard nothing of Lord Hanwell who had been sent to join the Captain as Lord Talbot's representative. None of the English soldiers I attended knew about him but that was not surprising as they had been on the field of battle while he presumably remained within the castle. I also thought of Jasper Coote confined in a cell, perhaps ignorant of exactly what was happening yards from the town.

After two hours of unremitting labour I bound the arm of a soldier who wore the crest of the castle's Captain. I believed all within Castillon's walls had remained safe, so far at least, and I asked in French how he came by his injury.

'I went outside briefly,' he said, 'escorting Lord Anvelle to the river when he left. A French arrow caught me as I returned.'

I repeated the name to myself silently with a French accent. 'Lord Hanwell? He left the town?'

'It didn't do him any good, sir. He was killed as he climbed into the rowing boat. The fellow with him stabbed him. Then he grabbed the oars and made off across the water on his own. We pulled his lordship out of the river but he was gone, his chest split open.'

I steadied my hand as the bandage slipped. 'Who was this murderous fellow?'

'Some Englishman who'd been shut in the dungeon but his lordship had him released. They were to leave together.'

'Jasper Coote,' I muttered. 'And he escaped?'

'Yes, I think that was the name. We couldn't spare men to pursue him. I think he will be safe now, on the other side of the Dordogne. I think he must have had scores to settle with Lord Anvelle.'

'Indeed yes,' I said.

Moreover, I thought, now he is free he will have scores to settle with others too – and I will certainly be among them.

Chapter 10

Andy Armstrong was true to his word and roused me from fitful slumber on the floor of the great hall, where a hundred or more soldiers had found temporary resting places. He was no longer wearing full armour, simply a padded jerkin like any humble foot-soldier. I followed him silently through the postern gate of the castle and down the ramp leading to the river gate in the town walls. A guard was waiting to let us pass and we clambered onto the shingly foreshore of the river, heading downstream. We had no torch or taper but there was an occasional beam of moonlight and my companion seemed to know his way without artificial aids.

'Do you swim, Doctor Somers?' Armstrong hissed.

I winced. 'It's years since I tried and I was never adept.' I wished he had told me earlier what he had in mind. I would not have built up my hopes of escape.

He gave a low chuckle. 'I guessed as much. Don't worry, I've no wish to complete our journey drenched to the skin. Just be careful not to slip into the water. It's little more than a raft we've got, with a paddle to direct it across on the ebbing tide. You'll need to keep your balance.'

I grinned weakly in the dark, not appreciating his attempt at humour, and stumbled on over the pebbles and mud until we reached a tumbledown shack above the waterline. Armstrong quickly lifted some broken wall planks, which appeared to have collapsed along with the roof, and hauled out a substantial structure of logs strapped together and covered in some black caulking material.

'Had this put here as a precaution: last line of defence in case the old Earl needed to slip off unseen. Now you can take his place. Basic lesson in my line of activity, this is: don't leave yourself without an escape route.'

I helped move our humble vessel into the water and scrambled aboard as Armstrong pushed off using his paddle. The current was running swiftly and my steersman seemed content to let us be carried out into the centre of the river which alarmed me considerably at first. Keeping my balance was no trivial matter but I understood I must prevent my weight falling too much to one side. Then, when Armstrong judged we were past the turbulence nearer the shore, he began to use his oar to ease us slowly towards the southern bank. With gratitude, I appreciated that he knew exactly how to manage our primitive conveyance and he sensed that my nervousness was subsiding.

'All under control, Doctor,' he said. 'Now we can talk. I trusted you from the beginning but I had to keep up the pretence. It comes as second nature to one like me. You realised I've been a spy for Lord Talbot, finding out all I could about the French army and their intentions. I suffered for it, I can tell you – much good it's done.'

He stopped speaking for a moment while he manoeuvred the raft towards a gently shelving bank on the south side of the Dordogne. 'That bastard Bartley hated me, jealous probably, and when he claimed I'd stolen a chicken, Lord Talbot had to have me thrashed. Otherwise, if I'd been given special treatment, Bartley would have worked out what I was up to and he wasn't the sort you'd confide in, unreliable. Trouble was when he flogged me, as you spotted, I'd been whipped only a week or two earlier, by the French in Angoulême. Luckily they assumed I was a worthless beggar, not an agent for the English, otherwise they'd have had my head off. But the two beatings knocked me back a bit, so you must have thought me weakly.'

He helped me off the beached raft and pointed to a building in the distance, faintly visible in the first glimmer of dawn. 'We can get horses at that farm. I must ride directly to Bordeaux to see Lord Palgreve. The French'll encircle the city and call for its surrender. We'll have to evacuate sometime but I hope we won't need to do so in a panic. The French will take all the fortresses the English hold. They'll line up the cannon and one after the other the gates'll be flung open.' He looked at me meaningfully. 'Including at Cadillac.'

'Sir Guy Binwood is treacherous and I suspect Jasper Coote has gone to join him.' I explained about his escape and Lord Hanwell's murder.

Armstrong whistled. 'Wish I'd known how dangerous that bit of scum was. While I was snooping I gathered there was a network of those helping the enemy, including English traitors. I deduced it was centred on Cadillac but I couldn't spare time to go there so I asked Guillaume Coustances to see what he could find out. I knew he visited a harlot there. I'll carry guilt for his death with me always now. As soon as I can I must visit Marie to check she's all right. After a catastrophe like this there'll be unruly bands of armed men harassing peaceful folk until order's restored.'

'You're fond of Madame Coustances?'

He gave a brusque nod and took hold of my arm. We had reached the farm and he conducted his business with the farmer hurriedly, giving him a handful of coins.

'I think I should go to Cadillac,' I said. 'Binwood and Coote could still do damage.'

'They could but you'll not stop them on your own, Doctor. It'd be stupid to go there. Come with me to Bordeaux. Have to bow to the inevitable in this situation.'

I knew he was right and acknowledged it. 'You mentioned seeing Lord Palgreve. Is he reliable? He wanted you executed for Bartley's death.'

'Oh, yes, he's loyal to King Henry: not the brightest beacon of the nobility and quick to take offence, but I have credentials from Lord Talbot to show him. He'll recognise necessity. Besides, Lord Clinton will have command of the English in Bordeaux, not Palgreve. He knows me.'

'Somerset's son?'

'Somerset's bastard,' he corrected me, looking over his shoulder. 'Wait! Get into the trees over there.'

We galloped into the copse he indicated and from there I glimpsed what he had seen. In the distance, behind

123

us, half a dozen French knights were riding furiously south with banners flying. We would have found ourselves in their path.

'As I thought'. Armstrong said. 'They'll cross this tongue of land between the Dordogne and the Garonne and lose no time in investing Cadillac. But your charming acquaintances, Binwood and Coote, will be given free passage by their seditious contacts. It's my guess they'll soon be on their way to England and they'll be found at Richard of York's side within the month. We'll follow the Dordogne to the estuary and find a boat to take us direct to Bordeaux.'

As we rode on I reflected on these rapid moves by the French. 'They'll let their soldiers rampage and terrorise the locals, won't they, to bring the population to heel? That's why you want to be sure Madame Coustances is safe. I understand: she's an admirable woman.'

Andy Armstrong grinned at me. 'What I hope for is that your mate, the wheelwright, got away from the battlefield and went straight to the farm. I fancy he's sweet on Marie. He'd be good for her.'

I turned my head away, astonished, urging my horse forward through a tangle of long grasses. It seemed I had been too full of my own brooding fancies to realise what must have been under my nose but I was puzzled by Armstrong's apparent approval.

*****

News of the disaster at Castillon reached Bordeaux before our arrival and a ship had already set sail to inform King Henry of the dire news. Measures were in hand to thwart panic reactions in the city, redoubling guards at the gates and preventing travellers without authority entering or leaving its precincts. Moreover, Lord Clinton had impounded the sailing gear from provision-vessels anchored in the estuary, whether from England, Spain, Holland or Flanders. If there had to be an evacuation, it was to be orderly and it would not take place until English honour had been upheld by resisting a show of force from the French, at least for a decent period. Within a few days the enemy duly arrived on the right bank of the Garonne and, facing each other across the expanse of water just north of the city, blockhouses were erected by both sides to posture and glower at each other. There was no immediate attempt by King Charles's men to cross the river.

I returned to my old lodgings and was fully occupied tending wounds and calming uneasiness while Armstrong was closeted with the English leaders. I gathered Lord Palgreve did not demur at his attendance at some of their debates and he was accommodated in the palace itself, no longer the shadowy misfit he had previously seemed. I was grateful that he had rescued me from the battlefield but I was still wary of him.

Meanwhile battered and disheartened men continued to find their way to the city after tortuous journeys from the battlefield at Castillon. Most bore injuries and all were shocked by what had befallen the English army. Through the long hours while I examined and treated a stream of patients, I looked for those I recognised, hoping for information, fearing as the days passed that my friends were irrevocably lost, steadying myself to mourn. Rendell I had known since he was a mischievous urchin of seven or eight. Piers, upright and idealistic, had shared many undertakings with me over the past three years. Johnny Tate I had at first mistrusted but he had saved my life. Each evening I flopped exhausted on my pallet but my sleep was disturbed by grisly, frightening dreams.

As we feared, news was brought of attacks on the populace in the countryside, mostly at some distance from the city, and on the fourth day after our return Andy Armstrong arrived at my door bearing safe conducts for us both to leave Bordeaux by the south gate and return before dusk. He was rueful that he had not visited the Coustances farm more expeditiously but I supposed he had been given no choice in the matter. In answer to my question he told me Minette might well be with her step-mother as he had learned she disappeared from Bordeaux before most of the garrison departed for Castillon. He had no definite information about her whereabouts but did not appear greatly concerned.

Armstrong was in armour again, as a precaution in case we encountered ne'er-do-wells, and while it seemed overdramatic, I welcomed feeling secure in his company. We went on horseback, even though it was so short an expedition, and at first everything had the appearance of normality. I began to relish the prospect of meeting the engaging Marie Coustances again, irrespective of other admirers she might or might not possess. Then as we approached the entrance to the farm lands the scene around about us changed.

The fields were deserted, with hayricks tumbled, and we exchanged worried looks before we came to the smouldering remains of outhouses and barns. On the undulating ground the vines had been trampled and, ahead of us, the farmhouse door hung crookedly from one hinge, concealing what lay within. We jumped from our saddles, causing my ankle to creak and wobble, and we ran inside.

The interior had been looted, furniture smashed and the modest contents of shelves scattered on the floor. We picked our way over broken earthenware and upturned cooking pots to where we knew she would be. We said nothing to each other. The flimsy door to the bedroom had been shattered and there was a streak of dried blood on the lintel. The rushes on the floor had been crushed and pushed aside by a charge of boots; the hangings had been ripped from the simple tester. In the midst of this disorder, Marie Coustances lay spread-eagled on the bed, her dress ripped apart, smears of filth disfiguring her nakedness, and from below her chin a veil of gore covered her breasts from the gash which had severed her windpipe.

But she was not alone. As my eyes took in the atrocity which had been perpetrated, I realised that her left hand lying over the side of the bed was clasped by the stiff fingers of another. I moved round and dropped to my knees beside Piers Ford, my treasured friend since I met him in the confusion of Jack Cade's rebellion. The good, honest wheelwright, who was tormented by mankind's inhumanity and longed for peace, had been savagely assaulted and mutilated. It seemed probable he had been compelled to witness the rape and murder of the woman he wished to help before he was brutally slain, but he had struggled to reach her and hold her hand. He had come with me to France, giving time for Bess Willoughby to reconsider his offer of marriage, hoping she would accept him on his return. I would never know whether he had relinquished hope of Bess, overtaken by affection for Marie, nor was it my place to speculate. What I knew was that I had lost a dear comrade, along with a woman about whom I had indulged pleasing though idle fancies.

Andy Armstrong was sobbing and I knew he would blame himself for failing to defend Marie against the demons of the world. It was my role to try and help the afflicted – the living afflicted – so I went to him and led him out into the sultry air.

'We must look for Minette,' I said. 'She may be lying anywhere, abused and killed like Marie.'

He cleared his throat as if remembering something and wiped his face before turning to what needed to be done. 'Minette,' he said with a sniff. 'Yes, we should look for her and fetch help to take the bodies. Dear Christ, I give thanks Master Ford was with Marie at the end. She would have known there was love in the world, not just barbarity. That's a small comfort.'

I thought his words sensitive and magnanimous.

Armstrong could ride more quickly without me at his side so I suggested he should return to Bordeaux to report while I started to search the farm. By the time he returned with a priest and the Sénéchal's men, I had combed the house and moved into the yard and its ruined outbuildings. Then we all fanned out across the fields and vineyards until dusk fell but there was no sign of Minette. We had no way of knowing whether this was a hopeful indication that she had not been present when the farm was raided. More likely she had been carried off by the ruffians to suffer further atrocities.

That evening Armstrong asked to join me in my lodgings and I produced a flask of wine, recognising he needed company to help him come to terms with what we had seen, as I did. He drank deeply, then set down his cup and fixed me with rheumy eyes.

'No need for deceit now, Doctor. I've had to pretend too much perhaps, but that's all over. I want you to hear the truth.'

I mumbled something about being honoured if he wished to confide in me, completely unprepared for what he was about to say.

'Marie was my sister, half-sister, much younger than me of course. My father went to fight in France when I was a little lad, left me with my mother on Tyneside. Later she died and my Da wed a French girl. He stayed over here, came to Aquitaine, and he had me brought to live with them. Marie was a tiny wee thing. He told me to protect her – sod it, I failed.'

He coughed and drank again. I did not interrupt.

'That's when I first met Guillaume Coustances, boys together. But later I went north to join the English army when it was fighting in Normandy – I was attached to Lord Talbot's troop. You can guess the rest. When I came back here last autumn the Earl was determined I should gather intelligence for him. I had contacts and spoke French and the local dialect as well as English. He gave me confidential commissions and they were hazardous. I didn't want my relationship to Marie known; might have put her and Guillaume in danger. I helped them when I could but got them to swear they'd never say who I was. Much good those precautions were.'

His voice faltered and I put my hand on his arm. 'You mustn't blame yourself. There's nothing to suggest the raiders attacked the farm because of your link with it.'

'Maybe, but I sent Guillaume to his death in Cadillac. I'll always carry that burden.'

I drew a deep breath. 'Two years ago I was responsible for the death of a good man who accompanied me to a dangerous meeting. He threw himself in front of me and died on my behalf. I had no right to live while he was killed.'

Armstrong's expression was bleak. 'Right has nothing to do with it. Like as not, these things are random. A priest might say there was a purpose behind our survival. I'm not sure life's that orderly. You cast horoscopes, as a physician?'

'I can of course but seldom do. They help to identify toxic imbalances in the humours which govern a patient's health or condition a malady, but the medicine I learned in Padua concentrated on what we can determine from examining our patients' bodies and their bodily functions. That seems to me good sense. As I know to my cost, afflictions of the mind are outside our comprehension to remedy successfully but I'm still doubtful that the constellations in the sky can help.'

'You're a bold thinker, Doctor, and a practical man. I like that.' He poured himself more wine.

We sat together quietly until his head drooped onto the table. Then I helped Andy Armstrong across the room to sleep on the pallet which had belonged to Piers while I lay sleepless on my bed, unable to set aside the awful revelations of that day. Hopelessness enveloped me.

*****

News reached us as the weeks went on, reporting the surrender of various towns to the French. A few of the most strongly fortified castles continued to hold out although their eventual fate seemed inevitable. Cadillac

129

was among them, held by Captain Gaillardet who was now unencumbered by the presence of Sir Guy Binwood. I was not surprised to learn that Sir Guy had taken himself off from the town as soon as news of the defeat at Castillon arrived. Whether or not Jasper Coote joined him, I could only guess.

Some supplies continued to reach Bordeaux by water but increasingly hunger threatened its inhabitants as the besiegers tightened their grip beyond the walls. Bands of unruly scoundrels, taking advantage of the breakdown in law and order, continued to harry the countryside and refugees streamed to the gates of the city. Its future remained in jeopardy and Armstrong told me he expected the French would make overtures to agree capitulation before the end of September.

I fulfilled my role, shared the diminishing rations of all city residents, and generally felt listless, almost unconcerned about what might befall me. Return to England was fraught with uncertainties. Would I be taken in charge, accused of murder, or had the efforts of my friends at home averted that risk? What had I to look forward to, a widower with limited resources, lacking a patron and incurring the animosity of potentially powerful men? If there was a violent struggle for Bordeaux, I might in any case be prevented from escaping by land or sea and who knew how the French would treat captives? There was no comfort in the alternatives.

Bitter winds driving up the estuary and sudden squalls of rain were intermingled with spells of early autumnal beauty, the changes as unsettling as the prospects facing us. Then came a week of astonishing upheaval: removing from me any semblance of choice, resolving my indecisions without my agency, hurling me into a mental maelstrom. I became a pawn without any impetus of my own. Yet, before I was swept away by what some would call Fate, I received a blessing which compensated for much which was to follow.

I hardly recognised them as they approached me in the street near my lodgings. They had just entered the city through the river gate and, on seeing me, these skeletal figures began to wave while I stared uncomprehending at first. Then with incredulous joy I ran forward with arms outstretched.

The taller figure was hobbling, leaning on a slender forked tree trunk as a crutch, swinging his left foot which scarcely touched the ground. Beside him, the shorter man had once been of a sturdier build but he had lost much weight and his face was drawn, lacking the rubicund glow which lit his roguish countenance in the past.

'Rendell! Johnny! Is it really you?'

'Yeah, we've been unavoidably delayed in arriving.' In spite of his pallor Rendell had not lost his wry humour. I embraced him. 'For once it's me has to be grateful because Johnny Tate here saved my life. Mind you, he then buggered up our chance of a quick escape by breaking his leg. Still, we've made it now. God, it's good to see you, Doctor Harry! We didn't know if you'd survived.'

It came as a shock that they had despaired of my survival as I had of theirs.

We talked late into the night, exchanging news, and I learned of the perilous weeks they had spent since they escaped from the battlefield, tramping on foot, avoiding capture, drinking from streams, eating berries, sleeping in woods and ditches: all of which became more problematic after Johnny's accident.

Rendell told most of their story. 'I'd been fighting hand-to-hand outside the walls of Castillon when a cannon blast threw me off my feet and I was knocked out cold. I don't remember anything until my guardian angel here slung me over his shoulder and headed for the river. Bloody good swimmer, he is. He got me across the Dordogne despite me being half-conscious and arrows shot all around us. Then we stumbled our way into some undergrowth where we could rest until I came to myself without my head spinning. We picked our way upstream

131

for a couple of days. We thought we'd a better chance of escaping the French search parties going in the opposite direction. After a bit we turned south, hoping we'd cut across to the Garonne, but Johnny got it into his head to climb an apple tree in the yard of a tumbledown farm.'

Johnny held up his hand to acknowledge his error. 'Loaded with fruit, it was, but the branch I stood on was weak and I fell awkwardly. I heard the crack and knew my leg was done for. Luckily Rendell's learned a bit from watching you, Doctor, and he managed to splint it roughly using our belts and a broken fence-post. We had to hole up for a while until I could manage to hobble; that's why it took us so long to get here. I'm beginning to put weight on my foot now and then. I know I'll always have a limp but I should be able to get around.'

'I'll check it over and give you some exercises to strengthen your leg. It looks as if Rendell's done a pretty good job in the circumstances.'

I gave them all the news I had, whether cheerful or depressing, and I described the atrocity at the Coustances farm. Neither Rendell nor Johnny had met Marie but they were dismayed to learn how Piers died barbarously at her side. They bowed their heads for a few moments and Rendell's voice was husky when he spoke.

'There's been no trace of Minette?' he asked, deducing the answer. 'Poor girl.' He changed the subject to comment ironically on Andy Armstrong's double life before enquiring about our prospects for evacuation from Bordeaux.

I shrugged. 'Armstrong says the English lords will negotiate surrender of the city in return for agreement allowing us all to take ship for England. I'm not sure it's where I want to go.'

'Probably won't be given an alternative,' Johnny said.

What transpired cannot have been what he had in mind but he never spoke a truer word.

Over the next week provisions became noticeably scarcer in the city. Armstrong reported there were upwards of three thousand English troops lodged in Bordeaux and as many fighters from elsewhere in Aquitaine. Scores were crammed into the new blockhouse but others had to find quarters among an increasingly uneasy populace who did not welcome extra mouths to be fed. We were not starving but our rations were cut back and I felt enervated and apathetic about the future.

It therefore startled me when I was summoned to attend Lord Clinton in the palace and was escorted to his office by armed guards. The acting Commander of the English garrison was accompanied by Lord Palgreve: not an encouraging sign, I feared. I hoped it was my medical services which were required.

Lord Clinton's expression was grave and he did not waste time on formalities. 'Doctor Somers, a ship sent on behalf of King Henry himself is lying off the estuary. Emissaries have come to me with a royal command that you are to be taken to that vessel and thence conveyed to England. You are to collect your possessions and leave Bordeaux immediately. Guards will accompany you to your lodgings and an armed posse will attend you across country to where a small boat can take you to the ship.'

I shut my eyes. Lord Clinton had not specified that I was under arrest but it was clear to me I was to be arraigned on the charge of murder with which I had been threatened when I left England nearly a year previously.

'Must I go alone?'

Lord Palgreve replied to my pointless question and sounded quite congenial. 'You may take your physician's assistant and any attendant that you have – provided they can be ready to leave at once. I wish you a fair voyage.'

Since Ned Bartley's death Palgreve had disliked me and I imagined he was enjoying this pretence of urbanity, relishing the knowledge that I was about to receive what he saw as my just deserts. I thanked him humbly.

By great good fortune, both Rendell and Johnny Tate were at our lodgings and, swallowing their astonishment, they seized the opportunity to travel with me. Within the hour we had left the city, Johnny riding pillion with a burly officer. I was mounted on a fine horse, as was Rendell, temporarily designated my assistant, but we were clearly under guard. There was no time to see Andy Armstrong although I left a message for him.

I had survived the horrors of warfare, assault and treachery but must now face the perilous reckoning which awaited me in my homeland.

Part 2 Westminster, Windsor, London and East Anglia 1453-4

Chapter 11

We landed at Southampton after an unremarkable crossing during which Rendell alternated between pleasure at returning to England and raw prickliness. I understood his ambivalence. Johnny Tate was consistently calm and self-contained, determinedly testing his leg as it grew stronger. I could not forget the horrors I had seen on the battlefield and at the Coustances farm and I missed Piers with his matchless combination of idealism and common sense. I tried to focus my mind, moment to moment, on my comparative freedom while aboard ship, where I was treated firmly but with respect. I recognised these might be my last days at liberty, perhaps simply my last days, without qualification.

A troop of men in royal livery met us on the shore, which was alarming because it indicated I was viewed as an important prisoner. Presumably for ease of riding, I was not shackled but the formidable escort was sufficient to dispel any thoughts of escape. Rendell and Johnny were told they must remain with me until we reached our nameless destination; then they would be free to leave. Neither demurred. Rendell in particular was amused by his designation as my assistant and pontificated on his skills as a bone-setter, chatting amicably with our guards.

As we circuited below the town walls, I identified the roofs of Winchester where I had once lodged for several months, and then we were climbing the ridge, heading towards the north-east. We travelled by easy stages, spending one night at a priory near the village of Basing and a second at Kingston where we crossed the Thames. I concluded that we were bound for Westminster, where the King's Great Council customarily assembled and where no doubt justices would be convened to pass judgement on me. There was a dreadful inevitability about what would follow.

My surmise as to location was correct and not reassuring. The Palace of Westminster was indeed our destination and the bustle of servants and delivery wagons at the gate confirmed that the court was in attendance. We rode under the great entrance arch into precincts which evoked a variety of memories for me and at once, as expected, I was separated from my friends. Oddly, I was escorted to a room in the range of buildings which I knew contained the Queen's apartments. The attendants were courteous and I was given a bowl of water to wash the splatter of the road from my face and hands. I was offered food but declined it, fearing my stomach was too tense to eat and might rebel with messy consequences. Later I was taken along passages to an antechamber where I was asked to wait while a man at arms kept guard by the door. My apprehension grew minute by minute although I tried to lull myself into placid resignation.

At last I was summoned into the adjoining room and there received a shock which jolted me out of my melancholy lassitude, shattering my preconceptions. A man wearing fine robes rose from his desk against the side wall and strode to embrace me.

'I'm glad to see you, Harry. You look out of sorts but I hope that's just the effect of a tiresome journey.'

'Sir Nicholas! I had no idea I was to meet you.'

I became aware that at the far end of the chamber a second man was sitting, a nobleman, flamboyantly clad in velvet and silks, with a jewelled collar and a resplendent chain of office round his neck. I looked more closely and bowed low in a turmoil of emotions, before Edmund Beaufort, Duke of Somerset and Constable of England, King Henry's favoured adviser and mortal enemy to Richard, Duke of York.

'Welcome home, Doctor Somers,' he said. 'You were present at Castillon, I understand. You've served your

King faithfully. John Talbot thought highly of you, God rest his soul.'

I muttered 'Amen', hardly able to speak in my surprise and confusion. I had served Somerset in the past and his greeting sounded sincere but I could not comprehend why I had been brought to see him. Sir Nicholas Chamberlayne, Somerset's man of business, was a friend: certainly he had been a friend. I was nervous. Much could have changed in a year and I was ignorant of the shifts in power and allegiances which might have taken place at court during my absence from England.

'You look baffled, Doctor Somers. As well you might. I'm sorry we couldn't explain why your attendance was so urgently required when you were fetched from Bordeaux. It was essential to maintain the utmost secrecy: imperative no hares were set running, no hint given of the crucial commission you're asked to undertake – the greatest challenge to your professional expertise.'

'I'm wanted as a physician?' Incredulity caused me to gasp. 'Who is to be my patient?'

Sir Nicholas pushed a stool towards me 'Sit down, Harry. 'Your patient will arrive at Windsor within a few days. You will journey there and share care of him with half a dozen quacks who have failed to make any headway in treating him during the last two months. His condition creates a conundrum for all of them and a crisis for the realm. You have experience, regrettable experience, which may be relevant in this strange case.'

I had begun to tremble as I interpreted what he was saying. 'My patient is...?'

'His Grace, King Henry, sixth of that name.' Somerset's tone was solemn. 'He has lost the power of motion, speech and, it appears, comprehension. He stares vacantly into space and responds to none of the expedients used by your fellow physicians. His servant feeds him as if he was a baby and indeed his behaviour is entirely infantile. He is carried from place to place. He sits and stares and eats; then he sleeps – that's all.'

Sir Nicholas continued the account. 'You can imagine, Harry, what dangers might arise if anyone outside the circle serving his Grace were to learn of his illness. The members of his immediate household are sworn to keep silent but how long the secret can be preserved is doubtful. The court is already restless with concern about what we have called a minor ailment. Her Grace, Queen Margaret, is desperate to find a cure before her enemies seek advantage from the King's disorder. She authorised me to send for you.'

This was the most improbable of all the improbable statements I had just heard. 'Queen Margaret authorised my attendance?'

Sir Nicholas smiled. 'Old grievances are swept aside by this catastrophe. You have experience of treating disturbances of the mind. Her Grace will receive you this evening to confirm what I have told you.'

'The King's mental state sounds very different from the affliction which troubled my late wife and medicine offers little to guide us in seeking to correct imbalances of the mind. Of course I'll offer all the help I can but I beg you not to think I have remedies unavailable to colleague physicians.' There was a note of panic in my voice.

'You'll do your best. That's what we ask.' Somerset rose to his feet and we all stood. 'Call for whatever you need. Do you wish your attendants to travel to Windsor with you? Their absolute discretion will be required.'

'I shouldn't wish to detain them, my lord. It may be easier if they leave me without details of my commission.'

'Rendell Tonks is one of them I believe?' Sir Nicholas was always well informed. 'Duke Edmund has offered to take him into his personal service. Tonks can report to his captain at the Somerset lodgings in the City.'

'That's kind. I'll tell him.' I bowed to both gentlemen but Somerset had one thing more to say.

'Don't be concerned about the violent events which occurred before you left London for Aquitaine. They have been fully explained without any adverse implications for

138

you. Nevertheless, have a care for yourself, Doctor Somers. I imagine your methods may differ from those of His Grace's established physicians. They may not disguise their spitefulness if they think you are unfairly favoured. More seriously, if word slips out to Richard of York's cronies about the King's affliction, as inevitably it will at some point, it may be more than spite which threatens you. Welcome back to your homeland, Doctor.'

I had not previously attributed a capacity for ironic humour to the Duke. It was definitely not encouraging. I had exchanged one set of anxieties for another.

*****

With shameful negligence I had forgotten about the Queen's pregnancy. I was startled to see she must be near her time but Westminster was the obvious choice for the birth of an heir to the throne. It would be natural for her to want rest during these final weeks of waiting but her formidable resolve would not allow her to evade the challenge confronting her. It soon became clear that her anxiety was outweighed by her determination.

'Doctor Somers,' she said as I straightened from my obeisance, 'Duke Edmund has informed you of his Grace's indisposition. He was taken ill at our hunting lodge at Clarendon and he remains there for the moment but I have ordered that he be brought to Windsor where his privacy can more easily be secured. I am advised his physicians have bled and purged him unremittingly while the priests have sprinkled holy water and prayed over his impassive body; but all to no avail. In the past I have had cause to censure your behaviour, Doctor, but, if you can achieve some improvement in his Grace's condition, you will earn our gratitude and bring England joyful deliverance from danger. I think you understand me.'

'Your Grace is magnanimous and I'll do my best but the condition you've described is unknown to me. Although I've attempted to treat disturbed minds, the circumstances were different. What my limited experience suggests is that any remedy, if one is possible, will not come quickly. Any gains will be made little by little.'

This was not what she wished to hear and she compressed her lips. 'We shall endeavour to be patient. The smallest hint of progress will give us hope. May God guide you, Doctor Somers.'

Her invocation may have been intended to end my audience but I needed to see what else I could discover to help a diagnosis. 'Your Grace, may I ask how King Henry seemed in the days before he was taken ill? Did his affliction come on suddenly or had he shown signs of unusual behaviour?'

She stared at me as if I had offended against good manners but answered thoughtfully. 'For some weeks his Grace had been mournful since we heard that the infidels had taken Constantinople. As a devoted servant of the Lord God he was pained by that blow to Christendom and spent much time in prayer. Then, only a day or two before he was lost to us, news arrived of the battle at Castillon and the Earl of Shrewsbury's death. His Grace was consumed with grief. Is it possible there is a link with what happened to him subsequently? The other physicians have not suggested it.'

'We know almost nothing about the workings of the mind but it seems to me logical that there is a link. When we receive a blow to the physical body we are bruised and our bones may be broken. Perhaps when a man's spirit is buffeted by successive ill tidings, the mind can be similarly bruised. If the injury is severe a sensitive mind's reaction might be so drastic that it closes down some functions. I have no proof of this and I've never encountered the phenomenon but it seems plausible.'

'You are imaginative, Doctor Somers, but I comprehend your theory. If it is true, would the condition be reversible?'

'I do not know, your Grace. I hope a period of calm and rest could help in time to restore the mind's lost balance but any improvement might occur slowly. It isn't possible to promise anything.'

She did not hesitate. 'Very well: follow your theory and do what you can. I shall continue to pray for His Grace and I shall invoke Heaven's blessings on your endeavours.'

She moved ponderously to the door which her attendants flung open while I hastily bowed. She was not a woman to forgive offences easily and my offence in winning the affections of a high-born French lady in her service, when she came to England, had been indefensible in her eyes. It was a measure of the calamity facing the crown that she was willing to temper her displeasure for the sake of expediency.

I went to the servants' quarters to find Rendell and Johnny who appreciated immediately that a weight of apprehension had been lifted from my mind. Rendell rejoiced that I was not to be held accountable for the violent deaths which took place before we left England, especially because similar accusations had been laid against him. Both my friends accepted without question that I was required to discharge medical responsibilities and they were happy to move on to the City of London, where Rendell's sister, Grizel, and her husband, Thomas, lived. Rendell was enthusiastic about becoming one of Somerset's bodyguards and he suggested Johnny might also find a future under arms. I doubted that would be Tate's preference, in view of his injured leg, but his experiences in Aquitaine had made him fidgety and I suspected he was apathetic about returning to his trade as a skinner on his lord's estate.

A letter was brought to me later in the evening which Sir Nicholas with characteristic efficiency had intercepted before it could be taken aboard ship for Bordeaux. It was from Perkin, my steward at Worthwaite, and it was dated four weeks previously. I read it hurriedly to myself but Rendell fixed me with a penetrating stare.

'Well, what news does he give you?'

'The manor is in good order. The harvest was reasonable, young Georgie continues to excel in helping Perkin, Dame Elizabeth is rheumaticky but cheerful. I fancy what follows is the nub of what he wanted to tell me.'
I read the next section aloud.

'I regret to inform you that the young woman, Mistress Bateby, has left Worthwaite after an altercation with Dame Elizabeth. I trust this will not cause you concern, Doctor Somers. I was always unclear how long she would stay with us and she had become increasingly restive. She received communications from friends of hers and took herself off when they sent a conveyance for her. She may have returned to the service of Duchess Cecily of York, from whence I believe she had come before you first met her. Dame Elizabeth and I sometimes found her a difficult guest to please but I believe we fulfilled our duties appropriately.'

'Poor old Perkin!' Rendell laughed. 'Ursula Bateby must have been a terrible trial for them. If she learns you're back, she'll be battering on your door. I doubt even dragons could keep her out.'

'Quiet! Ursula Bateby mustn't find out where I am.'

Johnny Tate, knowing little of the background, entered into the light-heartedness of the moment. 'And when you move on from your new commission, Doctor, is contact with this lady to be resumed then?'

I felt myself flush but Rendell had plucked up courage to ask the question I dreaded.

'Does Perkin have news of the household at Hartham Manor?'

I owed him the truth and took several breaths before reading out what would torture him.

'Lord Fitzvaughan and his family are in good health and Lady Eleanor was gracious enough to pay us a visit recently. At the Feast of the Blessed Virgin Mary Mistress Judith was brought to bed of a sturdy son and both have prospered. Lady Eleanor is most considerately mindful that this child is her late kinsman's bastard.'

The door slammed as Rendell dashed from the room and I held up my hand to prevent Johnny following him.

'Give him a moment of quiet. He needs to reconcile himself with what can't be changed. If you'll go with him to the City, to see him join Somerset's troop of soldiers, I'd be grateful. When he's established there, it may be easier for him to accept what he abhors.'

Johnny nodded but, notwithstanding my counsel, he went after Rendell. I read Perkin's letter once more and began to wonder what exactly his final comment about Lady Eleanor Fitzvaughan's mindfulness might mean.

*****

I had ventured once before to the bastion of Windsor with its broad, squat towers, overlooking the Thames, but I did not know it well. I was impressed by the lavishness of the decoration in the guest apartments where I was to be accommodated, along with the other doctors, in chambers designed for visiting nobility. The intention was that, during our occupation of these desirable rooms, few nobles would be in residence, but the duration of our stay must be uncertain. In the meantime, before the arrival of the entourage from Clarendon, I could enjoy a short respite in which to set aside the agonising memories of Castillon together with the recurring fear that I might still be arraigned for murder.

An hour before noon on the appointed day the King's retinue rode slowly into the upper ward of the castle to be received by the Constable. A strong band of outriders surrounded the curtained litter and a bevy of physicians, priests and acolytes swelled the train of attendants who shielded the royal patient from view as he was taken into his private lodgings. I waited nervously while the travellers were refreshed until I was summoned to his apartments in the Rose Tower. There I was introduced to three brother physicians and two surgeons, all of whom acknowledged

143

me with distinctly unbrotherly coldness, which did not surprise me. I gathered they had been told that, under Queen Margaret's decree, they could observe while I examined his Grace but they must not make pronouncements until I had concluded.

Despite the description I had been given of King Henry's condition, when I entered the royal presence I was appalled by the sight of the simulacrum of a monarch he had become. He crouched rather than sat on an upright chair, staring straight ahead without apparently taking heed of anything. His eyes were blank, unfocussed, his cheeks hollow and he seemed scarcely to breathe. His chest rose and fell so slightly that I feared at first he had no pulse. His face had been wiped clean but I could see damp spots on his velvet robe where the broth fed to him had dribbled down his chin and the linen at his throat was grubby. His elbows and forearms rested on the wooden arms of his chair but they lay at an unnatural angle and I presumed an attendant had placed them in position. England's sovereign ruler had no power to control movement of his limbs.

I knelt observing him closely for several minutes. I moved my hand in front of his face and spoke loudly close to his ears but I could mark no reaction. He was entirely locked within the carapace of his body, oblivious of everything external. When I had seen him in the past on formal and ceremonial occasions, he showed little energy but he radiated gentleness and piety. Now there was nothing. I had read an account by the other doctors which reported no obvious abnormalities in his bodily functions and I conducted my own examination to confirm these findings. It seemed unlikely the root cause of his affliction had a physical explanation. Questions which I could not answer flooded into my head.

Was it really possible this stupor was an instinctive protection against the overwhelming abominations of the world which tortured his soul? Had his mind ceased utterly to work or was it simply refusing to manifest itself

144

to others? In the deep, imprisoned recesses of his mind, was he conscious of things he could not express? No answers to these questions were known to medicine.

I re-joined the group of physicians who had watched me with unconcealed disdain.

'Well, young fellow, what can you contribute to our counsels?' the eldest doctor sneered. 'You're said to be experienced in treating possession of the mind. Is that so?'

I did not intend to dissemble. 'I've never encountered a case like this. I was honoured to attend the late Cardinal Beaufort of Winchester in his final days when he grew frenzied and I cared for my own late wife whose mind was sadly disturbed and her behaviour erratic. Neither experience is directly comparable to his Grace's condition but they may offer pointers to guide me.'

'We need to bleed his Grace again.' A short assertive man had become impatient. 'I maintain we should put leeches to his scalp once more and draw off the hot blood from his brain.'

'On the contrary, he should be purged vigorously.'

'An herbal bath and administration of brewed syrup may be...'

'Perhaps a less spicy diet...'

'Powdered pearls are said to be...'

Several doctors spoke at once. I cleared my throat and bowed to the assembly.

'Her Grace, Queen Margaret, has authorised me to determine the King's treatment for a short period so, by your leave, brothers, I shall try a different approach.' I turned to a servant. 'Would you please ask musicians to attend his Grace to play muted but cheerful airs. Our patient may show no signs of hearing them but music can penetrate the heart and calm fervent emotions. It's worth testing whether it can soothe the innermost spirit trapped inside the King's unresponsive body.'

'Rubbish!'

'Piffle!'

'Poppycock!'

I spoke over the protests. 'I found the sound of the organ was beneficial to pacify the late Cardinal's troubled mind even in his greatest distress.'

'You said yourself the case was different.'

'It will do no harm to try. It doesn't appear that your forceful treatments have had noticeable success so far. I accept that it may take weeks to achieve any response but I'll draw up a course of mild treatments to calm and support a distraught mind. No more intrusive interventions will be imposed for, shall we say, a month?'

They muttered their disgruntlement but, under the Queen's direction, they were bound to accept my prescription – at least for the time being. I could only pray it might prove efficacious but it would at least save the wretched patient from suffering more barbaric usage. That alone, I considered, might be enough to justify my involvement in trying to solve this bewildering enigma.

Chapter 12

My colleague doctors made no secret of their scorn for an interloper foisted upon them, restricting their conversation with me to basic courtesies. Only the unassuming Michael Retford expressed interest in my studies at the University of Padua and asked about my experience in treating Cardinal Beaufort. He described himself as an herbalist rather than a physician but I found his willingness to listen to novel theories and learn from practice refreshing. It was obvious he was viewed as a junior contributor to the counsels of the others, so we were both on sufferance as far as our superiors were concerned.

Michael had been sent to Clarendon when the King was taken ill but he had lived at Windsor for several years, preparing basic potions and unguents required by the royal household and its guests. I welcomed his congenial company and we took to walking together in the afternoon in the little cloister where we could converse in private. We were relaxed with each other and exchanged guarded comments on the King's ailment and the obstinacy of medical men who resisted admitting their ignorance.

'Queen Margaret's time is imminent,' I said one day in mid-October. 'I hope they deliver a healthy child. Many years have passed without a direct heir to the throne.'

Michael Retford gave me a strange look. 'I'll say "Amen" to that if all is as it's made to appear.'

'What do you mean?'

'You've been across the sea, caught up with warfare. You've maybe not heard the gossip in the taverns and marketplaces.'

'About...?'

He looked round to make sure we were not overheard by any of the attendants or canons from the nearby chapel. 'There's chatter about who sired this child. King Henry is reputed to live like a monk and in eight years of marriage Her Grace has remained barren, until now. Need I say more? Idle tongues wag at less than this.'

'I assume the gossip suggests a name?'

'For the man who may have cuckolded the King? Who other than the Duke of Somerset?'

I had heard slanderous allegations in the past about queenly favour accorded to Edmund Beaufort. They originated with Richard of York's adherents and they fostered his interests. 'Let's hope the gossip dies away after the... Dear heaven!'

'What are you thinking?'

'If a boy is born, an heir, it would be usual for the child to be brought to the King, his father, to be acknowledged publicly before the court.'

'Christ! Can King Henry manage that? At the very least, someone would have to lift his hand to place it on the baby's brow.'

'I don't think that would count.'

'The sceptics will revel in the scandal.'

'Perhaps we'd better pray for a girl.'

We broke off from our improper speculations and turned towards our lodgings. We entered the middle ward at the moment a royal messenger thundered through the Norman gate and leapt from his saddle, running to speak to the King's Constable. Michael and I glanced wordlessly at each other. A little later it was announced that the Queen had been brought to bed of a boy who was pronounced robust and likely to live. Following these jubilant tidings the palace bells began to ring, echoed quickly by those of churches in the village of Windsor and across the river. A speedily assembled procession of canons made its way into the castle's chapel, chanting psalms of praise.

The messenger also made it known that at the direction of the royal mother the child's principal godfather was to be Edmund Beaufort, Duke of Somerset. Queen Margaret was not noted for her sensitivity to the opinion of others but, in the circumstances, I judged her choice of sponsor for her son extraordinarily crass.

*****

The foreboding I had expressed to Michael Retford was proved accurate. Protocol required that Prince Edward of Westminster be acknowledged publicly as heir to the throne by his father and the infant was to be brought to Windsor for the ceremony. According to custom, representatives of the lords spiritual and temporal were to be present as witnesses. I realised it was far too soon to expose the King to this scrutiny and what was required of him was beyond his competence. Nevertheless, I did my best to prepare him, hoping against hope that he might touch the child even if he could not speak. In the days before the event I escorted him to sit outside in the mellow autumn sunshine, lulled by calmly joyful music, and I spoke to him repeatedly about the blessing God had conferred on England in the birth of his son. I had no confidence that my words meant anything to him.

The deputation of peers duly arrived, together with Queen Margaret, Prince Edward, his wet-nurse, maids, pages and a bevy of servitors. With formal ceremonial they were brought before the King, who sat huddled in his chair staring into space, and obeisance was made by all present. Inevitably they secured no flicker of recognition from their liege lord but, resolutely unperturbed, the Duke of Buckingham advanced, holding out the swaddled babe, and he begged King Henry to bless the child. I held my breath, praying desperately for a miracle, for the movement of a hand, a grunt of recognition, the hint of a smile, but the King remained impassive, paying not the slightest attention to what was happening.

Queen Margaret had always been a woman of spirit and she was not easily thwarted. She strode forward to take her child from the Duke's arms, bending to kiss the infant brow. Then, spreading her skirts, she sank to her knees and in her turn offered the prince to her husband. She spoke softly.

'Dear lord, your Grace, this is our son. We have named him Edward in honour of the saint you venerate, whose abbey overlooks the place of our boy's birth at Westminster. Give him your blessing.'

For a tantalizing moment King Henry's eyelids fluttered and he glanced at the child held out to him. Then he cast down his eyes and bowed his head. He made no sound and I doubted he had registered anything. Shortly afterwards his Grace was carried to his bedroom by an attendant, his head nodding against the chest of the fellow who held him. He had become as much an infant as the baby he failed to acknowledge.

The representatives of church and state looked at each other in consternation, white-faced, aware now of the catastrophe facing them. The pretence that the King was merely suffering a mild indisposition had been demolished. Her sovereign lord lived and breathed but England was bereft of an effective ruler. Without the authority of the crown, the country risked becoming prey to rival marauders, ravaged by their hostility. Had I survived the violence in Aquitaine to encounter similar savagery in my homeland? In the pit of my stomach I felt nauseous.

*****

In the aftermath of the disastrous ceremony, I had my own preoccupations. Although I always argued that any improvement in the King's condition would come slowly, my efforts were judged a failure by my colleagues. I could hardly appeal to the Queen, now returned to Westminster, who might blame me for her own humiliation, so I yielded to the censure of self-justifying physicians eager to rubbish my unconventional treatment. I regretted the implications for our patient's welfare but recognised this was an argument I could not win, certainly not in the short term.

The most senior of the doctors, who consistently disparaged my approach, was John Arundel, Warden of the Hospital of St. Mary of Bethlehem, where he claimed to have studied illnesses of the mind. He barred me from further experiments with music and quietude, imposing instead a regimen of bleedings, potions, laxatives and administration of a treacly medicine derived from roasted snake skin. Arundel insisted that only by such means could the corrupt humours be expelled from the King's body but, as an adjunct, he was content for the priests to resort to exorcism. I could not condone imposition of these fruitless remedies and poured out my discontent to Michael Retford.

'Be patient, Harry. You can be sure they won't achieve any alteration in King Henry's condition, except perhaps to make him withdraw more thoroughly from the world. You couldn't blame him if he did. When that happens, I'd guess they'll become desperate and be willing to let you try again. Either that or they'll get bored with achieving nothing and call you in to take over the thankless task.'

Michael was perceptive and I chuckled. 'That's not exactly reassuring. Besides, I can't bear to let them hurt the harmless loon. Our task should be to protect him. Arundel intends to cauterize the King's scalp to dry out wet matter at the back of the brain which he contends affects the memory. It's a wild theory with nothing to recommend it. Can you imagine how painful it will be?'

'If the King screams they'll count it a success, proving he can still feel pain. Why don't you seek permission to leave the castle for a while? It would be good for you to get away. You've got friends in London, haven't you? Go and visit them.'

It was good advice and fortunately Sir Nicholas Chamberlayne had remained at Windsor. When I described my position to him he was sympathetic.

'It actually fits in rather well,' he said with a grin. 'I'm returning to court myself and you can accompany me

– at my request, so the worthy doctors can't pretend you're running away with your tail between your legs. You'll be able to visit your friends in the City but there are also enquiries you can make on my behalf while you're at Westminster. You can imagine what a ferment of gossip there'll be, now word is out about His Grace. The adventure in Aquitaine is over too. Bordeaux and the other towns have surrendered and the remaining English garrisons are embarked for return to these shores. What a moment for Lords Clinton and Palgreve to bring their weary followers into harbour!

'Richard of York is expected to arrive at Westminster imminently with his entourage so Somerset is concerned to out-flank his enemy's manoeuvres. You'll be good at ferreting out any hints of mischief. You've done that sort of thing before. We'll be kept informed about progress here and you can return to Windsor when the time seems right. Duke Edmund will explain everything to Queen Margaret, don't worry.'

I did not doubt Duke Edmund's influence with the Queen but I wondered whether Sir Nicholas realised how scurrilous some of the reported gossip might prove to be. He clapped me on the shoulder in friendly fashion.

'Lady Maud's at court,' he said. 'She'll be glad to see you again.'

It was over a year since Sir Nicholas, then recently widowed, had wed the former Lady Maud Fitzvaughan, whose first husband, Lord Walter, had been killed in Normandy. The Fitzvaughan title had then passed to the husband of Maud's daughter, Lady Eleanor, and Maud did not relish the position of dowager in her son-in-law's house. She was a spirited woman who had overcome adversity in her own life and deployed her wilful pride and enduring beauty to secure what she wanted. I met her first as a callow youth, and she it was who introduced me to erotic delights. Subsequently, there had been a time, before I met Kate, when Maud was my occasional mistress. That was all in the past and I felt no lingering temptation towards dalliance with Lady Chamberlayne but the prospect of meeting her again was intriguing.

It would be more problematic if an encounter with Lady Maud caused me to meet Bess Willoughby who attended her. Bess's husband, Robin, had died defending me from my enemies and she could not forgive me for placing him in danger. I acknowledged my responsibility. Piers Ford had paid court to Bess when she was widowed and I had hoped she would accept him when he returned from Aquitaine. Now that could not be.

Deep in the recesses of my memory, and stifled for so long, was the recollection of the chaste love I had felt for Bess when we both served in the household of the late Duke Humphrey of Gloucester more than a decade earlier. My affection had been reciprocated at the time and, if a wretched mischance had not occurred, we would have married. It was provoking to think how our lives over the last twelve years would have been significantly different, had we done so: provoking but pointless speculation, I concluded.

*****

After my unprofitable musings about past loves and my lack of success at Windsor, I welcomed immersion in the hurly burly of life at the palace of Westminster. Nevertheless, I was ill prepared for the succession of former acquaintances I encountered there. Some were well-intentioned but would be predators, great and small, were gathering to secure advantage for themselves and perdition for their enemies. The Dukes of Somerset and York were the principal players jostling for supremacy but their minions were not slow in looking for their own opportunities to prosper.

My first encounter occurred when I had been summoned, imperiously, I thought, to wait upon Lady Maud and was passing along the corridor near the Queen's apartments which led to the Chamberlayne lodgings.

153

Completely unexpectedly, a graceful figure glided from a doorway and a well-remembered, pleasing voice greeted me.

'I knew you would come, Harry Somers. I conjectured I should meet you at Westminster more quickly than if I waited in the back-waters of Suffolk.'

'Mistress Bateby.' My mouth was dry. 'Perkin told me you'd left Worthwaite. I didn't know you were at court.'

'Duchess Cecily of York recalled me. She wished me to return to the Queen's service. You'll remember she sent me to her as a tiring-maid once before. This time I've been provided with my own maidservant to enhance my status and I'm unencumbered by the duty to report on my royal mistress. I simply brought the Duchess's felicitations on the birth of the Queen's son. I suppose I was part of the birthing gift from Richard of York and his wife. Duchess Cecily observes the courtesies whatever the animosity between her husband and the Queen.'

I bit back a comment on the double-headed nature of this gift. Ursula Bateby had been a spy for York's acolytes, including her loathsome lover, Stephen Boice, when she served the Queen previously. 'I'm sure you find the court more congenial than my modest manor in the back-waters...'

She touched my arm and drew me into the doorway. 'I'm deeply grateful for the sanctuary you gave me at Worthwaite when I was destitute after Stephen Boice's death. I agreed to come here because I thought I would be reunited with you all the sooner. I sensed you wouldn't hurry to return to Worthwaite.'

I shivered at her choice of words. 'I won't delude you, Mistress Bateby, my experiences in Aquitaine have affected me. I don't yet know how much I've changed but I'm not ready to resume the life I led.'

She lowered her eyes. 'You mean you have no desire to revisit my bed?'

'Forgive me; I didn't expect to meet you here. There's much I haven't resolved in my mind. Please excuse me. I'm going to an appointment.'

'With my lady Chamberlayne?' Do you intend to cuckold Sir Nicholas as you did the woman's first husband?'

Her voice had risen and I was bound to protest, appalled that she had discovered so much about my past, but there was something admirable about her boldness. 'I beg you to speak quietly. There's nothing between Lady Maud and me.'

She came close, looking up at me through her eyelashes in a way I remembered. 'I'm glad. I confess I've hoped you would become my lover, Harry Somers. I've waited a year since you killed my protector. I bore witness on your behalf, explaining that Stephen's death was an accident after he drew his dagger on you and the fire broke out which consumed him.'

I was bewildered and responded guardedly. 'That's all true.'

'Not quite, as you well know. Gilbert Iffley has pressured me to withdraw my statement sworn before the justices and to assert that I saw you murder Master Boice in cold blood. The justices could be persuaded to accept that I'd been too afraid to testify against you previously because you threatened me, a defenceless woman.'

I stared at her, uncertain how to interpret her words. 'You ordered me to kill him in cold blood, as I recall. I merely gave quietus to a dying man, ablaze from head to foot.'

'Have a care, Harry. The world is changing. Very soon Richard of York will be pre-eminent in the realm and Gilbert Iffley will be at his right hand. Stephen was brother to Gilbert's wife and she wants you brought to the gallows. I've resisted their pleas but if you cast me off, I may be forced to comply with their demands. Where else can I look for protection? Do you understand me, Harry? You must be prepared to recognise me.'

'What do you mean "recognise"?'

'I beg you to take me as your acknowledged mistress, dear physician. It would be enough to secure my position and I could defy Gilbert Iffley's taunts.'

The gentle trap was sprung and I was snared, for I liked Mistress Bateby and wished her no harm. All I could do was to prevaricate. 'You must let me consider. It's sudden. I can't give you an answer now.'

She lifted my hand and put it to her breast. 'You are lodged with the Somerset entourage. Tomorrow night or the next I shall come to you – with discretion but not observing the strictest secrecy. I shall excite your passion as I did once before and I think you will then find it easier to accede to my request. Will you give me permission?'

I inclined my head and she gave me a gentle push to send me on my way. Her nervous giggle echoed behind me. 'I will be yours alone, Harry, if you will have me.'

*****

My interview with Lady Maud Chamberlayne posed no such impossible choices but it was disconcerting. She was of noble blood and had always been my superior but in our fluctuating relationship the differences between us had usually been overlooked. This was no longer the case. Her demeanour made clear that she had consigned the past to oblivion and, although she was kindly disposed towards me, she was bestowing a grace which I could in no way reciprocate. It irked me a little and I could not resist baiting her.

'Gossip suggests Richard of York will arrive shortly and assert his right to act as Regent during the King's illness.'

'Indeed yes,' she said with a condescending smile. 'The Council will attempt to repulse him but he will prevail.'

I was surprised she appeared so obtuse because her ready intelligence had always been part of her attractiveness. 'York's bound to move against Somerset if that happens. Sir Nicholas is one of Edmund Beaufort's closest supporters. Don't you fear he'll suffer if his patron is disgraced?'

'Oh, Harry,' she trilled merrily, 'what a dull bumpkin you're become. Nick has had feelers out to York's cronies for months. He'll know when the moment is right to cut the bonds with Somerset.'

'He'll switch allegiances?'

'Our allegiance is to poor, saintly King Henry. We must merely decide how best to demonstrate our loyalty in these unsettling times.'

'Of course.' I found her pragmatism unnerving. 'Forgive me: I'm not a courtier, just a humble physician.'

She stretched languidly in her chair, reminding me of what delights lay beneath that rippling skirt and low-cut stomacher. 'You should take a mistress, Harry: some modest maiden who serves one of the lesser noblewomen perhaps. A temperate, unassuming soul would be good for you. I'll see if I can find one for you.'

When I made my escape Maud reiterated her promise to find me an amenable doxy. It was very clear she did not have someone like Ursula Bateby in mind.

*****

Next morning I joined Sir Nicholas in the antechamber outside the hall in which the Great Council was meeting. Richard of York's followers were everywhere, disciplined and formidable, and I glimpsed the Duke himself when he entered the meeting, stern-faced and, I intuited, implacable. We could hear no raised voices through the heavy doors, just the mumble of debate, until one man's vigorous tones throbbed with derision even if we could not discern his words.

'I don't recognise the speaker,' I whispered.

'It's that mischief-maker, John Mowbray, Duke of Norfolk. He's always been a friend to Richard of York.

Listen! There's a murmur of assent to what he said. Somerset won't have it all his own way without the King to back him. This could be risky for him.'

Sir Nicholas sounded unconcerned and I would have been confused by his nonchalance had Lady Maud not advised me of his readiness to change sides if it became expedient. Soon afterwards the scrape of benches on the tiled floor and the stamp of the guards' feet as they came to attention indicated that the doors were about to be opened for a break in the proceedings. A nobleman in his mid-twenties strode from the council chamber ahead of others, a handsome fellow who did not conceal his arrogance. I fancied I had seen him at court in the past but he had not cut so impressive a figure as he did now. I could not put a name to him and raised my eyebrows in query to Sir Nicholas.

'Richard Neville, Earl of Warwick, eldest son of the Earl of Salisbury and nephew to Richard of York. He gained the Warwick title by marrying Anne Beauchamp who brought him vast wealth along with her late father's earldom. He's not a man to be trifled with although he's still quite young.'

'I remember Warwick was opposed to York a few years back.'

'He was scrupulously neutral until the King found against him in a dispute he had with Somerset over some land. Highly injudicious, that decision was: looked like favouritism by the King and offended a man of great potential. What's that?'

Sir Nicholas span round to question something he had overheard and gripped my arm. 'They're saying Mowbray has demanded Somerset's impeachment. It's to be considered further when they re-assemble. I must go to Duke Edmund.'

I nodded as he swept into the council chamber where Somerset had remained. I moved in the other direction, following the crowd. Small-beer was offered for refreshment in the adjoining room and I took my turn to fill a cup when I felt fingers grasp my shoulder.

'I cannot tell you how joyful it makes me to find you here, Harry Somers. You have been missed.'

I drew myself up and faced Gilbert Iffley, Baron Glasbury, master of irony, who at different times had adopted the roles of both nemesis and saviour towards me. 'Baron, I surmised I might encounter you at Westminster.'

'This is the moment we have prepared for, Harry: the opportunity we've craved. Richard of York's hour has come. You're not too late to benefit. Despite yourself, you've aided the Duke's interests in the past. You are part of the pattern we have woven.'

'You know very well I complied with what you and Boice wanted of me under duress, knowing the harm he'd already caused my wife. Now Kate is dead and you have no hold over me.'

'I wouldn't put it quite like that.' The silky tones caressed my hearing. 'But this is no time to argue. Come with me to an assembly that's about to convene while the Council stands adjourned. It will give you food for thought: an assembly of Neville kindred. You will be welcome.'

'I have no Neville blood.'

'But your poor, sweet wife had, Harry, as indeed has mine. As, of course, had my wife's brother, the late lamented Stephen, whom you killed. Come.'

The emphasis of his final words and a flick of his eyebrow were full of malice. The middle of a heaving crowd of excited courtiers was no place to engage in rational disagreement and I did not wish to draw attention to myself. I sighed and reluctantly let Iffley lead me from the room.

Chapter 13

The network of Neville connections was intricate and spread widely through the nobility and gentry of the shires. If they chose to make common cause they would be a formidable force, although in the recent past squabbles between different branches of the Neville kindred had led to violence. I could identify many of the men squeezed into the guardroom where the meeting was to be held and knew others by sight. There were no surprises until I caught sight of one man standing on the far side from the door: a man disastrously out of context, so far as I was concerned, and I quailed. Jasper Coote stared at me and his hand went to his belt where no doubt a dagger was concealed. Gilbert Iffley followed my gaze and smirked.

'Ah, yes, you have encountered that gallant officer, haven't you? And his uncle, I believe, Sir Guy Binwood?'

'I didn't know Sir Guy was his uncle.' I bit my tongue to suppress an exclamation of horror that the traitors were at liberty and apparently well regarded by York's friends. After the death of Lord Talbot and his son at Castillon, no one had been in a position to take action against them. Yet they would be well aware that I suspected them of treachery.

'They're both Nevilles on their mothers' sides. Such a prolific tribe, aren't they? Their womenfolk breed at threefold the rate of less favoured dames: York's wife foremost among them, fecund and delightful. Look, Warwick's about to address us. Listen carefully, Harry.'

The young Earl rose to his feet with easy elegance, the personification of confidence and power. His smile was vulpine.

'Dearest kinsmen, you are welcome. We meet at a moment of crisis and there are matters which I'm bound to share with you, matters which place our land in peril. You know of our beloved King's serious indisposition. You know also that the Queen has been brought to bed after long years of barrenness and has produced a boy, said, very properly, to be the son of her royal husband. I grieve to suggest to you that this may not be true, that the child of her body was not got on her by King Henry but by her cursed paramour, that creeping louse, Edmund Beaufort.'

'This is malicious tittle-tattle,' I said to Iffley but he put his finger to his lips.

'The child was presented to the saintly King,' Warwick continued, his voice trembling with assumed emotion. 'Held out to him by my lord, the Duke of Buckingham, and then by the infant's mother. King Henry refused to acknowledge the boy as his heir. He turned his eyes to the ground and made no response because he understood the foul trick perpetrated on his royal person.'

'This is nonsense,' I mouthed but dared not utter.

Iffley shook his head. 'Listen.'

'Pardon, cousin, but is there proof of this serious allegation? Do the Queen's ladies confirm that Somerset has visited her bed?' I could not see the speaker but admired his pluck.

'Pah! They'll bear witness when they see their mistress disgraced.' Jasper Coote's voice was unmistakeable.

Whispered allegations of the Queen's infidelity had circulated for years among those who disliked her and York's agents had sought evidence to give them substance. Indeed, Ursula Bateby had been infiltrated into the Queen's household originally with instructions to find proof, but she had been unable to do so. From all I had seen of her, I believed Margaret of Anjou was far too wily and calculating to risk her position, and probably her life, for the transitory pleasures of erotic passion.

Others were voicing cautious scepticism and the Earl of Warwick began to sound vexed. 'The Frenchwoman was barren for more than seven years after she wed the King. It seems fortuitous that she should conceive just as her husband loses his wits. How do we know this baby came from her womb? Couldn't it be a changeling brought into the Queen's bedchamber after she had imitated pregnancy while King Henry ailed?'

Iffley tutted in annoyance and he was not the only man present who considered Warwick had overplayed his hand with this alternative proposition. Nevertheless the Earl had sown seeds of doubt and as the meeting broke up and members of the Great Council re-assembled I detected widespread unease among my companions. I tried to slide away inconspicuously when Baron Glasbury left me but my movements had been marked by the man I wished to avoid.

Jasper Coote was quickly at my side, spitting venom. 'As you well know, physician, there are matters between us which demand resolution. You discredited me in the Castle at Castillon, caused me to be tortured and nearly led to my execution. You are my enemy and I shall exact retribution with your life.'

I had to brazen out this encounter. 'We should be clear about the facts. You were a spy intent on betraying your King and you later killed your overlord, Lord Hanwell. I understand you serve Richard of York and pursued underhand activities with the French on his behalf, so perhaps you had authority for these questionable deeds. That doesn't exonerate you from your guilt in my opinion but in these uncertain times we might be wise to set aside personal animosities.'

It took very little to rile Jasper Coote. 'How convenient, you cowardly leech! I shall set nothing aside. Don't think you can shelter under Baron Glasbury's wing. You imagine you're clever to make his acquaintance, I suppose, because he's high in Duke Richard's esteem. I saw you fawning on him. I shall expose you as a spy from Somerset's camp and then he'll be happy to see me cut your throat. Get out of my way.'

I had taken a risk in annoying him but he reacted instinctively, without consideration. He was not a bright man. I could hardly prevent myself grinning. 'Master Coote, I've known Gilbert Iffley for the last ten years.

There is little you could tell him about me he does not already know. He has harassed and menaced me and also saved my life when it suited him. I don't think I've exhausted my usefulness as far as he's concerned and if you expose me to him, as you put it, he's likely to laugh in your face and then forbid you to lay a finger on me.'

Coote's mouth fell open and I hurried back to join Sir Nicholas Chamberlayne without waiting for a riposte. I was under no illusion. I had bought time by invoking Gilbert Iffley's dubious patronage, which I loathed, but Coote's hatred was in no way moderated and one day he would seek his revenge.

*****

Sir Nicholas was white-faced and knew what was to come before we saw the party of royal guards sent from the council chamber with drawn swords. We watched them march along the corridor, headed by their captain, and they wheeled with immaculate precision towards the Queen's apartments.

'I could have wished a different location,' Sir Nicholas said with a sigh. 'It shows vainglorious disdain that he should venture there at such a moment.'

The news was soon cascading through the palace. On the authority of the Great Council, Edmund Beaufort, Duke of Somerset, had been arrested in Queen Margaret's lodgings and taken to the Tower of London. He would be impeached, charged by Mowbray with the loss of the King's domain in Normandy, stripped of the office of Constable and incarcerated to await sentence for his crimes. Richard of York was triumphant and would seek to be named Regent during the King's incapacity. Bystanders had only to wait, eyes cast down, while events played out as was ordained. With varying degrees of openness, courtiers protected their own interests, recognising where in future power would lie.

Sir Nicholas was not directly prejudiced by Somerset's arrest but he decided it was opportune to absent himself from Westminster until after the festivities at Yule, so he and Lady Maud departed for their manor at Harrow. He invited me to join them but I was not ready to revisit the place where Kate had died and so much that was dreadful occurred. Many lords and their servitors left Westminster but the Queen's household remained, as did some who felt more secure in its precincts. I welcomed time to think without the usual bustle of the court and hoped to offer my services as physician to those remaining in the palace. I also intended to call on my friends in the City whom I had neglected for too long.

My mind was churning with anxieties. What would it mean if York became Regent? I believed him fair-minded and competent but he would need the assistance of his underlings and they included too many people I did not trust. Gilbert Iffley had been affable when I encountered him and might have decided I was no longer important to his schemes. But that could change and, if he saw a use for me, he would revert to the menacing manipulator he had always been. Ursula Bateby had indicated that the allegations arising from Stephen Boice's death continued potentially to hang over me and Iffley had been trying to revive them.

Then there was the presence at court of Jasper Coote, and presumably Sir Guy Binwood, whom I knew to be traitors. They seemed to enjoy York's trust and would be eager for any opportunity to punish me. I was known to have served Somerset in the past and I was a friend of his follower, Sir Nicholas. Caution suggested I should disappear, hide at my manor of Worthwaite in Suffolk until more stable times came about. Yet I might be obliged to return to Windsor, should the Queen insist, and, if I could be given a free hand, the physician in me wished to see what might be done to alleviate the King's strange paralysis of mind and body.

For me it was a time of intense uncertainty and heightened emotions, amplified by the torment of my recent experiences. I was free from the horrors I endured in Aquitaine but subject to weird tricks of memory and disturbing dreams. I needed to absorb myself in my work but found too little to keep me occupied in the largely vacated palace. Perhaps inevitably, in this situation, I took the line of least resistance. One immediate and enticing diversion was available and, jettisoning prudence and decorum, I threw myself into the pursuit of pleasure, finding solace in Ursula Bateby's ready embrace. I decided I was content to live light-heartedly while the world around me settled to its new equilibrium – whatever that would prove to be.

I did not enquire how Ursula was able to slip away from the Queen's apartments with apparent ease. Her serving maid, Mary, was a tight-lipped, sly-looking girl who doubtless understood how to organise what her mistress requested. She herself was a resourceful and engaging woman who knew how to deploy her charms as skilfully as a trained swordsman wields his weapon. She had many connections at Westminster: some, I admitted, might be undeclared to me, but she insisted she had no other lover since she became my mistress. I did not underestimate her capacity for deviousness but, in the wildness of those days, I did not care and devoted myself to the unfamiliar gratification of desire. We both found joy in our intimate encounters and she was a witty companion. It was simple to lose myself in temporary infatuation. Nevertheless, I held onto a residue of good sense.

Although I was growing fond of her, I made no promises to Ursula about the future of our relationship and I thought her realist enough not to look for a long-term commitment. She seemed to revel in the lack of secrecy surrounding our arrangements, which was an unorthodox attitude for a young woman at court, and she chuckled with glee when she overheard a laundry maid describe her as 'Doctor Somers' wench'. She claimed this was a status worthy of high regard. She had, of course, been Stephen Boice's mistress and suffered gross abuse at his hands, so her contented mirth was perhaps forgivable. I did not choose to probe too deeply into her motives.

*****

As the period of festivities drew to an end my laggard conscience pricked sufficiently to impel me towards the City of London and the home of my old friends, Thomas and Grizel Chope. Thomas had shared many of my adventures and rescued me from danger more than once. He had done well as a craftsman, rising from humble and challenging circumstances to become a respected master carpenter and guildsman in the City with premises near the Tower. Grizel, his wife and Rendell's sister, was capable and wise, the mother of a lively brood of children, always ready to support and advise a friend without fear or favour. Maybe I was intuitively afraid of her home truths while I indulged my dissolute mood and that was why I neglected to make an earlier visit. It was an omission I soon came to regret.

I took a ferry from Westminster to London Bridge on a crisp bright morning and walked the rest of the way along streets I knew well but in which I now felt myself a stranger. I pondered but did not understand my sense of separation from my surroundings.

I presented myself at the house, surprised to find the sideway into the yard locked, and gathered at once from the maidservant's sombre character that this was a household in mourning. I moistened my dry mouth to ask what calamity had occurred when the door to the workshop opened and Rendell emerged. He looked at me with fury.

'So you've deigned to come? I thought you'd be here weeks ago. We heard you were at court with Chamberlayne. One of Thomas's vintner friends made a delivery to Westminster and recognised you.'

166

'What's happened? I didn't know there was trouble?'

'Trouble? Come in threes don't it? First the baby born a year ago died; then Griz lost the next that was still in her belly. Now Griz herself is dying.'

'What? Oh God, why didn't you send for me? What's the matter with her?'

Thomas had followed Rendell into the house. His eyes were not hostile, simply bleak with misery. 'You can examine her, Harry. She'll be glad to consult you but we've no reason to doubt our local physician. You only have to look at her to see. She's being eaten up inside. It's destroying her. We're going to lose her.'

'Oh Thomas...' I needed to pull myself together, to adopt a professional stance but these were my oldest friends and I could not be dispassionate. 'I'm so sorry.'

'Sorry! Fat lot of good that'll do.' Rendell was as distressed as his brother-in-law but needed someone to vilify. There was only me.

Slowly I pieced together the sad history of the last few months in the Chope household. Grizel had been ailing for some time but it had not seemed serious at first, attributed to the weariness of frequent child-bearing and grief at losing the baby who had always been frail but seemed to be growing stronger. Now the malignancy of her malady had become evident and everyone realised the inevitable outcome. Fortunately the three boys and little Margery were thriving and Thomas was prosperous enough to employ nursemaids to care for them but that did nothing to assuage his heartache. After more than a decade of their marriage I could not imagine him without his adored helpmate.

Later I was allowed to see Grizel and she expressed no recriminations for my dilatoriness in visiting her family, receiving me with calm appreciation. Her body was wasted, her face shrivelled like a much older woman's, and her eyes were sunk within dark sockets; yet her spirit was undimmed. Her pale lips curved into a smile and she spoke with a burst of energy.

'I feared I wouldn't see you again, Harry. It's good you've come. I know you've all manner of duties. Help Thomas if you can, when I'm gone. I know he'll suffer – but he's got the children to provide for. It's them I most worry about. Hal and Dickon need a firm hand while Tom could do with a bit more confidence. Most of all, little Margery will miss her mother... It'll be such a male household as she grows up.'

A tear trickled down beside her nose and I took her hand as she winced. 'I'll do whatever I can. I'll speak to Thomas. Are you in pain? Perhaps I can give you something to help.'

'That'd be good. I wish I was leaving you in happier circumstances. You don't look well yourself, Harry. You're still grieving for Kate?'

'There's been so much that was upsetting: Kate's awful death and all the losses in the fighting across the sea. In time I hope I can rebuild my life.'

'I think back sometimes, lying here, remembering when we were all at Duke Humphrey's palace at Greenwich. I was a child when I met you, a scruffy little serving maid, and Rendell was a ragamuffin. You were good to us. You should have married that pretty girl who went to serve Lady Maud Fitzvaughan.'

'Bess? Bess Barber as she was? I hoped to wed her at the time but it wasn't to be. She married someone else and was happy. It was probably best for her.'

'Who can tell? I wish Rendell had found a real love, not just fly-by-night fancy women. I wish I could go, knowing he was suited.'

I nodded but did not say I had hoped he was suited. 'Try not to fret about things you can't change. You've counselled us all so often we'll still hear your voice in our heads, cautioning us not to do whatever we've set our minds to.'

Her parchment-like cheeks crinkled with merriment. 'Thank you for making me laugh, Harry. You always had my measure. God bless you.'

She closed her eyes and slipped into half-sleep so I kissed her brow and went to mix a potion which might give some relief from the worst spasms of pain.

I stayed talking with Thomas until the sky began to darken. I felt sure he would handle what confronted him with wisdom and do honour to the wife he loved deeply. Rendell had gone while I was with Grizel. Thomas told me he had abandoned his newfound position in Somerset's household when the Duke was arrested but the Governor of the Tower of London had allowed him to resume his earlier position as a guard at the fortress which was conveniently near to the Chopes' house. Thomas also had news of Johnny Tate, who stayed with them briefly before returning to the late Lord Hanwell's demesne in Hertfordshire, his home before he followed his overlord to Aquitaine. I hoped he had settled back contentedly into his occupation as a skinner but doubted it was the best use of his considerable talents.

I returned to Westminster, chilled in body and soul, and that night I sobbed impotently in Ursula's arms. I found it soothing to have her company while grieving for my friends' unhappiness but I could not banish the knowledge that Grizel would disapprove strongly of Mistress Bateby's velvety hold over me. Yet Ursula displayed sensitivity, understanding my need to spend time alone, and for a while she ceased to pay her intimate nocturnal visits, waiting patiently for me to call for her.

*****

Weeks passed and the first warmth of springtime brought buds to open and green shoots to appear between cobbles in City streets. It did nothing to allay the sombre atmosphere afflicting the Chope household. I visited when Grizel was close to death and a few days later I walked with

Thomas in her cortege, accompanied by an enormous crowd of his fellow guildsmen and other friends. He would not lack for sympathy and support. Rendell acknowledged me curtly but did not stop to speak and I could do nothing to rid myself of the fear that Grizel's death had broken a bond with my old friend. It was my duty to make sure this did not happen.

Sir Nicholas and many other courtiers returned to Westminster and were soon distracted by developments they had not foreseen. Queen Margaret, resolute as ever, drew up a protestation addressed to Parliament demanding that she be named Regent: overtly attempting to thwart York's ambition. Sir Nicholas tutored me on legal niceties, asserting that the Queen's claim, based on her husband's illness and incapability, was unjustified by precedent in England. Queens had only ever been given the power of regency when their husbands were absent from the country. Moreover, the fact that Margaret of Anjou's protestation quoted laws from other jurisdictions did not make it more welcome to the English peers. Formal and binding decisions were needed on these issues. Parliament had been prorogued when the King was taken ill, but it was now imperative action be taken to prevent Henry's stupor also paralysing government of the realm.

The Council evaded the delicate subject of the Regency but instead agreed to nominate York as the King's Lieutenant, a title and position given in the past to the King's representative in his domains across the Narrow Sea. This would mean a new Parliament could be called with the Duke presiding at the opening of its deliberations. It offered a neat way forward but I could see the device fell short of the unambiguous endorsement of York's precedence which he obviously coveted. Much remained unresolved and I was troubled about what would happen next, for the sake of the rudderless country.

I too felt rudderless, reluctant to commit myself to York's cause, yet wishing him well if he truly acted with integrity. Above all, my mind was burdened with despondency after Grizel's death and I had no inclination to dwell on things I could not influence. I could see no way to break the iron grip of the melancholy which oppressed me.

Chapter 14

Gilbert Iffley waylaid me after dinner in the great hall and insisted that I accompany him to a meeting in the City. He gave assurances of my safety and promised to escort me throughout the proceedings. In spite of his accustomed guile, I knew him well enough to accept his word on this occasion and, even though I felt listless, I was inevitably intrigued by his request. It was a novelty to regard him as close to the seat of power rather than a scheming dissident.

We took a barge from Westminster and as we glided downstream on the ebbing tide, I began to wonder whether, after all, this was a trick to take me to the Tower to join the Duke of Somerset in confinement. I was relieved when we pulled towards the northern bank as soon as we passed the friary of the Dominicans but I looked at Iffley in surprise when I realised we were making for the water-gate of Baynard's Castle where my first patron, the late Duke of Gloucester, had kept his City lodgings.

Baron Glasbury was amused by my confusion. 'Richard of York is using Baynard's Castle these days. It'll be like old times for you, won't it? Don't fear, you'll be quite safe. The Duke wishes to see you.'

'Why didn't you tell me that?'

'You'd have refused to come.' He pushed my back to encourage me up the slippery ramp leading to the entrance and I reconciled myself to the forthcoming encounter.

York was ensconced in one of the chambers I remembered, indeed where Thomas had once installed new panelling. Iffley was admitted to the meeting immediately while I waited to be summoned, declining with instinctive caution the refreshment offered by attentive servants. It was not long before I was ushered through the heavy doors and bowed low in front of Duke Richard and a large assembly of his advisers. I registered a blur of faces, identifying only the handsome young Earl of Warwick, standing near York who was his father's brother-in-law. I concentrated my attention on the Duke sitting on a throne-like chair.

'Doctor Somers, we are grateful you've come.' He had an agreeable voice and could use it to convince listeners his words were sincere and directed personally to each individual. 'I'm informed that you have attended our dear but afflicted royal cousin at Windsor.'

If this interrogation was to draw on my medical knowledge, I was content. 'It's three months since I did so, your Grace. Several other physicians and surgeons have charge of the King's health. My contribution was unnecessary in their view.'

'You advocated different treatment from theirs? Did you achieve results?'

'None of us did, your Grace. We don't comprehend the workings of the mind enough to be confident how to treat its disruption and the King's malady is unlike anything we've experienced. I'm certain that if an improvement can be brought about in his condition, it will take time.'

'And can improvement be brought about, by whatever treatment?'

'Your Grace, there is no certainty.'

'But in your considered opinion? You will not be held to your prognosis but I should be glad to learn it.'

'There's no evidence to back my opinion. It's little more than a hunch but I believe some improvement may occur. King Henry remains in a satisfactory physical condition and he's utterly calm. I don't hold out hopes of a complete recovery, although it may be possible, but I wouldn't rule out some improvement.'

'Thank you, Doctor Somers. That's clear and honest. I've seen you before, I think?'

There was no point in dissembling. Iffley would have briefed him 'Once in Dublin, your Grace, and a few times when I have been in attendance at the court.'

173

'You've not chosen to join our company?'

'Your Grace, I've had obligations to other overlords at various times but my service is always to the King.'

'Well said. We respect your scrupulous loyalty. I take it you would willingly serve those with legitimate authority to act in the King's name?'

I breathed in deeply. 'In all lawful matters, your Grace.'

I heard Iffley snort but Duke Richard smiled. 'And if Edmund Beaufort were to be lawfully found guilty of illegitimate acts, you would quit his service?'

'Your Grace, I'm not bound to the Duke of Somerset's service. I served him briefly but that is in the past.'

York nodded 'Good. Thank you for your attendance, Doctor Somers, you've assisted our counsels. I hope to see you again.'

He rose, we all bowed and the Duke left the room with a handful of advisers. He had confirmed my impression that he was by nature fair-minded but his animosity towards Somerset was undisguised. I turned to Iffley, ready to move back to the antechamber where I had waited, but a strident voice cut through the murmur of conversation around us.

'That man's a negligent physician! Worthless. Refused me treatment. Denied me help. We shouldn't listen to him.'

Sir Guy Binwood strutted forward, his eyes narrowed with spite. Clearly he resented the fact that I had escaped the death he contrived for me at Cadillac. 'Well, Somers, you can't deny it. You refused to treat me for the stone in Aquitaine.'

I stood my ground. 'That isn't true. I declined to cut you because it's a dangerous operation to cut for a bladder stone and I'm not a skilled surgeon. I gave you something to ease your discomfort. That was my proper role.'

'A measly, useless mixture – a quack's remedy.'

'What was the potion you prescribed, Doctor Somers?' To my surprise it was the Earl of Warwick addressing me as he turned aside from his companions.

'My lord, it was saxifrage tempered with wine and pepper, drunk warm. It's been found helpful by others afflicted with the stone.'

Warwick gave a roar of laughter and punched Sir Guy on the chest. 'That's the very mixture you recommended to my father to ease his belly pains. You're traducing this doctor's reputation. Whatever you've got against him, it's not his inadequacy as a physician. Baron Glasbury, see Doctor Somers safely back to Westminster. We may have need of him in the future. We've few enough around us with single-minded integrity.' He shot a meaningful look at Binwood.

I bowed to the Earl and Gilbert Iffley hustled me through the throng of amused onlookers while Sir Guy glared at me with hatred. He was not a man to endure humiliation lightly and because Warwick was too elevated a target for his outrage, I could expect him to vent his fury with double intensity towards me. At least there was no sign of Jasper Coote.

*****

Within the week it became clear that, despite what scandalous backstairs gossip might assert, the legitimacy of Queen Margaret's son was not to be formally questioned. Parliament, under York's guidance, created baby Edward Prince of Wales and Earl of Chester. Duke Richard accepted he was no longer heir presumptive to the throne and declared that actions he took as the King's Lieutenant were explicitly on behalf of the crown. I thought this a shrewd move for, if Henry's incapacity continued, Richard would hold effective power and could demonstrate his competence without being portrayed as challenging the King. Surely, in these circumstances, even

175

if Henry recovered, York's reputation would be enhanced and he might expect to keep royal favour?

For a few days the atmosphere at Westminster seemed calmer and during this time Sir Nicholas held a small gathering in his lodgings to say goodbye for the time being to his son by his first wife. Nicky was now fourteen and had been a page attending the Duke of Somerset for nearly two years but with Edmund Beaufort languishing in the Tower, and continuing uncertainty as to his fate, the boy's future was precarious. Sir Nicholas judged it wise to move his son elsewhere and I admired his skilful diplomacy when I heard Nicky was to join the household of the Earl of Warwick.

The Earl was five or six years younger than me and I thought his inexperience had shown when he let his dislike of Somerset lead him to defame the Queen with wild and contradictory accusations at the meeting of Nevilles. On the other hand, he had impressed me recently when he dealt commandingly with Sir Guy Binwood's mendacious slurs. I was pleased that he chose to join me soon after he entered the room at the Chamberlayne assembly.

'So many wily dispositions are being made, Doctor Somers, so many auspices examined, in order to profit from the changes around us. Casting horoscopes is something you do as a physician, I suppose?'

The last person who said something of the sort to me had been Andy Armstrong and for a moment I wondered what had happened to that inscrutable fellow.

'My lord Earl, it's necessary to determine the balance of a man's humours in order to treat him appropriately but I don't put exaggerated reliance on horoscopes. I've not found them entirely dependable.'

'I applaud realism, Doctor. It's my guiding principle. I judge as I find. If I'm slighted or unjustly treated I consider that my contract with the man who scorns me is terminated.'

Was he explaining why he had shifted his allegiance to support York's cause after King Henry disillusioned him? It seemed strange that he should speak so revealingly to an insignificant physician he scarcely knew. I speculated whether he might be less self-confident than he appeared.

'You're not attached to any household at present?'

'At her Grace the Queen's request I may be summoned back to Windsor to attend the King. It's a loose commitment but I have no other.'

'You're a man of property yourself, I believe?'

It was unnerving to find the Earl had learned something of my background. 'I hold a small manor in Suffolk but I see myself as a physician above all things. That's the vocation for which I trained.'

'In Padua as well as Oxford, I hear. And you served in the household of the late Duke of Suffolk, earning many complimentary comments on your skill.'

'My lord, I'm flattered you've heard good reports of me.'

'Not just of your medical skill. You've solved mysteries as well – a highly desirable accomplishment.'

'I'm an unwilling investigator, my lord, and any success I've had has been largely incidental.'

He laughed but did not challenge my comment. 'You're also a man of action when necessary. You helped rid the world of two base rogues in Stephen Boice and the Earl of Stanwick.'

Gilbert Iffley was his informant, without any doubt, and this was not comforting. 'A series of dreadful events led to their deaths.'

'Tactful too! They were villains. Stanwick was a danger to the peace of the realm and an enemy to all right-thinking Nevilles. On behalf of my kindred, I'm grateful to your man for eliminating his pernicious influence. Boice was a jumped-up merchant of no account to me but I understand he had done you and your late wife harm. I applaud your action.'

177

I mumbled something indistinct, uncertain how to respond to Warwick's plaudits, and he beamed at me.

'You're a good fellow, Doctor Somers. Maybe I should appoint you as physician and potential investigator in my household. That would keep you close to governance of the realm and I might benefit from your wise counsel to temper the exuberance which sometimes carries me away.'

It was strange to be patronised by a younger man, however high his birth, and I did not know how seriously to regard his proposition. 'My lord...' I stuttered. 'I'm overwhelmed.'

He smiled beneficently and went to join the circle round Sir Nicholas, leaving me perplexed. I judged him a man of noteworthy potential, capable of recognising and learning from his own errors. It could be intellectually rewarding to serve him but, after the mischances I had suffered and the melancholy I felt, I feared it might be too late for me to recapture the vigour and optimism I would need to match his. In any case, his comment was probably no more than a pleasantry.

I moved across the room towards a courtier I knew when a number of other people also changed their positions and, without either of us intending it, I came face to face with Bess Willoughby, in attendance on Lady Maud Chamberlayne. I bowed and she flushed but she did not turn away as once she would have done. Lady Maud waved a languid hand to indicate Bess was free to converse with me.

'Mistress Willoughby, I trust you are well; and your children.'

'Thank you, Doctor Somers. Anne and Rob are at the Chamberlayne manor-house in Harrow. I hope to see them again in a few days.'

Although stilted, they were the first civil words she had spoken to me since her husband's death and I waited for her to berate me afresh for that terrible occurrence. She lowered her eyes.

'I was very sorry to hear of Master Ford's death in Aquitaine.'

'It was tragic. I miss his friendship.' I had never known how she really regarded Piers Ford and wondered if she would hold me responsible for his death, simply because he had decided to accompany me to Bordeaux.

'I'm riven with guilt,' she said. 'I hold myself to blame for Master Ford leaving England. I'm sure you know I declined his offer of marriage. It was too soon after losing Robin – but I could have been kinder. Master Ford was a fine man.'

'You're in no way to blame, Mistress Willoughby. Piers knew he'd approached you too soon. He wanted to absorb himself in helping others until he could ask you again. That's what he did in Aquitaine – help others. He died helping others.' I did not propose to give her any further details but it was clear her sorrow at Piers's death had softened her attitude towards me, which I welcomed.

She sighed. 'You know well enough, Doctor Somers, life can be very cruel. I would not have accepted Master Ford, had he lived to offer me marriage again. I esteemed him but he could not take Robin's place. I'm fortunate that I have my position with Lady Maud and am not dependent on finding another husband speedily. Yet the knowledge I would have rejected him a second time only makes my feeling of guilt the greater.'

Her words came in a rush and they tugged at my heart. 'Piers in no way blamed you. He understood. He wouldn't want you to feel guilty.'

She gave me a searching look. 'Perhaps I've been too ready to attribute blame in the past. Master Ford's fate has taught me that. I cursed you, Doctor Somers, for causing Robin's death but I know you weren't responsible. Robin chose to go with you to that dangerous encounter and he chose to defend you. It was Robin's nature.'

'Your reaction was natural and I do bear some responsibility. I shouldn't have asked Robin to go with me.

It would lighten my spirit if you felt more cordially towards me in the future.'

She smiled wistfully. 'I have much to thank you for, Doctor Somers. You saved my children from villains on that awful occasion when your wife died. You have suffered dreadful loss. We should offer each other kindness.'

'I'd be happy if we could. There's misery enough around us.' I told her of Grizel's death and the bereft Chope family, for I thought she might recall the little maid in Humphrey of Gloucester's household when we were young. Her eyes filled with tears.

'Please give Master Chope my sympathy. I remember him and Grizel well. Rendell Tonks too.'

I was stammering my gratitude when Lady Maud bore down upon us, with the customary rustle of silks and clinking of jewellery. She commandeered Bess Willoughby's services and shot me a glance which managed to combine amusement with vitriol. Despite the sombre theme of my conversation with Bess, I returned to my quarters with a lighter step and merrier heart than I had felt for a long time. My rapprochement with the woman who had first won my heart was precious to me.

At my invitation, Ursula had recently resumed visits to my bed but I was glad she did not come that night. I was in reflective mood. Grizel's death and the shattering of Thomas's settled world had already jolted my complacency. Now I reflected on Bess Willoughby's continuing loss. At least both Bess and Thomas had years of happiness in their marriages to recall. Because of Kate's mental frailty my own memories were doubly painful, both for what I had lost and for what might have been.

Perhaps, I mused, I should not disregard the opportunity to build a new life with a woman I found pleasing enough, albeit conventions would be broken by that union. Because of her chequered background, most of my acquaintances would not consider Ursula a suitable wife for me, and that posed concerns. I was not swept away by overpowering passion and I valued the opinions of friends I had known for many years. I had suffered in the past as a result of unwise actions.

In consequence, although I was attracted by the idea of marrying Ursula, I backed away from the complications it might entail and, reprehensibly, I let things drift. She was a forthright woman but she never alluded to marriage and I doubted she thought it remotely possible. Perhaps, I told myself, she saw our liaison as a fleeting diversion and might tire of me, so I lazily shirked coming to a decision.

There was a further complexity to consider. Richard of Warwick's flippant suggestion that I might join his household was tantalising. I had served in the households of noblemen previously and enjoyed treating the variety of patients from scullery maids to the greatest in the land, with their wide range of medical conditions testing my skills. If there were to be the prospect of a similarly honourable, fulfilling position in a noble entourage, I should not dismiss it. But could it be reconciled with taking Ursula Bateby to wife?

*****

Unanticipated events can influence the affairs of realms and individuals alike and the sudden death of Cardinal Kemp, Archbishop of Canterbury and Lord Chancellor of England, proved the point. By creating vacancies in two crucial posts, it brought to the fore issues which might have been conveniently ignored for longer, but for both new appointments the King's authority was required. There was no obvious way forward so Richard of York hurriedly called together a group of lords and bishops to decide what should be done. They drew up articles to be read out to the King and the day after Kemp's demise a delegation journeyed to Windsor to advise their sovereign of the crisis and assess his condition. York was not part of the delegation but his wife's nephew, Warwick, was

181

included and, at Duke Richard's request, so was I. My remit was to report my medical opinion of what I observed. Thus I was drawn back into the tangle of state proceedings.

We arrived when the King was at table, being fed by servants, and we watched respectfully, alongside the bevy of doctors I remembered, while he ate his dinner. The visitors noted with pleasure his healthy appetite for the food placed in his mouth. He did not speak but this did not occasion comment as he had never been talkative. What concerned the dignitaries more seriously was that, when they read out the articles affirming allegiance and setting out the problems caused by the Cardinal's death, he gave no sign of comprehension. The representatives asked that the King be taken to another room, hoping the movement might waken his senses, but it achieved nothing.

Warwick and the others took refreshment before we set out on the road again and I took the opportunity to draw Michael Retford aside for a private conversation. He looked wan and I suspected care of the invalid was becoming a burden to all the physicians, surgeons, herbalists and attendants who served King Henry. Michael listened to a brief summary of my life at Westminster and I detected a glint of envy in his eyes but I had omitted reference to the incidents with Jasper Coote and Sir Guy Binwood as well as to Grizel Chope's death.

'Has nothing at all changed in King Henry's condition during the past four months?' I asked.

'At first we all strained to discern some trace of improvement. John Arundel was sure the blood-letting and cauterising was having an effect, insisting an eyelid fluttered or the mouth curved into a smile, but if there were such movements they were involuntary and had no significance. As the weeks have passed we've all grown dispirited, knowing we've accomplished nothing at all. Most of the doctors spend less time at the castle now, slinking off for their own pursuits. The only good thing is that the poor King is left unpummelled and suffers fewer incisions into his scalp, so if Dame Nature will cure him in due course she has a better chance of doing so without their interventions.'

I grinned at his gentle humour. 'And you, Michael, are you frustrated at this thankless task you've been handed?'

'If I had nothing else to do, I'd be tempted to shrink into myself like King Henry. Fortunately there are many in the castle and the village who call on the services of an herbalist, so I don't feel wholly useless. I still think your diagnosis was most likely to be correct and more time is needed. Will you be coming back to Windsor?'

'I don't know. There's a faint possibility of doing something else which would be tempting. Arundel and the others wouldn't welcome me back, would they?'

'Not yet, but in a few more months I'd guess they'll be glad to hand over responsibility. They're giving me a freer hand already in what potions I prescribe. I'll follow your advice and if there's a chance you could help, I'll send a message for you to come. Should I send it to Westminster?'

I paused before replying but I wanted to share a confidence. 'Yes. It would be forwarded from there if necessary. There's a chance I might be serving the Earl of Warwick's household.'

Michael whistled. 'You've switched from Somerset?'

'Edmund Beaufort is in the Tower. My loyalty is always to the King and observance of the law but times are changing.'

I too could be pragmatic.

*****

Within days of the abortive visit to Windsor and my report on the King's unchanged condition, the Great Council resolved how to break the deadlock confronting them. They still denied Richard of York the Regency but

183

invested him instead as Protector and Defender of the Realm, resurrecting an office which my old patron, Humphrey of Gloucester, had held during King Henry's minority. If he was wise and acted with discretion, York would have all the power he craved, with no competitor. He would still act in the King's name but his authority would be supreme. The sands had shifted definitively under the surging tide of the Duke's dominance. I hoped he would use his position wisely, casting off the wilder acolytes who had blighted his reputation in the past.

York's first decrees were predictable, to secure his adherents in the vacant positions of state. His brother-in-law, the Earl of Salisbury, Warwick's father, became Lord Chancellor. His sister's relative by marriage, Thomas Bourchier, Bishop of Ely, was elevated to the See of Canterbury. The ascendancy of the Nevilles was assured. I thought sheepishly of the Prioress of St. Michaels' Convent in Stamford who hated the Nevilles, on behalf of her Percy kindred, and I wondered how the rivalry between those two great families in the north of England would now evolve. For complicated reasons, the Prioress had been effectively my mentor for many years but she disowned me when I insisted on standing by my fragile wife – who carried her own regrettable inheritance of Neville blood.

York's next move was understandable but could also be discerned as spiteful. Queen Margaret was ordered to reside at Windsor, caring for her afflicted husband, in all but name under open confinement, banished from Westminster. When I heard this news I envisaged, dishonourably, that it would bring me respite from the problem I faced with regard to Ursula Bateby, for the Queen's entire household would move with their lady to Windsor. It proved otherwise, however; indeed, York's decree expedited events which determined my future.

When we next met, Ursula seemed to acquiesce with the Duke's order more readily than I expected and for a moment I imagined she did not object to our separation. The illusion did not last. She rolled her eyes and put her hand to my neck, drawing my head towards her as if I was a pet dog she chose to fondle.

'With Queen Margaret in residence, the King's doctors will be compelled to heed her bidding and, as she approves of your advice, I fancy she'll order you to return to Windsor and take your place among them from time to time. That would be a joyful situation if I could remain there but I fear I shall be compelled to leave the Queen's service.'

'Why? What do you mean? Are you ill?'

She shook her head and did not reply at once. 'Duchess Cecily may take me back into her household. She has been kind to me. You'll recall I told you my husband was killed while fighting under the Duke.'

'But why should you leave the Queen?'

'If I remain, I will be expelled ignominiously from the royal household when she knows that I am pregnant.'

I reeled and gulped, totally unprepared for her announcement. 'Is it true?'

'It's early but it seems certain.'

I felt myself sway as all the ambiguities in my mind fell apart. 'Then of course, I must offer you my hand, seeking your consent to marry me. Oh, Ursula, a child...'

She gazed at me as if thunderstruck and I thought how modestly she viewed herself. She had disregarded the possibility that I might offer marriage and the respectability she had forfeited. I wondered what was in her mind while she hesitated. 'Do you think the Queen would countenance our marriage? You are her tiring-maid.'

She took a deep breath. 'Marriage is an honourable estate which she respects and you are as estimable a husband as any tiring-maid might aspire to – especially if her Grace remains ignorant of inconvenient particularities. You know how I lived as Stephen Boice's whore – and in the past there have been others. Can you really wish to make me your wife?'

'With all seriousness and solemnity, Ursula.'

She stroked my disfigured cheek, deep in contemplation, before speaking. 'I hope you will never have cause to regret your generosity. I swear I shall be a loving and devoted wife to you: a role I never supposed open to me. Nothing will prevent me fulfilling this laudable duty.' A mischievous smile curved her lips. 'You'll come to Windsor when you're sent for and our union will be consecrated. Then Gilbert Iffley will no longer be able to menace you. He'll understand that I would never testify against my husband. You'll finally be free from blame for Stephen Boice's death.'

I was immediately embarrassed. 'I never thought of that. It isn't why I'm asking you.'

'I know that, you sweet man. But it is a benefit. Just think: we shall be married in that handsome chapel at the castle and thenceforth enjoy all the blessed gifts which matrimony bestows. I shall lie with you as your wife and you will lawfully possess me. Oh, Harry...'

Her voice trembled but she put her arms round my neck and gave me a lingering kiss. Then she hurried away while I stared after her, startled, bemused and exhilarated in equal measure.

Chapter 15

The prospect of a child changed everything. Of course I felt a sense of obligation as well as affection towards the woman I had impregnated but duty was outweighed by sheer joy at the hope that, with God's blessing, I would become a father. The loss of Yolande de Langeais' baby six years earlier had been desperately painful and, combined with other circumstances we could not alter, the loss contributed to our parting. Later, during my marriage to Kate, I learned that one aspect of her mental affliction was terror at the possibility of giving birth and it seemed nothing could lessen her revulsion. Was it possible these accumulated sorrows would now be put behind me, together with the lingering fear that I would be charged with Stephen Boice's murder?

I told myself I must plan for my future as a married man and prospective father. My objective was always to practice medicine, using all the training and experience I had received. The question was how best to secure this. I had heard nothing from the Earl of Warwick and was forced to the conclusion that the enticing allusion to a post in his household had no substance. I began to revisit old plans from a time when I longed to establish myself in the City of London, independent of any patron, treating all who sought my services in exchange for modest fees. It was a dream I cherished but Kate had disliked the idea, believing it unworthy of a professional man who should be the confidant of some great noble rather than touting his services like a tradesman. Surely Ursula lacked such pretensions? Yet it seemed I must always torment myself. Would she truly be contented with domesticity and acting as my helpmeet in treating the ailments of the poor?

In all marriages there must be necessary accommodations to be made between the parties, I concluded pompously. Ursula and I knew each other far better than most newly affianced couples and the bedchamber would hold no surprises or anxiety. Life as a

City physician should enable me to break away from the festering antagonisms of rival courtiers and the wiles of their hateful acolytes. I would welcome that.

Ursula had led a turbulent life over the past few years. When we met, before I went to Aquitaine, she told me she had been widowed when a husband she did not care for was killed in a skirmish while fighting for Richard of York. Duchess Cecily had then sent her to spy on the Queen and she had been induced to become Stephen Boice's mistress. He had subjected her to base cruelty, but she showed herself resilient and gained satisfaction from taking her revenge. She was intelligent and, as my wife, she would no longer need to scheme to secure advantage. I would be able to provide her with a reasonable standard of comfort and, if she wished, she could become a respected dame in the locality. Our child – perhaps, our children – would strengthen our bonds. It was all possible.

In the days after the departure of the Queen's household from Westminster, while I awaited a summons to return to Windsor, I decided I should face some of my own demons. I must be ready to move into my new life unencumbered by ghosts from the past. Foremost among those demons was the need to visit Sir Nicholas Chamberlayne's manor at Harrow on the Hill where the appalling events took place which culminated in Kate's violent death and where she was buried. I had avoided returning there but now I knew I must do so in order to lay her more thoroughly to rest in my heart.

Sir Nicholas knew nothing of my commitment to Ursula but he welcomed my decision to go to Harrow and insisted on accompanying me. His wife had gone to their manor before Easter, declaring it was tedious to watch Richard of York's self-aggrandisement and she would welcome fresh country air after the foul stench of the court. I proposed to stay only one night with the Chamberlaynes and as soon as I arrived in Harrow I made my solitary pilgrimages to the site of Kate's death and her tomb in the hilltop church. I felt an unaccustomed sensation of peace after paying my respects and entered the curtilage of the manor-house to join my hosts in a contented frame of mind. It was not to last long.

Attendants were waiting at the gatehouse, with a groom holding ready-saddled horses, while a man dressed in a fur-trimmed gown strode towards them across the courtyard. I was startled to identify Gilbert Iffley but it gratified me that he was no less disconcerted to see me. For a moment his normal aplomb was ruffled and he paled but he quickly recovered his composure.

'Baron Glasbury,' I said, 'You did not expect to meet me here, I imagine.'

'Doctor Somers, to be sure, you have sad reasons to recall this place. My visit has been concerned only with matters of business, necessary but not on this occasion fruitful. I'm afraid I must be on my way. I have other engagements to keep before nightfall. God keep you.'

I bowed and watched the enigmatic Baron ride away with his entourage before I entered the main enclosure of the manor-house. The old tower at the heart of the complex, which was ravaged by fire before I went to Aquitaine, had been partly demolished. The family continued to use its lower floors and an adjacent building but a new construction had been started on the western side of the courtyard. This promised to be spacious with wide windows which were then becoming fashionable. Sir Nicholas had no shortage of funds, it seemed.

I was taken to my chamber and given water to wash. I changed my linen ready to sup with the Chamberlaynes but I was informed Sir Nicholas was occupied with public affairs and would be delayed. In the meantime Lady Maud wished me to take wine with her so I was escorted to her solar, with a sweeping view to the south.

The woman whose varying fortunes I had observed and influenced for more than ten years was resplendently arrayed. The finest Luccan silks shimmered as she moved and the gold filigree around her throat glistened in the low

189

sunlight beamed through the narrow side-window. The most flamboyant artefact was a headdress of incomparable grandeur which shone with the hues of precious stones set in a gilded circlet around the base of her cap. Rubies, emeralds and sapphires sparkled and I did not doubt they were genuine, costly gems, the costliest Sir Nicholas could afford. It was no wonder that, after all her tribulations, Lady Maud Chamberlayne looked joyful in her quasi-regal splendour.

I made my obeisance and only as I straightened my back realised her ladyship was attended by two serving women: one, the faithful Marian, who so conveniently suffered profound deafness, and had been present in the past at several of my less decorous encounters with her mistress. The other was Mistress Bess Willoughby who looked solemn but not unfriendly.

Her ladyship initiated our conversation without preliminary pleasantries. 'There is something I wish to say to you, Harry Somers, before Sir Nicholas joins us. My husband is a man of astuteness and skill but he is a man and therefore blind to some niceties of etiquette.'

I suppressed a sigh. 'In what have I offended?'

'Ha! You see, Bess, he nurses guilt.'

Mistress Willoughby blushed prettily and I wondered what banter had been exchanged between them at my expense. Lady Maud drew herself up in her chair and faced me sternly.

'It will not do, Doctor Somers; it will not do. You are belittling yourself, making a mockery of all your friends have done formerly to improve your situation in the world.'

For a moment I speculated whether my improvement had been the motive behind her intimate attentions to me in years gone-by and I must have grinned.

'Don't dare to express amusement! It's no frivolous matter for you to consort openly with a notorious harlot. By all means rut with her if you must, others have done so, but you should not allow her to boast of her association

190

with you as if she was an honest woman. The servants' corridors at Westminster are full of salacious gossip about your liaison. Isn't that true, Bess?'

Mistress Willoughby put her hand to her mouth in alarm and I was sorry Maud had revealed what her attendant probably disclosed under pressure. I smiled reassuringly at Bess.

'My Lady, I assume you are referring to Mistress Bateby. I'm well aware of her past life. She has been greatly wronged. One of her virtues is openness and she has no wish for a clandestine relationship, kept behind closed doors. If, after all she has suffered, she gains self-respect by being linked with a humble physician, while court gossips look for scandal among their colleagues, I do not demur.'

I was sorry Bess flushed to hear me speak of "court gossips" but I was annoyed by Maud's intrusive moralising and contempt. I drew breath to throw down my angry challenge by announcing my impending marriage to the disparaged Ursula when Marian scuttled forward to hold the door as Sir Nicholas rattled the catch before entering. She may have seen the handle quiver but the dreadful thought crossed my mind that she might not be as deaf as I had understood.

'My apologies, Harry, I hadn't intended to leave you in the she-wolves' den unchaperoned. Have they mauled you badly?'

'You're in time to find me in one piece but near to being savaged.' I answered in the same jovial tone, while trying to hide my relief at his arrival.

Sir Nicholas insisted on showing me the new building works, particularly the great hall which was nearly completed externally.

'I wish to have it panelled throughout on the inside,' my host said. 'It's my wretched luck that the carpenter who was to design and install it has just died suddenly before he had completed even a sketch. I'll have to find a new craftsman.'

'My oldest friend is a master carpenter in the City of London, much sought after by nobility and distinguished citizens. You could consult him. I can't promise he'd take on the work himself but he'd be able to travel here and back to his workshop in a day to see what's needed.' I gave Sir Nicholas the necessary details, hoping that Thomas might find it of interest to advise the Chamberlaynes, distracting him just a little from his terrible loss.

We went down to the hall for a fine supper enlivened by entertainments which did not stray too far towards the ribald and I was spared any further baiting by the ladies. Nevertheless I was unsettled by Maud's taunts and regretted that Bess had been embarrassed. I was glad to share a final glass of wine alone with Sir Nicholas who made no awkward references to my private life.

'I met Baron Glasbury leaving your manor-house,' I said, succumbing to curiosity.

For a moment Sir Nicholas paused, twisting his glass in his fingers. 'One is compelled to trade with the devil these days. He's a pernicious fellow, as you well know, but it's politic to maintain good relations with a variety of undesirables, to keep a foot in both camps. Too much remains uncertain. Glasbury came here of his own volition, intent on sniffing out treachery to Richard of York.'

'You haven't secured York's complete trust?'

Sir Nicholas laughed. 'A wise man knows how options can be kept open and York is no fool. In any case, Gilbert Iffley didn't find what he was looking for. I detected his chagrin and enjoyed it. He'll continue the hunt but I'm confident we can outwit him. Better watch yourself, Harry, now you've been seen visiting this vipers' nest. It's time for shrewd diplomacy. Don't commit yourself too far one way or the other.'

Perceptive advice, I thought ruefully, but not necessarily easy to follow.

*****

I found it difficult to sleep that night. The private guest room was little more than a cubicle off the main chamber, where the generality of visitors, merchants and tradesmen, were accommodated, and it was airless. In the early hours, sweating profusely, I dragged myself from the bed to open the communicating door and create a cooling draught. Perhaps some slight sound had disturbed me, or it could have been sheer coincidence, but across the larger room, beyond a number of occupied pallets, a man stood shielding the flame of a candle with one hand as he shrugged his bundle of possessions into a comfortable position on his shoulder. The light was enough for me to distinguish his features and my mouth fell open, although I was sufficiently conscious not to exclaim and risk waking the sleepers.

Andy Armstrong quickly put a finger to his mouth, causing the candle to flicker, before he turned onto the curving staircase in the corner of the room and tripped light-footed down the steps. He could not have discerned my features in the dark but no doubt he knew who was accommodated in the private chamber. He had not been surprised to see me.

I crept across to the window overlooking the courtyard where burning brands in a metal sconce threw enough light to reveal a tethered horse near the door from the tower. A moment later, Armstrong emerged, unloosed the halter and swung himself into the saddle. He looked up directly towards my window and touched his forehead respectfully before pulling down his hood to cover his brow. It was disconcerting that he expected me to be watching. The outer gate to the manor-house was already swinging open and in an instant Armstrong had gone. His horse's hooves were muffled and the hinges of the outer gate were well greased. His surreptitious departure had been carefully contrived.

Back in my bed, cooler but wider awake, I pondered the range of visitors to the Chamberlayne manor. Andy Armstrong was an experienced spy and might well be pursuing his craft, even if no longer in a military context. If so, who was he working for? Not, I imagined, Richard of York. Sir Nicholas had referred to Gilbert Iffley failing to find what he had come for at Harrow on the Hill. Was it an unfathomable and probably duplicitous individual the Baron hoped to discover there? Sir Nicholas was intent on keeping open all his options but it was a dangerous game he played. I was determined to avoid entanglement in such intrigues.

*****

I made a further pilgrimage to Kate's tomb next morning and agreed to join the Chamberlayne household for dinner at midday before I set off to ride back to Westminster. This enabled me to snatch a few words with Mistress Willoughby, apologising because gossip about my liaison with Ursula had put her in an embarrassing position.

'You know Lady Maud,' she said with gentle mockery, raising her eyebrows, 'at least as well as I do. She was bound to censure your behaviour and quote the chatter she'd heard. She enjoyed taunting you.'

'You don't think she was seriously affronted?'

'At the time she meant every word but she was amused to see you wriggle on the hook she'd baited. You are a paradox to her. She expects you to be admiringly envious of her newly acquired wealth and grandeur but instead you're consorting with a woman of low repute and seem oblivious of her good fortune.'

'That's a shrewd assessment. Does she realise you understand her so absolutely?'

Bess Willoughby smoothed her skirt. 'That's not a proper question to put to a lady's attendant.'

There was laughter in her eyes which gave me great pleasure after the hostility she had shown me following her husband's death. I tried to look contrite. 'I admit it, Mistress Willoughby. I shouldn't press you. I had hoped to see your children on my visit. I trust they're well?'

'Indeed, yes, but they aren't here. They left at Eastertide to stay a few weeks in Norfolk, at Hartham Manor, with Lady Eleanor and her family. They know the place well, of course, and there are young children for them to play with. Lady Maud proposes to visit her daughter for Pentecost. We leave in two days and I shall then retrieve my infants. That's scarcely the right word, though. Anne will be seven this year and little Rob had his fourth birthday before he left Harrow.'

She tried to disguise the tremor in her voice but it was obvious she was mourning Robin's absence and the loss to her fatherless children.

'There's a new baby at Hartham,' I said gently, hoping to distract her from her grief. 'Poor Judith, who served my wife with such diligence, has given birth, I understand.'

Bess nodded. 'She's a brave woman. She has called her son Roger after his father, despite the violence with which the late Earl forced himself on her and got her with child. I pray God the boy will not inherit his father's vile temperament.'

'Amen. The birth of his natural son has caused harm enough already. Rendell Tonks had hoped to ask for Judith's hand.'

'And he won't now because she was raped by a contemptible beast?'

'Rendell would happily fall on his knees before violated Judith but he can't bring himself to accept the Earl's bastard. Don't judge him too harshly. He's still young and has much to learn.'

'I will try not to judge him but there's enough wretchedness without compounding Judith's pain. Yet perhaps all isn't lost...'

195

Her voice tailed away. She clamped her lips and looked resolute. 'Will you visit your friend, Thomas Chope, while you're at Westminster?'

'Certainly. He was grateful when I gave him your commiserations. He was touched, in view of your own loss.'

'That small group who first met in Duke Humphrey's palace at Greenwich have had their share of adversities.' There were tears in her eyes again but she shook her head as if to disperse them. 'Just be careful, Doctor Somers, you don't add to your own quiver of sadness.'

I left Mistress Willoughby, delighted that we could now talk to each other as old friends but troubled by her instruction to me. Was she alluding to the possibility that I might marry Ursula Bateby? Would that union ruin my rapprochement with Bess? But Bess would surely understand about the forthcoming child? She clearly admired Judith for not rejecting the son she had been compelled to bear. Bess might blame me for making Ursula my mistress but perhaps she would respect my wish to accept my responsibility as a father. Her good opinion meant far more to me than Lady Maud Chamberlayne's acidic comments. I departed from Harrow without divulging my matrimonial intentions.

*****

The messenger from Windsor arrived before I left the manor-house. He had been first to Westminster and was sent on to Harrow because he was committed to deliver the royal command in person. At Queen Margaret's behest I was to present myself at the castle within three days, to attend my patient and 'carry out my duty' – a none-too-subtle reference to my nuptials, I presumed. I asked the messenger to convey my obedience and promised to be at Windsor in two days' time. My business at Harrow was concluded.

I turned out of the gatehouse into the high street of the village, determined not to dwell on the horrors which had occurred there when Kate was killed. Outside the inn a scruffy fellow was sitting cross-legged, observing those who passed him. I took him for a beggar and when he hailed me I extracted a small coin from my purse to toss to him.

'Thank'ee. Doctor Somers, isn't it? I've a message for you.'

This seemed improbable but I drew rein and he repeated the words he seemed to have learned by rote. 'Old friend, he said. If you'd care to stop for refreshment at the sign of the Green Hazel Tree in Willesden, he'll be waiting. He'd like a chat about your time together in the past, he said.'

Andy Armstrong knew I had recognised him and observed his stealthy departure from the manor-house. He must have learned I was on the premises but was due to leave the following day. Now he was giving me an opportunity to meet him in less constrained circumstances and I welcomed his thoughtfulness. I took out a second coin to reward his spokesman. The contrast between this unkempt fellow and the royal messenger amused me. I wondered if it denoted my improving prospects for the future.

It was a well-used road from Harrow leading to Westminster and the City of London so, travelling by daylight, no special precautions were necessary. The gates to both city and palace would not be closed until darkness fell and in early summer the hour for this was getting later. I would have time to drink a jar or two with Armstrong before completing my ride. I trotted contentedly towards my appointment.

Above the door of the Green Hazel Tree hung a battered but identifiable sign showing a verdant sprig of leaves, while to the side of the inn a less happy specimen of the actual tree grew. It had been pollarded once but such maintenance had been abandoned and the cracked bark of its trunk bore signs of mildew. The inn itself had a workaday look but it stood on a busy route and appeared to be well patronised. I entered, gave my name and said a friend hoped to meet me there. The potman nodded and pointed to an empty seat.

'He's occupied for a bit, sir. He asked that you sample some of our best ale while you wait. I'll show you upstairs when he's ready.'

I had no problem with this, provided I was not delayed for too long, and took a deep draught of the excellent ale. A short time later two men, who could well have been trained soldiers from their bearing, descended the staircase, glanced round the room, spoke to each other and left the premises. I hoped they were Armstrong's visitors and finished my drink before the potman beckoned me to follow him. Only as I stood up did I appreciate just how strong the ale was, but with concentration I could make my way up the stairs without wavering. I assumed that the heat of the crowded tap-room had contributed to the dullness in my head.

The door to the right on the landing, which had been pointed out to me, stood open and I entered without a second thought. An attendant closed it behind me while I was trying to make out shadowy details, focussing on a figure who rose from a chair by the window and extended a hand to greet me. I opened my mouth to address him by name but it was not Andy Armstrong and I shut my lips tightly.

'Who did you expect to meet, Harry? I trust you will tell me. Take a seat.'

The mellifluous voice of Gilbert Iffley, Baron Glasbury, was loaded with irony. I cursed the carelessness which had led me into his trap and struggled to clear my mind.

'Baron, I admit I didn't know but I should have deduced from the quality of the ale it was someone with exceptional tastes.'

Iffley grimaced. 'You should have drunk more of it. Maybe you wouldn't be so guarded if you had. I don't want to delay your journey but it's time we came to an agreement. You can help me. I surmise that while you were at Nicholas Chamberlayne's manor you met a particular fellow guest. Someone you'd met before?'

'There were several visitors doing business at the manor. I didn't meet them and I was lodged separately. Why are you asking?'

'Too ingenuous, Harry, by far. I went to Harrow intent on exposing a villain who was known to be there but he'd been hidden and I had to leave empty-handed. It seemed likely you would fare better. If I'm right in my supposition, he's someone you met in Aquitaine.'

'I've no idea what you're talking about, Baron.' His obvious curiosity about Andy Armstrong made me resolved to reveal nothing.

Iffley sighed extravagantly. 'What do you owe this man, Harry? Or are you part of his network?'

'What network?'

'Is it possible you actually don't know? I thought Sir Nicholas would have confided in you? The man I'm seeking is a spy-master, working for Somerset. He has organised a network of spies in every household of potential allies, every household not wholly committed to Richard of York's interests.'

'Somerset's in the Tower,' I said with exaggerated idiocy. 'How can he be involved in such arrangements?'

'André Chartier is his agent and provocateur.'

'André Chartier?'

'You know perfectly well who I mean – or if you don't, you'll soon find out. I have here documents which would lead to your arraignment for the murder of my good-brother, Stephen Boice. They contain Ursula Bateby's revised testimony to that effect, retracting the statement she gave under duress, which exonerated you. If you wish to prevent me laying her evidence before Duke Richard, you will do as I tell you.' He paused dramatically.

My stomach churned with relief and subsided in resignation. His reference to Ursula's revised testimony was a ruse, a threat he had held over me but it was now void. She was too canny to have signed documents which might rebound on her as well as me and now she never would. The Baron was unaware of our impending marriage and I was not going to enlighten him. If it gave me the means to undermine his hold over me once and for all, I would relish outwitting him.

'Which is?' I asked casually.

'Damn you, Harry Somers; has the ale made you completely thick-headed? I want this rat, Chartier, caught and strung up on the nearest gallows but I also want proof of which great households are prepared to dally with him and join Somerset's conspiracy. There's one such household on which you're qualified to report.'

'I've just been to Harrow and I assure you I found out nothing of use to you.' I felt no pang of conscience in lying.

'Not Harrow, not the Chamberlaynes, but a related household of greater distinction: Hartham Manor in Norfolk where Lady Maud's daughter lives with her beloved, wayward husband, Lord Gaston Fitzvaughan. We have reason to believe Gaston is part of a seditious intrigue against Richard of York. You will go there and you will seek out evidence so the plot and its instigators can be destroyed.'

'And if I decline to go?' The question expected of me.

Iffley ran his fingers over the pack of documents. 'It will be you facing the gallows, Harry, after you are dragged before the justices accused of murder. I shall regret losing you. I enjoy our stimulating encounters, although you have disappointed me with your obtuseness on this occasion.'

'Blame your ale, Baron. But I understand your terms and I'm bound to accept them. I will go to Hartham Manor and make enquiries but first I'm commanded to present myself at Windsor. I don't expect to be there more than a week or so. After Pentecost I will go to Norfolk. I trust that will suffice.'

He beamed at me with sickening self-satisfaction while I adopted an expression of unhappy acquiescence. It was not entirely false. For the moment it was expedient to humour him but Pentecost was a season for marriages and my marriage to Ursula was now absolutely essential.

Chapter 16

While I was away at Harrow Ursula suffered loss for her maid-servant, Mary, had sickened unexpectedly and died. It seemed she had consumed fungi gathered in the woods near the castle which proved toxic. Ursula shook her head sadly when she described the girl's rapid deterioration.

'She was a shy little creature and never inspired confidences between us but she served me obediently and it's dreadful to think of her miserable death. She was in great distress.'

'Poor child; she can't have realised what dangers lurk at our feet and in hedgerows. I'm sorry there's this sadness clouding our wedding day.'

Ursula smiled bravely. 'It mustn't spoil our happiness. We can be excused from dwelling too much on sorrow at our time of joy.'

I squeezed her hand and kissed her, admiring her resolve. I would ensure she acquired a new serving-maid as soon as we were wed.

The Queen did not grace our nuptials in person but gave us her good wishes and a generous gift to celebrate our lawful union. Ursula was thrilled by this mark of royal favour, as much perhaps as by her endorsement of respectability as a married woman. There was no doubt about her pregnancy. When we lay together, the thickening of her body was already apparent, at least to a physician, and I cherished her for the life she carried. She accepted that I must soon leave her to travel to Norfolk but she did not demur. Doubtless, in my absence, she would enjoy boasting to her companions of how she cajoled me into marriage and I did not begrudge her this satisfaction.

On Doctor Arundel's instructions I was not permitted to see the King and I feared I would need to leave Windsor without the chance to assess the patient's current condition for myself. Ursula was having none of this, however: outraged by my treatment, she took steps to ensure the Queen was made aware of it, whereupon I was abruptly summoned to Queen Margaret's presence in the King's apartments. I was struck by the simplicity of the Queen's gown and plain cap, realising she was dressed in a similar fashion to the nursing sisters in attendance who assisted with care of the invalid. This was the role she had embraced diligently for herself.

'Why did you not inform me yourself, Doctor Somers?' Her tone was peremptory. 'I required your attendance here for medical reasons, not merely to gratify personal desires in the marriage bed.'

'Your Grace, the other doctors don't seem to have understood this but I didn't like to challenge them. They would never disobey your commands.'

She sniffed derisively. 'You are too good-natured. You damage your own interests. I shall issue clear directions to Doctor Arundel together with the consequences of thwarting my will. You will see the King within the hour and report back to me. I will confide to you in the meantime that since I have been at Windsor I've endeavoured to follow the painstaking approach you advocated for care of my husband. There have been no more egregious interventions to purge or bleed him without good cause.'

'Your Grace, I'm honoured by the trust you've put in me.'

'Return when you have seen the King.'

Arundel and the other physicians shuffled round me with insincere apologies, chastened by the Queen's fury, and I had ample time to examine King Henry before returning to the Queen's lodgings. This time she was more richly clad and attended by a flock of her own ladies including, unobtrusively, my wife. She indicated they should withdraw to the far side of the room and spoke to me in a low voice.

'Well, Doctor Somers, what did you notice?'

I had been preparing my reply while crossing the courtyard. 'Your Grace, King Henry looks in bodily health, well-fed, more colour in his cheeks than when I saw him last. He's being assiduously cared for and he seems calmer than I remember.'

'Nothing more?'

'Your Grace, I mustn't encourage false optimism. One flicker of an eyebrow, a slight twitch of the lips cannot be taken as sound proof of returning intelligence.'

Her voice sank to a whisper.

'But you discerned such a flicker and twitch?'

'I discerned the impression of those movements, your Grace. They may be meaningless. It's too soon to be sure.'

Queen Margaret's eyes held mine for a moment. She was still a woman of startling beauty and I was spellbound by her look. 'We understand each other, Doctor Somers. We shall continue to follow your prescription. You will say nothing.'

As I gave my word, the Queen bade Ursula stand forward. 'When you return from the journey you are to undertake, do you intend to remove this serving woman from my household, Doctor Somers?'

'We've scarcely discussed our future domestic arrangements, your Grace, but it's always been an ambition of mine to practise as a physician in the City of London.'

Ursula had adopted the posture of a modest tiring-maid, hands clasped and eyes lowered, but I caught her momentary frown. It was unfortunate to be divulging plans in public which we had not yet discussed but I felt bound to give the Queen an honest answer.

'That is a creditable ambition, fitting for one of your background, Doctor: as is your marriage to my serving woman. May God bless you.'

When we met in our chamber that evening, Ursula was cheerful, revelling in the Queen's approval of our marriage, teasing me gently for not sharing my plans with her, ready to await my return from Norfolk before considering the possibilities further. I was grateful for her forbearance but she had not detected the underlying reprimand in the Queen's words addressed solely to me.

Margaret of Anjou could be pragmatic if it suited her purpose but she did not forget slights or what she saw as impropriety. Her endorsement of my marriage to Ursula was meant to remind me of the gross offence I had committed seven years earlier in winning the heart of the highborn French Countess Yolande and aspiring to wed her. The Queen was prepared to recognise my medical standing and had no criticism of my marriage to Kate, who had been my social superior, but she would never fully forgive my presumption in bedding a French noblewoman.

Before I left Windsor I had to suffer one other difficult encounter, this time with my friend, the herbalist, Michael Retford. I was pleased to see him again and to find him prospering but he was obviously uncomfortable speaking to me. I guessed the reason and would have preferred not to unsettle our careful conversation but Michael felt bound to be explicit.

'Of course I wish you well in your marriage,' he said awkwardly, 'but I was surprised to learn of it. Mistress Bateby, as she was, had not seemed a likely bride for you.'

'Because she was my acknowledged mistress? It isn't usual to marry one's paramour? An unnecessary nicety?'

Michael reddened. 'Not that. I shouldn't say more. You're married now and I hope she'll be a loving, loyal wife to you.'

This was aggravating and I was irritated. 'Do you have reason to doubt it? I know of her past life and the trials she's faced. Throughout everything she's kept the patronage of Duchess Cecily of York and the Duchess recommended her to the service of the Queen, despite her stained reputation. I'm not alone in admiring her qualities.'

Michael bent down to pick a sprig of rosemary from a bush in the border beside us. 'Forgive me. There's always tittle-tattle in the castle – more than ever since the Queen came here with her household. Mistress Somers is a very comely woman and unusual in her openness. That's enough to set tongues wagging.'

It was strange hearing an allusion to "Mistress Somers" who was not Kate. 'Don't listen to them then. At any rate, when I return from Norfolk I intend to take Ursula away from here, away from the court and the gossip-mongers. It's intolerable that she should be made the subject of envious slander. Excuse me, I must go.'

I stalked off, revealing my irritation, but I heard Michael's sigh and that stayed with me, more troubling than his ignorant innuendo.

*****

I went first to Westminster to inform Gilbert Iffley that I was on my way to Norfolk and assure myself that no hint of my marriage had yet reached his ears. I found it satisfying that he would realise he had lost his hold over me while I was far away, ostensibly still complying with his directions.

Richard of York and many of his closest followers had left Westminster bound for the north of England where the perennial rivalry between the Nevilles and Percys had erupted into open violence. It seemed the Duke was determined to prevent an escalation of this trouble and his rapid action contrasted with the negligent attitude of the King's advisers towards such incidents in the past. It promised well for York's effectiveness, provided he did not show overt partiality for one side or the other.

The Earl of Warwick had ridden from Westminster with his uncle but was reported to be returning to the castle in the Midlands from which his title was derived. Of course, I thought wryly, Warwick Castle was where his household was based, where no doubt he had the services of a long-established physician. There had never been any real prospect of him offering me a position. I had let wishful thinking delude me. So be it: I was now intent on securing my own future.

I rode into the City of London before taking the highroad north-east. I called on Thomas but, as I might have foreseen, he was occupied with clients, instructing apprentices and listening to a fellow guildsman's troubles, all at the same time. The children were well, he insisted, and he was so busy he had scant time to grieve. I was not sure this was a desirable situation but I could do nothing to remedy it. I did not linger but before I left the workshop I learned Rendell was still at the Tower and had acquired some special responsibilities which absorbed his interest. That, at least was good news.

My route into East Anglia was familiar although I had not travelled it for more than eighteen months. Every stretch of countryside and stopping place was redolent with memories of earlier expeditions but I was prepared for this. The only town I wished to avoid, which was not on my route, was St. Albans where, on my last journey south, I met a strange old monk who prophesied violence and destruction would break out in the vicinity of his abbey. I had been transfixed by his words, even while attributing them to wandering wits, but I had gone on from St. Albans to the horrors which awaited me at Harrow on the Hill. There was no good reason for my resurgent qualms but I was disinclined to revisit the scene of that perplexing encounter.

The day before arriving at my little manor of Worthwaite, I called, as had been my custom in the past, at the castle of Wingfield, principal seat of William de la Pole, the late Duke of Suffolk whom I had served. His widow and the youthful second Duke were not present on this occasion but my old friends in their household welcomed me. Doctor Leone, the Italian apprentice who had become my assistant and then succeeded me as the de la Poles' physician, was ebullient. I knew he had married the serving maid he courted for many months and he was now the father of a small daughter who entranced him. Happily

207

uxorious and besotted with his offspring, he gave me hope for my own domestic serenity.

I also sought out Father Wilfred, the chaplain at Wingfield, who knew much about my past joys and sorrows. He had buried my tiny son, born before his time, then assisted Yolande's escape from danger to the protection of her brother in France and marriage to a suitable nobleman. Father Wilfred had kept my secrets and respected my intentions. Years later he had supported me when I faced the agonies of Kate's mental turmoil. Now I wished to tell him of my remarriage, of Ursula's chequered history and my hopes for a new life with her.

As always Father Wilfred listened attentively and blessed me. 'You never choose the smoothest road, Harry,' he said, 'but your heart is your guide and it is honourable. Nurture your new union and have patience. Scandalous chatter soon dies away with nothing fresh to feed it. I encountered Mistress Ursula when she was staying at your manor. Whatever may have befallen her previously, she struck me as a capable, well conducted woman. I pray you will make each other joyful.'

I thanked Father Wilfred for his understanding but was surprised when he had something else to tell me.

'It's a coincidence, Harry,' he said. 'No more than two weeks ago, a fellow called here enquiring the way to Worthwaite, where he hoped to find you. I gave him directions but explained you hadn't been at the manor for many months. I expect he went there anyway and Perkin will tell you more but I thought I'd mention it. He was from Burgundy.'

'A Burgundian? I don't know anyone from Burgundy.'

'Maybe he'd heard of your reputation as a physician. Perhaps Duke Philip is in need of a household doctor?'

We laughed at this flight of fancy and spent a pleasant evening together, over a jug of ale, while Leone retired early to his quarters to supervise care of his fractious daughter who was teething.

*****

Next morning I rode beside the modest stream known as the River Waveney until I reached the boundary of my land, a small enough plot compared with the great estates in the neighbourhood. I could see labourers working on the higher ground, driving sheep together prior to shearing, I presumed, as I strove to remember what Perkin had meticulously taught me. Nearer the house it was quiet and I paused to look at the enclosure which we had fashioned as Kate's garden where she would sit when she was calm. She had helped design it and I heard in my mind her excited voice when I first suggested creating a physic garden. 'Betony and mugwort, comfrey and chamomile,' she had trilled, remembering the properties of herbs she learned in the early months of our marriage when she had been in reasonable health and we were happy.

I shook myself and brushed away a tear. I must be business-like to encounter Perkin, my valued steward, and Dame Elizabeth his wife. Tears were soon in evidence, however, when they greeted me: initially on their wrinkled faces and then on mine. Only young Georgie Antey, whom I had sent to Worthwaite for his own safety, and who had proved an invaluable assistant for Perkin, stayed dry-eyed but there was no hiding his pleasure in seeing me. He looked on me as his patron, which was humbling.

Throughout this genuinely cheerful reunion I could not help but suspect that, although they were all glad to see me, they would prefer it if my visit was not too long extended. The manor was well organised and efficiently run. A resident owner with his own profession to pursue added nothing beneficial to its operation and, in the past, had too often caused complications. From the moment I crossed into my own domain I also realised that

209

Worthwaite was burdened with too many conflicting memories for me to wish to live there again. All it had meant to me, all that joy and grief, must now be set aside. They would have no part in my future life.

I took care not to refer to Ursula. Perkin and his wife had found her a problematic guest and I did not wish to embarrass them. After I had gone from Worthwaite, they would learn of my remarriage but I did not intend that my new wife would intrude again on their quiet existence. In this at least I was confident Ursula and I would be of one accord.

Perkin did not mention a visit from the Burgundian Father Wilfred had spoken of, so I asked whether any callers had enquired for me recently. It was Georgie who answered.

'A fellow come from Burgundy, Dijon, I believe. I took him for a travelling merchant. He knew you were not at the manor but asked if you'd told us when you'd be coming. I couldn't help him there, of course. He said he was journeying to the north of England. He had business with the Earl of Salisbury, I think. He'd made a diversion here because he had greetings for you from someone of your acquaintance. I didn't think it was my place to ask who it was.'

I laughed. 'Very discreet of you! I can't think who the acquaintance might be but I've heard the French King is trying to negotiate a settlement between Duke Philip and rebels in his town of Ghent. Over the years I've met several Frenchmen who might represent King Charles in an embassy to Burgundy. Perhaps it's one of them who travelled here.'

I thought no more about it and settled to listen to an hour or more of Perkin reporting on the number of lambs born in the spring, the weight of fleeces sold, the qualities of the new agent buying wool in the neighbourhood and the trouble the miller encountered with a broken mill-sail. Georgie presented me with the registers he kept, recording transactions, debts incurred and discharged, and purchases made to provision the farm. Dame Elizabeth insisted on showing me the preserves in her pantry and introducing me to the new house-servants she had engaged since I was last at the manor. I felt wholly superfluous to the smooth running of Worthwaite and was content that it was so. I announced my intention to travel on to see Lord Fitzvaughan at Hartham Manor after two days.

Dame Elizabeth fluttered her hands. 'Lady Chamberlayne is there at present, I believe, visiting her daughter and grandsons. Lord and Lady Fitzvaughan have often asked for news of you, Doctor, while you were across the sea in the fighting. They'll be glad to see you safe and sound. Mistress Judith too. She's a precious member of the household and her baby son...'

Perkin coughed and shook his head, preventing his wife saying more and I decided it would be prudent not to ask her to continue. I would form my own opinion about Judith and the late Earl of Stanwick's bastard when I saw them and understood better their position in the Fitzvaughan household.

That night, in the bed I had shared with Kate, I slept badly, fragmentary dreams waking me several times. I was eager to be on my way, leaving behind all that Worthwaite represented in my mind. Every step I took now would lead towards my new life.

*****

I had seldom felt so welcome. From the keeper of the gatehouse to Lady Eleanor herself, everyone greeted me with genuine delight. What I had done to defend Lord Fitzvaughan's wife and children, and the personal grief I had incurred as a result, was known to all. Probably the tale had been embellished in the telling to those who had not been present in Harrow more than eighteen months previously, but I was looked upon as the family's champion. I was uncomfortable with such adulation but rejoiced to see them prospering. At least the presence of Lady Maud ensured my exuberant reception was tempered with a degree of acidic disdain and in the circumstances I appreciated her astringency.

I was entertained by the ladies while Lord Fitzvaughan was detained by business. I met again his eldest son and heir, Walter, now approaching his fourth birthday, and little Gastie, as he announced himself, fully two years old and very lively. Bess Willoughby was present with her clever, observant daughter, Anne, and Rob, who was beginning to resemble his dead father so closely that Bess must be torn by conflicting emotions to see him.

A nursemaid set down before me a good-natured infant of some nine months or so who crawled rapidly to grip my leg and attempted to haul himself upright while uttering enthusiastic but incomprehensible sounds. I looked round in puzzlement, for the child was obviously of some account within the household, until Lady Eleanor realised the reason for my confusion.

'Doctor Somers, may I present my kinsman, Roger of Ravensmoor.'

This was the late Earl of Stanwick's bastard, Judith's son, and he was referred to by the name of the estate in the north of Yorkshire which had been left to Eleanor when the title of a landless earldom passed to his father, Roger Egremont. I peered round in case I had failed to recognise Judith.

'Roger's mother has asked to meet you privately. She's waiting in the anteroom. She did not wish to disgrace herself with excessive emotion in this gathering.'

Lady Eleanor's words were spoken with kindness but the suggestion that Judith feared losing her self-control was worrying. As Kate's devoted attendant, she had endured a multitude of trials without denting her optimism or equanimity.

'I've only been here a few days but in this remote spot we await the latest news from Windsor and Westminster with impatience.' Lady Maud was speaking, bored with our absorption in the children. 'I expect letters from Sir Nicholas daily but perhaps you can forestall what he'll have to tell?'

I controlled my rapid breathing. Sir Nicholas was conscientious in securing intelligence and relaying gossip; he would speedily report my news. 'His Grace, King Henry, remains unchanged but is receiving good care under the supervision of the Queen. I shall go to Windsor when I return to the south. I've recently married again. My wife is one of Queen Margaret's tiring-maids.'

It was Bess who gasped aloud and Lady Maud who exclaimed in disgust. 'Dear God, a tiring-maid! Not that woman we spoke of? A woman with the reputation of a harlot? Have you lost all semblance of dignity?'

'Mother, that is offensive.' Lady Eleanor rounded on Maud in a manner I would have found amusing in other circumstances. I was too conscious of Bess's distress as she clenched her hands to her chest in an attempt to stop herself shaking. Lady Eleanor turned to me. 'Who is this fortunate woman, Doctor Somers, who has won a hero-physician as husband?'

'She was a widow, my Lady, formerly known as Mistress Ursula Bateby. She stayed for some months at Worthwaite while I was in Aquitaine but you may not have encountered her.'

I expected an eruption of scorn and fury from Maud but she said nothing. Instead she tossed her head, nearly displacing her elaborate headdress, and swirled from the room in silent contempt, allowing Bess to follow her in evident relief.

'Ah!' Lady Eleanor exclaimed, misunderstanding her mother's reaction. 'I think you were meant to pine for her ladyship who's no longer attainable as your companion.' She regarded her mother's discomfiture as a pleasurable joke.

Soon afterwards I was shown into the anteroom to meet Judith who looked as calm as I remembered. She was plainly dressed but her gown was of fine material and she

213

was carefully groomed. She smiled as I entered and held out her hand but did not speak. I sensed that words were trapped inside her and she had asked to see me privately because I might help her express what she could not say in front of others.

'I'm so glad to see you, Judith. Perkin had kept me in touch with your news.'

'You've seen my son?' Her voice was flat.

'He's a healthy, forward lad. Lady Eleanor called him Roger of Ravensmoor.'

'Her ladyship insists that as the Earl's bastard, he's entitled to the designation. She wishes him to be brought up with her own sons.'

'You don't agree? Does she wish to part you from him?'

'No, no. She treats me with consideration. But I fear for Roger if he has his father's temperament. He will see the Fitzvaughan boys inherit all that legitimate birth brings them while he is given an empty title, even more worthless than his father's earldom which will not be his. I don't want him to grow envious and vicious. I would rather take him away to know nothing of his inheritance, to assume he was some humble man's child, to live a quiet, contented life in ignorance of how he was conceived. Lady Eleanor won't hear of it.'

'Some men inherit their parents' nature; some don't. We have no idea what influences the outcome. It's in God's hands. We can't be sure what action would be beneficial or harmful. But the boy carries noble blood. Doesn't that give him a right to know who his father was?'

She sank onto a stool. 'I don't know. He didn't ask to be born but I bore him. Must the sins of his father be visited on my son? I cannot hate my child. I want only to protect him.'

'We can't be sure how best to do that. I'd like to see you find happiness, Judith. Might it be easier if you let Roger become more fully part of the Fitzvaughan household? If you were willing to let him...'

She looked up at me sharply. 'Is that your own thinking, Doctor, or has...?' She faltered and her inability to speak his name told me all I wished to know.

'Rendell loves you, Judith. He would ask for your hand on the instant if you were unencumbered but he'd find it difficult to nurture your rapist's child.'

The way I had expressed myself was crude but direct and I felt awkward. After a pause Judith got to her feet. 'Thank you, Doctor,' she said. 'There's comfort in knowing the truth. I could love Rendell and to wed him would be my dearest dream. I know that. But I'm no longer free. I can't deny my child.'

'Perhaps you need time to think. Don't do anything precipitate. You may feel differently. Remember I'll always be a friend you can consult, if you wish.'

She smiled. 'I appreciate that. I've always esteemed you, Doctor, for how you cherished Mistress Somers even when she was at her most troubled and unkind. I trust you will find contentment for yourself.'

I did not tell Judith of my remarriage although I was ready to do so. We were interrupted by an attendant who announced that Lord Fitzvaughan was now free and anxious that I should join him. We both knew I was bound to oblige my host.

As I accompanied the servant along the passage to Gaston's study, the fellow spoke to me in a low voice. 'You might like to know, sir, his lordship isn't alone. He has a visitor who's anxious to meet you. He's been at the house a couple of days hoping to see you.'

I nodded my gratitude for being forewarned and prepared to meet the mysterious Burgundian who, evidently, had not yet travelled further north as Georgie believed. I was duly intrigued.

The door of the study was flung open and when I was announced Gaston de la Tour, Lord Fitzvaughan, advanced with open arms to greet me. The man who years ago had detested me and sought my death was now my committed and grateful supporter. I was happy to greet him but my glance strayed over his shoulder. Behind him, ensconced on a wooden settle, nursing a beaker of wine and a self-satisfied smirk was, I conjectured, no emissary from Burgundy but the inimitable Andy Armstrong.

Chapter 17

Gaston clasped me in his arms before indicating his guest. 'Harry, you've met Master Andreas, I believe.'

'Albeit, by a different name which doesn't serve at present.' Armstrong stood and bowed. 'You glimpsed me in another house, Doctor Somers, when it was necessary for me to depart by night and I couldn't reveal that I knew you. I'm involved in clandestine matters, as I was in Aquitaine, even if of an altered nature. I use several names.'

Gaston handed me a stoup of wine. 'We can trust you, I know, Harry. Master Andreas controls a network of agents who keep alive the Duke of Somerset's interests and plan for his restoration to power when the right moment comes.'

This was exactly what Gilbert Iffley had sent me to Hartham Manor to confirm. My marriage had released me from the Baron's menaces and I had no intention of betraying Lord Fitzvaughan, but it was ironic that Baron Glasbury's mission had proved so easy to accomplish.

'Do you truly believe Somerset's hour will come again? York is firmly in control.'

'If the King were to recover...'

'His condition shows no material change.'

'You've seen his Grace? As physician?' Gaston was excited.

'Yes, I speak from personal observation. Besides I hear York is diligent in resolving long-standing difficulties which beset the realm, reconciling the Nevilles and the Percys in the north. Why should you want to undo such good work?'

Armstrong put down his wine and stood up, his expression belligerent. 'Have you joined York's clique, Doctor?'

'No, although I've been pestered to do so. It might amuse you to know Baron Glasbury wished me to come here precisely to report on Lord Fitzvaughan's association with Somerset's friends. He was hoping I might catch a spy-master he referred to as André Chartier.'

Andy Armstrong moved with whippet-like speed, snatching a dagger from his belt and lunging towards me, but Gaston had drawn his sword as quickly and pushed me aside. 'Patience, Master Andreas; Doctor Somers is no turncoat. Does Glasbury have some hold over you, Harry? Are you under duress?'

I smiled at Gaston. 'The Baron believes he has the means to control what I do but I've neutered the effectiveness of his threats. I shan't betray you or Master Andreas but I do question whether it's desirable to disturb the peace of the kingdom when it seems to me progress is being made in establishing good government.'

'By a faithless villain who aspires to seize the crown!' Armstrong's outrage was not mollified.

Lord Fitzvaughan had his own reasons to oppose my pacific aspiration. 'John Mowbray, Duke of Norfolk, is York's ally. He's my enemy and has done me wrong, as you well know, Harry. I shall never give him or his cronies my support, whatever achievements they claim.'

I spread my hands in a gesture of surrender. 'I understand I shan't prevail in my arguments but I fear for England if all our leaders share your views and cherish their quarrels as precious possessions. I don't want to see the bloodshed of Castillon replicated in our countryside.'

Armstrong grunted and sat down, thrusting his dagger back into his belt. 'You're a physician, not a man of action. You can indulge these fanciful notions. I should have remembered what that Prioress lady told me.' I stared at him in surprise. 'Prioress in Stamford. She gave me an audience. Said she knew you but you'd proved a disappointment. You had the chance to be at the centre of affairs with the ear of great men but you'd thrown it away because you were pig-headed.'

'She said the same to my face, two years back. She cultivates her own secular animosities. She's kin to the Percys. Is she part of your network?'

'You shouldn't ask that, Doctor, but I had occasion to visit Stamford before I came here. If you've got access to his Grace, the King, you could send us reports on his condition. All Queen Margaret's communications are intercepted but we could get news from you direct to Somerset.'

'He's a prisoner in the Tower.'

'Do you suppose we haven't got contacts there? You underestimate us. One of our friends is a mate of yours, that bright young fellow, name of Tonks.'

'Oh God,' I thought but did not say. It fitted with what Thomas had told me. It was all too likely Rendell would enjoy playing the go-between but it was a dangerous pastime. 'I'm not one of the King's regular physicians. My approach differs from theirs but none of us has brought about any improvement.'

Armstrong was sharp-witted. 'But you've seen the King? How did that come about? They sent for you from Bordeaux, didn't they? Was that Somerset? Or have you got the patronage of Queen Margaret herself? Christ, why didn't you say so, you dolt? I might have skewered you when you're a friend. Are you going back to Windsor?'

I wanted to extricate myself from these exchanges. 'I'll only be in Windsor briefly. I've married a maid-servant in the Queen's household and am taking her to London where I plan to work as a physician. I intend to have nothing more to do with the court or great men. I'll simply pursue my profession.'

'But a great woman will send for you if she decides it would be useful. I'd heard Queen Margaret was directing the King's treatment since she went to Windsor. She's following your guidance, isn't she? You're better at this game of concealment than I am, Doctor Somers. Here, shake hands. I misunderstood what you were trying to disguise.'

I took his hand and Gaston slapped us both on the back, bewildered and impressed by our conversation, of which, I suspected, he understood only a little.

We were soon joined by Sir Jacques d'Avranches, Lord Fitzvaughan's intimate companion, and it emerged that he knew Armstrong from time spent in Normandy. This squared the circle neatly in my mind. With his many names and guises Armstrong was a man of the shadows but, like spiders inhabiting dark corners, he was a formidable exterminator, spinning threads in which to entangle his prey. He was handy with a dagger too and I no longer doubted whether he might have killed Ned Bartley in Bordeaux. It was entirely credible.

When our conviviality came to an end Armstrong took my arm and suggested that before he left Hartham Manor the following morning I might call at the servants' quarters where his own attendant was lodged during their stay. 'You'll remember him, Doctor. He's a good soldier and I'm glad of his support. Johnny'll be glad to see you.'

'Johnny Tate?'

'Who else? Damned resourceful, he is, and well-intentioned. Unlike some we knew, eh? You've come across Jasper Coote at court, I take it? I hope your milk of human kindness stops flowing when it comes to him. He certainly wishes you harm. Watch your back when he's around. Don't forget what I've said.'

My undertaking to remember his words was regretful but sincere.

*****

I was delighted to see Johnny Tate before he rode away with Master Andreas, or whatever he was known as that day, and Johnny exclaimed with pleasure when he recognised me.

'Returning to work as a skinner had lost its attraction?' I asked with a grin.

'Not only that but the new Lord Hanwell's a miserable brute. He's making life hard for those in the village, taking over common land and wanting more labour on the demesne from his tenants. When Andy

220

appeared, after tracking me down, and asked me to be his bodyguard and assistant, I jumped at the chance – despite my wonky leg. We're on the move most of the time. It suits me.'

'You've been to Stamford, I hear.'

'Just called in there on our way south from Yorkshire. Right up to the city of York we went, to see the Earl of Northumberland.'

'Henry Percy himself? Of course. Was this before or after Duke Richard of York reconciled the Earl with his Neville enemies?'

Johnny pursed his lips. 'Well now, we were with the Earl before Duke Richard arrived but we had a pretty good idea what their meeting would achieve. Henry Percy's sons had been more than usually rowdy and had to be punished, he knew that. But he's no more reconciled to the Nevilles than a huntsman to the stag. He doesn't exactly love Richard of York either.'

I was sorry to hear that my hopes of peace between rival nobles were based on self-delusion but shrugged the notion aside. I wondered if Johnny appreciated the dangers in Armstrong's ambiguous role and whether he was putting himself in peril.

Johnny nodded cheerfully, reading my thoughts. 'I got the taste for danger in Aquitaine, you know. I reckon Andy spotted that.' He picked up his bundle of belongings. 'On the move again, we are. I dare say we'll cross paths somewhere else, Doctor Somers. You're in the same game, aren't you?'

I was uncertain what this cryptic question meant but I waved him off as he went to join Armstrong who appeared to be dressed as a cleric. If only, I reflected, this play-acting was all a jolly charade with no risk of ending in bloodshed on a battlefield or in a dark alley.

*****

I stayed two more days at Hartham Manor. During that time I had a private discussion with Lady Eleanor whose continuing devotion to her husband and tolerance of his nature always impressed me. She had shed the romantic illusions she entertained as a youthful bride but she regarded Sir Jacques d'Avranches as a respectful friend while Gaston continued to treat her with courteous attention.

'I have hopes I shall bear him another child,' she said. 'I should like a daughter. I'd make it my ambition to be a different sort of mother from my own.' She blushed and giggled. 'You won't divulge my disloyalty, will you? Lady Maud and I have little in common and you've displeased her by remarrying without consulting her. I'll be glad when she returns to Harrow.'

I understood her sentiments but I wanted to ask her about a particular member of her household. 'You've been kind to Judith,' I said. 'She's in a difficult position. She's torn between wanting to care for her child and wondering what would be best for him.'

Eleanor set down the embroidery she was holding and put her hands in her lap. 'Men of the nobility often make provision for their irregular offspring as well as their legitimate heirs. I approve of that. Roger, Earl Stanwick, was my kinsman and my father may have been harsh to disinherit him of everything except an empty title. I feel I owe his son an obligation.'

'Judith was not an acknowledged mistress. He took her by force.'

'Judith was wronged but I still recognise an obligation to her son. I've no intention of separating them but wish Roger to be reared as becomes his inheritance of Stanwick blood. Judith will be accorded an honoured position as his mother, irrespective of how he was conceived.'

'Judith needs time to come to accommodate herself to your wishes, my Lady. She has an admirer who might feel able to ask for her hand if she was not burdened with her child.'

Lady Fitzvaughan's eyes flashed with unusual anger. 'You mean that rough soldier who slew the Earl? He acted with correct valour on Judith's behalf but that in no way gives him the right to aspire to wed her. The mother of Roger of Ravensmoor is far above his station. I trust you will inform him accordingly, Doctor Somers.'

I hid my shock and dismay for I had never expected Lady Eleanor to express such an opinion. Her own background was hardly conventional but her parents both had noble forebears and clearly for her that was the significant consideration. I did not attempt to argue.

I saw Judith again briefly when she reiterated what she told me previously. I had no stomach to disclose Lady Eleanor's opinion. Probably she already knew it and telling her would have done nothing to ease her predicament.

I encountered Lady Maud Chamberlayne only in company, exchanging brief, genteel salutations which preserved our dignity but, I sensed, betokened the end of any closer bond. It remained to be seen how her husband would relate to me as the manoeuvring for power among the King's advisers developed.

Lord Fitzvaughan and Sir Jacques were happy to share a jug of wine with me each evening. They were grateful for help I had given them in the past but needed nothing from me in the present. Gaston was appreciative of the trick he believed I had played on Gilbert Iffley by marrying Ursula so she would not bear witness against me, but he clearly regarded her as unworthy of esteem. I felt a gulf had opened between me and my old friends at Hartham and I had a premonition that I would not visit their manor again.

There was one person from whom I wished to part on more cordial terms and I sought out Mistress Willoughby in the garden of the dower-house which she had created years ago. She saw me approaching and held out an armful of lavender.

'The plants are not tended as they should be,' she said. 'I am turned gardener in consequence.'

'A most proficient one. I took cuttings from this garden for Kate's bower at Worthwaite. It soothed her, sitting among the flowers.'

Bess looked at me wide-eyed and her breathing was laboured. 'You've really married again? You've married Mistress Bateby?'

I remembered how upset she appeared when I made my announcement to the ladies of the household and the astonishing idea came into my mind that she might regret my marriage because she still cherished tender feelings towards me. I had never contemplated that possibility and it caused me to shiver with alarm. If it was true, what had I thrown away? Was this why she would never have accepted Piers? My whole world seemed to somersault and I struggled to maintain a calm demeanour.

'I have. I'm sorry if it surprised you.'

'I suppose it shouldn't have been a surprise. It was well known she was your mistress. You are a kind man and would wish to act honourably. I hope you will be happy.' Her voice caught and she tried to disguise her emotion with a cough.

'You find it difficult to like her?'

'Like? I hardly know her. It's not my place to like or dislike her...Oh Doctor Somers, I hope you will be happy. Please excuse me.'

She stumbled into the dower-house and although I put out my hand to take the door, she let it close in my face. I stared after her, riven to my heart, utterly perplexed as to whether my surmise was correct, grieving that I had caused her distress.

Over the next twenty-four hours I thought constantly of how deeply I had loved Bess when we both served in our youth at Duke Humphrey's palace at Greenwich. I revived neglected memories and treasured them while recognising this was an indulgence I must put behind me. I did not see Bess again at Hartham Manor and

224

when I rode from its gatehouse I determined to thrust away vain regrets for a love thwarted many years earlier.

I did not intend to return to Worthwaite but took the direct route south to St. Edmundsbury where I would spend the first night of my journey. I was familiar with the road and it was all too easy to let my mind wander. Within five minutes I had abandoned my resolution to forget Bess and could think of nothing else.

*****

The inn was one I had stayed at many times and the town had been the scene of several important episodes in my life. After supping in the tap-room with a multitude of other travellers, from middling merchants to wily pedlars and itinerant craftsmen, I went out into the yard for a breath of air. The stench of the midden was overpowering and I decided to stroll across the square fronting the inn while the dying rays of the sun lit the western sky. There were few other onlookers to appreciate its magnificence. I stood beside the massive entrance gate of the abbey and, momentarily dazzled, closed my eyes.

The sack thrown over my head was thick and rough to the skin but I had no chance to wrench free from it because my arms were seized from behind and my wrists quickly bound. With sedulous efficiency my only weapon, the little knife, was detached from my belt. I tried to shout for help, though I doubted that anyone would choose to intervene, but my head was wrenched back and a gag fastened on top of the sack. It forced the vile-tasting hessian into my mouth and made me retch as I wondered whether I was about to be garrotted. The similarities with the assault I suffered at the huge hands of Madame Claude's protector in Cadillac were disturbingly vivid. This time my assailants seemed to be of average size but there were more of them.

At first I expected my purse to be ripped from my belt but it quickly became apparent that simple robbery

225

was not the objective. These were seasoned ruffians and their business concerned me, not my possessions.

I doubted enough air would reach my nostrils inside the sack for me to breathe for more than a short time. Perhaps it was simply intended to asphyxiate me; but I was not left in peace to perish. A kick to my belly caused me to crumple and my feet were briskly strapped together. At least three aggressors must have taken part in this scrupulously crafted attack and, until I was writhing uselessly on the ground, it was conducted in silence. Then I heard hooves and a clipped voice.

'Strap him to Adam's horse. We leave at once.'

I was flung across a sturdy horse while Adam, whoever he was, mounted behind me. He was not as burly as my captor beside the Garonne. I made a vain attempt to cough and gulp, shamming shortness of breath, in case my new custodian might be concerned if I expired while in his charge.

'Quit that.' The voce was gruff and uncompromising. 'You won't choke. There's an air-hole at the back of your head. Now lay still or you'll taste my whip.'

Within moments we were at one of the town gates. I was unclear which direction we had taken but the gatekeepers obviously expected us. I heard the creak of hinges and the rush of wind as we trotted towards the opening gate. The custodians of law and order at the entrance had doubtless been well bribed. My mind was clear enough to wonder why they had bothered to shroud my head. Even though there would still be daylight, no one would interfere with a posse of soldiers, perhaps clad in Richard of York's colours, conveying a trussed prisoner to face justice. If only that were the prospect facing me, I mused, but knew it was not.

I heard the swish as Adam lashed the horse and we shot forward with terrifying speed. The hooves of several other steeds accompanied us. I formed an impression that we soon left the highway, following a circuitous route, twisting and turning, possibly along a track between hedgerows which muted the sound of our passing. Then I deduced we were passing under the shade of large trees with creaking boughs and certainly at one point we plunged through a muddy area where the squelching ground slowed our progress. Denied sight, I was acutely conscious of noises, straining my ears when I thought I heard the faint jingling of bridles in the distance but it soon faded.

I was in considerable discomfort. My wrists and ankles were chafed by the tight ropes binding them and my left foot was numb but the real pain was in my neck and shoulder. My head hung down beside the horse's flank, bouncing with each stride and jarring the muscles which should support it in more normal positions. We were travelling considerably further and at greater speed than when I was abducted in Cadillac. I knew it was bizarre that I should be comparing these unsavoury experiences in such a dispassionate manner. I had miraculously escaped from the first experience but dared not contemplate the likely ending of the second. I felt my head grow fuzzy as the journey continued and again wondered whether the air reaching my lungs would be sufficient to keep me alive.

At last there were indications that we were near our destination. We turned to the left and one of the riders dismounted to open a squeaky gate. We continued for a few yards and came to a standstill at a point where I could detect a glimmer of light through the sacking. I was hauled to the ground and made to stand upright, held by men on each side. As I listened intently I fancied I could hear the sound of water. I was dragged forward, up a slope, into an interior space which echoed with our footsteps.

'Who did you think you were about to meet, Doctor Somers? One of Somerset's spies perhaps? I'm sorry to disappoint you.'

No muffling could disguise Jasper Coote's sardonic tones. 'I would happily cut your throat,' he continued, 'but I've promised Sir Guy Binwood he should have the pleasure of eviscerating your guts. The poor fellow can't mount his horse at present. He's in great pain, all because of your negligence, physician. He's had to travel by litter. He can still wield a dagger though and he doesn't intend you to secure a speedy quittance. He owes you reciprocal torment. Your actions put us both at hazard in Aquitaine and you remain a danger to us.

This was the cue for Sir Guy Binwood's howl of fury. 'Bring him here. Remove the hood. Strap him to this hurdle.'

It could have been a barn. There was the smell of hay and manure. I had no opportunity to look in detail at my surroundings. I heard Jasper Coote's guffaw and glimpsed Sir Guy, grey-faced and rigid on his seat, clasping a long-handled poniard. In front of him was a wooden hurdle and I was forced backwards onto it. My feet were untied, my legs parted and bound separately to the struts.

'Bring him nearer, within my reach.'

For an instant, I remembered with yearning those friends I had been eager to leave at Worthwaite and Hartham and I mourned for Ursula and the child I would never see. Now I was facing an excruciating death, for there was no doubt at all what Sir Guy intended to do, and I shut my eyes. I heard the shouting, cheering I imagined, and saw a flash. I felt the sting of the blade. Then, mercifully, I lost consciousness.

Chapter 18

I had a fever. I was aware I had a fever long before I had strength to open my eyes or sustain more than a few moments of partial alertness. Sometimes phantasms appeared in front of me, old enemies and villains long dead, evil creatures with no name but exuding hatred, weird unrecognisable forms whose identity I nonetheless knew. For a time I thought I was in the Venetian states where I had studied when I first fled from injustice in England. Later I wondered if my mind was tricked into that delusion because I had been viciously attacked in Verona and nursed back to health by friends. There had been other assaults subsequently in my own country and other folk had nurtured my recovery but they did not inhabit my tormented brain as I lay in feverish confusion. It came to me during one instant of cognizance that I was dying and I had no power to remonstrate with my destiny. It seemed unimportant.

When I began to have moments of greater lucidity, it was Bess Willoughby's face which came to me, soothing my fear, but I soon realised she was only present in my imagination. Then there came a time when I awoke, aware of my surroundings, which I could not identify although they seemed vaguely familiar, and I gave a croaking cry to see who would come.

'Santa Madonna, grazie, grazie!'

At first Leone's voice seemed to confirm that I was in the Italian states but he was no longer the youthful apprentice I had known there. He was the mature physician who must have saved my life.

'Don't try to speak, Harry. You will be very weak. But you will now do well, I promise you. The fever has gone.'

'Wingfield?' I managed to whisper. Somewhere below my middle, I was very sore.

'Yes, they brought you here just in time. You lost much blood. Master Tate is most competent dealing with injuries. Like the battlefield, he said.'

Slowly over the next few days I learned the full story. As a precaution, Johnny Tate had been sent to follow me from Hartham Manor, on Andy Armstrong's instructions, after they found out that Jasper Coote and Sir Guy Binwood were in the vicinity. Armstrong did not expect me to be attacked but wanted assurance I had left the area without mishap. He berated himself subsequently for not accompanying Johnny as the number of my assailants presented an almost unsurmountable challenge for one man. Fortunately for me, Johnny was resourceful and as soon as he tracked my captors to the barn, he knew he must frustrate their intentions immediately. He hurled the blazing torch from the sconce beside the entrance onto the thatched roof and, as the flames took hold and men rushed out seeking safety, he dashed past them into the building.

'Master Tate described it all,' Leone said. 'He is most brave. The fire took hold quickly. There was hay in the barn. He was not quite in time to stop that brute's poniard striking you but it missed its target. If it had gone into your guts there would have been nothing anyone could do but it sliced along your thigh without cutting the main blood vessels.'

'My thigh? Where you...?'

Leone hooted with laughter. 'Where I had to cut you because your wound was inflamed and seared the flesh to stop it rotting. What was it, not three years ago? This time was much worse because it took many hours before you were brought here. Master Tate bound your leg and took you first to the monks at St. Edmundsbury. They thought they would be burying you but by good fortune Father Wilfred was visiting the Abbot and he knew you. He knew me too of course, so you were trundled in a litter, very ill but breathing, and I did what I could and sewed you together. I thank God, all is well.'

230

'I thank God and you too, Leone. Johnny isn't here now?'

'No. He and Master Armstrong both came but they needed to go on their way. Master Tate was well advised to be made scarce in case he was recognised and accused of killing the brute who tried to murder you.'

'Sir Guy Binwood is dead?'

'Yes, that's the name. He was unable to move easily and Master Tate cut him down. The others, they escaped. Now you must rest. I will come later to change your dressing. My wife will bring bandages and you will meet her. I am most happy.'

Whether Leone's happiness referred to my recovery or his beloved wife, I did not know but, on his behalf, I gave thanks to God for both. Later, I asked Father Wilfred to visit me so he too could share my gratitude and my prayers. On successive days the chaplain called, as I grew stronger, until he judged it was time to give me the news he was keeping for me.

'We didn't inform your steward at Worthwaite or your friends at Hartham Manor of your injury until Doctor Leone was satisfied you would survive. It wouldn't have helped you to have a pack of agitated well-wishers at your door when you were so ill. I've told them now that you are recovering. They may wish to come to see you.'

'Tell them there's no need. I was on my way back to Windsor. It's my wife who will be concerned. I've been away much longer than I planned.'

'Mistress Somers knows what has happened and by now she will be joyful that you are recuperating. I have sent messages to her at Windsor every day. She wanted to come here but I begged her not to undertake the journey. She told me she was with child.'

I sank back in my chair, freed from the one anxiety which troubled me. ''That was good of you.'

'I'm sorry the one who was so concerned to visit you could not delay longer but I have his message.'

'Who do you mean?'

231

'His name is Robert de Beaune. He is from Burgundy. He hoped to meet you but he had to return to Westminster and thence to the Burgundian court.'

'I don't know him. Why did he wish to see me?'

Father Wilfred smoothed his cassock and his eyes twinkled. 'Not long ago he'd been in France, part of an embassy from Duke Philip of Burgundy to King Charles who is seeking to bring about peace between the Duke and his rebellious subjects in Flanders. He was to travel on to England, on a mission for the Duke. He mentioned this to a member of King Charles's court who asked him to take a message to Doctor Harry Somers, if he could contrive to meet you.'

I was still mystified why any of my casual acquaintances in France should try to contact me. 'Who was it?'

'A noble lady you met in Aquitaine, I believe: the marquise de la Baule.'

'By all the saints! Yes, I did meet her last year. She's at the French court?'

'She apparently spoke highly of your courtesy and helpfulness in Aquitaine but the message she wished to pass on concerned another lady.'

I felt cold and imagined the blood draining from my already pale cheeks. I did not speak.

'The comtesse de Saint-Etienne is the lady's title now. I recognised the name she had when she came to England as a widow, when the Queen married King Henry: the comtesse de Langeais.'

Yolande. How extraordinary that the message should come from the lips of Father Wilfred who knew our history. 'Is the comtesse well?'

'She is and delights in her little daughter, according to the marquise de la Baule. The Count de Saint-Etienne has retired from the French court and his family were about to move to one of his estates when the marquise saw them. The ladies spoke together privately and the comtesse confirmed her fond feelings for you. The marquise thought you would like to know this.'

I attempted to laugh but the sound was strangulated. 'The marquise de la Baule is a mischievous woman, raking the ashes of what happened when Yolande was in England. How could she confide such a personal matter to a Burgundian messenger? It was indelicate, unseemly.'

Father Wilfred looked at me closely, trying to gauge what I really felt. 'I believe your secrets are quite safe. Robert de Beaune is a high-ranking official of the Burgundian court and he struck me as a man of integrity. His main mission in England was to see the Earl of Warwick, to interest him in joining the crusade against the infidel which Duke Philip intends to lead one day.'

'The Earl of Warwick?'

'He is the foremost Earl in the realm. It seems Duke Philip has obtained good reports of his valour.'

'On the jousting field perhaps. He's untested in battle.'

Father Wilfred recognised my wish to change the subject and we did not refer again to the comtesse or the marquise. Nevertheless when he left me he gripped my hand and spoke words which I only half-understood.

'You should take comfort, Harry, from the message of the seraph to the prophet Isaiah: he carried a live coal to purge the iniquity of a sinful man. It cauterised to permit healing. You should comprehend the treatment. Do not dwell on regrets.'

In my bemused state I recognised Father Wilfred's intention to offer solace. Even so, I wished I had never received the message from Robert de Beaune. As with my innocent reminiscences of Bess Willoughby, I had long since set aside my doomed passion for Yolande and now was no time to be reminded of it. As soon as I was strong enough I would return to Ursula, my wife and the mother-to-be of my child. There was much in her past she wished to forget, whereas I had memories to treasure, but they were now no more than shadows of dreams. Together we would build a new future anchored in what was real and present, where we could both find fulfilment.

*****

It took longer than I hoped for me to regain sufficient strength to journey south. At Leone's insistence, I restricted the time I would be on horseback by travelling slowly to Ipswich and embarking there on a ship which took me to London. Once in the City, I called on Thomas who was as usual immersed in his business and the affairs of his guild. It was clear this obsessiveness served to conceal the enduring pain of his bereavement. I was pleased that Sir Nicholas had contacted him and he had undertaken both to design and oversee the installation of panelling in the new hall at the Harrow manor-house. He was touchingly grateful to me for giving him this opportunity to concentrate on something novel and challenging.

Thomas asked me to examine young Dickon who had been ailing and was relieved I could confirm it was a childish malady from which the boy was already recovering. I could tell Thomas was fearful that if one of the children fell seriously ill he would be lost without Grizel's practical skills and good sense. Hoping to reassure him that I might be at hand to help him in such an eventuality, I spoke of my hope to set up my practice as a physician in the City, which we had often discussed in the past. He nodded but made no comment and I did not like to trouble him with discussion of possible premises. He was preoccupied with his own concerns and I considered it would be insensitive to dwell on the implications of my remarriage.

I lodged for two nights at an inn in the City and, with some trepidation, met Rendell to share a flask of ale. He knew about the attack on me and Sir Guy Binwood's death because he had met Armstrong and Johnny surreptitiously on a handful of occasions. He was revelling in his role as contact between them and the more senior members of Somerset's entourage in the Tower.

'Got to see the Duke himself a couple of times when there were special things to report – like when Andy installed a spy in the Duchess of York's own household. You've no idea the information that comes through the network. Somerset's kept up to date and we can get messages to key people up and down the country.'

'Somerset must be in danger, surely? One day he'll be taken to court charged with all the crimes he's alleged to have committed. When he's found guilty, by a group of his peers who support Richard of York, he'll be executed.'

'They say York's not certain of getting a majority of nobles on his side. That's why he's delaying. Meanwhile, the King may recover.'

'It's more than two months since I saw King Henry. There were no signs of recovery then.'

'You going back to Windsor?'

'After I've been to Westminster.'

'You'll send word what you find?'

'That's what Armstrong asked me. If there were to be a significant change in the King's condition, I don't suppose it would stay a secret anyway. I'm sure York has as efficient a network of spies as Somerset.'

'So you'll send word?'

'If there's anything worth reporting. I'm a double agent. I'm to see Gilbert Iffley tomorrow. He commissioned me, with menaces, to spy on Lord Fitzvaughan and his contacts. Fortunately his menaces are now void.'

Rendell looked puzzled so there was one piece of information which had not reached him. 'The menaces concerned getting Ursula Bateby to change her evidence and contend I murdered Stephen Boice. She won't do that now because she doesn't exist.'

'She's dead?' Rendell's mouth fell open and I dared not imagine what he was thinking.

235

'She's very much alive and with child but her name's Ursula Somers.'

'Christ Almighty! You've married her? I knew you would, you bugger. Pretending you wanted to avoid her!'

'These things are complicated.' I swigged my ale and looked Rendell in the eye. 'I saw Judith at Hartham Manor. She's in a difficult position.'

'That's a bloody understatement!'

I ignored his exclamation. 'Lady Fitzvaughan wants the boy to be brought up with her own sons. He's known as Roger of Ravensmoor. Judith isn't sure what would be best for him. She feels her responsibility as his mother.'

Rendell's face had turned scarlet. 'Would Lady Fitzvaughan take the brat so Judith could be free of him?'

'She might be willing but Judith won't part with him.'

'Does she know how I...?'

'I told her how you felt. She was happy you still cared for her but said she couldn't deny her son.'

'Stupid, stupid scruples! Can't she see? Oh God, I hope she thinks about it.'

'I'm sure she will but you might think about it too, Rendell. There could be another way forward.'

'Never! I'm never bloody taking that rapist's sprog.'

I thought he might storm from the room but when I made no further protest he sat silently, swilling his ale before drinking deeply. No purpose would be served by telling him how Lady Fitzvaughan had denigrated any idea of Judith wedding a common soldier. These were not circumstances in which an insult might provoke Rendell into defiance. Instead we talked of other things before he returned to his duties at the Tower, a little drunk but quite controlled. He had matured but the conundrum he faced would have tested the sagest logician and Rendell would never be that.

*****

I do not think of myself as an arrogant man but I wanted the satisfaction of rebuffing Gilbert Iffley by demonstrating that I had broken free from his threats. He had taunted and intimidated me so often in the past, perhaps my foolhardiness was understandable. At least I had the intelligence to insist on meeting him in a public place at Westminster: in the gallery where I had often conversed with Ursula, where we could speak to each other quietly while the business of the palace went on around us. It proved a wise choice but a desperately unwise meeting. The repercussions of my bravado were to bring misery and change the course of my life.

It was apparent at once that he was not pleased to see me and I assumed this was due to my marriage. By way of greeting he glared at me. 'You look like a living cadaver, Somers. Your face is as grey as the clouds over the Thames. You nearly died, I hear.'

'My full recovery will take time, Baron, but I'm well enough. I wished to tell you in person that I went to Hartham Manor as you requested. I fulfilled my commitment to you but I have nothing further to report. We've come to the parting of the ways. I shall be leaving the court and the service of great men and will have no more to do with you. You have no hold over me any longer.'

I should have realised he was seething with pent up fury and I had given him the excuse to vent it. His chin jutted and the veins in his throat stood out like knotted twine but he kept his voice low, spitting his anger in my face.

'So you've come to gloat, you pathetic bastard! You've married Boice's whore and think that will save you from retribution. You pitiful idiot, did you lose your mind when you began sniffing up Ursula Bateby's skirts? Your wits are as broken as your body or are they lodged solely in your prick? You came here to exult in your triumph. Perhaps you imagined I hadn't learned of your nuptials. Dear Christ! Did it never occur to you who sent Jasper

237

Coote to cut you to shreds? There was no need for that sad bag of guts, Binwood, to have gone with him. He brought his fate on himself but Coote should have skewered you as soon as he found you outside the walls of Saint Edmundsbury's abbey.'

I tried to walk away but he grasped my shoulder, squeezing hard, and his voice acquired a sharper edge.

'You're right to think I have no further use for you but greatly mistaken to imagine you've escaped. Hitherto I've only toyed with you. Now I promise you'll feel the full force of my hatred.' He twisted a strand of my hair hanging below my cap. 'Maybe it's just as well you've survived this time, Harry. You remember your first wife, don't you: the mad woman? Well, I shall delight in torturing your mind more than your body. You're a fool, physician, and I swear you'll suffer incomparably for your smugness.'

He tugged my hair viciously and strode along the gallery, pushing past attendants in his way, scattering a group of alarmed pages. I leaned against the wall for a moment with my eyes closed, calming myself. I had been more than a fool; I had been careless, blind to what I should have questioned, self-congratulatory when I should have been sceptical. I should have wondered how Coote knew I was in Suffolk. I should have appreciated how outraged Iffley would be by my attempt to trick him and how skilful he was in employing pawns to do his bidding. He had threatened me often enough but never before had he looked at me with such loathing and contempt. My moment of ill-considered triumph was obliterated and I was in dire peril from this most resourceful of enemies.

I straightened my cap and found a smear of blood on my fingers where Iffley yanked out hairs by the roots. I had no idea what mental suffering he would devise for me but feared he meant to harm Ursula. Above all else, that must not be.

I went directly from the palace and took a boat upstream as far as I could. Then I hired a horse and, although in pain, I rode like the madman Iffley had foretold I would become, for Windsor.

*****

My wife was unharmed, glowing with joy to greet me, her pregnancy well advanced. We held each other closely, rejoicing that we were both safe after such turmoil and worry, but I did not breath a word of my meeting with Baron Glasbury. The castle was suffused with the warmth of early autumn and the dying sun illuminated the changing colours of the leaves on the trees beside the walls. It was difficult to equate the happiness of our reunion and our glorious surroundings with the horror of Gilbert Iffley's malice. I resolved to set aside all thoughts of the future and let unaccustomed contentment sustain me.

Ursula shepherded me to our quarters where she insisted I refresh myself and don clean clothes. I was amused by her determination to see me fitly arrayed before we appeared in the hall for supper with the Queen's household but slightly puzzled by the urgency of her directions. When at last she was satisfied with my appearance, she smiled at me as she lifted the physician's gown to hang more neatly on my shoulders.

'You're to attend Queen Margaret in the King's lodgings directly Vespers is over. See, they're coming from the chapel. Go now. Her Grace was most insistent she wished to confer with you as soon as you were ready.'

I trudged across the courtyard, piqued by this royal command which gave me no time to recover from my exertion on horseback or prolong my reunion with my wife. Nevertheless I was impressed by the enthusiasm with which Queen Margaret received me and her instruction that I accompany her at once to the King's chamber. Her cheerfulness removed any anxiety that His Grace's condition might have deteriorated but I was baffled when I saw him, for he looked exactly as I remembered and I could think of no reason for this impulsive visit.

239

I followed Queen Margaret as she approached his chair and dismissed the musicians who had been playing softly. I stood back when she knelt at her husband's side and watched as she stroked his hand and murmured into his ear. For some time nothing happened and I began to feel embarrassed but then I saw what she saw. The King turned his head and looked at her, his eyes focusing, and his lips trembled briefly into a gentle smile. It was over almost as quickly as it occurred. The Queen rose, summoned the King's attendants to join him and led me from the room.

'You marked it, did you not? It's happened several times now. It is significant.'

I bowed. 'It's certainly encouraging, Your Grace. Your personal contact with your husband has made the difference. But there's a long way to go to bring about sustained and meaningful improvement. I pray your efforts will continue.'

'They will, Doctor Somers. I have renewed hope. I use your methods, you understand, and am fortified to see them begin to succeed. But we must tell no one of this development. We shall keep it close among King Henry's servants. Wider communication could be dangerous. We must be patient – and persistent. I need you here now, Doctor Somers, guiding my every step. It is my wish that you will not leave Windsor until His Grace regains his full senses and resumes his proper place as sovereign of this realm. Come: you will accompany me to pray for our endeavour.'

I bowed to signify my compliance with her wishes. I thought King Henry's full recovery unlikely and I still aspired to set up my practice as physician in the City but, in view of Gilbert Iffley's spleen, secure residence in Windsor Castle for the immediate future offered many attractions.

Chapter 19

On a morning when November mists hung low over the river while the towers of the castle shone in the sunlight above the murk, our daughter was born. She was a healthy infant and Ursula, although exhausted, showed no signs of sickening. My wife was content that we named the child after my long-dead sister, Alys. It seemed a fitting tribute to my unhappy sibling but I prayed her little namesake would be spared the anguish she suffered and be blessed with good fortune. Because I was a physician, the nursemaid grudgingly allowed me to cradle the swaddled baby in my arms and, in that moment, looking from the tiny pink face to Ursula's weary but jubilant expression, I was at peace.

Every day I spent hours at King Henry's side, sometimes alternating with Queen Margaret, sometimes accompanying her. We read to him, organised rotas of musicians to play and arranged for him to be carried from room to room, varying the background of which he was almost certainly unaware. Her Grace held his hand, wiped his face and put her cheek to his in a manner I found very moving. We celebrated small successes when the King showed glimmers of sentience but they were random and could be followed by several days in which he remained locked within himself. If this was to be the rate of progress, I thought privately, King Henry was unlikely to have advanced far beyond the gestures of babyhood before he was taken from us in old age. I contrasted his almost static condition with little Alys's noisy, restless growth.

I was sitting by the King, bleary-eyed after a night disturbed by my four-week-old daughter, when he drew himself up with a sudden movement which caused me to falter in the fable I was reading aloud. Then his mouth opened and a sound came from it, not a grunt or groan but, I was confident, an attempt to speak.

'Ma...Ma...Mar...'

I signalled to the attendant by the door. 'Fetch the Queen. Ask her to come quickly.'

Although she responded at once, the royal patient had subsided into lethargy when the Queen joined us but I urged her to fondle his hand, even to cuddle him. I wondered if I was breaching the accepted rules of etiquette to make such requests but she did not complain at my impertinence. Boldly, in front of me, she kissed his lips and was rewarded by a bewildered gasp from her husband and the repetition of his effort to speak her name.

'Ma...Mar...Marg...'

He said no more that day, nor for several days, but we treasured the encouragement it gave us to persist in our task.

I confess I was often bored during those hours I spent at the King's side, even though I had Ursula and Alys to return to and cosset. I would have welcomed the opportunity to offer medical services to others in the household at the castle but the place was crammed with physicians, surgeons and herbalists. On the Queen's instructions, they saw the King only occasionally, so they had ample time to advise and treat the ailments of servants, soldiers and labourers. My role was exclusively to attend King Henry. I knew I should be grateful but I could not dismiss fear of what might lay in store for my family when eventually my services were no longer required.

I was able to renew my friendship with Michael Retford which gave me pleasure. I was ready to set aside annoyance at his reservations about my marriage to Ursula and when he mumbled an apology for speaking crassly to me, I reassured him.

'I repeated gossip,' he persisted. 'I should have known better. Mistress Somers is charming and a devoted mother. I'm happy for you. I was upset at the time we spoke. I'd taken a liking to your wife's little maid, Mary. She talked to me now and then, seemed at ease with me. She died so suddenly. In my sorrow I was ready to question everything. Forgive me.'

'It's all forgotten, in the past. Let's move on.'

We chatted inconsequentially but I could see Michael was holding something back from me and in due course I asked him what it was.

'I didn't want to speak out of turn again,' he said. 'But perhaps you should know. A week or so before you returned to the castle, someone was asking about you, down in the village. I was treating an old retainer from the royal household who lives there and this fellow accosted me, asking if you'd returned to Windsor. He looked like a soldier to me, an officer probably, but he didn't wear the favours of any particular lord. I wasn't comfortable to tell him anything so I just said you'd been injured and I didn't know if or when you'd be coming back. It's worried me since then in case he was a friend of yours.'

'I'm sure he wasn't. He wasn't a Burgundian either, I suppose?'

'A Burgundian? No, he was English. Of good birth and education, by his accent.' Michael was flustered.

'It's all right. I'm joking. A man from Burgundy had been looking for me some weeks ago but he left a message which I received. This is clearly someone different. What did he look like?'

'A handsome fellow but conceited, I'd say. He was irritated by my assumed ignorance and treated me with contempt.'

'You're excellent at assessing character. It sounds like Jasper Coote, the man who tried to kill me, who'll try again. He wants me dead. He must have learned I was recovering and wondered where I was. He'll be back and he's very dangerous.'

Michael smiled. 'I'm glad my instinct hasn't failed me. I was sufficiently concerned to speak to the Constable of the castle. He instructed that the man was never to be admitted to its precincts.'

I hugged my herbalist friend. 'You're a marvel for intuition.'

Later I went to confide more fully in the Constable. He was aware of my standing with Queen Margaret and assured me that anyone enquiring for me would be apprehended and kept close until I vouched for the person. Windsor Castle had become my refuge and I welcomed the security of its walls.

*****

For good or ill, news arrived from Westminster regularly. Among less tendentious material I received an unsigned missive which obviously came from Gilbert Iffley and it froze my blood as I read it.

You fool, you did not acknowledge you were to attend the King. This allows you the possibility of delivering to his Grace the service you declined when you attended the late Duke of Suffolk. Your cooperation could change everything. It gives you one last opportunity to revoke for ever that outcome I foretold. For the sake of all you love, fulfil your duty.

I understood the enigmatic communication perfectly. More than once, Iffley and Boice had tried unsuccessfully to persuade me to poison the master I then served, thereby removing Richard of York's hated rival at the time. Kate had suffered for my refusal. Now I was being offered the safety of my family in exchange for a still more heinous crime – the murder of an anointed king.

I could not prove who had sent me the letter, nor could I substantiate to a court of law how it should be interpreted. In any case, with Richard of York supreme, a court of law would recoil from considering uncorroborated calumny. Iffley knew I would not kill my patient. It was merely an added torment. His threat continued to hang over me. I burned the letter in a futile gesture: as if its destruction obliterated its message.

There was a flurry of alarm and outrage from the Queen when we heard that Somerset was to appear imminently before the Council to answer the charges laid against him. This had already been long delayed but yet again the specified date came and went and nothing happened. In another respect, however, York took determined action and incurred Queen Margaret's fury. An Ordinance issued by the Council at his behest concerned the management of the King's household, or rather its diminution, in the interests of economy and efficiency. It resulted in the reduction in size not merely of the King's household but of the Queen's and the infant Prince Edward's as well.

Queen Margaret raged at the insult to herself and the subtle undermining of her son's position. It was irrelevant how many underlings were adequate to serve her as befitted her royal status. Any intervention by Duke Richard touching on her personal standing intensified her hatred. Nor was she content simply to rail impotently at the slight to her honour. She believed she held in her hands the means to counteract the Ordinance and reduce York to the cypher she wished him to be. Her efforts to energise the King were redoubled and my attendance on the patient during his waking hours became almost constant. Tiny signs of life behind the blankness were enough to fire her optimism.

There were no further reports suggesting Jasper Coote might be in the vicinity of Windsor but a fortnight before the Feast of the Nativity I was invited to meet a visitor received by the Queen who claimed he knew me. I conjectured it could be Sir Nicholas Chamberlayne, still maintaining contact with the crown as well as the Duke of York, but it was a cowled friar who came forward to greet me. The face beneath the hood was weather-beaten but cheerful.

'Doctor Somers, I was distraught when I learned of the assault you endured and the fever that followed. I thank God you're restored to health.' Andy Armstrong crossed himself ostentatiously.

'Thank you, brother. Brother...?' No one else was present and I could not hide my merriment.

245

'Brother Andrew from Richmond,' Armstrong intoned, 'in the north, whence I've come. I had business with Earl Percy of Northumberland but I hope it impresses you to know I have spies even in Neville households. I've amassed much useful information.'

'Which you've reported to the Queen herself? You're privileged to be given an audience.'

'You see her every day, I'm told.'

'As her husband's physician.'

Armstrong grinned. 'You do excellent work, I hear. May God bless your endeavours and bring about the miracle we pray for.' Again he made the sign of the cross.

I was diverted by the seriousness with which he inhabited his assumed role and bowed my head respectfully.

'Your irreverent young mate, Rendell Tonks, is invaluable to our operation. He has the ear of Somerset himself. Clever move, that was, to infiltrate him into the Tower.'

I had no wish to claim responsibility for Rendell's position. 'Is Johnny with you? He saved my life at St. Edmundsbury – for the second time.'

'He's not come to Windsor but he'll be joining me again when I return to London. He'll be glad to hear you're prospering.' Armstrong came closer and his voice changed. 'I asked you at Hartham Manor if you'd switched your allegiance to Richard of York. Why didn't you tell me you'd married Ursula Bateby?'

'I didn't imagine you'd ever heard of her. And I still haven't altered my allegiance.'

'Are you dim-witted? You've married a woman who was Duchess Cecily's agent in the Queen's household.'

'My wife has no such role any more. The villains who tried to control her actions no longer have power over her.'

Armstrong bit his lip. 'So that's the game. You've seduced her mind as well as her body. Well and good. The girl, her maid, died, I'm told?'

Was there nothing the wretched man did not know? 'Mary? Yes the poor child poisoned herself accidentally with toadstools.'

'You've proof?'

'I wasn't here. It was while I was away. Why are you asking?'

Armstrong stuck out his chin and the corners of his mouth turned down. 'It was mightily convenient for Mistress Somers to lose Mary when she embraced her new husband's interests and threw in her lot with the Queen. She'd probably worked out that the girl had been engaged to spy on her. Duchess Cecily or her advisers suspected Ursula Bateby could no longer be relied on so the girl was sent to serve her and report back about her behaviour. When York's men heard Bateby had married you it confirmed their fears. And Mary died. Was that coincidence?'

I struggled to stay calm. 'What else? Are you implying Mary was murdered? It seems Somerset's adherents and York's are all engaged in spying on each other's conspiracies. It's bizarre. It feeds these far-fetched ideas. Ursula and I are done with this macabre fantasy. We shall be leaving the court to live quiet lives away from quarrelling nobles and their acolytes.'

With slow deliberation Armstrong shook his head. 'I'm afraid you'll never escape those who want your services, Doctor Somers, unless perhaps you abandon everything and flee across the Narrow Sea. You won't do that, I think. But I don't want us to fall out. I've made no allegations. I have no proof, any more than you have. All I would counsel is that you be aware of strange coincidences, shall we say? Are you certain that the infant is yours?'

I flew at him with a clenched fist but he was much too agile and experienced to allow me to hit him. He grasped my wrists and forced me to my knees.

'Don't be a fool, Doctor. Think it through. I've no reason to suggest the child isn't yours but you know your

247

wife's history. She's dazzled you when you need to be alert. You'd have done well to keep her as your concubine.'

Firmly but not roughly, he pushed me to the ground and turned on his heel. I was not yet restored to my full, puny strength and could not immediately pull myself upright. In any case, during those brief moments after he had gone, I had no stomach to pursue him. I leaned on a table, taking deep breaths, steadying myself before I left the room.

The allegations he had refrained from making explicit were diabolically offensive and untrue; I was certain of that. I trusted Ursula and I had come to love her. I must not allow myself to doubt. Yet how could I forget what Armstrong had implied? What new torture was I to undergo? Had I survived physical battering in order to be torn apart by mental agony? That was what Gilbert Iffley promised but he could have no part in Andy Armstrong's insinuations. Had Baron Glasbury turned necromancer to foresee my destruction through the agency of a man he did not control?

*****

Inevitably it was the paternity of my daughter which obsessed me. Why should Armstong have put doubt in my mind? Was it simply because Ursula had been another man's mistress when I first met her? She had freely told me she entertained others before we were committed to each other. She had been frank and I believed her. If a woman's reputation is deemed to be sullied, does it mean no accusation is too grievous to hurl at her? Or could there be more? Was it known that she had continued to consort with another while she was seeing me?

I could not bring myself to share my terror with Ursula and seek her reassurance. I could not bear to think of her lying to me, nor could I face either her scorn or her confession. I was a coward and I despised myself for entertaining even a jot of mistrust.

I cradled Alys in my arms, peering at her sweet face. Surely, her chin was a tiny replica of my mother's? The long fingers on her chubby hands were like mine? But I knew babies change in appearance as they grow and parents inspect them closely to note fleeting resemblances to kinsfolk. Superficial similarities meant nothing. My daughter carried no disfiguring birthmark like the purple stain on my cheek but that was a cause for rejoicing, not suspicion.

It began to prey on my mind that Mary's demise could have a relevance to my profoundest fear. Armstrong had said she was spying on her mistress. If so, she would have known of any improprieties Ursula committed. This could have been a more potent motive to close the girl's prying eyes than any concern about reports sent to Duchess Cecily. It would mean Mary had been silenced to safeguard a secret I was meant never to discover. That was an unbearable thought.

On the Eve of the Nativity as I walked with Michael Retford in the cloister, I determined to broach the subject which tormented me, although I dared not do so directly.

'I've been pondering all the tribulations of the past year,' I said. 'There've been so many, from affairs of state to the domestic. I regretted I'd not been here when the little maid, Mary, died. I might have been able to save her if I'd realised at once what she'd eaten. Sometimes immediate vomiting can be induced or antidotes administered.'

Michael looked at me guardedly. 'I wasn't present, of course. I believe Mistress Somers summoned one of the physicians in attendance that day but it was too late.'

'I scarcely knew the maid but you told me you liked her. I believe she lived in the household of Duchess Cecily of York before she came here? That was a sheltered way of life, perhaps?'

Michael stared at me, reading my mind. 'That's what was odd. Mary was a village girl. The Duchess took her into service at Fotheringhay Castle after her mother died. Mary would have known which mushrooms were good to eat and which must be avoided. She talked to me about the properties of wild plants. It's how she came to speak to me in the first place, when she heard I was an herbalist. She was interested in such things'.

'You avoided saying so to me but you suspected she was fed the poison by another person? Did you mean intentionally?'

He spread his hands and shrugged. 'It's an awful thing to suggest. I'm sure it must have been an accident. But, yes, I think someone else gave her a dish to eat.'

'How terrible! Poor Mary.'

I shrank from enquiring further and Michael probably knew no more. Had it been Ursula who gave Mary the dish which killed her? And if so, was it remotely possible my wife had not known what that dish contained? I dared not seek the answer.

*****

On the Feast Day of the Blessed Nativity the King attended Mass in his chapel with members of his household ranged behind him. I noted from a distance that he moved his head a number of times and afterwards when he was carried into his apartment his eyes were open, darting from side to side as if with purpose. In accordance with daily routine, he was settled into his chair, fed with a spoon and soon fell asleep. I had permission to slip away to bid my wife and daughter the joys of the day but I returned to attend my patient later in the morning.

Queen Margaret and some of her attendants were with King Henry but when she saw me she beckoned with her usual imperious gesture and I hurried forward. 'Observe his Grace carefully,' she instructed.

Initially I saw nothing worthy of comment but then his back stiffened and his shoulders squared in a way I had never observed before during his illness. I glanced at the Queen whose lip trembled but neither of us expected any further revelations. It was adequate progress, worthy of celebration on that Holy Day.

I detected minute twitches in the lower part of the King's face, a tremor of his chin, one hand raised an inch, the lifting of a foot; and then the miracle began to manifest itself in front of us. His Grace gave an enormous yawn as if awakening from deep sleep, which indeed he was, and he stretched out his arms, flexing his fingers. As one, we witnesses held our breath, no one moving, until, when the King rose gracefully to his feet, we all fell to our knees. He glanced around at the sprigs of holly adorning the top of the panelling.

'What day is this?' he enquired in a clear voice.

'It is the day of Christ's blessed Nativity, your Grace,' Queen Margaret said with remarkable composure. 'And God has restored you to us in his great mercy.'

King Henry blinked. 'Have I been indisposed? My mind is fuddled and I feel stiff. I have no recollection. I see I am in my castle of Windsor. I don't recall coming here. It's of little account. I feel much rested and in good spirits. My sweet Margaret, you must tell me what has transpired.'

Slowly, the tale was told and the King listened in astonishment, dazed but entirely lucid in his speech and in control of his body. We onlookers gaped in amazement, some clearly frightened by a spectacle vouchsafed through divine intervention, some beginning to weep in relief and gratitude. I felt myself shaking, unable in any way to explain what was happening, chastened to realise the inadequacies of our medical understanding, humbled by the possibility that the care I had prescribed for the patient had contributed to this extraordinary outcome.

Of all the affecting scenes on that Feast Day, the one which touched me most deeply occurred when Queen

251

Margaret brought the infant prince and set him on his father's lap.

'This is our son, your Grace, born just over a year ago. See how advanced he is, already he can totter a step or two before he tumbles to the ground and sits there chuckling.'

'Dear Heaven and I did not know. Our son! What is his name?'

'He is named Edward in honour of the royal saint you much revere.'

The King rose, handing the child to the Queen, and clasped his hands together in prayer. 'Glory to God in the Highest; I would have chosen no other name. You bring me great joy, my sweet wife.'

'Will your Grace lay your hand on our son and recognise him as your heir, to confound all your enemies and those who would challenge your sovereign rights?'

Without hesitation King Henry laid his hand gently on the boy's forehead and raised his voice. 'This is my true son and declared heir to my realm, Prince Edward. May God bless him and keep him safe!'

We all echoed, 'Amen'; and I prayed in my heart that I might be granted the King's confidence in affirming to myself the legitimacy of my daughter's birth.

*****

The festivities that day were unmatched. They took place in an atmosphere of awe, so obviously were the participants in the presence of something inexplicable and wonderful. I rejoiced with everyone else; for who could not rejoice at that happy sight? With medical prudence, I cautioned against the assumption that the King's recovery would necessarily be permanent but no one was inclined to listen to my whining at that time of celebration. Yet my heart was riven by fears, not just for myself and my family, but for the peace and prosperity of the kingdom.

Gilbert Iffley would hold me responsible for the King's recovery, when it was my patient's demise he desired. I had rebuffed his barbarous commission and he would credit me with healing that shattered mind. He would have no hesitation in punishing me. The only faint hope of escaping his venom would be to leave court and disappear into a humble, anonymous way of life where it might not seem worth his while to pursue me. I did not rate my chances of success at all highly.

Prospects for the country were no less frightening. The head of the realm was restored to us but the restless limbs of the body politic were not tamed. Richard of York had been an effective, judicious Protector of the Realm but, if the King's recovery persisted, he would not be allowed to continue unopposed as chief adviser to the crown. Queen Margaret's triumphant rancour would see to that. Old rivalries would be given new imperatives. New hostilities would be fostered in the volatile, bitter atmosphere.

In a dreadful premonition, I foresaw disaster striking England as the nobles who vied to govern in King Henry's name fought each other to the death. Would it really come to that? I remembered the strange old monk at St. Albans Abbey who three years ago had prophesied violence and destruction in the land. In my uneasy imagination it seemed I had inherited his mantle of despair.

Chapter 20

The news rippled out from Windsor, borne to friend and foe alike by agitated messengers, and within days Richard of York presided over his last meeting of the Great Council. He was still designated Lord Protector but it had become an empty title, soon inevitably to be rescinded. The King grew stronger day by day and, encouraged by the Queen, he began to exert his will: which reflected hers. I did not voice my misgivings that his Grace's recovery might never be permanent or complete, that he might relapse if affairs of state put too great a burden on him. I had only instinct to inform me and that was no basis for disillusioning those who rejoiced in the turn of Fortune's wheel.

Ursula understood the reason for my melancholy but she knew me well enough to realise I was troubled by personal concerns as well as the dangers facing the kingdom. Always courageous, she set herself to draw out what, otherwise, I would have left unsaid. One evening in our chamber, with Alys slumbering beside us in her cradle, my wife took my hand in hers.

'The royal household will move from Windsor within the month,' she said. 'Is this the opportunity you've wished for, to establish yourself as physician in the City of London?'

I sighed. 'I hope so but it can't happen at once. Queen Margaret has made clear she wishes me to continue serving the King, at least until his health is more secure.'

Ursula smiled which surprised me. 'So we shall remain at court for the time being?'

'I took it as a royal command. I'm sorry.'

'There could be benefits. I predict Richard of York and his acolytes will take themselves off, back to one of his castles or to Ireland. We shall be free from the threat

Baron Glasbury and others continue to pose while they remain at court.'

I had not told Ursula of Gilbert Iffley's wild menaces when I last saw him but she knew his nature. 'You're right. If the King makes good progress, I hope I can retire from the court later in the year.'

'But something else is disturbing your sleep, Harry. I thought at first it was the difficulties you faced in bringing the King to health but the night-dreads persist, don't they? What are you not telling me?'

'Nothing...you're imagining...' I could not lie to her. 'Only foolish fancies. Perhaps I'm weary after so many frustrating weeks at the King's side before he showed signs of improvement.'

'Perhaps, but I think there's more. It's Alys's name you murmur in your half-sleep.'

My alarm must have been obvious. 'Do I?

'What is it you fear? Has she some hidden flaw that I don't know? I beg you to tell me. It's torturing me.'

I felt guilt for causing needless worry. 'No, no, she's a robust healthy child. We are fortunate...' I could not prevent the catch in my voice.

'Then what?' She paled. 'Oh Blessed Mother Mary, is it possible? What have you heard? What evil is being spoken?'

I shook my head but could not frame words.

'There are always rumours at court, bad-mouthing, we both know that. I was engaged to spread calumny against the Queen. Are wicked slanderers trying to tarnish Alys's birth?'

In misery, I nodded dumbly.

'Why did you not tell me? Oh, Harry, what pain you've suffered from these lies! Upon the cross, I swear I've lain with no one but you since I became your mistress, long before Alys was conceived. Did you truly doubt me?'

Tears ran down my cheeks as I tried to express the extremity of my remorse. 'Forgive me. I should have dismissed the vile insinuations. I shouldn't have let them fester. I should have trusted where I loved.'

Ursula lifted my hand and kissed the palm. 'It's natural. You've suffered in the past. I know Kate's illness led her into depraved behaviour.'

'You are not Kate. I'm ashamed.'

My wife held my eyes with hers but her hand quivered as it clutched mine. 'You're forgiven, Harry, with all my heart and I've given you my oath. My past life dishonours you, I freely admit, but I am faithful to the man I love who offered me marriage despite my association with Stephen Boice – and other sinful couplings. Alys Somers is and always will be your daughter.'

What a ridiculous fool I had been to nurture my fears in secret! I reproached myself for doubting her but Ursula's words were all I needed to drive the detestable delusions from my mind.

*****

Within a few weeks we left the sanctuary of Windsor and Richard of York's protectorate was ended. King Henry was reinvigorated and, doubtless urged on by the Queen, he revoked most of the decisions York had taken. The Earl of Salisbury was dismissed as Chancellor, as were other place-holders appointed by Duke Richard.

By the beginning of March we were lodged at the palace at Greenwich, erected during my boyhood by my first patron, Humphrey of Gloucester. The Great Council had been summoned to assemble there and I was positioned at the back of the chamber beside the clerks, discreetly placed at the request of Queen Margaret in case the King's strength failed. It did not.

York was present in the chamber along with a score of peers and ten bishops. Their followers were crowded outside the door, ready to be summoned to do their lords' bidding. I heard the gasps and groans when these attendants caught sight of the noble Duke who was escorted by servants in royal livery to join his fellows. As he entered the chamber, Somerset bore himself proudly, unbowed by more than a year's imprisonment. His normal weathered complexion had faded and his velvet jerkin hung loosely on his lean frame but he appeared healthy and he had lost none of his glib fluency. He knelt before the King, flinging out his arm, pointing towards Richard of York without turning his head to glance at his enemy.

'Your Grace, God has looked mercifully upon your realm to restore you to us as our beloved King and governor. I bring to you my complaint against the man who was designated to act in your name during your illness and who detained me unjustly in the Tower of London. Charges were mooted but never brought against me in a court of law so I have never been given the opportunity, rightfully mine, to plead my case. I have been denied the right of the humblest Englishman to face his accusers before an impartial judge.'

King Henry held up his hand and spoke more firmly than had been usual before his malady. 'Cousin of Somerset, I know you as a true and loyal subject. You are guilty of no crime, your bail is discharged and you are free. Your dispute with Richard of York is hereby referred to eight noble peers whom I shall designate. They will arbitrate between you. Both noble Dukes, of Somerset and York, will be bound over to the value of 20,000 marks to adhere to the findings of the arbitration. So it shall be.'

Two days later Somerset was restored to his position as Constable of England and York was stripped of the Lord-Lieutenancy of Ireland and the Captaincy of Calais. Notwithstanding the King's words, there was no effective arbitration. Royal preferences were explicit. There was no impartial judge. The successes York had achieved in enhancing the rule of law and settling long-running feuds were set at nought. Duke Richard won no favours for his exertions as Protector. He was summarily ejected from the King's inner circle and replaced as pre-eminent adviser by his bitter rival. One coterie of cronies was superseded by another.

In the days before York and his friends left the court, I encountered the Earl of Warwick once more and he was affable. He took the trouble to draw me aside but his brow was furrowed.

'I'm glad to see you, Doctor Somers, but I hope you won't remain at the court much longer. You'd be wise to seek your patients elsewhere.' I must have shown my uncertainty as to his meaning and he put his hand on my shoulder. 'You're spoken of as the physician who brought about the King's recovery and there are those who aren't pleased by your achievement. I don't think I need say more but take my hint and leave royal service.'

'That's my aim, my lord. Whatever's being said of me, as if I had some marvellous remedy for the King's ailment, is quite untrue but I understand your warning. I'm grateful. I hope to leave the court and set up my practice in the City of London.'

'Good, do so without delay. I heard you've already suffered grievously at the hands of Jasper Coote.'

'I did, my lord, and was lucky to survive. Sir Guy Binwood was killed in the fracas.'

'The common weal is the better for it. Fortunately, Coote is travelling in the north of England at present on Richard of York's business but who can tell what may happen after the ill-advised events of recent days? The chances of peacefully resolving all that stands between the Duke and Somerset are receding fast. Get away from court, Doctor Somers; it's not the best place for you.'

I bowed as he hurried along the corridor, hailing some and ignoring others as he passed through a throng of courtiers. I was glad he wanted to help me but disturbed by the implications of his message. Somerset's restoration and the ejection of York's friends should offer me security but Warwick's advice was far-sighted and wise.

The court moved to Westminster where I hoped it would stay for a settled period. That would enable me to seek premises in the City and install Ursula and Alys in them as quickly as possible. I had been well rewarded by my royal patient and could afford to engage house-servants to assist my wife and a nursemaid for my daughter if Ursula wanted help with the child. The life I had dreamed of for so long was nearly in my grasp but the urgency to give it reality was greater than it had ever been. Only by cutting myself off from the court and disappearing into an unobtrusive way of life might I escape Iffley's vindictiveness.

*****

A packet of letters from Hartham Manor came to me at Westminster. There was happy news that Lady Eleanor was with child again. This pleased her and it signalled that Gaston had not abandoned her bed completely. He too was proud that he was to be a father once more and he spoke affectingly of his hopes that his wife's pregnancy would be straightforward after the distress of the miscarriage she suffered three years previously. The Fitzvaughan boys, Walter and Gastie, were both sturdy and bright. So too, I noted, was the infant referred to as Roger of Ravensmoor.

A small sealed note among the other correspondence attracted my attention and I opened it hurriedly, knowing it was from Judith.

I trust you will not object to me writing on my own account, Doctor Somers, although I am sure Lord Fitzvaughan will tell you we are well. Everyone continues to be kind to me and they make much of my child but I am now resolved that we cannot stay at Hartham Manor. I fear for Roger if he is brought up as if he were a noble. If I could find a position as nursemaid or lady's attendant, somewhere I could take Roger with me, I should be content. I beg if you hear of such an opportunity, you will mention me and let me know. Your grateful servant, Judith.

I felt a lump in my throat reading the letter. I could not tell if Judith's decision was wise or what would be best for her son but a mother's love was surely bound to be significant. If only I could find her a suitable position in the City, Rendell might reawaken his affection for her – and perhaps come to accept the child. I grieved for my friends whose lives had been blighted by that abhorrent abuser, Roger Egremont. Perhaps the most obvious possibility should be explored? Might not Thomas Chope's household benefit from her caring and competent services? Rendell would be sure to encounter her if she was lodged with his late sister's family.

I ventured into the City, intending first to call on Thomas but when I arrived at his house a journeyman carpenter whom I did not know emerged from the workshop.

'I've heard your name, Doctor Somers,' he said after I announced myself. 'Master Chope is away at Harrow on the Hill where he's supervising a big job in the manor-house – panelling, matching shutters for the windows, specially ordered furniture: it's taking much of his time. He's hired me to oversee the younger apprentices and keep the business going while he's not here. My name's Nat. He'll be sorry he missed you.'

'I hope to be living nearby soon. I'm looking for premises. You could tell him that. Do you know if his brother-in-law, Rendell Tonks, is still a guard at the Tower?'

'He's not, sir. He came to tell us. He's one of Somerset's bodyguards, now the Duke's been released. You'll find him at the Duke's house by the river.'

'I know it. Are Master Chope's children well cared for, do you know?'

'There's a bevy of maids and the little 'uns are thriving. The boys are in and out of the workshop. That eldest one, Hal, has a rare talent for designs. He'll go far.'

I thanked Nat for his news and promised to call again as soon as I could. I was cheered to find Thomas was prospering but it seemed unlikely he had need of Judith's services. I was entertained to imagine the extent of refurbishment in hand at the Chamberlaynes' manor-house. Lady Maud was responsible for that, without question. Fleetingly I felt sorry for Sir Nicholas and more so for his purse.

I visited three buildings in the City where accommodation was available and one of them seemed suitable for a physician's use: the ground floor of a house owned by a goldsmith's widow who lived on the upper floor. Unfortunately there was a drawback which prevented me taking it on the spot. I would need to consult Ursula, for it was uncomfortably close to the scene of Stephen Boice's death. The house on Tower Hill which had such unpleasant associations for us both was badly damaged by fire on the night Boice died and a new construction now filled the space. The house of the goldsmith's widow faced it across the square. Ursula was a practical woman, not overly superstitious, but it was likely she would be recognised in the neighbourhood, as indeed might I. On balance it might be best to look for premises further afield.

When I turned back to return to Westminster I took a route which passed the entrance of Somerset's house at Blackfriars where I enquired at the gate for Rendell. To my delight he promptly appeared from the guard-room, full of cheerful self-importance.

'Sergeant Tonks, at your service, Doctor Somers. Reinstated in my old position in his Grace's personal troop.

'That's good news. I'm glad your attendance on the Duke in the Tower has been recognised.'

Rendell rubbed his nose. 'Yeah, quite interesting, that was. I saw Andy Armstrong a week ago. He was heading north again to join the Earl of Northumberland. That's where he came from originally. His family had always served the Percys until his father went to fight in France and stayed there.'

'Yes.' I had no wish to discuss the man who had questioned Alys's paternity. 'Do you expect to remain in the City? I imagine Somerset will grip the reins of government firmly.'

Rendell pinched the end of his nose which suggested he was about to say something especially confidential. 'He may have a hurdle to overcome first. Richard of York and his buddies who've headed off to their estates are getting out their banners and polishing their armour. We're wise to them, though. It's not been announced yet, but the court's going to move to Coventry. We'll be well placed there to cut the buggers off if they march for the City.'

'By force of arms?'

'What else? It's the only way to settle it. We'll show who's master. That's why Andy's gone to rally the Percys.'

'You sound eager? Didn't you have enough of battle in Aquitaine? This will be Englishmen against Englishmen: brother against brother, literally in some cases.'

'Yeah, well, I ain't got no brothers. No sister either, since we lost Griz. I ain't got anyone to worry about. No girl, not even a bloody floozy at the moment. Got nothing to lose.'

It was not the time to mention Judith. Much of Rendell's bitterness derived from her situation and his reaction to it. I was horrified that it was driving him to seek violence as a welcome release for his anger. I knew frustration could make him reckless but to express my concern would risk annoying him more.

'I hope fighting can be avoided,' I said lamely.

I felt affectionate responsibility towards Judith, who had cared with such dedication for my afflicted Kate, but I did not contemplate engaging her as nursemaid in my own family. I told myself it would be premature to think of such a thing before we had our own home but I knew in my heart I recoiled from the idea for reasons I chose not to analyse. She and Ursula were both strong-

262

minded women and I found it difficult to imagine them sharing care of my daughter in harmony, even without the complicating presence of Judith's little son.

To assuage the guilt I felt, I wrote to Judith promising to look out for a position which might suit her but in the meantime I offered her a home at Worthwaite if she felt it necessary to leave Hartham Manor. She and baby Roger could stay there as long as they wished but I suspected it was closer to the Fitzvaughans' residence than she would prefer. I wrote also to Perkin although it was hardly necessary to ask him to make Judith welcome if she chose to take up my offer. Dame Elizabeth would be pleased to have Judith back at the manor, as she had been when she cared for Kate.

*****

Summons were despatched for the Great Council to meet in late May but York and the Nevilles were not invited. Predictably Somerset wanted to avenge himself on those who had imprisoned him and to bring about Duke Richard's destruction once and for all. Rumours were circulating at court, said to emanate from Somerset's supporters, claiming that York aimed to depose King Henry and rule England in his own right. I did not believe this allegation but it signified how intense the animosity between York and Somerset had become and how Edmund Beaufort, with Queen Margaret's backing, wished to bring matters to a head.

At Somerset's behest, York was summoned to appear before the King in Leicester accompanied by only a small retinue. I doubt anyone believed he would comply with this order and reports were soon received in Westminster confirming Rendell's prediction. York and the Nevilles were on the road from the north with considerable numbers of armed supporters. Unsurprisingly therefore his Grace, King Henry, accompanied by Somerset, prepared to travel to Leicester with an army equipped for war in case that proved necessary.

My despair grew that recourse to violence would not be avoided and I begged the Queen's permission to leave royal service. She was ambivalent in her reply and spoke of retaining me 'at a distance' to be recalled urgently if required to attend the King. This was not ideal but it was as much as I could hope for and I concluded it was a feasible arrangement. It was therefore imperative to settle quickly on accommodation in the City where we could make our home as soon as we left court.

Ursula did not dismiss the premises of the goldsmith's widow out of hand, although she was wary of the location, and she agreed to come with me to view them before making a final decision. We left Alys with the palace nursemaids and Ursula rode pillion as we made our way into the City and towards Tower Hill. She gripped my arm when we approached the row of houses across the square which now included a façade with wider windows than the old building demolished by the fire.

'It doesn't look the same. That's a mercy,' she said. 'I think I could reconcile myself to living opposite. Who owns it now?'

I opened my mouth to admit I did not know when a groom appeared leading a horse to the front of the building and a man emerged ready to mount. 'Dear God!'

I tried to turn but the newcomer had seen us and he lumbered forward, fingering his whip. I thanked the saints that a good number of people were in the square.

I inclined my head slightly. 'Baron Glasbury.'

'By Christ's Body, you're become bold, physician, riding with your doxy within yards of the place the pair of you killed my good-brother, Stephen.'

Ursula was trembling but it was essential to control my fury. 'You're mistaken in everything you say, Baron. Mistress Somers and I have business nearby. I'm sure we all regret this accidental meeting. Good day.'

Gilbert Iffley scowled at passers-by glancing towards us but it was clear he did not wish to attract attention. 'Don't think you've escaped the retribution I promised. I gave you the means to avert your fate and you scorned it. You've brought about your own reckoning. In a short time, when larger matters have been resolved, I swear you'll reap the harvest of my wrath. You and your woman will suffer. I curse you both.'

He hauled himself into the saddle and urged his horse into a purposeful trot. Onlookers were muttering, peering at us with interest, but I ignored them and rode away in the opposite direction. Only when we were several streets from the square, did I draw on the reins and turn to Ursula who was in tears.

'What has he threatened, Harry? Why didn't you tell me?'

'Vague threats, that's all. We were safely out of his way at Windsor. It's all bluster and rage. But it's a damnable nuisance he's still using the house on Tower Hill. We'll have to look elsewhere. Never mind, better to find out now than after we'd taken the place opposite: despite this disagreeable encounter.'

I attempted to seem cheerful, hiding the dismay I felt, but Ursula was not comforted. She found it difficult to frame words between her sobs.

'It was wrong. It could never be. I'm fated to pay for it. Holy Mother, protect us. Take us away, Harry. Take us away.'

The events leading up to Stephen Boice's death played out in my mind. If the fire had not started he would have killed me, I had no doubt of that. Such guilt as we bore derived from legitimate self-defence and its consequences. But Ursula had a troubled spirit beneath her calm good sense. Her desperate plea reinforced my resolve – to go away, from the court, maybe from the City. But where could we confidently look for safety?

265

Chapter 21

News was received that York and his friends were rallying at Royston, less than fifty miles north of London. They sent His Grace the usual protestations of their loyalty, complaints that they had been excluded from the Great Council and demands for the punishment of traitors. This provoked a foreseeable response. The command was given for the vast royal retinue under arms to march north from Westminster and at this point I was ordered to attend the Queen.

I was disconcerted to find her dressed for travelling and she wasted no time in giving me my instructions.

'Doctor Somers, there's no time to lose. I cannot accede to your request to leave the court until the present emergency is past. You will prepare yourself at once and ride with the King's personal troop. We cannot be certain how his Grace will react to the sight of battle and I require you to be nearby to care for him if he quails. Once the present danger is over, the security of the realm assured and our enemies defeated, you will be free to leave us. Do you understand?'

'Perfectly, your Grace.' There was no other answer. 'You are also leaving Westminster?'

'Of course. I ride with the King within the hour. My ladies will accompany me but I excuse Mistress Somers who may remain with your child and the royal nursery.' She lifted an object from the table beside her, unfurling a cloth which covered it. 'See, I have my own breastplate fashioned by the armourer. I will not shrink from joining my husband on the battlefield if need be.'

I sensed she would not welcome an expression of hope that fighting might be avoided. 'It's very fine, your Grace.'

She waved me away and I hurried to fetch my instruments and a change of clothing. I bade a hasty goodbye to Ursula and concentrated on telling her I had the Queen's agreement to leave the court when the present danger had passed. She saw through my abbreviated summary at once.

'Did her Grace define what would constitute the present danger's conclusion? Never mind, my love, I understand you have no choice. God keep you safe and bring these troubles to a speedy end.'

I kissed her, once for herself and once for Alys, and then made for the courtyard where I was provided with paniers for my possessions and a reliably steady horse which suited me well.

It was to be expected that Somerset's contingent would be close to the King and I saw Rendell in martial array following his lord. I believed he caught sight of me but he gave no acknowledgement and I knew he would not wish me to intrude on his military duties. Another good friend was more forthcoming and I welcomed Sir Nicholas Chamberlayne's company as we rode in snaking formation along the highway known as Watling Street.

'I wasn't sure I'd see you here,' I said guardedly.

'I'm reinstated as Somerset's man of business so it's proper for me to go with him. I've received a knight's training even though I don't frequent the jousting field, let alone the battleground. You've seen more of bloody combat than I have.'

'I don't want to see it again. Can battle be avoided?'

'Unlikely but there'll be the habitual exchange of meaningless courtesies first: more oaths of allegiance, more forswearing of traitorous disloyalty.' He caught my eye and grinned before speaking in a low voice. 'You're thinking I might have found myself riding with our opponents if the King's recovery had been more protracted. It's true of many here, who have their interests to protect.'

'You'd serve Richard of York if he had the supremacy?'

'I'm Somerset's sworn man but there isn't room in the realm for both him and York. That rivalry needs to be settled for the benefit of the entire kingdom.'

I knew many would agree and see recourse to arms as justified if it brought lasting peace. But at what price, I wondered. And could an outcome which eliminated one or the other of the main combatants truly lead to peace? It might solve the immediate dispute but it would not prevent new quarrels arising and might encourage more violent exchanges in years to come. I pondered in silence after Sir Nicholas left me to ride at Somerset's side; he was once more the consummate courtier and acolyte.

We halted for the night at the little town of Watford where we took refreshment and the King received a further missive from Richard of York, duly reaffirming loyalty and demanding the arrest of Somerset. The unacceptable demand cancelled out the pious affirmation. More significant than the message was the information that the messenger had come from Ware, only fifteen miles to the east. York's army had not rested at Royston. They were within half a day's ride of the King's force and there was no likelihood that we could slip past them and continue on our way to Leicester without an encounter.

The order was given that the ladies would remain at Watford overnight but the army would advance at once to St. Albans. There we would occupy the town atop its little hill. I was told it would be easily defensible against an enemy forced to attack up steep inclines and needing to cross a deep encircling ditch. I was assured this was an impeccable military tactic and I understood the logic, but I had qualms which owed nothing to military considerations.

Alone in that huge assemblage of excitable, nervous warriors, I heard in my mind the words of the old monk in the abbey of St. Albans who had alarmed me with his prophecy. *The violence will begin here, outside these walls, and you will minister to the fallen.* It had seemed improbable, weirdly prescriptive. Now I realised it was about to be enacted.

*****

The Queen had instructed me to stay within reach of the King so I was less than comfortable to learn that, if a battle took place, he intended to don full armour and position himself at the head of his troops in the centre of the town. This was unprecedented and seemed most unwise in view of his delicate condition and instinctive dislike of combat, but I knew any protests I made would be overruled. I was taken to see the market place in St. Albans where the royal bodyguards were expected to take their stand. There were stalls and workshops nearby as well as the Castle Inn where I might find cover but if hand-to-hand fighting reached the market place, conditions would be cramped. There could be less scope to tend the wounded than I had at Castillon.

It was seven in the morning when I heard trumpets and realised that a herald had been admitted to the town bearing another message from Richard of York. Foolishly I dared to hope for a moment that, even at the eleventh hour, battle could be avoided but I was rapidly disillusioned.

'Shadowplay, Doctor Somers, nothing more. Vestiges of more chivalrous days – or so we're told. Play-acting, I call it'

I span round at the familiar voice. 'Andy!'

'Ridden down from the north with my liege lord, Henry Percy. This is where Richard of York gets his come-uppance. All I've been preparing for has led to today's confrontation. We've assembled scores of England's nobility to fight for the King. York has only two or three men of note. His army is just a rabble of inexperienced commoners. They'll never break through the barriers to get into the town, don't worry.'

'I hope you're right.' It was no time to indulge the animosity I still felt towards him.

'The badly injured can be taken to the abbey when it's over. There'll be other physicians there with the monks who have knowledge of healing. They'll treat wounds in the refectory. Why don't you join them?'

I shrugged. 'I have to stay near the King.'

'Have you now! I'm honoured to be speaking to you, royal physician. Tell you what: they'll be exchanging heralds and messages for at least an hour. Come with me to the abbey and I'll show you the whole configuration of the armies from the tower. The Abbot intends to watch the whole business up there.'

I had no wish to enter the abbey or view the battle-lines and I was not at ease with Andy Armstrong, as ever a law unto himself. Nevertheless I could think of no reasonable excuse and let him conduct me along Holywell Hill. I dreaded meeting the prophetic monk I encountered previously, but recalled that part of his prophecy foretold he would not live to see the day when violence began in the town.

Abbot John Whethamstede was welcoming and accompanied us to the top of the abbey tower where he had established his eyrie from which to watch whatever befell. He rejoiced to hear that I had served the late Humphrey of Gloucester in my youth for the Duke had been a generous patron to the abbey and his body now lay in the vault below the shrine of Saint Alban himself. It was near there that that I had met the old monk but I made no reference to him. The Abbot was also glad to have Armstrong explain the disposition of the armies as they were drawn up before the start of hostilities.

'We've got the advantage, your reverence,' Armstong said cheerfully. 'York's herd won't succeed in breaking into the town. They're marshalled over to the east and south-east. There's a couple of lanes they can take leading up the hill but both are closed by barriers where they cross the great ditch. Bars and chains block entry and our men will be massed behind each barricade. York's mob'll never pass.'

The Abbot nodded. 'Between the lanes the fields stretch steeply right up to the ditch with its palisade.

270

That's a formidable obstacle, I imagine, difficult to climb. Above there, gardens lead to the houses on Holywell and St. Peter's Streets.'

'We'll have archers posted all along on the slope above the palisade. They'll shower arrows down on any fools trying to reach it. No one could get through.' Armstrong sounded supremely confident.

'There're no cannon to worry about?' I ventured a question.

He shot me a knowing look. 'Neither side's got artillery. There's no Jean Bureau here.'

The Abbot was peering hard at York's troops. 'Are they in three companies?' he asked.

'Usual formation, your reverence. You can see the banners of York himself and the Earl of Salisbury at each end of the battle-line. I reckon they'll each try to force a passage along one of the lanes. They're both experienced soldiers. They'll put up a fight. We'll concentrate our defence on those barriers.'

I pointed to a host of red-jacketed archers and foot-soldiers clustered in the central area facing the ditch and palisade. 'Whose are those men?'

Armstrong gave a dismissive chuckle. 'They're the Earl of Warwick's men. I suppose they're meant to distract our defenders on the slope above the ditch. Not that they can achieve much. Just for show really. The Earl's still wet behind the ears, never fought a battle in his life.'

Wet behind the ears was not the impression I had formed of Richard Neville but I was not going to challenge Armstrong's opinion. 'I must be getting back to the market square,' I said. 'If possible I'll come to the abbey after the fighting.'

The Abbot gave me his blessing and I hurried away. Armstrong did not come with me.

Across St Peter's Street from the Castle Inn men were setting up the Royal Standard and mounted nobles were gathering, together with their personal guards, although they had not yet pulled down their visors. Sir

Nicholas Chamberlayne was talking to a resplendently clad and notably good-looking fellow of about my age. He beckoned me.

'My lord, this is the physician who's attending the king: Doctor Somers. Harry, do you know the Lord High Treasurer, the Earl of Wiltshire? We're directed to take our places here to await the first assault.'

I bowed to the Earl wondering how long his elegant features would remain unblemished. 'Battle is inevitable?'

Sir Nicholas nodded. 'You've not heard the King's reply to the rebels? He's never sounded so incensed, almost vindictive. He declared he'd destroy every mother's son. Those captured in the field are to be hung, drawn and quartered as an example to all would-be traitors.'

'That won't discourage York's followers, I presume?'

'By no means. If anything it may encourage their fury. They'll say it's better to die on the battlefield than suffer a shameful death in captivity.'

'Hark!' The Earl of Wiltshire lifted his gauntleted hand and there was a moment's quietness while others in the market square listened intently. From beyond the houses lining Holywell and St. Peter's Streets we heard shouting, rising in a crescendo.

'It's begun,' Sir Nicholas said. 'To our positions! God be with you, Harry.'

I moved to the entrance of the Castle Inn and was invited to join the landlord and his serving men in an upper room overlooking Shropshire Lane which led down to the ditch and palisade. It was one of the lanes Andy Armstrong had pointed out, heavily barricaded at the foot of the slope where it crossed the ditch. On the town side of the barrier the King's archers were massed, already launching a hail of missiles on the attackers. Beyond the obstacle, wave upon wave of York's men surged forward, only to be beaten back. Further to our right we could glimpse Sopwell Lane where the pattern was repeated.

Church bells sounded the alarm in the town and reinforcements for the defenders streamed down the lanes to support their comrades. There were casualties among the King's soldiers but the barriers held firm and the assault showed signs of faltering.

'The bastards'll have to give up soon,' the landlord said with satisfaction. 'They can't make headway up either of the lanes.'

An elderly potman grunted. 'Wouldn't be so sure, master. They face the gallows and disembowelling if they're caught. That's a powerful incentive to keep fighting.'

'What's happening over there?'

A sharp-eyed serving lad directed my attention past Shropshire Lane, into the meadows below the ditch and palisade where a wedge of red-clad footmen, fronted and flanked by bowmen, was moving steadily forward. They were just out of range of the defending archers higher up the slope and the emblem of the ragged staff was raised over their lines. I caught my breath. 'Warwick,' I murmured.

Trumpets rang out and the wedge began to charge ahead, racing for the palisade in close formation. Inevitably there were injuries from the defenders' arrows but Warwick's archers loosed their own to cover red-jacketed foot-soldiers and mailed knights, also on foot, as they flung themselves into and across the ditch. Then, incredibly, men were swarming up the embankment, clambering over the palisade, crashing through the line of defenders, pounding over the gardens towards the centre of the town. 'A Warwick! A Warwick!' resounded triumphantly from the invaders who knew they could turn the tide of the battle.

'Downstairs!' the landlord shouted. 'Bolt the shutters. Lock the cellar door. Let in only the King's men.'

Useless precautions, I suspected, in the face of frenzied warriors, whichever side was victorious. I followed the inn-keeper downstairs and looked out into

273

the market place. A posse of red-jackets emerged onto Holywell Hill and turned to scurry down Shropshire Lane while in the distance another group ran to the left in the direction of Sopwell Lane. The tactic was clear. Warwick's men who had broken through were attacking defenders from the rear and once the barricades were breached the main body of York's army would surge into the heart of the town.

Large numbers of Warwick's followers were now swarming across the market place towards the Royal Standard beneath which their consecrated King sat on his horse, surrounded by royal bodyguards. There too most of the nobility were clustered, their banners fluttering, their armour gleaming as the sun rose through clouds to its midday zenith. The fighting grew in intensity and I watched in horror as arms were severed, brains spilled and chests pierced. I had seen such things at Castillon but this was acutely painful because I recognised many more of the injured and fallen. It was the conflict between kinsmen I had long feared.

The landlord of the Castle Inn grasped me by the shoulder to haul me back and bar the door but at that moment we were both pushed aside while half a dozen knights burst through the entrance, seeking shelter. Buffeted by elbows and with kicked shins, I staggered out into the vortex of the battle. I had no choice. My duty was to be within reach of the King and I could but trust that my physician's garb would give me protection from swirling maces and slicing blades. I knew it was a futile hope and flattened myself against the outer wall of the inn.

I heard a shout in the distance, in what I thought was Warwick's voice: 'Spare the commons. Aim for the lords!' I applauded the intention but deprecated all the violence.

Arrows were showering down on the King's bodyguards and I saw three of them fall in the mêlée. The circle formed under the Royal Standard, around their sovereign lord, had been augmented by soldiers in

Somerset's livery and I wondered for a moment whether one of them was Rendell. Then there came a shriek of indignation and a roar of fury from the guards and I realised the King himself had been injured. I was on the wrong side of the street but I must attend him.

Grasping my physician's bag above my head I ran headlong towards the incident and somehow I was granted passage although an arrow skittered to the ground near my feet. The King had been lifted from his horse and was hurried into a neighbouring house with blood oozing between the plates of his armour on one shoulder. His eyes were wild but it was wrath not madness which possessed him. 'It is foully done to smite an anointed King!' he cried.

When his armour was unbuckled and I could see his wound I sighed with relief. 'There's a lot of blood, your Grace, but the wound isn't deep, just a long graze, in no way life-threatening. It must have been a glancing blow from an arrow which skidded from the base of your neck to the shoulder. It'll be painful for a while but it will mend. This balm is astringent and will sting but it'll help the bleeding to stop.'

The King nodded and shut his eyes when I applied the unguent but he opened them as I bound a dressing over his shoulder. 'It is sacrilege to strike a King,' he said in a firm voice. 'What days are we come to that sworn liegemen cause their royal master's blood to flow?'

No one dared attempt an answer.

We had taken refuge in a tanner's shop, smelly but secure, and the owner brought a flask of wine to refresh us. Outside, the sounds of battle continued but before long they diminished and one of the King's men at arms sought admittance to bring news which was dire but not unexpected.

'Your Grace, the battle is not yet over but I fear the day is lost. Many noble lords have yielded up their lives: Henry Percy, Earl of Northumberland, and my Lord Clifford among them. The Duke of Buckingham lies near to death, pierced by three arrows. He has been conveyed to the abbey.'

King Henry turned to me. 'Will you attend him, Doctor Somers? Do what you can to ease his pain. I shall do well now you have patched me.'

I bowed and moved to the door, escorted by the man at arms, but as we stepped into the roadway he put his arm across to prevent me going further and I quickly understood why. Across the street the door of the Castle Inn was flung open and the group of knights I had seen enter now debouched with drawn swords, intent on cutting their way through the enemy. This time I recognised them as Somerset and his closest retainers. Rendell was not among them. They fought courageously but they stood no chance against the greater number of Warwick's men positioned opposite the inn. They were cut down mercilessly, Edmund Beaufort among them. No one man would be able to claim the credit for dispatching Richard of York's most bitter foe, because six or seven struck Somerset, plunging their weapons into his cadaver.

I staggered back into the tanner's shop, blurting out what, to the King, was the saddest news of all for he greatly esteemed Somerset. He bowed his head and crossed himself but before he could speak armed men broke into our sanctuary and within moments the victors of the day were lining the walls. The three commanders clattered into the royal presence and I caught my breath. Was it possible they would add regicide to treason? Nothing now seemed unthinkable.

Richard of York, the Earl of Salisbury and his son, the Earl of Warwick, were bespattered with mud and gore. They had not shunned the fiercest personal combat, leading their troops by example, striving to achieve the utter rout of their hated rival: and they had succeeded. Yet it was immediately clear from their faces that they understood the enormity of what they had done: coming in arms against the King, committing unquestionable treason, placing themselves beyond the normal

276

expectations of mercy and forgiveness. In unison they sank to their knees before their royal master.

'We crave your pardon, your Grace,' York said. 'We are appalled your life was put in peril. That was never our intention. We had no ambition to take up arms against you, most sovereign lord, but against those traitors to the crown who had gained your ear. Somerset is now dead and you are rid of his pernicious advice which polluted the good name of your realm. We beseech you to accept our penitence for imperilling and distressing you and we beg you to admit us to your favour henceforward.'

King Henry stared at his kinsmen wearily but he was in full possession of his faculties. He lifted his hand. 'I pray you will cease these acts of violence and restrain your people from further depredations. Let no more harm be done and I will take you to my grace.'

He had little choice in the matter but the three suppliants bowed their heads in assumed contrition and humility before standing.

'The wounded have been taken to the abbey,' the King said. 'Let us join them.'

Royal henchmen helped their master to make his way from the tanner's house and I followed. Quickly York moved to the King's side, escorting him through the town in a potent display of supremacy. The Earl of Warwick winked at me.

'Well done, Doctor Somers, you played your physician's role bravely. Let's go to see who else has lived to squabble over division of the spoils.'

It would be enough, I thought, to discover which of my friends had survived that dreadful day. There would be no spoils for any of them who remained loyal to the King. And no one could tell if this would prove to be the end of warfare within the kingdom, an isolated and regretted aberration – or simply the opening foray in a continuum of violence.

Chapter 22

The scene in the market place and Holywell Street was horrific. Bodies lay strewn where they fell and servants were searching for their masters, disentangling the injured but living from the limbs of the deceased. This was expected but there were other troubling scenes. For the most part, the citizens of St. Albans had played no role in the fighting, cowering behind barred doors, shielding families and possessions. Now they were exposed to the fury and greed of victorious warriors. Whether or not they had actively supported the King, they became prey. Houses were ransacked, booty carried through the streets and maid-servants were dragged from inadequately secured cellars. Townsfolk bold enough to remonstrate were beaten and knifed. To his credit, York shouted angrily to his officers to quell the disorder and eject the looters but I feared they would have limited effect.

The atmosphere in the refectory of the abbey was calmer but poignant. Most of the wounded conveyed there were nobles and knights but a few common soldiers had been brought in by the monks. Although the main target of the attackers, as expressed by Warwick, had been the lords, arrows, however well directed, can be indiscriminate in the havoc they cause. The King was glad to rest and take sustenance while I obeyed his instructions to examine the Duke of Buckingham.

The Duke was seriously hurt, struck by three arrows. The monks tending him were pessimistic about his chances of survival and I shared their concern. The wounds to his body were highly dangerous and the barb which ripped open his face would leave a lasting memento of the battle – if he lived. Lord Dudley had been similarly struck on the cheek. Surely, to sustain such mutilation, these men must have put up their visors? I did what I could to ease their pain and encourage healing, moving along a line of recumbent figures, recognising several of England's pre-eminent nobles. A few with only minor abrasions and cuts had also made their way to the abbey and I began to note those of the King's supporters who were absent, perhaps because they were beyond mortal assistance. I was working alongside the abbey's Infirmarian and I put my worries to him.

'Have you seen the Lord High Treasurer, the Earl of Wiltshire, or Sir Nicholas Chamberlayne?'

The monk looked down as if embarrassed but when he faced me there was a twinkle in his eye. 'May God forgive me if I disparage anyone, by implication if not directly.'

My expression would have revealed uncertainty as to his meaning and he elucidated in a low voice. 'My lord of Wiltshire left the abbey some time ago, quite unscathed and wearing a monk's robe and hood. He slipped down to the river south of the abbey. I surmise he was well away from the battleground soon after York's men entered the town.' The Infirmarian paused until amusement overcame his scruples. 'It's rumoured, shamefully, that he was afraid of losing his beauty.'

I grinned. 'He is a very handsome man. Was he alone when he made his escape?'

'I couldn't say. We were bustling to prepare for the injured. One of the brothers may know.'

I speculated whether Sir Nicholas and maybe others had accompanied the renegade. It would be accounted treacherous defection and cowardice by the King's supporters but for those who were reluctant to commit themselves wholly to one side or the other, there would be logic in flight. With York as victor, the deserters might reap rewards from their ignoble behaviour.

I had no time to reflect further as I moved on to a collection of ordinary soldiers, deposited just inside the door of the refectory, who had not yet received medical attention. Their injuries were at least as severe as those of the nobility. Arrows pierced quilted jackets more easily than plate armour but for the most part they had not been hacked so brutally by swords and maces. Some were past hope but many would recover even if they were maimed. I bent over each man, feeling for pulses, bathing, applying balm, binding wounds, in a few cases stitching a slash to help healing. Blood obscured features before they had been swabbed and this was the case when I knelt by a groaning patient whose right cheek was covered in gore. I lifted a dripping cloth to clean the wound and my hand shook.

'Rendell!' I resisted my alarm, controlling my voice. 'Lie still: let me find what the damage is.

'Doctor Harry, thank God. I can't see.'

The blood from his right cheek had congealed across the other side of his face and I gently sponged his left eye. His lips twitched in a slight smile. 'Praise the saints and you, Doctor. I thought I was blind.'

'No, the damage is all on the right cheek. It has affected the right eye. I'll need to bind it. We won't be able see how bad it is until the rip in your flesh heals.'

As always Rendell was sharp and would not be hoodwinked. 'Have I lost an eye?'

I coughed to smother a sigh. 'You may have done. I can't tell yet. You're whole everywhere else. I'll do what I can.'

'Lost me looks too. Marked for life.'

'It'll proclaim you an intrepid warrior.'

He flinched as I dabbed his eye socket. 'Somerset fled into the inn. Some of us were left outside.'

'Somerset is dead and York has won the day. The world has changed around us. We'll be moving out of St. Albans in the morning. I'll get a litter for you so you can rest.'

'Christ, no! I ain't going in a bloody litter, like a namby-pamby. Ouch!' He had tried to lift himself on his elbow but it was painful.

'If you want your face to heal, you'll do as I say. I'll ride beside you as much as I can. We've got to make sure infection doesn't set in.'

He closed his good eye and I squeezed his shoulder before leaving him. It would be horribly difficult for someone of Rendell's temperament to accept the disability he had suffered. All the folly and ruination of warfare which I had dreaded was encapsulated in the shattered face and fractured vision of my young friend.

*****

The victorious commanders presented themselves at the abbey, demanding that the Duke of Buckingham be surrendered to them, along with Somerset's badly injured son, the Earl of Dorset. The King was in no position to refuse and carts were provided to convey the incapacitated nobles to prison. I doubted whether Buckingham would survive the journey.

I was exhausted and flopped onto a pile of sacks to rest as much as I could before we set out for London in the morning. Even so, I arranged to be roused during the night so I could check on the most seriously injured patients. Although he was not in the worst category, I took the opportunity to visit Rendell and was pleased to find he was managing to sleep. I walked into the cloister to breathe fresh air for a few minutes, away from the stench of blood and liniment, and to escape the moaning of those in agony. I sat on a stone bench built out from the wall and shut my eyes. I was quite unaware of soft footsteps padding towards me but I sensed the flutter of a robe. A cowled monk stood in front of me.

'Doctor Somers, by all that's holy, this is good fortune to come across you.'

I staggered to my feet, suppressing irritation. 'Andy, I didn't know you were in the abbey. Are you injured?'

'Nothing more than a scratch or two. But I'm not here officially, so to speak. I won't be in the procession wending its way to Westminster with Richard of York preening himself at the King's side. I've duties to perform

281

elsewhere and I'll be sliding out of the postern gate within the hour. I'll be joining Johnny Tate. He's unharmed, you'll be glad to know.'

'I am indeed. Henry Percy was killed, I heard.'

'Yes, I mourn him. He was a generous lord. How did you know about Sir Robert Ogle?

I stared blankly at Armstrong. 'Who?'

'Formidable fighter. I knew him years back. It turns out he was leading the men under Warwick who won the day by storming the palisade and breaking into the town. I'd dismissed Warwick as a commander because he had no experience in battle but I could tell you thought differently. Did you know about Sir Robert Ogle?'

I laughed. 'I'd never heard of him. I've learned to respect Warwick, that's all.'

'Clever move of his, certainly. Ogle will have been responsible for the tactics but Warwick will get the plaudits – the victorious commander of the central division. Will you take service with him now?'

'I've finished with serving nobility. I hope to practice as a physician in the City, attending all who need care. Yesterday has confirmed my intention to have nothing more to do with fractious lords turning brother against brother. I'm a physician and that's all I want to be.' My truculence was strengthened by my distrust of Andy Armstrong.

His face in the moonlight was luminous. 'I wish you success, Doctor. But I wouldn't take a wager on your future position. I need to make myself scarce. I probably won't see you again for some while. There are sons who were made fatherless in the streets of this town and they will seek their revenge. My task is to rally them. I'm glad to have met you and I wish you well. Remember the advice I gave you after Castillon: don't ever leave yourself without an escape route.'

He glided away and I sank back on the bench. He had confirmed all my fears that the blood staining the cobbles in St. Albans' streets would not be the last spilt in the King's realm. Self-seeking rivalries would reassert themselves and the desire for reprisals would drive men's action. I thought of Ursula and Alys and swore to myself that all my energies would henceforth be directed to my profession and their welfare. I was blessed to have a loving family, after so long, to put at the centre of my life. I must extricate them from danger and find somewhere to shelter them in obscurity. Surely, with York's victory, Baron Glasbury would be fully occupied without troubling himself about me? With his ambitions achieved, he would lose nothing by shrugging me aside as not worthy of his continued attention. I dared to hope so.

*****

On the road south from St. Albans the victorious troops were joined by contingents led by the Duke of Norfolk and the Earl of Shrewsbury, the late John Talbot's eldest son and heir. They had not joined the battle but were ready to acknowledge York's authority. Other opportunists came flocking. King Henry rode flanked by York and Salisbury while Warwick, as the foremost Earl in the kingdom, preceded them at the head of the procession bearing the sword of state. No onlooker would have the slightest doubt who now controlled the affairs of the realm. The Queen and her ladies were summoned from Watford to join the company and they took their places silently as ignominious adjuncts to the champion's triumph. I kept well back, riding with the litters and carts which bore my patients towards Westminster and reunion with their anguished kin.

We paused at Watford for refreshment while the ladies were escorted to their places and it was there I encountered Jasper Coote. He wore York's colours but his immaculate appearance confirmed that he had not taken part in the battle. I wondered whether he had been sent to cajole the Earl of Shrewsbury into committing actively to Duke Richard's cause. Unless there was a good reason, I would have expected Coote, a seasoned fighter, to have been present in St. Albans. Whatever my speculations, I did not intend to enquire and hoped to escape his notice but he bellowed at me across a crowd of thirsty soldiers quaffing their ale.

'Don't think our quarrel is ended, quack. You owe me a life and I shall take it.'

I turned my back on him. It was unlikely he would attack me in such an assembly and it seemed best to ignore his threat. A few heads lifted to appraise him and there would be many witnesses to attest I had done nothing to provoke him. My main misgiving was whether Gilbert Iffley was nearby, intent on using Coote once more as his catspaw, planning to implement his vengeance.

A commanding voice rang out, causing more heads to turn than Coote's aggressiveness. 'This is no time for petty squabbles, fellow. Doctor Somers is a respected physician, under my protection. Be off with you.'

The dismissive, derisive tone would have riled Coote far more than my attempt to ignore him but the Earl of Warwick was the hero of the day and it would be unwise to argue with him. I bowed as Richard Neville came to my side.

'You didn't heed my advice to quit the court, Harry. You were perhaps foolhardy but there's many a man who gives thanks to heaven that you were there to bind his wounds and staunch his bleeding.'

I acknowledged his generous comment. 'I was required to attend the King in case his health deteriorated. Fortunately it didn't and I was free to help whoever I could.'

'For both of which eventualities we are glad. We trust the King will now benefit from disinterested advice given by honest counsellors and you will be free to pursue your profession as you wish. I'll urge my uncle of York to send Coote back to the north to vent his spleen on the Percys, not you. God keep you.'

284

I was honoured by Warwick's interest in my welfare but feared his intervention with Jasper Coote would exacerbate, not mollify, the officer's hatred. The idea of dispatching the wretch to the far north of England was one I strongly supported – but it did not answer the challenge posed by Gilbert Iffley. Fortunately the Baron did not appear to be in Richard of York's retinue.

We continued on our way to Westminster without incident and Ursula ran into my arms when I dismounted in the courtyard of the palace. In her embrace I laid aside my worries and gave silent thanks that my return was so contented: both my wife and child were well.

I made sure that the injured in my care were taken to their lodgings but Rendell had no home to go to and, after his sister's death, no one to tend him. Without Grizel, I could not deliver him to the Chope household, busy with its own concerns, and he was unwilling to show himself elsewhere until he knew whether he would suffer permanent limitations to his eyesight. I blessed my sweet wife who agreed he should lodge with us while his wounds healed.

Ursula had other joyful news to give me in the form of a letter from my old friend, Master John Webber, the apothecary who lived near Newgate and supplied me with herbs and potions over many years. John knew of my wish to establish myself in the City and he wrote to inform me that premises adjoining his were to become available shortly. He suggested that, if the accommodation pleased me, he and I could work more closely together and develop our practice jointly. It was more than I could have hoped for and I was elated.

Ursula accompanied me to see the narrow-fronted house by Newgate. It was of modest size, its exterior plain and the furnishings which were available for us to purchase were simple, but it was adequate for our needs. There were domestic offices in the basement and, at ground level, chambers which would serve for a consulting room and study. Although there was only a small space in which to store my supplies, the proximity of John Webber's premises meant I would not need to keep a large collection of ingredients and mixtures under my roof. I was fully satisfied. Upstairs there were suitable living quarters for my family with a pleasant solar at the highest level which looked out across the City wall and gave a glimpse of distant fields. Ursula was delighted with it and imagined herself sitting at her spinning like a noble lady in a fable, looking out towards the countryside.

'Dreaming of her chosen knight performing valorous deeds? I'm not sure I want to encourage that idea,' I said with mock disapproval.

'You are my knight, you nincompoop, and you perform valorous deeds every day as a physician.

I drew her into my arms and kissed her, temporarily bereft of speech in my happiness.

I contracted to take the premises from the Feast Day of St. John, in a month's time. Then we joined Master Webber and his family for a celebratory meal.

*****

Without delay, new dispositions of power were made at Westminster. Richard of York was installed in the office of Constable of England, vacated by Somerset's death. His brother-in-law, Henry Bourchier, replaced the pusillanimous but handsome and unmarked Earl of Wiltshire as Lord High Treasurer. York's nephew, Richard Neville, Earl of Warwick, was to take up the potentially lucrative Captaincy of Calais, in recognition of his crucial role at St. Albans.

The King had no option but to confirm these appointments and he consented to grant a general amnesty for all offences against the Crown in recent weeks. Forgiveness came naturally to his peaceful temperament but he viewed Somerset's death as murder, so it was doubtful whether his commitment to pardon on this occasion was heartfelt. Queen Margaret certainly did not hide her fury and vengefulness but she was powerless. After King Henry had fulfilled his role as cipher, legitimising actions taken in his name, York had him conveyed out of London to Hertford Castle where he and the Queen were to live in honoured seclusion.

The slate, it was stated, had been wiped clean and, when Parliament met, its enactments purported to consign the events at St. Albans to oblivion. All was, by statute, declared to be harmonious within the realm. No one involved in the battle was to be impeached, vexed, harmed or molested in their bodies, goods or lands. Commendable toleration would heal all divisions.

And yet... I doubted whether years of rivalry and hatred could be ended so easily. Across the country, sons who had lost their fathers would be nursing their wrath, rebuilding their resources. The injured Earl of Dorset, now assuming his father's title as Duke of Somerset, the new Earl of Northumberland and the late Lord Clifford's heir might bide their time, but they would not relinquish their right to seek a settling of scores. This should be obvious to any thinking person and I had privileged knowledge to buttress my conclusion. Andy Armstrong was charged with sustaining their enmity, planning the circumstances of their revenge, and his capability should not be underestimated. Masquerades and mischief-making were second nature to him.

Most of my patients from the battleground were now in the hands of other physicians or buried beneath the earth. Against all expectations, the stricken and disfigured Duke of Buckingham had made a good recovery and he might be a voice for calm and good sense, as he had often been in the past. But I had no confidence there were many others to support him in pursuing compromise and reconciliation.

I thanked God that I would be spared involvement in any sequel to the battle of St. Albans, safe with my cherished family in the little house close by the City wall at Newgate. My previous life had tangled me too closely in affairs of state. This had brought me benefits and professional satisfaction but it put me in frequent danger, threatening me with death more than once. I was ready to exchange that former existence for the serenity of a loving marriage and the quiet execution of a humbler role. Indeed I recognised I was becoming almost obsessive in my yearning to be done with the past and to find fulfilment, above all else, in the untroubled faces of my precious wife and little daughter.

Sir Nicholas Chamberlayne had reappeared at court, ready to make his accommodation with Richard of York and pledge his support for the new power-brokers with the ear of the King. There was some ambiguity, I heard, about whether he actually fought at St. Albans and a garbled account circulated saying he had been dispatched from the town with an urgent message for the Duke of Norfolk whose forces did not arrive until after the battle. Whatever the truth, Sir Nicholas was unbowed and seemed to enjoy the favour of the King's new counsellors. He did not seek me out and I made no attempt to contact him. I was uncomfortable with the miasma of disloyalty which hung over him – and, to be fair, over many more.

The only cause of personal regret I carried with me related to Rendell. As the weeks went by, his tattered cheek was healing. It sported a dramatic jagged scar which he accepted with pride as evidence of his soldierly prowess. Sadly, however, when the bindings were finally removed, it became clear that he would never regain the sight of his right eye. He was a fit and strong young man who would be competent to pursue many occupations with only one eye, but Rendell had acquired no other skills, devoted since boyhood to life as a man at arms. He might still be employable for guard duties but to his chagrin he would surely be inhibited on the battlefield. He had not always proved resilient when suffering ill fortune and I feared for his state of mind when he appreciated the full consequences of his loss. Hoping to soften the impact of that knowledge, I asked him to stay longer with us and to help prepare the Somers residence to receive its future occupants. I think he regarded it as an amusing pastime but he showed himself proficient in organising workmen and scheduling alterations. It was, I supposed, not unlike planning a military operation but I did not develop the analogy.

Chapter 23

Rumours of great men's affairs reached my ears but they were not my concern while I was touting my physician's services in the locality and hoping to benefit from John Webber's good offices in promoting my skills. It was a slow business to build up a reputation and acquire a clientele, especially among those of limited means who were unused to consulting a professional man. I was willing to charge only modest fees to such people but that made some good folk charier, not reassured. I needed time and word of mouth to gain their confidence.

I knew I must be patient and not allow myself to be distracted by events at court. Nevertheless, I learned with apprehension that the Earl of Warwick had so far refrained from sailing for Calais because his Captaincy was not recognised by the garrison there, which continued to obey the orders of dead Somerset's deputies. A straw in the wind of wider problems to come, I thought, but already I felt far removed from these anxieties.

My misgivings were not always justified. The Constable of the Tower readily took Rendell back into service with the guards and, for the time being, the impact of my friend's permanent impairment was overshadowed by his pride. He liked the adulation of non-combatant colleagues who missed the encounter at St. Albans and continued to regard his prominently scarred face as a worthy memento. I believed he would need to come to an accommodation with changes to his life in the longer term but I had done all I could to help him. Sometimes I was too much given to fretting on behalf of others. Perhaps I did so to balance unaccustomed enchantment in my own life.

A flurry of communications from East Anglia reported Judith's departure from Hartham Manor. Her own letter was full of gratitude and accompanied one from Perkin recording the pleasure he and Dame Elizabeth had gained from her arrival at Worthwaite together with a wide-eyed, mischievous two-year old boy. A missive from

Lady Eleanor Fitzvaughan was less cordial. She berated me for encouraging Judith's inappropriate decision to remove Roger of Ravensmoor from his family's home. She sympathised with the young woman's predicament but obviously thought her own offer to rear the infant with Gaston's children was the proper way forward. In her view the child's inheritance of noble blood from his father, however ill-begotten his birth, should outweigh other considerations. She was puzzled and offended by Judith's rejection of her generosity.

I was hurt by Lady Eleanor's arrogant tone. I had done much to help her in the past and respected her customary good sense and fair mindedness. I reminded myself that she was in the early months of pregnancy and might be troubled by sickness or other discomfort which caused her to express herself with unusual bitterness. I hoped she would soon reconsider her attitude, softening her displeasure towards Judith and restoring me to her favour. I was sorry I had vexed her but did not dwell on my regret; it did not accord with my new contentment.

With diligence Ursula set about turning our lodgings into a comfortable home. She engaged the services of Betsy, a maidservant who was a competent cook, and a lad who came daily to help with heavy tasks. From day to day new drapery, cushions and even a turkey carpet were delivered to embellish plainly furnished rooms. My wife showed impeccable taste in her choice of accessories but she was a careful business-woman, paying heed to the finite resources of my purse and securing several advantageous bargains. Sometimes she had a dreamy look, as if she could hardly believe the joyful situation in which we found ourselves, and I shared her incredulity after so many trials. Occasionally I realised she had tears in her eyes and was touched by her humility in the face of good fortune.

I learned before we left Westminster that Warwick had been as good as his word, securing Jasper Coote's departure for the north of England. There had been no sign of Gilbert Iffley and I failed to establish whether he had been in arms at St. Albans. York's followers had suffered few casualties but I wondered if Baron Glasbury could have been one of them. At all events, it was encouraging that he had disappeared from my sight, as I hoped he would if I slipped into a quiet life with no active links to great men.

I took Ursula and Alys to meet Thomas Chope and his family and was reassured to see how well they were. The boys appeared to be absorbed in their own pursuits and the eldest, Hal, was soon to be apprenticed to a high-class worker in wood who designed and fashioned decorative bosses and pew-ends. The lad's talents were well matched to this artistic craft and he was excited about entering his chosen trade. Dickon, more stolid, seemed content to stay beside his father's workbench and was already learning to use a carpenter's tools. Young Tom, who had always been more timid than his brothers, was proving to be studious by nature and continued to attend the guild school. There was even talk of him taking clerical orders in due course; Grizel would have been very proud.

Only Margery showed signs of missing her mother. She would not look at us at first, her eyes resolutely cast down, and it was clear she found the presence of our baby troubling. Her only sister had died when she was little more than Alys's age and I was sorry for the small girl who lacked a mother in that robustly male family. Margery declined to speak to us until Ursula coaxed her with a tale of a doughty maiden who saw off a dragon after her brother ran away. Slowly the child raised her head and looked at my wife longingly.

'Tell me again,' she said and Ursula complied.

I teased Thomas about his swelling paunch. He was a few years older than me and was entering middle age as a prosperous and distinguished guildsman. I was pleased for him but it was cruel that Grizel was no longer by his side.

'I'm thinking of marrying again,' he said as if reading my thoughts, taking me quite by surprise. He flushed. 'Maybe next spring. I'll have finished all the work out at the Chamberlayne manor by then.'

'That's splendid,' I said for want of anything more pertinent to say. I wondered for a moment whether his intended bride was a much younger woman, perhaps the daughter of one of his colleagues in the guild. I hoped she would be kind to Grizel's children. I hesitated to enquire and he did not volunteer further information.

Thomas laughed, flexing his shoulders. 'It's good to see Margery with Mistress Somers. It underlines what she's missing. She could do with a sister too.'

I punched his shoulder lightly, amused that he was planning so far ahead. 'I'm glad to see you in such good spirits. We've both had sorrows in the past but new life is possible.'

*****

In the early days of autumn when a lowering sun bathed the roofs of City buildings in a golden glow, I received a visit from Andy Armstrong. My resentment towards him had faded but my greeting was half-hearted. I did not wish to be involved in his secretive activities or even to know about them and I was uncomfortable that he had managed to track me down without difficulty. His visit seemed innocent enough, without any ulterior motive, and he was not in disguise, so I relaxed while he reminisced about our time in Aquitaine. Then he sank back on the settle in my study where my patients were invited to sit and watched me in silence for a few moments.

'Bit of luck it was that Richard of York sent the King and Queen to lodge at Hertford Castle.' He smirked but realised from my expression that I did not follow his logic. 'Johnny Tate comes from near there. He's back at his trade, supplying skinned rabbits and pelts to the castle. It's a convenient way of passing messages in and out: keeps Queen Margaret in touch with royal supporters.'

'You're still engaged in your old trade?'

293

'You don't approve? It's not everyone who's content to buckle down under Richard Plantagenet, you know. St. Albans wasn't the end of the story. It just opened a new chapter. Resources need to be built up and plans carefully laid. I'm a humble go-between, facilitating arrangements. There are scores to be settled.'

'I regret that. I want nothing more to do with it. York's a competent man. Now Somerset's gone, the kingdom might benefit if York was accepted as the King's chief counsellor and recriminations were set aside.'

Armstrong snorted, making no attempt to hide his disdain. 'You sound like our pious King Henry himself. He'd prefer reconciliations all round. Queen Margaret's made of sterner stuff. I can imagine her riding into battle, clad in armour, leading her warriors against her bitter foe. She's an indomitable woman.'

I shook my head sadly, recognising the truth of his words, while he regarded me more benevolently. 'I didn't come here to embroil you in matters you find distressing. You're a physician and must hold to the principles of your craft. I came to give you a bit of news and to ask you to receive a visitor. A Burgundian I've been acquainted with for several years.'

I was thrown off balance by this announcement and instinctively reluctant to pursue it but Armstrong was determined to complete his mission.

'Robert de Beaune. He tried to meet you a year ago but was forced to leave a message with a cleric. He doesn't know if you received it. Now he's visiting England once more and would like to see you.'

I bit my tongue, thinking quickly. 'I received the message and was grateful to him. He doesn't need to seek me out again. I'm sure he has far more important commissions to fulfil.'

Armstrong grinned. 'Oh, I think he's got new information for you this time. He mentioned a lady, the marquise de la Baule. You'll remember her, I'm sure.'

'She's a mischief maker. She presumes on our slight acquaintance in Aquitaine, when I acted on Lord Talbot's instructions and enabled her to return to the French king's domain.' I did not wish to go into further details.

Armstrong gnawed his lower lip, evidently curious, but after a pause he shrugged. 'Robert de Beaune has business with a goldsmith in Cheapside tomorrow morning. He'd like to call on you afterwards.'

'I may still be occupied with my patients.'

'I think he'd be prepared to wait.'

It would be churlish to persist in raising obstacles so I said no more and Armstrong rose to leave. 'Her Grace, the Queen, will be pleased to hear you're establishing yourself in the City. You have her favour.'

'I'm honoured. Please convey my gratitude and service to her Grace.' It was a turn of phrase, a courtesy expected of me and I thought no more about it.

'She'll appreciate your commitment.' Another courtesy: although he sounded unnecessarily grim.

Only two patients called at the house next morning and their ailments were not serious. I had balsam to hand for one of them and made up a purgative for the other. I had promised to call during the day at a nearby house where an elderly man was still weak after recovering from a fever. I was tempted to visit him immediately and thereby risk missing the intrusive Burgundian but I lingered, reluctant to act rudely. Or so I rationalised to myself.

Shortly before midday my visitor arrived and the conventions of hospitality meant I was compelled to invite him to dine with us. Ursula joined us for the meal and for its duration Robert de Beaune was the perfect guest. He was a large, florid man, widely travelled, used to mixing with high nobility, urbane and ready with an amusing anecdote to enliven discussion of any subject. Yet he lacked haughtiness. He was gracious to my wife, complimenting her on our unassuming repast, and I warmed towards him for his natural courtesy which treated a physician's spouse with gallantry fit for a noble lady. Ursula was accustomed to enduring ill-natured condescension from worthies who considered themselves superior to her. It was a joy to see her respond to the Burgundian's eloquence with unforced charm and wit.

After we had eaten, Ursula left us menfolk to finish our wine and I readied myself to receive some impish message from the marquise de la Baule but Robert de Beaune was in no hurry to deliver it. He discoursed at length about the glories of the Burgundian court, its affluence and splendour. He proclaimed Duke Philip's estimable qualities as a Christian ruler, patron of music and art, who had extended the territories he governed well beyond those he inherited. Duke of Burgundy, Count of Flanders, Artois and Franche-Comté, since the death of his father some thirty-five years ago, he had added titles and lands to his honours, including Brabant, Hainault and Luxembourg. Nominally he held most of his fiefdom from the King of France and he observed the ceremonial niceties of this subservient relationship but no one was misled. Philip of Burgundy was a glittering power in his own right among the rulers of Europe.

Robert described the flamboyant feast the Duke had held the previous year when he proclaimed his intention to go on crusade to recover Christendom's holy cities. The entertainment apparently included a naked girl from whose right breast jets of hippocras spurted. She was guarded by a live lion which may have been a sensible precaution given the enthusiasm of the audience. What the Pope might think of this demonstration of piety, I could only speculate. I was more interested to hear about the tapestries, sculpture and paintings Philip commissioned and the library he had created which reminded me of my first master, Duke Humphrey of Gloucester, who offered patronage to innumerable writers and learned men from many countries.

'You'd approve of Duke Philip's bounty to his people,' Robert continued. 'As a physician you'd applaud his provision of free medical attention for the poor in Dijon where he has his great palace. He's provided civic baths and brothels too.'

I did not enquire whether these came within the remit of the Dijon physicians but I was fascinated to learn about this eminent Duke of whom I knew little. Even his principal advisers seemed to share both his wealth and his compassion. His Chancellor, Nicolas Rolin, had founded and endowed a magnificent hospital where the poor and sick could be tended in the small town of Beaune, Robert's own birthplace. If only English nobility were so dedicated to aiding the unfortunate, I thought, rather than indulging their self-interested rivalries. It would be an honour to serve as physician in such a compassionate institution.

'I was at the French court again earlier this year, representing the Duke,' Robert's tone of voice had altered and I knew what this change of subject must portend.

'King Charles is supreme in his realm since the English left Aquitaine. Forgive me: I know you were present at Castillon. I pass no judgement, you understand, merely report the position as I found it. In fact King Charles has his own troubles and they lie close at hand. His son, the Dauphin Louis, is perpetually at odds with him. Not a happy state of affairs. Still, although that situation was germane to my mission on behalf of Duke Philip, it has no relevance to the message I bear for you.'

I braced myself. I did not wish to be reminded of comtesse Yolande or to hear about her from this stranger's mouth. Her part in my earlier life was sacred to me but it was in the past. Now we had both moved into different phases of our existence. I had rejoiced to learn the previous year that she was well and living contentedly but further provocative bulletins would be unhelpful.

'I encountered the marquise de la Baule once more when I was at the French court.' Robert smiled at the recollection. 'She is a woman of remarkable talents but, as you know, she suffered great grief following the cruel death of her beloved friend in Aquitaine. I was overjoyed to see how her disposition has improved since I saw her last. She has a new companion – you understand my meaning – a young woman who was placed in her care and it seems the attraction is mutual. She is rejuvenated by this passion and she attributes the opportunity to find fresh purpose in her life to you, Doctor Somers.'

'The marquise is a lady of extravagant emotions. I did very little to help her but I'm obliged for her kind thoughts and pleased she has found a new meaning in her life.' I found myself copying Robert's way of speaking.

'She has sent a more tangible earnest of her sincere gratitude.' Robert de Beaune drew a purse from the pouch at his waist and handed it to me. 'She is a wealthy lady and you need feel no embarrassment to receive it.'

I loosened the cords binding the purse, chinking the coins inside as I did so, and I glimpsed the rich glow of gold. 'She's lavish in her generosity. I don't deserve this.'

'She believes you do and that justifies the gift. She bids you to remember the chateau by the Garonne sometimes in your waking reveries. Think of it as a talisman to bring you good fortune equal to hers: a talisman, she repeated. That is all the recompense she seeks. She does not wish you to write to her. I will convey your thanks.'

I cleared my throat before I could speak. 'I'm stunned. It's unexpected and undeserved. I'm her humble servant.'

'I will inform her.' He rose to his feet. 'I am delighted to have met you, Doctor Somers. I was distressed to have missed you last year and then to learn of your sad injury. I hope to meet you again.'

Despite my best intentions I could not resist making the enquiry. 'There was no other message? That was all the marquise asked you to transmit to me?'

'That was the entire substance of her commission, except to repeat that all was well. You may have full

298

confidence in my ability to communicate precisely what I am instructed to deliver.'

I feared I had offended him but he laughed it aside and left the house in good spirits. He announced he was journeying to meet the Earl of Warwick in his eponymous castle. Last year it had been the Earl's father, Salisbury, he visited; now, after St. Albans, the son's enhanced reputation merited Duke Philip's greater interest. It did not occur to me at the time to wonder how Andy Armstrong had encountered Robert de Beaune. Later I conceived the notion that both men were 'agents' for their paymasters and I speculated whether there might exist some fraternity of spies within which they conversed amicably, irrespective of allegiances.

I stared at the golden crowns in the marquise's purse and blessed her liberality but in a corner of my perverse heart I regretted she had not sent me even the briefest of news about the comtesse de Saint Etienne: except, perhaps, the indication that all was well.

*****

It was only a week after the Burgundian's visit that another caller came to the house requesting my urgent attention. I presumed the fellow had some ailment and ushered him into my study. He was bundled in a thick hooded cloak with his old-fashioned headdress pulled down over his brow and its lengthy hanging scarf wrapped round to envelop his neck and chin. There was a nip in the air on that late October day but I suspected he was suffering an ague. As soon as I closed the door he addressed me.

'You are Doctor Harry Somers, lately come from Westminster and Windsor?'

'I am. Did someone send you to me? How can I help?'

He did not reply at once to my questions but threw back his hood and undid the ties of his cloak. The device on the badge which sparkled in the folds of his cap was repeated in golden filigree on his chest. The royal coat of arms was unmistakeable.

'I am come from Hertford,' he said, 'at the command of her Grace, Queen Margaret. She requires your attendance in person. Your sovereign lord has need of your services.'

I slumped in my chair. So, my caution about the permanence of the King's recovery was well founded. 'I'm sorry to hear that,' I mumbled. 'How long is it since his Grace's condition deteriorated?'

'I understand he began to decline over the last sennight.'

I sighed, realising that Andy Armstrong had probably been sent to seek me out at the first sign of King Henry's illness, so they knew where I was when the crisis arose. 'I'm no longer attached to the court.'

'Her Grace commanded me to say she understands your position and the interruption this imperative will cause to your practice in the City. She is nursing her royal lord but wishes to have your advice readily at hand. You will of course be richly rewarded. I am to escort you to Hertford without delay. Please make your requisite arrangements but it is essential no one in your household discloses where you have gone or for what purpose. We travel incognito.'

I registered that the King's incapacity was being kept secret from his principal adviser for as long as possible. That was not reassuring.

'Forgive me: I must speak with my wife. I'll have refreshment brought to you while I consider the matter.'

The messenger bowed. 'Of course, thank you. You appreciate it is a royal directive, Doctor Somers.'

I drew Ursula into our bedchamber to explain the exigency which had arisen. My outrage grew as I summarized what I had been told, trying to bolster my instinctive defiance.

'I shall refuse to go. I'm not in the King's service. I've escaped those commitments. We came here to lead humble lives, free of directives from our superiors. Who knows how long I would be required to leave you? I'm only starting to establish a practice here. How could it survive my absence, compelled in such an arbitrary manner?'

Ursula put a hand to her forehead and swallowed before answering. 'You are King Henry's subject, Harry. He can command your attendance – or Margaret can on his behalf. God knows, I don't want you to go to Hertford but neither do I wish you thrown into the Tower for defying your sovereign's order. You have no choice. It's a mercy we have funds to keep your household from starving while you are gone. Betsy is invaluable to run the house and John Webber and his wife are at hand to aid me if problems occur. If necessary I will engage a nursemaid, as you once suggested, to help care for Alys when I have to be elsewhere. You need have no concerns on our behalf but you must go.'

There was incontrovertible truth in her words and, despite my anger and fear, I was bound to comply. She did not know and she must not know what terrified me. I had never confirmed that Gilbert Iffley died at St. Albans and it seemed probable some rumour would have reached me if he had. He could be lurking at one of York's castles – Ludlow or Fotheringhay perhaps – or he might have been sent north, along with Jasper Coote. In either case he would return. If he then discovered I was treating the King again, and especially if the patient regained some semblance of health, Iffley would renew his virulent threats against my family. I had begun to be easier in my mind, daring to believe he viewed me as beneath his contempt, become too worthless to merit reprisals. Now the horror had been re-awoken and I must live with it.

I returned to my study as the royal messenger was finishing his meal. 'I'm just assembling the remedies I wish to carry with me. My wife is bundling up my clothes. I shall be ready to depart before the church bell chimes for Nones.'

Queen Margaret's emissary stood and bowed. He had expected no other response.

As I rode from the house on the horse my escort provided, Ursula and I blew kisses to each other. She held Alys in her arms and encouraged my daughter to wave a little hand to wish me God Speed.

Chapter 24

Hertford Castle, I learned from my escort, was a minor royal residence used mainly to provide overnight accommodation, a day's ride from London, for those travelling north. It housed longer-term occupants from time to time and had been granted to King Henry's late mother, Catherine de Valois, on her marriage to his father. Apparently our King had spent much of his infancy there as it was to Hertford his mother initially withdrew after the death of great Henry, fifth of that name. I wondered whether his Grace had any memories of this early sanctuary before Queen Catherine remarried, below her station, and consigned her son to the care of nursemaids and governors.

It appeared sturdy enough, with outer walls of flint and an imposing gatehouse opening from the town square. Inside these defences it had a more homely appearance with timber-framed buildings adjoining a central keep. A postern gate gave access to a stream which, I was told, was the River Lea, more familiar to me further south where the route to East Anglia crossed it. When we entered the courtyard of the castle I could hear faint strains of a harp and a citole. I nodded my approval silently but could not prevent a wave of annoyance passing through me. Queen Margaret knew exactly what treatment I would recommend. She did not need me to be present in person.

I was bidden to attend the Queen as soon as I had refreshed myself. I found her sitting with the King who looked much the same as he had done at Windsor, in a condition of baby-like dependence. That episode had lasted nearly eighteen months. I bit back words of frustration and resentment as I made my obeisance.

'Your Grace sent for me. I'm sorry for the cause. Did King Henry's condition deteriorate suddenly?'

'Doctor Somers, I'm obliged you have come. His Grace showed few signs of impending relapse before he sunk within himself. Of course his experience in the midst of battle at St. Albans and the death of our dear friend, Somerset, must have preyed on his mind.'

'As the loss at Castillon distressed him before his previous illness. I believe your Grace has made a shrewd diagnosis.'

She smiled, enjoying the flattery. 'You taught me, Doctor Somers, how calamity might have overpowered his loving nature.'

'It was only a theory but I still find it credible. I surmise from music I heard on arrival that you are content to follow the treatment I advised previously.'

Queen Margaret tossed her head. 'Some of the other doctors who were at Windsor have come and they continue to advocate their vile treatments which I refuse to countenance. I need your medical backing to withstand them.'

Given the Queen's indomitable spirit, I thought this improbable but I could see that my fellow physicians might be glad of my presence so I could take the blame for failure. They would consider that the King's reversion to babyhood prejudiced the earlier achievement for which I was given credit and they would squander no regrets on me.

'I can offer no new advice but neither can I promise success a second time.'

'I understand that. It's my impression that his Grace is not so deeply lost to us as he was last year. I have mentioned this to no one else but I note blinking and trembling lips which did not occur for several months after I joined him at Windsor. You must examine him, Doctor Somers, and give me your judgement.'

The Queen withdrew and his Grace's body-servant assisted me in undressing the patient for examination. It was all depressingly familiar and I was careful not to let wishful thinking impel me towards an optimistic interpretation of natural reflexes. And yet...: I sensed the Queen could be correct in what she observed but I cautioned myself against building hope on such frail foundations. I desperately wanted to believe improvement might come more quickly this time. I wanted to be free, to go home to the City, to my physician's practice, to Ursula and Alys, but I must not let my longing influence my professional opinions.

Shortly after I arrived in Hertford a message was brought from Westminster. Parliament had been prorogued after its activity in July but it was due to reassemble on the twelfth day of November. His Grace was requested to attend, as convention dictated, but there was no chance he could fulfil his role. A reply was therefore sent, to be read out to Parliament, explaining the King was unable to be present for 'certain just and reasonable causes'; such was the cryptic phrase chosen to describe the circumstances. In consequence, Richard of York was commissioned to act in Parliament for King Henry on this occasion. No further details were set out but it was obvious what conclusions would be drawn from the King's absence.

Sure enough, news was brought that Parliament had wasted no time in reappointing York as Protector and Defender of the realm, according to the recent precedent. No public announcement was made about the King's health and it was not thought necessary to send a deputation of nobles to wait upon him, as they had at Windsor. Clearly the King's principal advisers were confident they knew what such visitors would find and the Lord Protector could only gain from his Grace's prolonged incapacity.

For me, the months I spent at Hertford were a tedious imposition. There was no one in the royal household whose friendship I sought, no Michael Retford to share my confidences and laughter, and the hostility of the other doctors never abated. I was the butt of their snide comments, derided for persuading the Queen to reject their trusted remedies in favour of lackadaisical nonsense, as they saw it. I was trapped and I was exiled from my family.

Ursula wrote to assure me all was well at our home and she had good support. She had engaged an experienced nursemaid, recommended to her, and Alys had taken to this Jane with gurgling delight. I missed the first anniversary of our daughter's birth but was charmed to read that she was now pronouncing 'Mama' loudly and persistently. I rued the likelihood that she would not add 'Papa' to her vocabulary until I returned to be a constant presence in her life. My joy that fatherhood had come to me after so long had its corollary. I begrudged being unable to observe every moment of the infant's development.

Just before the Feast of the Nativity I had rare contact with the wider world beyond the town of Hertford but it was a mixed blessing. Johnny Tate had a delivery of rabbit skins to make at the castle and I joined him afterwards in a nearby hostelry. He seemed cheerful and busy, pursuing his trade as a skinner but also undertaking missions for Andy Armstrong. He was upset to hear of Rendell's injury.

'Bloody unnecessary fighting,' he said. 'Let the sodding lords battle it out if they must without involving honest common men. I didn't drag Rendell Tonks from the carnage at Castillon in order that his fellow countrymen could half-blind him a year or two later.'

'Too true – but he's resilient and he's managing better than I feared. He's serving at the Tower.' I paused but I could not resist sharing my concerns. 'Don't Andy Armstrong's activities make renewed fighting more likely?'

Johnny wiped a sleeve across his ale-damp lips. 'I don't get involved with what he's up to. I just help him out from time to time: acting as escort on journeys, running the odd errand, passing messages to and fro. With my gammy leg I'm more restricted than I was but I like a bit of activity, makes a change from sitting at my workbench all day. Soldiering gave me a taste for something a bit lively.'

I nodded. I could not blame him. He was bright and resourceful, capable of handling more complex challenges than a village skinner could expect to face. He had proved his worth in dire circumstances on two occasions when he saved my life.

'I went north with Andy not long ago. I've got bad news for you, I'm afraid. Andy asked me to tell you.'

Puzzled, I set down my beaker and stared at him. I could not imagine what news he might have gleaned which would concern me personally.

'We called at Richard of York's castle of Fotheringhay among other places as we were coming back south. Andy had messages to deliver to a confidential contact. I didn't enter the castle but Andy said there was a man there you knew: Baron Glasbury. Fortunately Andy was disguised as the latest character he's adopted, Father Ambrose. The Baron apparently only knows his Frenchie name of André Chartier and didn't suspect anything when they briefly crossed paths.'

So the Baron had not died and he remained York's loyal acolyte. I was still puzzled. 'That must have been a nail-biting encounter for Andy but hardly too surprising. Gilbert Iffley is liable to be found at any of York's residences. He has a wide ranging role on behalf of the Duke.'

'So I gather. We couldn't discover what his purpose was at Fotheringhay but there'd been a meeting there the day before. While I was hanging about waiting for Andy, quaffing ale at the tavern in the village outside the castle, I met someone who'd been present and was just leaving the neighbourhood. He recognised me from Aquitaine, I'm afraid. I had to make up some story about a cousin near Peterborough who'd ordered fancy kidskins from me. It was Jasper Coote.'

'Coote! Dear God! You were in terrible danger. He must have known it was you who rescued me from the barn and killed Sir Guy Binwood?'

'I don't think he did. It was a great scramble when I charged into the barn. The roof was already on fire and the men inside were jostling to get out: Coote included, though

I had no chance to study what he did. I was concentrating on Sir Guy and dragging you to safety. I fancy that, if Coote had time to think at all, he supposed I was just the anonymous vanguard of a bigger group come to rescue you.'

'That's a blessing.'

'Up to a point, because when I met him at Fotheringhay he associated me with you from Aquitaine. He remembered how I'd worked with you when you investigated what had happened to the so-called spy beside the Garonne. There was hatred in his eyes as he referred to you. He called you the Duke of Somerset's contemptible lackey, fit to share your late master's fate.'

I shook my head. 'I was never Somerset's lackey. But I don't doubt Coote wants me dead.'

'Does Baron Glasbury want that too? It sounded as if they'd been plotting your destruction from what Coote told me – gloatingly.'

'The Baron's been lying low recently. He certainly has a serious grudge against me but it's more his style to torment and torture his prey rather than put them out of their misery. He's engaged Coote's services before. They're a dangerous combination.'

'You must be very careful, watch your back. You need a bodyguard.'

'I'm safe enough in Hertford, serving the royal household.' I recognised the risks I might face when I returned to London but I did not refer to them.

Johnny looked me straight in the eye and I recognised his perceptiveness. 'If I can help, let me know. When I'm not at home on Lord Hanwell's estate, Andy can always locate me.'

He said it with a grin as if he was joking but I knew he was not. Nevertheless I brushed it aside. 'A physician with a bodyguard! That would be a novelty but I'm not sure it would reassure my patients.'

We both laughed.

There was no sudden restoration of the King's senses that Yuletide but little by little he became more aware of his surroundings and responded to the Queen's ministrations. By Candlemas it was apparent that he was conscious of what we said to him and, although he did not speak, his eyes were alert and showed understanding.

I dared to hope I would be able to return home before long. This had become both more urgent and more hazardous since my conversation with Johnny Tate. If Gilbert Iffley had renewed his intent to punish me, he was likely to persecute my family as a means to cause me suffering. I dreaded hearing that Ursula or Alys or both of them had been carried off and were at the mercy of fiendish men. Yet, if the Baron and Jasper Coote were resolved to harm me personally, I would be more exposed to their machinations in London.

The Queen was kept regularly informed about Richard of York's actions as Protector and it appeared he was behaving cautiously. The creation of Prince Edward as Prince of Wales was ratified and he was granted the dukedom of Cornwall and the earldom of Chester to provide him with a fitting income as he grew older. Well and good: but Parliament was concerned with financial matters on a larger scale and this proved controversial. In order, they claimed, to restore the royal finances to an acceptable level, the Commons sought to recoup most of the grants made by the Crown since the beginning of King Henry's reign. This device had been used previously as a way of raising revenue when the beneficiaries of such grants were compelled to pay up to retain the lands they had acquired under royal dispensation. The Lords, however, whose interests were most affected, were unwilling to support the move by the Commons. Deputations duly arrived at Hertford begging for the King's intervention.

I was in attendance on the King when a group of infuriated nobles made their plea to him and I sensed he was concentrating purposefully on their words. His lips moved as if he was mouthing in repetition what they said but he made no sound. The Queen remained calm, not attempting to encourage or deter him, but she became visibly indignant when reference was made to York's arrival at Parliament, attended by an armed escort.

'Your Grace,' the spokesman of the Lords explained further, 'the Duke of York and his nephew of Warwick must have been accompanied by a retinue of some three hundred soldiers. These would not have been sufficient for them to enforce their will on a reluctant House so it seems probable their principals believed they themselves might need protection.'

Queen Margaret raised her eyebrows. 'York is unsure of himself? Is that what you are implying?'

'There are rumours circulating at Westminster that the King may not in fact be seriously indisposed, that he may attend Parliament in person. Indeed, that's why we are come to petition his Grace, to beg him to exert his authority and make known his wishes in this delicate business. It challenges his royal entitlement to give and withhold grants at will – a matter of prerogative.'

King Henry's fingers grasped the arm of his chair and, while the Queen and I held our breaths, he rose jerkily to stand. 'You may tell my loyal Lords,' he said in a tremulous, cracked voice, 'that I will come.'

The King sank back on his cushions but he held his head high and his eyes were focussed. The Queen clasped her hands reverently but her expression was one of sheer triumph. The nobles fell to their knees, uttering thanks to God and invoking His blessings on their Graces and the whole realm. They were then courteously but firmly ushered from the room while I handed my patient a cup of wine fortified with herbs.

'Your Grace may wish to moisten your lips.'

'Well thought of, physician,' he said and turned towards his wife. 'We must order our departure for Westminster without delay.'

'Indeed we must, my sweet lord. With your renewed energy we shall resume our proper positions and Richard of York can return to his castle at Ludlow, shorn of the Protector's title. I pray he may obtain his just deserts for his despicable and treacherous aspirations. Doctor Somers, once again our trust in your wisdom has been justified. You will attend the King when he goes to Westminster but you will then be free to return to your family – with our gratitude.'

I bowed and withdrew, my mind churning with unanswerable questions. For how long would the King's mental stability hold? How would York react to his demotion? Would the Queen's intransigence encourage fresh belligerence from her enemies? Was recourse to renewed combat now a greater or lesser risk? And would this changed situation bring me respite from Gilbert Iffley's threats? Would he and Jasper Coote remove themselves from court? Could I at last live peaceably in my home, practice my profession, care for my wife and daughter? Despite all my doubts and reservations, the wraith of hope fluttered in my heart.

*****

They were safe; they were well.

Next morning I would return to Westminster and stand quietly in the shadows while King Henry discharged York from the role of Protector. Thereafter, his Grace intended to dismiss Parliament and set out on a royal progress, re-establishing law and order across the country. I was not required to accompany him. My task completed and, for the moment at least, my erstwhile patient was exhibiting the same burst of energy which accompanied his previous recovery. It was my devout prayer that he never relapsed again.

311

In the meantime, before I was released from royal service, I could spend the night at home with Ursula and Alys. As I embraced them I gave silent thanks for their well-being: Ursula radiant and openly rejoicing; Alys a little timid at first with the arrival of a stranger she might not recall – four months being a significant chunk of an infant's life. Tentatively, she allowed me to cuddle her and bounce her on my knee until after a few minutes she vouchsafed a quizzical smile. She cast a glance at her mother, seeking reassurance, before opening her mouth to gurgle and then to attempt the unfamiliar sound.

'Pa-ppee,' she said solemnly and my joy was complete.

Chapter 25

With judicious appreciation of the changed situation, Richard of York resigned his position as Lord Protector, without awaiting dismissal, and I was delighted that, with equivalent good sense, King Henry confirmed the Duke in the lieutenancy of Ireland and allowed him to remain on the Great Council. If this presaged an attempt by both parties to work together for the benefit of the realm, it could only be applauded. Yet the Queen's stony expression suggested she was not reconciled to the foes who had killed Somerset and this did not bode well for peaceful relations in the future.

The King acquitted himself with dignity and resolution when he addressed Parliament so I had no concerns that he was sufficiently restored to health to dispense with my services. I was duly released from my charge and received reasonable recompense for my care. I crossed the courtyard at Westminster to seek a wherry making down-river to the City, while wondering whether this would be the last time I was present in these august precincts. This was my hope, my ambition, and I thrust aside a multitude of reminiscences and perverse regrets.

A nobleman's barge, emblazoned and caparisoned with red pennants, was making ready to cast off from the jetty. I paid it no attention but stood back to await the humble vessel for hire standing offshore until its pretentious neighbour had glided away. An imperious voice calling my name roused me from day-dreaming.

'Doctor Somers! Are you bound for the City? Come aboard quickly. It's months since I saw you.'

I should have recognised the banners with the device of the ragged staff. I bowed hurriedly and took hold of a retainer's proffered arm as I climbed onto the Earl of Warwick's ostentatious craft. 'My Lord, I'm grateful.'

'Once again you've succeeded in restoring our beloved King to his people with his spirit strengthened and his health unimpaired.' Richard Neville was at ease among his followers but he leaned towards me with a chuckle to add a further quiet comment. 'My uncle of York must curse your medical talent but I won't hold it against you.'

'I can claim no credit, my Lord, and I'm on my way home now, after finally leaving royal service, as you advised I should.'

'Until poor Henry's wits wander once more and you're recalled.'

'Heaven forbid – either eventuality.' I was uncertain of the Earl's mood and did not wish to be led into sensitive territory.

He smiled as if to set my mind at rest. 'Indeed. We have achieved a pleasant concord, have we not? I am permitted to retain the Captaincy of Calais and hope to travel there in person by and by.'

'You won't appoint a lieutenant to deputise for you?'

'As many have done in the past? No, I have a mind to take charge of my own small domain and sample the delights of maritime adventure from its well-appointed harbour. My departure is only delayed while negotiations continue with the merchants of Calais. They are seeking guarantees before they will pay the garrison considerable arrears of wages. Once Parliament has consented to grant security to these worthy traders, the soldiers will be paid and they in turn will surrender to my representatives. I don't wish to impose my Captaincy by force of arms against men who have right on their side in claiming money owed to them.'

'So it's not just a protest by the late Duke of Somerset's supporters objecting to a new master?'

He slapped me on the back. 'It may have started with one or two of the former Captain's cronies making a protest but the arrears are real and changed allegiances have their price.'

I considered him admirably pragmatic but he had more to say.

'I shall want to build up the garrison with men owing their positions to me. I'll be looking out for eager young fighters ready for action at sea, as much as on land. I'm planning to offer them excitement and the chance to make their fortunes while we defend the Narrow Sea for King Henry. If you know any likely fellows, send them to me with your recommendation.'

I thought at once of Rendell. 'I have a friend in the guard at the Tower who sometimes grows restless, although I've not seen him for some months. He lost the sight of one eye at St. Albans but he's otherwise in vigorous health. Your offer might appeal to him.'

I refrained from saying Rendell had fought in Somerset's retinue but Warwick was ahead of me and his reaction did not disappoint.

'I don't need to know which lord he followed in the battle. We all fought for the King, according to our beliefs as to what would best advantage the realm. Send him to me, Doctor.' The Earl's eyebrows fluttered. 'I suppose you wouldn't fancy a role as physician in a garrison of fiery soldiers and seamen?'

My heart missed a beat but his tone was jocular and I reminded myself that once before he had thrown out a hint which attracted me but was never meant seriously. 'I'm returning to the practice I've started to establish in the City. My wife and daughter are settled in our house by Newgate.'

He nodded. 'And I wish you success there, Doctor Somers, unencumbered by your foes.'

This pulled me back to earth. 'I heard news that Jasper Coote has ventured south again, at least as far as Fotheringhay.'

'You're well informed. I hoped you'd remained in ignorance about his movements. Luckily I learned where he was and I've arranged that he will accompany my uncle even further north than previously. York is to seek a settlement with the Scots' King James who's broken the truce with King Henry by sending raiding parties across

315

the Border. The mission should keep Coote out of your way for several months.'

'I'm grateful. The information I was given suggested Coote met Baron Glasbury at Fotheringhay.'

For a moment Warwick looked uncomfortable. 'I didn't know that. I thought Gilbert Iffley at Ludlow but he's one of my uncle's closest advisers and journeys at his lord's bidding. We shouldn't read malice into a casual encounter.'

I acknowledged his remark and did not choose to question it, though I was not convinced. We were almost at Blackfriars Steps where I would land, in order to complete my journey home on foot.

'Don't forget to mention my need to recruit young stalwarts to your friend,' Warwick shouted as I stepped onto the jetty.

'I won't, my Lord. I hope all goes as you would wish it in Calais.'

Then I strode out as jauntily as my uneven gait permitted. At last this was to be my definitive homecoming.

*****

I had met the little nursemaid, Jane, the previous day, after my arrival from Hertford. She seemed quietly competent and I was glad Ursula had found reliable help while I was away. Jane greeted me now with modest composure, as she opened the front door, explaining that Betsy had been granted leave to visit her sick mother a few miles away in the village of Islington. 'Mistress Somers is in the solar, Doctor,' she said, 'and little Alys too, bless her.'

After a word of thanks I bounded up the stairs and a moment later Ursula was in my arms.

'You're truly home for good, Harry?' There was a gurgle of laughter in her voice.

'I'm truly home for good.'

316

There were several letters awaiting my attention but none to cause me serious concern. Cheerful messages from Worthwaite confirmed that Judith and young Roger were happily ensconced at my manor, cherished by Perkin and Dame Elizabeth. A brief reference implied that there had been no reconciliation with Lord and Lady Fitzvaughan and there was no communication for me from Hartham, which I regretted. Sir Nicholas Chamberlayne, on the other hand, was fulsome in his appreciation of my medical skills, rejoicing in the King's return from Hertford. He spoke of his hope to journey north shortly with the Duke of York to treat with the King of Scots. Clearly Sir Nicholas remained intent on fostering good relations with all who might benefit him in the uncertain future. His diplomatic skills were never more in evidence.

It was the letter from Thomas Chope which startled me most. He had intimated previously that he was minded to marry again. This was natural and a matter for celebration but I had never imagined who his bride was to be. I stared at the words which evoked for me a multitude of memories and regrets.

I am honoured that Mistress Bess Willoughby has consented to be my wife. We remembered each other from the days of our youth at Greenwich, where of course you knew us both. Since then we have both experienced happy unions and great sadness at our losses. I met Bess again while I was working on the panelling at the Chamberlayne residence at Harrow, where she has been in attendance on Lady Maud. Soon she will be mistress of her own home once more, as Mistress Chope, and my house will be the richer for her presence and that of her children, Anne and Rob. My little Margery will be the happier for acquiring an older sister.

I beg that you and Mistress Somers will be present when we make our vows. You are my oldest friend, Harry, and Bess remembers you with cordiality.

Cordiality! I choked slightly as I read that word. This was not Thomas's language. I had no doubt Bess had composed the letter and I welcomed this reaffirmation of her forgiveness for my part in causing Robin Willoughby's death. The losses of both Robin and Grizel had been cruel blows and there was a wonderful symmetry in bringing their bereaved partners together. I recognised that Thomas suited Bess far better than poor Piers ever could, for all his idealism and devotion.

I wished the couple happiness but I could not forget how Bess had spoken unkindly about Ursula, prompted of course by Lady Maud. Surely she would not nurture lasting animosity towards my wife? I could not believe it was in Bess's nature to persist with hostility indefinitely. Conversely, I hoped Ursula would not associate Bess with the bad-mouthing she suffered at court. Was it too much to hope that four people who had borne burdens of personal grief, each of us bereft of a spouse, might find new pleasure in shared friendship?

Ursula showed no antagonism towards the participants in the forthcoming nuptials and I gained confidence that my worries were groundless. I recognised how sometimes, when there was no genuine reason for anxiety, it seemed I must invent one and I berated myself for stupidity. I must learn to accept contentment and kindness. There was ample evidence that Dame Fortune's wheel had turned auspiciously.

My homecoming was celebrated generously by our neighbours, John Webber and his wife. They held a dinner in my honour and invited several notables who might become my patients. I was given introductions to other distinguished City men and the prospects for extending my practice looked bright, although it would continue to be more challenging to attract humbler folk to my door.

It pleased me that I acquired a handful of patients in the poorer alleys behind our street, venturing there to see them rather than expecting them to cross what they might see as a physician's daunting threshold. I accepted only a nominal fee from this clientele, as I had always planned, but I still encountered wariness among those unused to confiding in a professional man. There were various self-appointed quacks in the vicinity who offered their own dubious remedies but the latent need for my services was great so I intended to persist in winning trust in the locality. My main regret was that I worked alone, with limited resources. I resolved to visit the charitable hospice of St. Bartholomew's which offered a refuge to the homeless and children of prisoners in the gaol by Newgate. There might be the possibility of linking my work with theirs. I remembered what Robert de Beaune had told me of the hospital built in the town of his birth and I longed to emulate that remarkable Burgundian model.

I was full of renewed vigour and determination so within two weeks of my return I was busily occupied, treating a range of conditions and revelling in my new-found autonomy. The court had left Westminster on progress to the Midlands and I understood York's entourage had moved northwards. For the first time in many years I felt at peace and in a month's time we would attend the marriage of Thomas and Bess. It seemed a symbol of new blessings bestowed on us all.

*****

What does it take to change a life? What harbinger infallibly suggests the maelstrom to come? Over the years I had experienced violent incidents which led to immeasurable change: the fall from scaffolding in a boys' prank which broke my ankle and left me with a limp; the brutal death of my sister which caused me to conduct my first investigation; the murder of my patron and friend, the Duke of Suffolk; above all, the disaster in which Kate died – all had changed the course of my life. Other decisive developments which diverted me from chosen paths had been more insidious, gradual and unperceived. None had been heralded in so ordinary a manner as that knock at the door one evening in early summer, when Ursula sat with her stitching and I was perusing John Webber's paper on the properties of cinquefoil and columbine.

Betsy was once again visiting her ailing mother, for whom I could hold out small hope of recovery, but I heard Jane bound down the stairs from the nursery to greet our visitor. I put down John's treatise and prepared to be summoned to meet some poor soul in need of a physician. The tramp of many feet mounting the staircase alerted me to the unexpected but I was unconcerned, imagining I was to receive a harmless deputation of guildsmen seeking my support for some charitable cause. Casually, I noted the absence of conversation as they approached and wondered why Jane did not precede them to announce their business.

The door crashed back against the wall as it was thrown open and half a dozen men with drawn swords erupted into the room. Ursula's sewing slid to the floor. I stumbled to my feet and, with rising nausea, recognised the leading intruder as Jasper Coote. He waved his arm to direct his followers to surround me.

'Sit down, Doctor Somers, or you'll meet with a nasty accident.'

I subsided, fighting to control my terror, incapable of speech. More men were pouring into the room, lining the walls, until finally two others made their unhurried entrance. The suavely elegant figure in front was Gilbert Iffley, Baron Glasbury, who could not suppress a malignant smile as he smoothed the folds of his velvet over-gown. The ponderous fellow behind him moved awkwardly, leaning on a stick, but I did not doubt his strength. His face was hideously mutilated, his mouth twisted into a permanent scowl. His disfigurement was much more pronounced than the birthmark on my cheek and I was sorry for him but, as she caught sight of this frightening apparition, Ursula leapt to her feet, screaming in utter panic, swaying before she fell to the floor in a faint. I rose from the chair but with four sword-points at my chest I was prevented from going to aid her although I found my voice to shout protests. Jasper Coote lifted her and thrust her back on her chair. He lifted a flagon of small ale from the table and sploshed the liquid over her face. With relief I saw her begin to rally.

'What does this outrage mean, Baron?' I addressed myself to Iffley. 'Why are you here?'

'For the sweet benison of retribution, Harry: long deferred but now in my power to deliver with fitting finality. For years you've scorned my offers to join the cause I serve. Despite the resultant harm to those you claimed to love, you repulsed my suggestions as to how you might benefit the realm. Above all you have twice used your skill to restore our beloved King to a semblance of his wits, cruelly hurling him back into the turmoil of public affairs, which distress him so. He would be better contented to spend his day in holy contemplation in a house of prayer. It's time you reaped your reward.'

The clever twisted logic fooled nobody present. They were all Richard of York's men. But the casuistry upheld the fiction of devotion to King Henry. Iffley delighted in fatuous masquerades, in self-justification, in taunting his prey. 'Besides which,' he added, 'you brought about the death of my good-brother, Stephen Boice, and you have escaped justice for your crime.'

Ursula had regained her senses and was listening with intense concentration to the Baron's words. She was very pale and clasped her hands together to disguise her trembling. If I was not allowed to assist her, Jane should be summoned; but Jane had not entered the solar with the intruders. She must have returned to the nursery to comfort Alys and for that I was thankful. Jasper Coote's fingers twitched over the hilt of his sword.

'If you have come to kill me, Iffley, get on with it and leave the house. You have no quarrel with my wife.'

He gave a roar of laughter but held up his hand to silence those of his followers who seemed to share his mirth. 'You know me better than that, Harry. Would a clean slash across your throat or a stab to the heart be fitting retribution? I don't intend to grant you instant release into God's judgement, even if you were then to spend eternity in the fires of Hell. The sentence I pass aims to ensure you suffer desolation on earth while you still live and I have the means of exquisite torment at my disposal. It was wondrously fortuitous that I travelled to Ludlow recently on Duke Richard's behalf and learned what the key might be to your destruction.'

Ursula gave a sob. Instinctively I stepped forward but the tip of Coote's sword ripped the sleeve of my jerkin and another man seized my arms. 'Don't be a fool, Harry,' Iffley said and looked over his shoulder as the door opened behind him. 'Ah, Jane, is this Doctor Somers' tot? She has her mother's hair, does she not?'

I struggled vainly in my captor's arms. Why had the idiot girl brought Alys into danger? How did Iffley know her name? 'I implore you, don't hurt the child. Do what you will to me.'

Iffley's tone was derisive. 'I'm no child torturer. I was merely inquisitive to see the fruit of your disgraceful union.' He strode across to Ursula and lifted her chin. 'You were Stephen Boice's whore, you slut, and you betrayed him. You were sent to court by Duchess Cecily to observe what misdemeanours might be taking place to the dishonour of our noble King. Instead, you became the subject of scandal yourself, disgracing those to whom you owed obedience.'

I opened my mouth to protest but Jasper Coote's fist closed it and split my lip. Ursula said not a word but bore Iffley's foul insinuations, looking across at me, tears welling in her eyes. Blood trickled onto my chin.

'You thought to hide your detestable sins, you callous bitch.' Iffley had dragged Ursula to her feet. 'You had no concern for others when your interests were threatened. When that little maid Mary was sent to serve you, you realised she knew more than was good for her and could destroy your new-found love-nest, so you fed her poison. Cold, calculated murder, no less.'

322

Ursula spoke no words of denial and her response chilled my blood. 'You have no proof, Baron.'

His smile was spiteful. 'Stephen taught you well, mistress. You've learned to cover your tracks. Unfortunately your precautions haven't been fool-proof. You never identified dear Jane here as a comparable threat to Mary.'

I could scarcely breathe as revelation followed accusation and Ursula's eyes were wild with fear. 'Jane?' she gulped.

The girl faced my wife with an insolent smile. 'Mary was my cousin, mistress. You weren't to know but I was sent to do her work and to bring her murderess just deserts.'

Ursula sank back on her chair, her face in her hands, and I did not stir. I was numb with terror, uncertainty and grief. Gilbert Iffley drew himself up and straightened the heavy gown on his shoulders.

'You may escape a court of law, mistress, but you know your duty and the vow you made. These men will escort you back to Ludlow.'

I was jolted into alertness. 'What nonsense is this? Do you propose to abduct my wife? You can't expect...'

'She is not your wife, Harry.' Iffley's voice came as a thunder-clap drowning my protest, leaving me momentarily speechless. He beckoned forward the mutilated giant who bowed to me with an insolent leer. 'Allow me to present Master Gregory Bateby, your whore's lawfully wedded husband whose union was sanctified several years ago by holy church and, he assures me, consummated with vigour. He has come to claim his conjugal rights, to rescue his errant bride from concubinage and restore her to his hearth and bed. You have no power to stop him.'

Ursula's face confirmed the truth of Iffley's assertion but my mind was working sluggishly. 'We thought Master Bateby had been killed in a skirmish,' I said feebly.

'Oh, Doctor Somers, she has curdled your wits. She has always known Gregory survived his injuries. She begged to be allowed to leave him, offended by the sight of his honourable scars, the heartless trollop. She was willing to barter an afflicted husband for an adventurous role as an agent at the court where she learned the arts of the temptress. She seduced my good-brother and very probably others, Harry, before she lured you into an unhallowed, adulterous liaison.'

I stared at Ursula, sitting with her head bowed, and I willed her to deny what Iffley had said. For a moment she did not move but then she slipped onto her knees and looked up at me. 'It's true, Harry. At first I did not dream of marrying you, never imagined it possible. But you cajoled me and your sincerity won my heart. I never wanted to deceive you.'

Gregory Bateby dragged her to her feet and wrenched her arms behind her back, forcing her to stand in front of him as if she were his shield. 'Tell this lecherous quack what you promised me when I let you go to Fotheringhay to receive instruction from Duchess Cecily before you went to court. Tell him, you faithless bint.'

Ursula's lips quivered as she faced me and spoke in a whisper. 'At Ludlow I promised to return to Gregory if he required it. I acknowledged I was his chattel. It was the price of my release. It seemed unlikely he would live long at the time.'

I shut my eyes. There was too much to assimilate, too many dreadful disclosures stripping bare my delusions. I clung to the reality we had shared, Ursula and I, denying what I could not absorb. My naiveté prevailed. I had to believe good might yet triumph, sinners repent, love overcome evil.

'Break your vow, Ursula,' I said. 'You've been used barbarously, forced to do cruel men's bidding and blamed for trying to resist. I love you and will stand with you. Come with me. We'll cross the sea, find a new life where our past isn't known. Live with me as my wife, the mother of my children. Your vow was a mockery of justice. You can't be bound by it. Come with me.'

It was Jane who gasped at the flurry of movement and Alys, suddenly startled from sleep, who whimpered. My daughter had been snatched from the nursemaid's arms and was clamped to his chest by Jasper Coote's left arm. In his right hand he raised a dagger. I roared in misery.

'Overdramatic, Jasper,' Iffley said with a sigh, 'but it makes the point. You have the choice, Mistress Bateby. You see how the child is wriggling. It would be all too likely she could suffer an accident if disorder broke out in this room. Your lawful husband will not take your bastard, that must be obvious, but if you go with him obediently the brat will be left with Doctor Somers who can decide what should be done with her.' He swung round to face me with a beam of delight.

'It occurs to me, Harry, there might be a refinement I could add. It would be more fitting for you to make the choice, not this deceitful woman. Choose who is more important to you: your whore or your daughter. If you are in thrall to the shameless harlot and ready to flee the country with her within the week, perhaps Gregory would accept a generous payment not to insist on her return, although she would of course remain his wife. If that is your choice, I would be willing to have the infant conveyed to Fotheringhay where she could be brought up to serve the Duchess – but there would be the danger that she might not survive the journey, you understand. Jasper would be her escort. Do I make myself clear? Alternatively, if you wish to protect the fragile life of your whelp, you can provide for her as you wish and part forever from your paramour.'

Iffley held up a hand to silence Gregory Bateby who was snorting with indignation and clenching his fists. The Baron wanted to twist the figurative knife in my heart. I had no doubt of his ultimate intention. 'Whichever choice you make, Harry, you will live with the knowledge of what you did, of the preference you showed for one or the other of your dependents.'

His face swam before my eyes in a moment of giddiness as bile came into my mouth. It was unthinkable I would endanger Alys but Ursula would be in danger at the mercy of a vindictive husband. If the child survived, I might succeed in a petition to the courts to reclaim her but Coote would remove that possibility. He would cut my daughter's throat. Yet, if Ursula was lost to me...?

While I tried to reason and conquer my nausea, the terrible choice was taken from me. Ursula broke free and swept forward to whisk our daughter from Jasper Coote's arm. She held Alys out to me. 'You will face no such appalling guilt, Harry. Baron Glasbury is wrong in fashioning the refinement, as he called it. The choice is not yours. It is mine. I am resolved to fulfil my promise. I shall go with Gregory to Ludlow. Provide for Alys, my love, and when the time is right, explain to her why I was compelled to leave you both. You have given me happiness beyond imagining.'

I took Alys in my arms and she snuggled quietly against my shoulder while I stroked her hair, mute with shock. Ursula and I held each other's eyes and all the world of our mutual understanding passed silently between us. We had no opportunity for a farewell of greater tenderness. Gregory Bateby seized her wrist and dragged her from the room, followed by Iffley's entourage, while Jane scurried out to fetch a bundle of Ursula's possessions. I stared and inhaled and was helpless. Jasper Coote remained, clasping his dagger and drawn sword, as if to protect the Baron who sat calmly at my table smirking at my powerlessness.

'I shall bother you no longer, Harry. You are worthless but you are free. Isn't that a comfort? I shall of course ensure that your ignominious situation is publicly known. I imagine it will cause both chin-wagging and head-shaking. How amusing!'

I shrugged, incapable of a considered response but I accompanied my unwelcome visitors downstairs to see them from the house, Coote following closely on my heels with his weapons at the ready.

'The Baron may have done with you, quack,' he said. 'I haven't. I swear I'll skewer your guts next time we meet.'

I knew this was more than bluster.

There were raised voices outside the door and Alys hid her face in my jerkin. In tones of outrage, John Webber was questioning the men who tramped out of my house. When he saw me he gave a gasp of relief but it was speedily replaced by a look of horror as he registered Coote's ominous appearance.

'What's happening, Harry? Some ruffian put Mistress Somers on his horse and rode to the gate with a crowd of others. Her maid's gone too. I've sent my man for the City guard.'

Jasper Coote twirled his blade and John stepped back but I shook my head at my neighbour. 'Nothing's amiss, John, nothing that can be put right by force of arms. I'll explain. Could I bring Alys into your house, to see Mistress Webber? I need her assistance.'

Laughing at my discomfort, Iffley and Coote mounted and followed their troop towards the City gate. John stared after them, thunderstruck by events he could not understand, until he saw how I was shaking. Gently he took Alys from my arms as I began to retch and he hurried to his door, shouting for his wife. I sank to my knees and spewed into the runnel by the roadway, emptying the contents of my belly and with them the illusions which for nearly two years had nourished my famished soul.

Part 4 London and across the Narrow Sea 1456-8

Chapter 26

Alys kept me grounded, half-rational, with a purpose to fulfil. She forced me to set aside my humiliation and grief: to plan, organise and care for her. Wholly dependent on me, motherless but deeply loved, she was all I had to cherish and I was the only person who could provide for her. A father's devotion and paternal obligation combined to become the overwhelming reason for my continued existence.

I could not bear to think about Ursula. My pain was too raw to try to understand what she had allowed to happen, the deception she practised, the murder she committed, the unsavoury future life she was prepared to accept with Gregory Bateby for my sake and Alys's. I never doubted that she loved me but I comprehended now how little of her complex nature I had ever recognised. As time passed I would think through every aspect of our relationship and try to understand her motives and her actions; but that time was not yet.

I knew I must not dwell on these matters until I had the mental strength to face their implications. Otherwise they might render me deranged, like poor Kate had been. On the brink of desperation, I sensed the existence of the abyss. Mercifully, for my sanity, I had duties on which I must concentrate: patients to attend and, above all, a daughter for whom I was entirely responsible. I was not overly troubled by Coote's threat against my life. Compared with more immediate problems, it posed a theoretical danger. Nevertheless it lurked ominously in my consciousness to disturb moments of repose.

Mistress Webber was assiduous in securing temporary care for Alys and Betsy, returned from her mother's deathbed, was competent to run the house. The apothecary's wife would willingly have engaged a permanent nursemaid for my child but, before I could agree to that, I knew I must ascertain whether an arrangement I would prefer was feasible.

I wrote to Judith at Worthwaite and explained the circumstances in painful detail. I owed it to her to be candid about my predicament. She had attended Kate with dedication during difficult years of my first – my only – marriage. I trusted Judith completely and made clear she was free to remain at my manor if she wished, but she and her son would be welcome beyond words if she chose to come to London. I wrote also to Perkin, stressing that no pressure was to be put on Judith but asking whether, if she chose to come to London, young George Antey could be spared for a few days to escort her on the journey. I consigned my letters to a messenger who travelled regularly between the merchants of the City and East Anglian sheep farmers so I had confidence they would be safely delivered.

There was no need to refer in my letter to what Judith might view as an impediment. It was obvious. Rendell Tonks remained a guard at the Tower of London and, while he stayed in the City, he might visit my house. It would be hard for her to avoid encountering him. If only the prospect of proximity could encourage a rapprochement, a stratagem to bring them together would have been both crafty and profoundly justified; but I had no such hopes. Indeed, remembering my conversation with the Earl of Warwick, I resolved to encourage Rendell to take service with him in Calais.

I arranged to meet Rendell at Thomas Chope's home. I needed to see Thomas to wish him and Bess well but I would not now attend their wedding. I was incapable of assuming a joyful demeanour on such an occasion and would be an embarrassment – an all-too-evident spectre at the feast. In fact our meeting of three old friends was uncomfortable enough. We were all facing significant changes in our lives but in such different circumstances that each of us struggled to relate to the sentiments of the others.

Thomas was, as I expected, exuberant about his forthcoming nuptials but, after I described Ursula's departure, he fell silent and stared down at his beaker of ale without drinking. I conjectured that he felt awkward listening to my miserable story when he had emerged from the gloom of his bereavement into the radiance of a new life.

I rallied sufficient good sense to tell Rendell about the Earl of Warwick's intention to recruit a fighting force before I mentioned my invitation to Judith. In response to the first item he looked thoughtful but expressed no immediate interest in defending the Narrow Sea. By contrast, when I spoke of my letters to Worthwaite he flushed and grew angry.

'Think you own her, do you, because she gave years of service to your family when Kate was feeble-minded?'

I was irritated but determined not to quarrel. 'Not at all. I made it very clear she's free to refuse and I'll accept her choice.'

'Rubbish! It's a ploy. Want to run everyone's life for them, don't you? Bloody interfering quack! Send me to Calais! Fetch Judith to London! You've made enough mess of your own affairs without ordering others about. I suppose you fancy the idea of rearing the two little bastards together.'

'Rendell!' Thomas had stirred from his stupor. 'That's uncalled for.'

'That's what they are though, ain't they? The Earl of Stanwick's ill-gotten brat, a rapist's spawn, and the daughter of a murderess who tricked a besotted clown into adultery.'

His words landed like knife thrusts. I staggered to my feet, incapable of coherent speech. 'How can you say..?'

Thomas was affronted but more level-headed. He seized Rendell by the shoulder and hustled him towards the door. 'Enough! You've gone too far. I know what you're thinking but you could be wrong. Leave the house now and simmer down. Don't you dare speak like that in front of my children or spread false speculation.'

Rendell drained his glass and I feared for a moment he would argue with his brother-in-law. I started to mumble that I would leave but Thomas's displeasure had its effect and Rendell gave him a curt nod before thundering from the room.

I was aghast, bewildered by what had happened, vaguely conscious that I had not understood something which had been said but Thomas was quickly consoling and apologetic. I let myself be soothed by his sympathy and then, inadvertently, he distracted me from the hurt Rendell had inflicted. His tone became solemn.

'Bess and I have done a lot of reminiscing as we got to know each other: from the early days when we were both at Greenwich but scarcely aware who the other was, through the years of our marriages up to the present. You've been a common thread in our lives, Harry. Bess told me how, as a young woman, she'd hoped to be your bride: before you went to the Italian states and, through mishap, she believed you died there.'

I nodded. 'True enough. A series of misadventures intervened. Happily, she met Robin Willoughby. She'll have told you she rightly blamed me for putting him in danger, years later, and causing his death.'

'She knows it was unjustified to blame you. She lashed out at you in her grief. She'd forgiven you long before I met her again at the Chamberlaynes' manor.'

'She told me so. I was hugely relieved. She's the last person I would want to harm.'

Thomas shot to his feet, frowning. 'Are you still fond of her, Harry? I know she esteems you. You're a free man. A distinguished physician. Perhaps it's you she should marry.'

The pain in his voice was chilling but I was astonished by his self-doubt. I flung my arms round him 'Don't torment yourself, Thomas. I have no claim on Bess's affections. It's half a lifetime since our timid courtship. I'm quite sure she'd be horrified to hear you speak of it as if there was an enduring commitment. It's not like you to imagine such a ridiculous thing.'

He grinned at me, shamefaced. 'Bit of a lovelorn old fool, aren't I?'

'What better to be,' I said, 'when your sentiments are reciprocated? God bless you both.'

I recognised from his expression that he thought he should not parade his happiness in the light of my misfortune and by tacit agreement our conversation moved on to neutral matters, trade, City business, taxation and the talents of the Chope children. This was safer ground for two men around middle age who at that moment were both liable to become inappropriately emotional.

Later as I trudged home through the City streets I rejoiced for Bess and Thomas. I had not been quite honest with my old friend when I implied my feelings for Bess had faded long ago. It was not yet two years since my visit to Hartham Manor when they had stirred again. If I had been free then, what might have occurred? But by that time Ursula had won my heart and, whatever the validity of my marriage vows, I had not been free. Like so much in my life, it was now all too late.

*****

When I heard nothing from Worthwaite after two weeks, I started to despair. Alys was becoming fractious with a stream of willing but unfamiliar, makeshift nursemaids. She cried for her Mama and looked at me warily when I tried to distract her with bouncing games and stories. What could I tell her that she would understand? How much, in fact, did I understand?

I had no energy to pursue my goals for broadening the scope of my physician's practice and encouraging consultations with poorer neighbours. I ministered dutifully to patients who asked for my services but had lost my enthusiasm to pursue more ambitious plans. My only meaningful task was to provide for Alys's welfare. If I failed in that, my existence would be entirely worthless.

Each evening, when I went to the apothecary's house to collect my daughter who spent the day there, I endured Mistress Webber's recriminations while she urged the necessity of engaging a permanent nursemaid. She knew I had written to a former member of my household but interpreted the lack of a response as proof of rejection. I became discouraged, fearful she could be correct, but granted myself another week before I would concede.

On the sixth evening after this I hurried the short distance from my neighbours' house to my front door ignoring a wagon clattering towards us from the City gate. With much hallooing, the driver drew up alongside but only when he jumped down from his seat did I recognise George Antey, now become a very presentable young man. He reached up to help his passenger alight and lifted a squirming toddler from her arms.

'George! Judith! You've come!' My voice was reedy with emotion.

'Is this the baby?' Roger of Ravensmoor pulled his mother's sleeve and pointed at Alys in my arms. 'Can she walk? Are you the Doctor?'

'Roger, that's rude. You're too impatient. This is Doctor Somers.'

'And this is Alys, my daughter.' I set her down on her feet where she stood unsteadily gazing in fascination at the little boy a head taller than she was.

'Ro...Ro...,' she stuttered and her unlikely champion put his hand on her shoulder.

'We look after you, Alys, Mama and me.'

'That's that then.' Judith was laughing as she grasped my hand. 'No hurdle to overcome there. I should have sent to say we were on our way, Doctor Somers, but we travelled quickly and you knew I'd come.'

'I... I hoped so... but I wasn't sure. I'm so glad you have. Come in, come in.'

At last after those weeks of anguish and uncertainty I felt a wave of reassurance as I ushered my visitors into the house. Betsy came running forward to show Judith the room set aside for her, George went to find stabling for his horse overnight and within a few minutes I was on hands and knees playing the part of a dragon. Alys was gurgling with excitement as I skulked under the table and the infant son of the Earl who, years before, had tried to kill me brandished a wooden pestle with which to defend his miniature lady in distress.

During the next few weeks, while still shattered by Ursula's departure, I began to find a semblance of equilibrium in my life. Judith had an instinctive understanding of my daughter's confused feelings as she gradually came to accept the loss of her mother and adapted to new circumstances. I watched with admiration when she calmed Alys's occasional tantrums and encouraged her from more frequent bouts of forlorn silence. Betsy took to Judith readily and together they managed domestic arrangements with smooth efficiency. As for Master Roger, he could be as rambunctious as any three year old lad but he never wavered in his staunch support for Alys which won my grateful appreciation. So long as she was healthy and well cared for, I would look for no other purpose.

Thomas and Bess Chope came to visit soon after their wedding and we spent a happy afternoon together. They brought with them only their youngest children, Robin Willoughby, now in his seventh year, and Margery Chope who was a year older. They were both gentle-natured, not seen as rivals by Roger, and the atmosphere in the nursery remained affable with squeals of delight enlivening the games.

Judith and Bess knew each other from Lady Maud Chamberlayne's visits to Hartham Manor and they were soon gossiping happily while Thomas and I shared a flagon of wine. He glanced towards his wife, and smiled to see her so animated, before leaning forward to speak confidentially.

'Rendell has left for Calais,' he said. 'The Earl of Warwick's captain jumped at the chance to recruit him and sorted everything out with the Governor of the Tower.'

Thomas sank back. I thought he had more to say but he crumbled the remains of a sweetmeat in his fingers and looked awkward.

'It's a good opportunity for him and he likes variety. He should enjoy it. I'm just sorry if he chose to go in order to avoid seeing Judith.'

Thomas raised his head. 'You don't need to feel sorry. He's had his chance with Judith. He's no reason to begrudge you what he's rejected.'

'Begrudge me...?'

He saw my incredulity. 'Rendell's not dim, Harry. He understood. We all do. There's no need for you to delay. You're not bereaved. You're free. It's what everyone will expect.'

I dared not leap to my feet as instinct demanded for fear of alerting Judith and Bess to our conversation. 'What are you saying? Judith and I aren't planning to marry. Our only relationship revolves around Alys.'

Thomas stared at me. 'It may have been crass of me to speak out so soon. Of course you'll want a decent interval to elapse but don't you think Judith is expecting to change her status by joining you here? Surely it occurred to you?'

'That's ridiculous. I'm sure you're wrong. It doesn't arise.'

Thomas compressed his mouth and shrugged. It was clear he did not believe me. After a brief pause he laughed. 'I spoke out of turn – much too soon. I won't say another word. But I'll take bets on the outcome in a year's time.'

Thomas was swept away by the euphoria of his own re-marriage and he meant well. I brushed his ramblings aside, confident I knew Judith's mind better than him. At one time when she served Kate, circumstances had led me to fear she nurtured affection for me but she banished that notion by revealing the attraction she felt towards Rendell. She was by nature steadfast and unswerving in her devotion. It would be inexcusable to put her in an untenable position.

Two or three months passed without any major disruptions in the pattern of life at my home and I settled numbly into a routine of work. There was sufficient demand for my services to keep me occupied but I still did nothing to further my earlier plans. I failed to visit St. Bartholomew's hospice, as I intended, putting it off from week to week, hoping my old enthusiasm would be rekindled as time passed. Yet everything relating to my practice, everything about the house, carried a potent association with Ursula and this was soul-destroying. How long, I wondered, did it take to refashion a broken spirit?

At the beginning of August I learned that the Earl of Warwick was finally preparing to depart for Calais with his wife and two small daughters. He was to take up his Captaincy in person and settle his household in this new domain. I welcomed the news. With York engaged on the King's behalf in the north and Warwick across the Narrow Sea, the prospects for quieter times in England seemed hopeful.

In the muggy heat of a summer evening John Webber and I strolled out into the fields beyond the Newgate. We made our way north to where the waters of the River Fleet ran clearly through the countryside before they became begrimed in the City. We watched lads splashing each other and skimming stones across the surface of the stream and we both, I imagined, were reminded of our own boyhoods. John's next words corrected this misapprehension.

'I'm sorry my wife upset Mistress Judith a few days ago. She meant no harm. It was an honest mistake.'

I immediately felt guilty for not knowing Judith had been distressed but was wary of disclosing my ignorance. 'What happened?'

'Women gossip. Can't stop them. I suppose my wife had chatted to her neighbours. I'm afraid you'd been the subject of their chatter when Mistress Som..., Mistress Ursula went away. Then Mistress Judith came and they couldn't help speculating. She's a fine woman, superior for a nursemaid. It seemed to them natural why you'd asked her to come. She'd served your household in the past. She has the little boy. It isn't clear if she's a widow.'

'What are you saying, John? What did Mistress Webber say to Judith?'

My apothecary friend sighed. 'She assumed the boy was yours. She implied it, I think, rather than making an allegation. But her meaning would have been clear and Mistress Judith was horrified. I'm afraid my wife compounded her mistake by trying to make amends. She expressed the hope that, in any case, there'd soon be a new Mistress Somers.'

'Meaning Judith?'

John shrank back, deeply embarrassed. ''Yes. I confess I had myself mentioned the possibility in harmless banter with my wife. I can only apologise.'

'No need, John. I can see what it looks like to the outside world but Judith and I understand each other. There's nothing intimate between us. It's a shame she was troubled. I'll speak to her.'

I offered my hand to show I bore no ill feelings and my friend clasped it eagerly before we spoke of other things. I did not wish him to know how badly equipped I was to deal with this new burden heaped on my shoulders.

Next day I felt bound to mention the matter to Judith. I was to blame and could think of only one solution but I was most uncomfortable, incapable of dispassionate judgement. I began tentatively, telling her John had apologised for something his wife had said although I went into no details. Her quick intuition focussed at once on her main concern.

'You didn't tell Master Webber who Roger's father was, Doctor, or how he was conceived?'

'Not a word. But I should have realised that bringing you here exposed you to this sort of tittle-tattle.'

'It's inevitable. I expected something of the kind. But it was a shock when Mistress Webber came out with a downright accusation so unexpectedly. I soon got over it and I didn't want you bothered by silly gossip.'

'I'm responsible for putting you in this situation. It's painful for you. Besides...what you say is true...speculation is inevitable. I didn't think. This is hardly the right context but...we're both mature people...if you wish it, I would offer...'

Judith rose from her seat, smoothing her skirt and blushing. 'No, Doctor, please don't say more. I appreciate your generosity. But you know where my heart is engaged. I bless you for the opportunity to live here with Roger and care for Alys. I want nothing else – as I cannot have the only marriage of my choice. You honour me with your chivalry. Forgive me for my churlish response.'

I felt overpowering, guilty relief. 'There's nothing churlish. I'm humbled by your honesty and how well you know yourself. I admit I scarcely know my own mind at present. So much has happened.'

My voice tailed away but there was no need to say more. What a fool Rendell was to snub this clear-headed woman who, for incomprehensible reasons, continued to love him with absolute dedication. Yet the passage of time might change many things. It was Judith's arrival so soon after Ursula's departure which fuelled idle, lubricious conjecture. We must wait in patience while chatter about my household became stale and petered out, as it assuredly would. Even so, I berated myself for obtuseness, self-obsession and an impotence I could not dispel.

*****

There were early signs of autumn's approach as I made my way home from the house of a silversmith by Grey Friars whose wife was nearing death. I had done what I could to relieve her pain and would call again in the evening. It was a familiar situation but one which I still found disturbing. Venting my frustration, I kicked a pile of newly fallen leaves, brought down outside a garden wall by the overnight wind. Then I crossed the road towards my house.

A lad I knew by sight, the local butcher's son, had brought a bag of oats to a fine horse tethered in front of my front door. He ran his hand over the grey's smooth shanks. 'You've a visitor, Doctor,' he said. 'He paid me to fetch this here nosebag. Nice gent.'

'Thank you. Stay with the horse to keep him safe and I'll give you something extra when my visitor leaves.'

The boy winked and saluted me as I hurried indoors to greet Sir Nicholas Chamberlayne whose crest adorned the saddle cloth. I had last seen him during my brief appearance at court after I returned from Hertford and I did not know whether he was aware of the change in my circumstances since then. Naively I underestimated his sources of information.

He strode forward, arms outstretched, as soon as I entered my study. 'Belated commiserations, Harry. I've heard Baron Glasbury guffawing about your humiliation, as he called it. What a confounded trick they played on you.'

I gave an unsteady laugh. 'I hadn't realised the tale of my matrimonial mishap had reached your elevated circles but I'm glad to see you.'

He had already been supplied with refreshments and I motioned him to resume his seat. He crossed his legs, revealing the rich silk lining of his over-gown, and beamed at me.

'I bring you greetings from the Earl of Warwick. I've had business with him recently. He's a young man of

339

great potential. I think I told you so before, months ago, so I can claim prescience now he's won credit from others.'

I nodded, hiding my amusement that Sir Nicholas still showed himself adept at trimming his sails to catch the dominant wind of great men's influence. 'I understand the Earl is now in Calais.'

'Indeed, yes, that's where he sent for me. My wife accompanied me. We've just returned. He wished to see me because he knew you were my friend. I have a message for you, one greatly to your advantage. He wishes you to join his entourage.'

I stared blankly for a moment while Sir Nicholas paused. 'He's heard of your difficulties and is appalled. He has his own reasons to detest Baron Glasbury. He wants you to serve his household as physician in Calais. There'll be the opportunity to attend members of the garrison who need medical care as well, though they have some sort of quack in attendance. He suggests you might find it congenial to make a new start in life there. He stressed your entire household as at present constituted will be welcome.'

Despite my confusion I registered that the Earl must be aware of the rumours concerning Judith, however extraordinary this was. Sir Nicholas grinned.

'I must confess the Countess of Warwick had a part in persuading him after my own beloved wife influenced her. Maud has sympathy with Mistress Judith's situation and she retains a kindness towards you, Harry.'

I could understand that Lady Maud might have fellow feeling with Judith because in her youth she too had born a child out of wedlock, although in very different circumstances. That she expressed a kindness towards me was more surprising but I suspected Sir Nicholas knew nothing of his lady's chequered relationship with me over many years before he met her.

'It's gracious of Lady Maud and the Countess to concern themselves with my future.'

Sir Nicholas chuckled. 'What man could resist the pair of them? But Richard Neville is no one's pawn. He sees where his advantage lies. He has excellent intelligence services, you appreciate, but they are not necessarily quite good enough for all his purposes. That's why your invitation comes with an additional request. He may be glad to call on your powers of investigation. He asked me to corroborate what he'd heard of them – which of course I was happy to do.'

My shiver must have been visible. 'I haven't carried out any serious investigations for a long time. It's not a role I'm anxious to resume.'

'In Aquitaine, I believe, you excelled yourself. The Earl is establishing himself in Calais and has widespread support but he believes there may be those lurking who would occasion him trouble. The possibility of acquiring a proficient physician with additional hidden skills is most appealing: in case he needs confidential enquiries handled with discretion. I trust you will agree, Harry. I've arranged that a ship will be ready to convey you from the City wharves in a week's time.'

How much this extraordinary invitation owed to the Earl, Sir Nicholas or their wives was an open question. Wheedled they may have been, but both men were astute and between them they had happed on a prescription which produced a powerful effect on me. It was unreasonably tempting and it was impossible.

'I can't just leave the practice I've begun to build here. There are patients to be tended. I lease this house. There are two small children in my household. I have obligations.'

'The Earl knows all this. The children will be welcome. He has two infant daughters of his own. They will all play together and share the nursery. As for your practice and this house, I will make all necessary arrangements for a suitable leech to take your place. You may depend on me. You've spent most of your professional life serving the households of great men. I make so bold to suggest it's your proper métier.'

'I can't uproot other members of the household who've recently joined me. They came willingly and my little girl is dependent on them.'

Sir Nicholas gave me a benevolent nod. 'Forgive me, Harry. While waiting for your return I made so bold as to mention my commission to Mistress Judith. You recall that I have met her in the past when visiting your manor and the Fitzvaughans. I was able to give her Warwick's assurance that the son of the late Earl of Stanwick will be accommodated in his noble household as she sees fit and she will be honoured in her own right. No pressure of any sort will be put on her. She made no comment because it must be your decision but I fancy the benefits of this move were not lost on her. She's a woman of acute intelligence.'

I put my head in my hands. There was too much to digest. 'I need to think, to speak to Judith. I'm overwhelmed, dazed.'

'Do so, Harry, of course. I shall stay the night at Westminster and visit you again in the morning.' He stood up and I moved forward to open the door for him. 'I urge you to consider carefully, my friend. You still have enemies this side of the Narrow Sea and I venture to suggest you are not in the strongest spirits to withstand them. It's my opinion this new beginning is exactly what you need. Ponder what I say.'

The Pale of Calais was England's crucial outpost across the Narrow Sea and the castle dominating the town was a military bastion. It formed the central hub of a chain of forts defending the harbour, its hinterland and the narrowest straits of the sea. Calais was a perpetual thorn in the flesh of France and its rulers. For more than twenty years, however, the immediate overlord of the territories surrounding it had been the acquisitive Duke of Burgundy who succeeded in extending his domain prodigiously while declaring himself a loyal Frenchman. The Captain of Calais must not only defend the Narrow Sea for England's benefit but juggle relationships with both France and Burgundy.

The castle was a fortress but also the residence of the Captain of Calais and his family, accommodating in suitable comfort the large and varied retinue this dignitary required. Outside its walls the town nestled, lively with merchants from a dozen countries seeking profitable trade, bustling with seamen, soldiers and ships' chandlers, enlivened by the ale-houses, itinerant entertainers and bawdyhouses to be found in any seaport. The town was also a centre for intrigue where whispered discourse on the wharves and in the taverns often concerned shifting allegiances between great lords and rival potentates as well as the inflated price of wool and the attractions of the latest hussy at the whorehouse.

The strange insularity of the place would be of interest to any newcomer but its special attraction for me was the chance to be inconspicuous. Within the Earl of Warwick's household I was introduced as a respected physician who had once served the late Duke of Suffolk and before him the Duke of Gloucester. I came as a bereaved husband, accompanied by my small daughter and her nurse who had tended my late wife. No chronology or superfluous complications needed to be explained. Judith was content. She was under the Earl of Warwick's protection and welcomed by the Countess to help care for the Neville daughters. Alys had been wide-eyed with excitement at crossing the sea and in Calais she was fascinated by the sight of the tidal swell regularly swamping the marshes beside the waterways. As for Roger of Ravensmoor – who was never to be so named – he was resolved to become a mariner or, sometimes, a boat builder: both improbable but harmless aspirations for this bright but problematic three year old.

Twice in the past I had left England in haste: for exile in northern Italy in my youth and four years ago to join the military expedition to Aquitaine. The sudden change in my circumstances this time differed from those earlier occasions because I now had responsibilities for my child and household but that did not account for my persistent melancholy. My recovery from the devastation of Kate's death had been painful, eventually eased by learning to love Ursula. Now, six months after my second, bizarre tragedy, I was still bereaved of the zest and resilience I possessed formerly. I accepted there could be no second miracle. I was henceforth reduced to an impassive player in other people's stories, detached from my own consciousness and likely to remain so for the rest of my existence. Calais offered a haven, a hiding place, and I looked for nothing more.

The Earl of Warwick was not in the town when we arrived. He had crossed to Sandwich on the English coast which was the main supply port for Calais. He was building good relationships with the authorities there which could be valuable in the future. When he returned he was bursting with ideas and enthusiasm to implement them, intent on using his absolute command in his maritime base to safeguard the sea and enhance his own reputation. I felt pallid and dismal beside him. Yet, despite the differences of status and temperament between us, Richard Neville seemed pleased that I had come. He had no personal need of my medical services but he evidently enjoyed our conversations and allowed me to share his confidences.

'I receive reports of the French King's growing power at sea,' he told me in one of our earliest exchanges. 'I'm clear he'll launch a major attack on England's ports before long and we're poorly equipped to defend them. We've only a handful of large vessels and a few merchantmen converted as warships. It's vital we build up our navy so the shipyards across the Narrow Sea are frantically fulfilling my orders. It'll take time before we're adequately prepared. Let's hope King Charles is distracted by his family problems and delays attacking us.'

'He's at odds with his son, the Dauphin, I've heard.'

'Have you heard where Dauphin Louis is now residing? No? He's fled his father's realm after the latest of their disagreements and taken refuge in the Duke of Burgundy's northern lands. He's ensconced in Brabant at the castle of Genappe. Duke Philip's given him a home and a pension – no doubt with an eye on winning gratitude from France's future King.'

'That's bold, surely, while the Duke still owes allegiance to King Charles?'

'His allegiance is only a matter of form. Philip has wealth and power. He's shrewd to court the Dauphin. Louis himself sounds a man of significance. He's about your age, Harry, and he's defied his father many times. I have to navigate my way through these unstable relationships, defending England's interests as seems best. At least it puts the quarrels between our home-grown lords in perspective.'

I was mildly shocked to hear him speak so lightly of the armed conflict at St. Albans eighteen months previously but appreciated the broader context within which he must operate as Captain of Calais.

'I shall return to England when required to attend the Great Council,' he went on, 'but I welcome my freedom to act without carping from tiresome officialdom. My uncle, Richard of York, is a man of integrity but some of his toadies are abominable and unscrupulous. You've suffered monstrous wrongs from Gilbert Iffley and some

345

months ago he sought to undermine my position on the Council. He alleged I was immature and owed my success in battle entirely to the experience of my officer, Sir Robert Ogle. It was a gross insult. When I heard how he'd treated you, I was determined he should not prevail in his vendetta.'

'I'm grateful, my Lord, but I'm astonished he should try to challenge your position. It must imply that he sees you as a potent threat to his own influence – with your uncle of York, perhaps.'

The Earl slapped his thigh with hilarity. 'Well said, physician. That's percipient. That's the insight I hoped for from you. I think Sir Nicholas Chamberlayne mentioned to you that I might call on your experience beyond the realms of medicine. I have no specific request at present but I trust you'll be willing to help me cross the choppy waters of political intrigue this side of the Narrow Sea.'

I gave him my commitment as a matter of course but later, reviewing in my head what had been said in our conversation, I marvelled that I did this so readily. Could I detect a spark of curiosity in my passive soul, engendered by the manoeuvres of foreign nobility and an instinctive liking for the clever young Earl whose service I had entered? At the time I deemed it improbable.

*****

During the winter months several vessels which had been patrolling the straits came into harbour and their companies of sailors and fighting men augmented Warwick's entourage. It was inevitable Rendell would be among the new arrivals. A day or two before the Feast of the Nativity, as I made my way beyond the walls of the castle where an apothecary had his premises, a familiar figure stumbled from the doorway of an alehouse. I raised my hand in greeting but he turned his back on me.

'Rendell! I don't know what I've done to annoy you but I'd like to put things right. I'm sorry if my presence here was a surprise.'

He swivelled, peering through bleary eyes. 'It weren't. I'd heard you'd come. Mates with the Earl of Warwick, no less. Good for you. Got a new wife too, I suppose, you stinking bastard.'

I rocked on my heels as Thomas's preposterous warning was validated. 'I've not remarried and have no plans to remarry. But don't take that to mean I've a doxy to warm my bed. Is that what you expected? That I intended to court Judith one way or the other when she came to London? It isn't true.'

He spat into the gutter and wiped his sleeve across his mouth. 'Why should I believe you?'

'Perhaps because you know I wouldn't lie to you. I was naïve, I'll grant you that. Neighbours in the City jumped to the same conclusion as you. It was unfair, uncomfortable. It was one of the reasons for leaving London.'

'She came to you willingly enough. Maybe it's her, angling for you.'

'You know Judith better than that. She came because Alys needs her.'

Rendell put out a hand to steady himself against the wall as a group of merry topers debouched from the inn. This was neither the time nor the place to engage in further conversation on matters of some delicacy.

'You have my word, Rendell. I've told you the truth. I need to collect some herbs from the apothecary along the road but if you're ready to give me the benefit of the doubt, join me for a drink some other time, just the two of us. You can find me at the castle.'

He burped and then spat once more, narrowly missing my foot. 'What a bloody honour! Fuck you!'

I did not attempt to respond. He threw an arm round the shoulders of a companion and they lurched off towards the harbour.

I reported my encounter briefly to Judith. She needed to be aware Rendell was in Calais and in an unforgiving mood. She bit her lip but did not comment. Neither of us expected him to take up my invitation.

For the next three weeks I was busy combatting an ailment which afflicted many of the children in the castle. It led to fever and inflamed throats and some of the little ones were badly affected. Most recovered but two infants in the servants' quarters died and anxiety was shared by parents throughout the household. Alys and Roger were both ill for a few days but responded well to my potions. The Earl's daughters were not exempt although the baby, Anne, had no more than mild sniffles. The condition of her four year old sister, Isabelle, was much more serious and I began to fear she would succumb. At last she rallied, however, and there was much rejoicing.

The episode gave me new insight into young Roger's nature. He had taken a liking to the Earl's elder daughter and became upset, after his own recovery, when he learned how ill she was.

'You make her well, Doctor,' he said, pulling my gown. 'You give her drink to make her better.'

'I'll do my very best. The drink is meant to help the fever. But sometimes it can't.'

'Make drink stronger?'

'That's a clever idea, Roger, but it doesn't always work like that. We have to concoct the mixture carefully.'

'Roger see?'

'Come and I'll show you'.

After that the small lad became a regular observer when I mixed remedies and explained as simply as I could what they were meant to do. He listened solemnly and took a precocious interest in the outcomes for those who were unwell. I was impressed by his seriousness and reported favourably to Judith on his intelligence.

'He's inherited your instinct to care for others in trouble,' I said, all too aware of her fear that he might inherit his father's brutality.

'The saints be praised if that's true! You don't mind him dogging your footsteps? You mustn't let him be a nuisance.'

'Don't worry. He's bound to find another obsession before long. In the meantime I'll encourage a wholesome interest in physic – but keep my ingredients under lock and key.'

It was good to see Judith laugh.

Soon after his arrival in Calais, Rendell appeared in the castle gatehouse: not in belated response to my invitation but to supervise guard duty. I had been attending the sickbed of the warden's wife in rooms above the gate and was descending the spiral when I heard familiar voices in the courtyard below. I stopped by a slit-opening in the wall and peeped down.

'Well, if it isn't Sergeant Tonks. I was inclined not to credit reports that you were in the town. I didn't believe you were so uncivil as to neglect your old companions.'

Rendell cleared his throat. 'I reckon you know why I haven't come, Mistress Judith. No use pretending. Has that sodding Doctor been pouring poison in your ear?'

'No, he hasn't and you're behaving like a silly dolt to indulge bigoted fancies.'

'Silly dolt! Well I won't waste your time, my fine lady.'

'You're not and I'm a simple nursemaid. There's no reason in the world we can't exchange courtesies. Where's the humour you used to display when we argued years in the past? It was all sport, to outwit each other then.'

I felt guilty as I eavesdropped but if I continued down the staircase I would arrive at a door into the courtyard near where they stood.

'I left what wits I had in Aquitaine,' Rendell said in a quiet voice and I wondered if Judith realised he was referring to the time when he learned of her pregnancy and Roger's birth. 'I can't bandy words with you as I used to. Can't pretend things aren't different now.'

'We can still acknowledge each other politely.'

'It don't come easy to me. Anyway, when the weather picks up, I'll be off to sea again.'

'And that can't come soon enough?' For the first time Judith sounded strained.

'Too true. Now I must inspect the sentries. I wish you well.' There was the hint of a tremor in his voice.

I waited on the stairs until Rendell had entered the gatehouse and Judith disappeared after crossing the courtyard. I hoped she recognised his last words as the concession I thought they implied. Surely there was sufficient misery in this life without my two dear friends creating additional grief for each other?

*****

The summons to attend the Earl in early spring was unexpected. It came in the midst of preparations for him to put to sea now the wind had changed direction. I hurried to his lodgings, hoping he was not suffering from some malady which put his plans at risk, and found him attended by a page I recognised as Sir Nicholas Chamberlayne's son, Nicky. The boy had grown much taller since I last saw him. The Earl hustled me into his study and beckoned Nicky to remain.

'I have need of those special services we spoke of,' he said without any preamble. 'There's a matter I want you to investigate, Harry. Urgently. I have to sail for Sandwich but I must be confident this business will be thoroughly looked into. There'll be gossip enough shortly.'

'What is it, my Lord?'

He flung himself into his chair and pointed to a stool for me. 'A body was washed up on marshland outside the harbour this morning: the body of a servant I'd sent to take messages into Flanders. He had a safe conduct to cross the Burgundian Duke's lands. Norbert had served me for years. He left here a week ago on horseback, for Ghent. I don't know if he arrived there. I'm told the body looks as if it's been in the water some while and his pouch is missing. I assume he'd been robbed.'

'Would his route to Ghent have followed the coast?'

'Perhaps part of the way. I expected him back by now so he may have been attacked as he approached Calais and his body cast out to sea. That would mean he was carrying replies to my correspondence which are lost or taken by those they don't concern.'

'It would be sensible to send another messenger to Ghent, to see whether your man arrived there and what messages he was given to bring back to you. Who was the correspondent you wrote to?'

Warwick rolled his eyes. 'That's the delicacy. My contact is Duke Philip's agent. He's providing assistance to the French Dauphin, Louis, sheltering in Burgundy's domain. Some of my letters concern the Dauphin. It's a confidential matter. I wouldn't want my approaches to become general knowledge at this stage. You'll appreciate the need for tact and the chance there's more to Norbert's death than common assault.'

'If your worst suspicions are justified, who would be most likely to want to intercept your messages and be willing to instigate murder?'

I knew the answer before he spoke.

'King Charles of France or his counsellors. He'd sent an army against his son before Louis fled to Brabant.'

'Was one of your letters addressed to the Dauphin personally?'

'Yes. The agent was to convey it to the Dauphin at the castle of Genappe. In itself it simply carried my respects. Nothing specific but an unauthorised reader might imagine an implication not spelled out.'

'That you – and England – might ally with Louis against his father?'

The Earl spread his hands on his knees. 'Who knows?'

'What is the name of the agent acting for Louis in Ghent? It looks probable I'll need to contact him.'

'He's from the Duchy of Burgundy. His name is Robert de Beaune.'

I swallowed an exclamation. 'I've met the gentleman in England.'

'That's lucky. See what you can find out. You have my authority to act as necessary. I'll write you a note confirming this and a safe conduct to enter Burgundian territory, as permitted by the Duke. My clerk will engage physicians from the town to attend to any ailments at the castle while you're absent and young Nicky here can give you any help you need.'

I bowed my head, sensing I was committing myself to something beyond a straightforward enquiry, suspecting without rancour that I had not been told the full story. 'I'll find out all I can. I'd like to see the body.'

'Nicky will escort you. It's been secreted in a warehouse by the harbour. You have my gratitude.'

Nicky looked intelligent and I took to him at once. He led me out of the castle by the postern gate and through unfrequented alleys to reach a building at the eastern side of the harbour.

'New wool will be brought here in a few weeks, after the shearing in England, but at the moment one storeroom is empty so that's where they've laid Norbert.'

He unlocked the door and took a step back as the pungent, sickening smell hit us. I knelt beside the corpse and noted that this victim had been longer in the water than Guillaume Coustances whose body I examined after it was thrown in the River Garonne. I did not wish to draw further parallels with my enquiries in Aquitaine. Whatever else may have happened to him, the cause of Norbert's death was easy to determine for the back of his head had been cracked open.

'Can you tell when he was consigned to the sea, Doctor Somers?' Nicky was peering closely at the victim.

'Not with accuracy. I'd guess two or three days ago. The body's been battered. Ah!'

I had lifted one of the man's hands and when I exclaimed Nicky dropped to his knees beside me. 'What is it, sir?'

I leaned over to inspect the victim's other hand. 'I believe this poor fellow was tortured before he was killed. Look: all his fingers have been crushed, viciously crushed. I don't think that could have happened by accident.'

Nicky pulled off the stained hose covering the man's feet and it was obvious his toes had been smashed with some heavy implement in the same way as the hands. The lad crossed himself.

'Heaven have mercy on him. Why should he have suffered such violence?'

I sank back on my haunches, speaking my thoughts aloud rather than putting a question to Warwick's page. 'Is it likely the Earl had given Norbert additional messages to deliver by word of mouth as well as the packages he carried?'

Nicky did not bat an eyelid. 'Very likely, Doctor. It would be normal. Not everything can be committed to paper when the subject is sensitive.'

'And enemies would be well aware of that? Have you any idea what the verbal messages were?'

He laughed. 'No, Doctor. They may have reinforced the Earl's good wishes to the Dauphin or they could have been directed to Duke Philip. The Earl's already been in touch with him.'

'And Robert de Beaune would communicate directly with the Duke?'

'I don't doubt it.' When I stood up the youth drew a cloth over Norbert's face. 'I can arrange with the Earl's chaplain for a quiet funeral, if you agree. There's no family in Calais.'

'Thank you. It would be helpful. If I'm to find out anything more, I'll need to make the journey to Ghent myself. I'll set out in the morning. Could a guide be found?'

'Of course. Leave it to me.'

As we emerged from the warehouse we heard distant shouts and bells clanging. Sails were swelling in the wind, pennants streaming, figures scrambling up the rigging of half a dozen vessels as they set their course out of the harbour. The small English fleet had put to sea.

Nicky locked the door before turning to me. 'This is a chancy business, Doctor. You should have an armed escort or you might be in peril. I'll arrange it. I wonder...'

His voice tailed away but I deduced what he wanted to ask. 'Would you like to come too? Would that be permitted?'

His face lit up with a beam of delight. 'Oh, certainly. The Earl said I must do everything to help you. I would have gone to sea with him but I don't care for it. When we crossed here the swell made me sick.'

I patted the honest fellow's shoulder in commiseration but experienced an almost forgotten and inappropriate twinge of excitement. Judith would certainly understand my commission and I hoped Alys would not be too upset by my brief absence.

*****

Our journey to Ghent was straightforward and, as I have never been a natural horseman, I appreciated the flatness of the terrain. We lodged two nights in modest hostelries and in both cases servants remembered Warwick's messenger staying with them on his way to Ghent. It was not the first time he had travelled the road and he was a sociable man, popular with his hosts who were dismayed to learn of his death. Significantly, I thought, no one had seen Norbert on his return journey to Calais.

I knew Ghent was a rich town of great importance, seat of the Counts of Flanders, at the confluence of several waterways along which were traded vast quantities of wool and cloth. Even so I was not prepared for the sight of the imposing stone buildings massed in its centre, churches,

354

towers, merchants' houses, all proclaiming to the humble visitor its wealth and arrogance. I dared not let my eyes be carried upwards for more than an instant, to contemplate soaring arches and fanciful decoration, for fear I would lose my companions in the bustle of the marketplace. I took hasty glances at the impressive port area, where narrow ships on a network of inland channels were loading and unloading cargo as busily as along the wharves on the Thames in London. Then in front of us was the great castle which was our destination.

The walls and towers of the Flemish Counts' castle were reflected in the waters of the River Lièvè, slightly distorted by ripples from passing barges. The edifice itself was solid, domineering and rather better maintained than the fortified palace in Bordeaux where many of Lord Talbot's officers had been billeted. Robert de Beaune was accommodated here while in Ghent on the Duke of Burgundy's business and it soon became clear he was accorded considerable deference. We were received by his attendant with formal courtesy while Robert was informed of our arrival but quickly supplied with perfumed water and towels to refresh ourselves when it was clear we were welcome. We were asked to wait while he finished a meeting and the soldiers escorting us from Calais were taken to the kitchens for food.

In due course Robert pounded into the ante-chamber, redder than ever in the face, and flung his arms around me. 'Doctor Somers, I am delighted, honoured, to receive you in the Duke of Burgundy's demesne. I had heard you were in Calais but had not expected you would venture into Flanders.'

I guessed that if he knew I was in Calais he was also aware of the change in my personal circumstances but he was far too much the diplomat to mention this. I indicated Nicky standing behind me. 'I've borrowed the Earl of Warwick's page, Nicholas Chamberlayne the younger.'

'Ah, yes, I've met the young gentleman's father. Sir Nicholas entertained me at his manor in Harrow on the Hill with his luminous lady.'

Luminous was a novel description for Maud but I must not allow myself to be diverted from my duty. 'I'm also pleased to renew our acquaintance but I regret the cause of my journey here is a wretched one.'

Refreshments were brought and we sat at table while I outlined the circumstances of Norbert's death. Robert's normally jovial expression disappeared under knotted brows and down-turned mouth. He munched a sweetmeat thoughtfully before commenting.

'Norbert certainly came to Ghent and brought the Earl's correspondence. I gave him packages for Warwick and also some verbal messages responding to earlier letters. Norbert told me he was returning to Calais by sea. He was to visit a friend who happened to be in Bruges and had offered him passage on a ship which was due to call at Calais before returning to England. I don't like the sound of this.'

'Did he mention who the friend was or anything about him?'

'He didn't give a name. He implied it was a merchant who called at Bruges from time to time. Whether the friend was false or Norbert was abducted from safety, it seems clear he was made captive, taken on board a ship and killed.'

'Also, I believe, tortured. Perhaps to make him disclose verbal messages he had been given.'

'Oh, that is terrible. But it is credible. And we can have no idea whether he divulged the information before he died.'

'Would it be highly inconvenient if he'd done so?'

'To a number of distinguished noblemen. Listen carefully.' Nicky stood up, expecting to be sent out of the room, but Robert shook his head and patted the stool the boy had occupied. 'As you know, the Dauphin Louis is at serious odds with his father, King Charles. King Charles is uncle by marriage to Queen Margaret of England; indeed he gave her in marriage to King Henry as a means of consolidating the truce between France and England. Queen Margaret is an assiduous correspondent with her dear uncle and is looking to him for support against rebellious English nobles: financial and armed support should it prove necessary. Need I say more?'

I understood. 'Logic suggests that those rebellious lords favouring the Duke of York, including the Nevilles, might welcome an opportunity to court the French Dauphin. King Charles is ageing and in poor health, I believe. One day Louis will succeed him. In the meantime the Dauphin takes pleasure in thwarting his father's schemes.'

'Exactly. You grasp the situation. The Earl of Warwick's verbal messages to me were along those lines and in return I was authorised to give him every comfort, on behalf of the Dauphin and of my own illustrious lord, the Duke of Burgundy.'

'I can see it would be inconvenient for such expressions of goodwill to become public but was there something more specific?'

Robert sighed. 'You are too quick, Doctor Somers. There is the suggestion of a meeting – Warwick, Duke Philip and the Dauphin. Fortunately no time or date has been proposed. I also gave Norbert verbal information for the Earl concerning French intentions to send their fleet in the summer to attack Calais.'

I could not prevent myself giving a faint whistle. 'The Dauphin has been willing to inform on his father's plans?'

'No, no. It's unlikely the Dauphin is privy to such plans. This is information I have obtained from my own invaluable sources. I have an effective network of contacts both sides of the Narrow Sea.'

I bowed my head in acknowledgement of my ingenuousness but Robert smiled and winked.

'The redoubtable marquise de la Baule, with whom we are both acquainted, now resides on her family's lands in Ponthieu, near Abbeville, not many leagues from Calais. She has installed herself in this secluded spot with her enchanting new companion. They cherish their privacy but are conveniently located for my agents to visit, in territory under the guardianship of my master, Duke Philip. She esteems him and is content to pass information to him from time to time.'

A tingle ran up my spine. Remembering how the marquise had been part of the chain passing messages between the English traitor, Sir Guy Binwood, and the French court, I was intrigued but unconvinced where that roguish lady's allegiance truly lay.

Chapter 28

I considered whether to visit Bruges before returning to Calais but decided it would be difficult to glean useful information there without exhaustive enquiries and I had urgent messages to deliver to Warwick. In fact, the Earl had already arrived back from Sandwich when we reached Calais, so I hastened to report what I had discovered and to pass on the warning about a planned attack by the French fleet. Nicky Chamberlayne accompanied me.

'I pray that in due time Norbert's death can be avenged: I owe him that,' the Earl said. 'They'll have got little information from him, I'm confident. He might have told them about the proposed meeting with Philip and the Dauphin, just to keep them happy, but there aren't any arrangements agreed yet which he could have divulged. Maybe his murderers thought he must know more and that's why they killed him.'

'You don't think they found out what he knew of the plans for an attack by the French fleet?'

'I suspect they wanted to know what I was plotting, rather than what Robert de Beaune had discovered, but they disposed of Norbert so he couldn't pass on any verbal messages any way. Maybe they hoped his body wouldn't be washed ashore. They can't have reckoned on my ingenious physician detecting the poor fellow had been tortured.'

'You believe they were followers of the French king?'

'Undoubtedly. Whether he was abducted before or after he met this friend in Bruges, we'll never know but it scarcely matters. It smacks of opportunism to me. Norbert had the misfortune to encounter one of King Charles's agents who took his chance to brutalise my servant in order to harass me.'

I was not comfortable with the coincidences this conjecture entailed but could think of no better explanation for the poor man's fate. 'Young Nicky has been a great help to me,' I said. 'He's a bright lad.'

Warwick grinned and punched the lad's shoulder. 'Good. I'm glad to hear it. He can keep his ears open for gossip around the town and report to you if he learns anything of interest.'

The Earl was occupied with plans for defence of the sea and was prepared to leave the sorry tale of Norbert's death more inconclusively than I liked. Nicky had other ideas, however, and in a few days he sought me out with an expression which managed to be both solemn and excited.

'The Earl and Robert de Beaune both assumed Norbert's body was thrown overboard from a French ship after he'd been killed. You thought so too, Doctor?'

'It seemed a reasonable assumption. What have you discovered?'

'French ships stand well offshore. They wouldn't come near Calais.'

I nodded, beginning to divine where he was leading.

'I've been chatting to a couple of old seamen down at the harbour – about tides and currents. If a body had been dumped out at sea, where a French ship should have been, it's most unlikely it'd be washed up on the marshes. That's more probable if the ship was inshore, just along the coast. The tide would have brought it in then.'

I stared at the intelligent young face. 'But no French ship would come that close in to the harbour at Calais.'

'Exactly. It must have been an English ship. There were several of them going in and out of harbour around that time.'

'And one of them might have been manned by supporters of Queen Margaret! They'd have been every bit as interested as King Charles to know what Warwick was discussing with Duke Philip and the Dauphin. If this is true, we don't want to alert them to our suspicions but can we find out any more about the English ships around Calais at the time?'

'The master of the harbour may have records but we can't just ask to see them.'

'Warwick could. He might well be interested in the movement of vessels in the vicinity of the harbour. He's charged with keeping the safety of the sea for English shipping.'

Nicky clasped his hands in delight. 'Leave it to me, Doctor. I'll ask the Earl to oblige.'

In consequence of these arrangements I spent an afternoon in Warwick's study poring over scrappy lists of ships entering and leaving the harbour over a number of days. The name of the sea-captain in each case was generally noted and sometimes other details, such as the port from which a vessel had come or whither it was bound. From the beginning I realised the exercise could prove futile as the ship in question might not have put into Calais at all but sailed elsewhere after depositing its human jettison in the sea. Then my eye caught a closely written entry and I had to still the pounding of my heart to read the words again.

The Silver Lady: Master and owner: John Porter, under lease to Father Ambrose. From Bruges. Onward to Weymouth.

It could have been a capricious quirk of fate but 'Father Ambrose' was one of the pseudonyms Andy Armstrong used. Moreover, I knew him to be an agent with half a dozen guises, working for Queen Margaret, and I was fully convinced he was capable of murder. It was horribly coincidental.

Weymouth seemed an unlikely destination for *The Silver Lady* but there was no proof it was accurate. It could have been fabricated because – I exclaimed aloud when I appreciated the fact – Weymouth would necessitate a ship sailing west along the Narrow Sea. More usual routes for English vessels took them directly to the Kentish ports but a ship following a westerly course might not track out to sea immediately. At first it might follow the French coast and no one in Calais would know if its master carried a safe conduct to make landfall in France. Was it possible Armstrong was now allied with the very agents he had sought to outwit when I first encountered him in Aquitaine? The answer was obvious. He was nomadic and evasive. He could easily have been in Ghent or Bruges. I also recalled that Armstrong was acquainted with Robert de Beaune who boasted of his contacts both sides of the Narrow Sea. I wished I had not identified so many unpalatable possibilities.

*****

The Earl's prospective meeting with Philip of Burgundy and the Dauphin did not take place, perhaps because of concerns about French intentions. Nevertheless it was clear the Duke wanted good relations with Warwick and in July he sent an embassy to the Captain of Calais, headed by his eldest son, Antoine, the splendidly entitled Grand Bastard of Burgundy. Philip was rumoured to have fathered a clutch of irregularly born offspring and they were recognised with honour and esteem, even granted their own livery. Warwick told me with satisfaction that his meeting with Antoine was cordial and promised well for friendship with Duke Philip. In the next few weeks, however, he had other preoccupations.

Since receiving the news about a planned attack, the Earl had his own agents monitoring movements by the French which might suggest the venture was imminent. In consequence, when he learned King Charles's fleet of more than sixty vessels was ready to put to sea from Honfleur, Warwick set out with the ships under his command to evade them. English naval power was not yet strong enough to withstand direct conflict with a powerful enemy and it was crucial no warships were lost until the number at the Earl's disposal had been increased. His tactic was strikingly successful in that the French failed to trace the English ships and soon abandoned the hunt.

Unfortunately there were wretched consequences for the English port of Sandwich, which was raided by the irate French commander thwarted of his seafaring prey. Booty and prisoners for ransom were carried away from the town and conveyed to France, stoking English indignation against the old enemy. Hostility towards Queen Margaret was also inflamed when rumours spread that she had personally instigated the attack by King Charles's men. Whether or not there was truth in this allegation, many in England were prepared to credit that she had no compunction in harming her husband's realm.

News of these events swirled round me as the months passed until I had been in Calais for a whole year. After the brief activity of my visit to Ghent I lived a quiet life, busy and satisfied with professional responsibilities. My domestic needs were amply catered for by the Earl's household, my daughter blossomed in the company of the other children and both Judith and her son seemed settled. Although I regretted abandoning my long-held goal to help poorer people in London, personal ambition had become meaningless to me. I was resigned to living out my days in quiet usefulness in this outpost of King Henry's kingdom.

There had recently been changes in the Countess of Warwick's domestic arrangements. The elderly senior nursemaid for the Earl's daughters was persuaded to take a less onerous role and Judith was selected to replace her. Judith would not accept the post until she had obtained my agreement but I was delighted for her. It was a great honour and Alys could continue in her care, together with Roger. The new disposition was very satisfactory and I thought of it as validating my decision to leave London for the sake of those dependent on me.

I had seen little of Rendell since the spring. He was at sea with Warwick's ships when they eluded the French and he subsequently took part in an escapade to engage with some Spanish vessels and capture their cargo. This triumphant freebooting was to provide the model Warwick developed the following year with considerable success: stopping, boarding and exacting tribute from foreign traders passing through the straits which England controlled. The Earl augmented his own substantial wealth and won support from his men who filled their purses. He also gained plaudits from English merchants whose livelihoods depended on secure trade across the Narrow Sea – and who relished the disruption of business suffered by their foreign competitors.

Rendell was in a remarkably good humour when I met him. Old irritations had been soothed by his adventures. He sported a few bruises from hand to hand encounters on Spanish decks but regarded them as of small account. I was pleased to find him cheerful and willing to share a jug of ale at a hostelry down by the harbour. Afterwards we walked to Fort Risban which protected the entrance to the harbour while he described alarming particulars of how to ram and shackle victim ships with grappling hooks. I admit I was only half-listening to this disquieting chronicle while I watched a party of women and children clustered on a small jetty not far ahead. Alys was there, and Roger, along with the Earl's eldest daughter and several of their playmates. I was relieved to note Judith was not one of the three nursemaids accompanying them.

We reached the landward end of the jetty as the nursery group turned back towards us and at least one of its members spotted me. Roger hurtled along the quay and grasped the sleeve of my gown. 'Look, Doctor, look over there: I found dead seagull.'

The rather pathetic remains of the creature lay on steps leading down to the sea. 'It is dead?' Roger queried, suddenly uncertain. 'You can't make it better?'

'I'm afraid it's quite dead, Ro-Ro.' I was glad my daughter's baby-name for Judith's son had become common parlance. 'No one could do anything for it.'

'You made Is'belle better.'

'Warwick's daughter?' Rendell was amused by this exchange and Roger looked up at him for the first time.

'What's the matter with your eye?'

'I can't see out of it any more. It was hurt by an arrow.'

Can you see with the other eye?'

'Yes but not so far round to the left.'

'Are you a soldier?'

'Yes – and a bit of a sailor now as well.'

'I like to be doctor best.'

Alys had toddled to join us, a few paces ahead of her companions. 'Papa, she squeaked, 'Ro-Ro naughty. He went down steps.'

'Alys, don't tell tales.' A father's admonition, which clashed with a boyish expression of indignation:

'I needed to look at seagull. To see if it was dead.'

The nursemaids had reached us and, after hugging the children, I bade Alys and Roger go with them on their return to the castle. Sergeant Tonks and I continued our walk to Fort Risban.

'He's a quaint little fellow,' Rendell said. 'Got a disciple, have you? Unhealthy ambition at that age, though: wanting to be a physician rather than a soldier.'

The paradox in what he said struck us both and we burst out laughing. I was profoundly relieved that he did not question me as to Roger's parentage.

*****

A week later Robert de Beaune arrived in Calais to see its Captain. I was cautious about making accusations which were based only on my conjecture but I advised the Earl to be chary of trusting him. I was startled by Warwick's peal of merriment and immediately felt it was I who was gullible.

'Oh, Harry, of course I'm guarded in dealings with our fine Burgundian friend. He's a diplomat and serves the most astute and glorious lord this side of the Narrow Sea.

365

He has his own objectives and we are merely players in the tale he wishes to tell. Nevertheless he's knowledgeable and when he chooses to impart information it's quite likely to be accurate. We must gain what we can from him and limit what we give away. Stay with me when I see him and judge for yourself.'

Robert de Beaune was genial as always. He had been travelling for some time and looked forward to returning to his own residence.

'Alas, it will only be my lodgings in Brussels,' he said with an exaggerated sigh. 'Duke Philip stays mostly in these northern territories nowadays. His presence is required there but I long to return to my native land, to his beautiful palace at Dijon and my own birthplace at Beaune with the magnificent hospice I told you of, Doctor Somers.'

'Where have you come from?' Warwick was not greatly interested in the ancestral Dukedom of Burgundy, a good week's journey to the south-east from Calais.'

'I crossed from England yesterday: a passable crossing with a kindly wind. I've come directly to see you because something I learned in Ludlow worried me deeply, given the esteem I have for your lordship.'

Neither the Earl nor I spoke but we must both have been surprised by the implication that news damaging to Warwick had emerged at Richard of York's headquarters.

'Your noble uncle was absent from his castle. I had business with underlings and I'm sorry to admit, Doctor Somers, that one was your old adversary, Baron Glasbury. I regret to say he is ill disposed to the Earl here as well as to his honoured physician. I imagine you are aware of this. What I learned, however was that the Baron is intent on direct interventions which would prove highly prejudicial.'

He paused for effect but again neither of us interrupted. 'The Baron has persuaded the Duke of York to make overtures to King Charles of France to see if he can break the alliance between that monarch and Queen Margaret.'

This unexpected announcement provoked Warwick's incredulity. 'That's ridiculous. There's no chance of success.'

'Indeed, my lord, and the Baron was certain you would object. Hence his secret plans to remove you.'

'Remove me? From Calais?'

Robert fixed his dark eyes on Warwick. 'From life, my lord.'

The Earl flushed but remained calm. 'My uncle of York would never countenance such a thing.'

'Which is why Baron Glasbury has set in motion his own arrangements. He has secured the services of a violent man, a known killer. You may have heard his name: Coote, Jasper Coote.'

'I am Coote's enemy,' I intervened, 'not the Earl.'

'The Earl has favoured you and stands in the way of Gilbert Iffley's pre-eminence among his uncle's supporters. That's reason enough for Coote's enmity towards his lordship.'

'Did you discover whether precise plans for my demise have been drawn up?'

'I think they have not, my lord, not yet. But I gathered you would be most at risk whenever you visit England's shores.'

'That figures: for I can throw a ring of steel around Calais to prevent Coote gaining access. I have no immediate plans to cross to England.'

'You would not ignore a summons to the Great Council?'

'When one comes, I'll go well defended. I'm grateful for your concern in giving me this news.'

The meeting was not prolonged. Warwick maintained his affability but Robert had no further findings to disclose to him. When the Burgundian excused himself I left the room with him, thinking the Earl might wish for a little solitude in which to ponder the prospect of an attack on his life from those he had regarded as allies.

After we entered the antechamber, Robert gripped my arm and spoke into my ear.

'Before I crossed the Narrow Sea to England I was in Abbeville, visiting the incomparable marquise de la Baule. She had another visitor. Both she and he send you their greetings.'

Surely this could not have been Jasper Coote, I thought in confusion.

'A gentleman we both know, with many talents and many appellations. He told me, when speaking to you, to refer to him as Andy.'

I gasped. 'Andy Armstrong was visiting the marquise?

Robert gave a thin laugh. 'A question of strange bedfellows, you think? There's truth in that. But allegiances change and agents can find advantage as well as piquancy in tangling with each other.'

My mind was whirring. Could Armstrong have been bound for Abbeville once before when he sailed into Calais and deposited Norbert's body in the sea? Robert's tone implied he had no inner knowledge of Armstrong's doings but was this contrived? My preoccupation almost led me to miss Robert's next whispered statement.

'The marquise asked me to pass on a message to you.'

I expected some further expression of her needless gratitude to me for helping her in Aquitaine but it was not that. What Robert de Beaune told me caused my heart to miss a beat and a shiver to pass through my whole body. I did not ask him to repeat it and he continued seamlessly to speak of another matter.

'The marquise extends an invitation to you to visit her home. Abbeville is no more than thirty miles from Calais. You will always be welcome there.'

I nodded casual thanks but was resolved to ignore the offer. All my concentration would be required to thrust the other information Robert had given me to the very back of my mind. It was provocative, tormenting and utterly irrelevant.

*****

After this uncomfortable visit, life in Calais continued serenely through the winter months. As ever I was busy at that season with a succession of minor ailments and the deterioration of patients in poor health with the coming of dank coldness. The Earl was occupied with plans for use of his augmented fleet when better weather came and did not call on my medical services. In my occasional hours of leisure, while Alys was entertained in the nursery, I was pleased to spend time with Rendell, billeted once more in the town until the warships were able to put to sea.

'I'm seeing a girl from the town,' he said one day, peeping at me slyly with his one good eye. 'Might get somewhere. Maybe I'll settle down with her. Let bygones be bygones.'

'Don't rush into anything.'

'I'm hardly likely to but you're not the best man to give guidance about the hazards of matrimony, are you?'

'Touché.'

Rendell was grinning and, although his barb struck home I knew it was loosed in jest.

We were walking in the smaller courtyard of the castle below the outer walls. Nearby stone steps led from the ground all the way up to the wall-walk used by the sentries. There was no one else about but I could hear children's voices faintly. A different sound caught my attention and I looked up as did Rendell and, when we identified the location and the source, we exchanged glances. Many years before, to my horror and alarm, an eleven year-old boy, for whom I was responsible, had clambered perilously along a ledge at the top of a tower in Padua to rescue a trapped kitten.

'No,' I said lightly, watching him evaluate the situation. 'Not this time.'

Then I noticed movement on the wall above this baby feline, which was similarly stranded on jutting stonework, and I exclaimed in terror. 'Oh, Holy Mother, no!'

A small head had appeared as a small body heaved itself onto the coping which topped the wall beside the sentries' walkway. There could be no repetition of a heroic rescue, however. This was no sure-footed eleven year-old but an infant who had not yet reached his fifth birthday and he was balanced precariously above a sheer drop to the ground, thirty feet below. My eyes closed momentarily as I felt myself sway, close to blacking out at the appalling prospect confronting us, but Rendell's voice dragged me to my senses. He was already halfway up the flight of steps.

'Sit down, Ro-Ro, and stay absolutely still. Speak quietly to the cat so as not to frighten it. Don't try to reach for it. It's too far. I'm coming to help.'

Heart-in-mouth again, as in Padua, I saw the child sink to his knees, leaning his head forward while he murmured reassuringly to the kitten. Thank God for his obedience. Then it was time to worry for Rendell's safety. He had almost reached the level of the animal and needed to step sideways from the steps to put his weight on a slightly projecting block of stone. From there he must balance and stretch upwards to retrieve the cat before trying to regain the staircase with a squirming bundle in his arms. I could not look at him.

Other heads had appeared above the wall and a mother's arm was now securely holding the boy crouched on the wall. I heard her calmly instruct the owners of small bobbing heads to stay still and hold their breath in order not to distract the would-be rescuer. Thank God for Judith.

Plaintive mewing drew my attention back to Rendell. He had plucked the kitten from its perch but did not attempt to return to the steps with it. Instead, gripping

370

the stonework with one hand, he stretched upwards with the other to deposit the creature in the cupped hands of a sentry who had come to straddle the wall and lean down. I had started to climb the stairs and put out an arm to steady Rendell as he took the last hazardous stride, on his blind side, back onto the step beside me. We continued together to the top, neither of us speaking.

A bevy of excited children and trembling nursemaids greeted us. Rendell lifted a small boy who clutched a quivering kitten into his arms. 'Well done Ro-Ro. You saved the day. You're a hero.'

'But I couldn't reach her.'

'You did exactly what was needed. You calmed the cat and that helped me do my bit.'

'You're hero, soldier funny-eye. I like you.'

Rendell ruffled the boy's hair before turning to Judith, showing no emotion. 'He's your son? This is Roger of Ra...'

'Roger is my son,' she said cutting across him, 'and I thank you for preventing him doing something foolhardy – as well as for saving the kitten. You put yourself in danger, took a risk. We'd brought the children to look out over the sea. It's the first clear day for weeks. The silly cat must have followed us and tried to run along the top of the wall. It fell.' She was speaking quickly and I sensed her discomfort. There was no banter; she was completely sincere. 'Excuse me: we must take these excitable children down to the nursery. Again, a mother's thanks to you.'

Rendell had flushed. He drew breath but did not say a word.

Chapter 29

A week later Warwick received a royal command to present himself in London for a meeting of the Great Council. King Henry appeared to be experiencing one of his occasional surges of energy. In a spurt of optimism he declared his intention to resolve all disputes and bring about permanent peace between his quarrelsome nobles. Safe conducts were issued to York and his principal supporters. There could be no question of the Earl disobeying such a summons.

Warwick described the position to me in a private conversation. 'I shall take six hundred armed retainers from Calais with me,' he said. 'I shall not ignore Robert de Beaune's warning although it would be a reckless deed for anyone to attack me when I'm in London under the King's protection.'

'The late Duke of Suffolk carried the King's safe conduct when his head was hacked off by English sailors.'

''You know how to reassure a man,' the Earl laughed. 'I'll take young Nicky with me as my page. It'll be a chance for him to see his father. Sir Nicholas will certainly be present. I gather he's been making most of the arrangements.'

Once again I was impressed by Sir Nicholas's ability to maintain good relations with both factions at the court.

'I think it may be best that you remain in Calais, Harry.'

Warwick sounded almost apologetic and I hastened to assure him I had no wish whatsoever to visit England while Jasper Coote regarded my life as forfeit to him. It was not my nature to court unnecessary danger, more especially since I had responsibility for Alys's care.

Rendell was inevitably selected to accompany the Earl and he was jubilant to do so after the inactivity of the winter months. He hoped to visit Thomas and Bess while he was in the City and promised to convey my good wishes to them. I wondered whether he would tell them of the Countess's second seamstress, with whom I had noticed him conversing several times since his exploit in rescuing the kitten. I wished it was a different courtship he could announce, but it was not for me to plan other people's lives.

I lifted Alys onto my shoulders down by the harbour as we watched the Earl's company embark to cross the Narrow Sea. The troops were a formidable sight, all bearing arms and smartly clad in their red jackets emblazoned with the ragged staff which proclaimed their allegiance.

'Rendy, Rendy!' Alys shouted, pointing at a familiar stocky figure. 'Rendy come back?'

'I'm sure he will. He's happy here. People like him.'

'Ro-Ro says he's brave but Dudith cries after she sees him. I seed her.'

I did not correct her grammar. For a moment I wished my daughter was not so observant and empathetic with the sorrows of others. These traits were wholly admirable but they might bring her unhappiness as she grew older. I hugged her.

*****

An outbreak of swine-pox in the town spread to the castle nursery and engaged my attention while the Earl and many of the garrison were away. Few of the affected children ailed badly but they were grizzly, itching and irritated. The nursemaids were weary from admonishing them and binding their hands to prevent the picking of pocks. Fortunately all in the castle recovered but a weakly infant in the fishermen's quarters succumbed.

I sat alone after supper most evenings and found myself thinking back over much that had happened to me. By now I could reflect on my relationship with Ursula without acute distress although I would always be puzzled by her enigmatic character. It would soon be two years since we were parted. I remembered Kate with sadness and deep affection, recalling the happiness we shared and the misery her troubled mind brought us both. Sometimes the memories I indulged were from longer ago but those I cast aside. They belonged to a different life of what might have been which was too painful to contemplate.

Warwick and his entourage returned to Calais after an absence of six or seven weeks. I was relieved to glimpse the Earl looking fit and unharmed and, being curious to hear what had happened in London, I was delighted that he summoned me to see him soon after his arrival. He received me unattended and there was no sign of Nicky.

'A farce, Harry, a farce, that's what it was. Excruciating! A "Love Day", King Henry called it. The day before this ludicrous event we'd come to some sort of hatched-together agreement – the payment of reparations to women made widows at St. Albans, the nominal settlement of claims and so on. Then in celebration the King had us all process through the streets of the City to St. Paul's where we marched down the cathedral aisle, two by two – holding hands. King Henry led the way, wearing his crown and the robes of state; then Queen Margaret came side by side with my uncle of York, each of them smiling viciously and exuding venom. My father followed, clasping the palm of young Henry, the new Duke of Somerset, whose Papa we killed at St. Albans. I was privileged to parade alongside that heap of dung, my cousin of Exeter whose gizzard I'd be glad to slit. Trailing behind us there were dozens of ill-assorted pairs pretending to look friendly under beetled brows. Why, if you'd been there, Harry, you could have accompanied Baron Glasbury.'

'I'm glad I wasn't. Did you encounter any violence?'

'As I suspected, it wasn't a good occasion to show hostility. The King was surprisingly lucid and enjoying his brief period of dominance. Antagonisms were suppressed but they'll be all the stronger when they burst out again. There was just one episode which made me think Robert de Beaune may not have been fantasizing about a threat that didn't exist.'

The Earl poured wine for us both but he did not touch his and after a pause he continued. 'I was lodged with my father's company at The Harbour in the City and when I first arrived the atmosphere in the streets outside was tense. Every noble who had come, whether supporting York or the Queen, was attended by hundreds of armed retainers and there was a real risk of violence. I ordered my men not to look for trouble and kept mainly to the house when not at court. But one night an interloper was disturbed in the garden below the window of my room. He carried a rope and was armed. When the alarm was raised he managed to get away over the wall but your excellent friend, Sergeant Tonks, claimed that he recognised the fellow from your time in Aquitaine. He swore it was Jasper Coote.'

'That's monstrous!'

'No harm was done and it was useless to make an allegation. We couldn't prove it was Coote. We doubled the guard and there was no recurrence but it gave food for thought. After the "Love Day", everyone kept up the pretence of amity but the joyful veneer was dented by an unexpected death – a natural death. Someone you knew quite well, I'm afraid.' He paused and sipped his wine while I racked my brain to think who it could be.

'At the "Love Day", the King was moved to elevate Sir Nicholas into the peerage as Baron Chamberlayne, in recognition of his services in organising the occasion and loyally working for the Crown over many years. The move was popular and there was genuine rejoicing. Sadly, though, three days later, Baron Nicholas suffered a severe apoplexy while at dinner and died at the King's table.'

I jumped to my feet. 'Oh, I'm sorry to hear that. Sir Nicholas was a good friend. I owe him much.'

'I thought so. The King grieved for him and quickly conferred the title on his son and heir. Nicky has remained in England to enter into his new dignity and I have lost my excellent page.'

The Earl continued to talk but I found it hard to concentrate on his words. I was mourning my friend and also thinking of Maud, now widowed for the second time. She had battled through much adversity, some of which she brought on herself, but her life had not been easy. Her happy marriage to Sir Nicholas, which gratified them both, had been all too short and it ended with cruel abruptness.

A few days later I caught up with Rendell who had other news to impart but sounded glum. While in London he had visited Thomas and Bess who were thriving, as were all the Chope and Willoughby offspring, and they sent me greetings. They were awaiting the birth of their first child together and were delighted at the prospect. I detected that Rendell found their harmonious household cloying and assumed his moroseness was due to this. I asked him about the incident in the garden of Warwick's lodgings.

'Yeah,' he said, brightening. 'I heard the guard shout and dashed from the house with two others. We'd drawn our swords. It was the sight of us that made the rogue turn tail. He must have thought there was only one man on duty. His hood shrouded his face but I heard him exclaim. It was Coote without a doubt, though I'm not sure the Earl believed me.'

'A foolhardy escapade, surely? Coote must have known Warwick would be well defended.'

'I reckon he wasn't planning to break in that night. He had a ladder at the wall and was checking the place out. Maybe he wanted to hide the rope somewhere to use another time, when he came back with a gang of cronies.'

'Which you foiled. Warwick was complimentary about that.'

'Was he? That's good but I'll be glad when we put to sea again. I could do with some action.' His tone reverted to gloominess.

I made an attempt to lighten his mood. 'I thought you might be glad to have time in Calais to renew your courtship of the seamstress maiden.'

Rendell scowled. 'Yeah, well, she's all right. I'm seeing her despite what bloody Bess said.'

Oh dear, I reflected. If Bess had chosen to counsel Rendell, I could imagine the gist of her advice. Bess, I remembered, had a high regard for Judith. I would probe no further.

'What about you then?' Rendell said with truculence. 'You intending to pay court to the new widow? You've bedded Lady Maud Chamberlayne often enough over the years before Sir – Baron – Nicholas swept her away. Maybe for a third husband she'd be willing to make do with a piddling physician.'

'I assure you she wouldn't and I'm not looking for a wife. What an idea!'

I was as disconcerted as I sounded and did not want to prolong this discussion. Luckily Rendell had something else to say although it was not information I welcomed.

'Met two other old colleagues in the City. Didn't know what to make of them. Andy Armstrong and Johnny Tate look to be as thick as thieves. Maybe that's what they are. Certainly I reckoned they were up to no good.'

'I can believe that. Tell me.'

'I met them by a fluke, down by the river at the tavern we always went to with Thomas. Johnny's left his lord's village for good, thrown in his lot with Andy. He said he likes the variety and it pays well. They travel about and meet people.'

'Did they say they'd been to France?'

'Yeah but not just France: Flanders, Brabant, Hainault. They ain't been to Calais though, as they might not get a friendly reception. They're working for Queen Margaret.'

Allowing for a tactical lie, it all fitted. 'Did Armstrong say much?'

377

'He chatted, like an old mate: reminisced about Castillon. He didn't speak about what he's up to now but I didn't expect him to. Hush-hush jobs and no questions asked, I'd guess.'

'I'm sure you're right.'

Rendell leaned towards me, biting his lip. 'Who's the bloke I've seen Judith talking to twice since I got back?'

It must have cost him a good deal to blurt out that revealing enquiry. 'What was he like?'

'Tall, well-built, about forty, dark hair, dressed smartish, looks like some poncey house-servant.'

I tried not to smile at this detailed description. 'I imagine you're describing Wat Weedon, principal pantryman at the castle.'

'High and mighty, isn't she now? Is she going with him?'

'I shouldn't think so, whatever that means. I saw him partner her in a dance-round at the Easter Day festivities.'

'Christ! Is he married?'

'Widowed. His wife died a few months before we came here. He has a grown-up son who helps the cellarer.'

'Why didn't you tell me?'

'I didn't know there was anything to tell. Or that you'd be interested.'

'I'm not.'

And Rendell turned on his heel and strode off with an attempt at jauntiness.

*****

I rarely received correspondence while in Calais and I eyed the two small packets which the messenger had brought with mistrust, sensing they boded ill. Eventually I opened one and found my deepest misgivings confirmed. It was brief and bore no signature but I never doubted Baron Glasbury was taunting me.

It might interest you to know, dear Doctor Somers, that your erstwhile whore, Ursula Bateby, is now become a widow in earnest. The wretched, cuckolded Gregory, died in the early spring at Ludlow. The woman may well be amenable, should you want her in your bed again. I bid you take your opportunity.

I swallowed bile in revulsion. Was Ursula party to this outrageous suggestion? Did they seriously think I might walk into a trap for the second time? Or was it simply a derisive gibe, a means to humiliate me? I thrust the letter aside and took up the second missive, thankful to think of something else. I read its message with a mixture of surprise and uneasiness.

Dear friend, Doctor Somers, I am perturbed not to have heard from you. I know Robert de Beaune passed on my message and, in accordance with my invitation, I hoped you would visit us. You have not done so and I fear this may be because once I told you falsehoods. When I misled you I was distraught with grief. I beg you to forgive me. Come soon. I long to renew our acquaintance and my sweet companion is agog to meet you. It will not be difficult. My family lands near Abbeville are but one day's ride from Calais. Bring your little daughter and her nurse. I should love to meet her. I will send my steward, René, so he can escort you on the journey. Do not disappoint me. Do not rebuff my humble request. Come soon. Bonne de la Baule.

I sighed. Unquestionably it would be ill-mannered to reject such a courteous plea and it was true the visit could be made without difficulty. I wondered whether the marquise's steward was the same René who had served her at the chateau near Cadillac. It was immaterial but intriguing. Finally I weakened, partly because I needed diversion from the other news, partly because of the invitation to bring Alys. It would be pleasant to spend two or three days with my daughter and take her to explore different territory for she had shown herself an intrepid little traveller. I knew Judith would be reluctant to seek

379

absence from her position or to leave Roger, while I recoiled from arriving with a second infant in my party. Everyone was content for me to take one of the younger nursery-maids to attend Alys. I consulted both Warwick and the Countess and then sent my reply to the marquise, full of obsequious apologies for my previous neglect. I arranged to visit Abbeville in a few weeks' time when the Earl and his men had put to sea again. Alys chafed at the waiting but was irrepressible with expectancy.

During those weeks I steadied myself to consider Ursula's changed circumstances dispassionately. In the course of our relationship I had come to love her with sincerity but that love had been shattered by her lies and deceit. Yet she was Alys's mother and I did not doubt she loved our daughter. If she was willing to renounce her duplicitous past, should I, for Alys's sake, seek to bring us together as a family, bound by lawful matrimony? I knew I could not do it. Although my intransigence made me feel guilty, I could not bear the thought of facing her again. I thanked Heaven Alys had adapted well to her changed life and persuaded myself that encountering Ursula might cause her unnecessary distress.

René was indeed the steward I met when I visited the chateau overlooking the Garonne after the marquise had left Aquitaine. He was rigorously correct and respectful in addressing me but seemed comfortable with his errand. Yet he declined to answer my questions about the household in which we were to stay three days. I concluded he was under orders to let me make my own discoveries. In fact Alys was so excited I needed to concentrate on keeping her still on the saddle in front of me, on the hack I had borrowed from the Earl's stables, until René offered to take her onto his more powerful horse. Within moments they were galloping ahead, my daughter squealing with glee, while I strove to quieten my panic at watching them.

I was surprised to see that the enclosed grounds of the marquise's home were strongly defended with armed guards manning the gatehouse and patrolling the walls. The manor-house itself was not so grand as the chateau near Cadillac but it was approached along an avenue of trees which gave it an air of importance. It was positioned in the middle of the demesne and had a distant view of the sea. Inside it was furnished resplendently with tapestries on the walls and fine tiling on the floor of the vestibule. A bevy of servants were on hand to receive us and Alys's eyes grew round with fascination.

The marquise de la Baule looked no older than when I had seen her previously. She exuded graciousness as she made us welcome, cossetting Alys who was immediately charmed. After we had refreshed ourselves and I changed into my best jerkin, dispensing with my physician's robe, I left my daughter playing happily with the affable nursemaid and went to re-join my hostess. As I expected, I was shortly to be introduced to the companion who had succeeded Mathilde de Crézé in the marquise's affections. She could not have been less like her predecessor.

I was struck by the young woman's beauty when she entered the room. It was undoubtedly enhanced by the services of a skilful dressmaker and coiffeuse but her delicate features had been bestowed by nature – or, as some would put it – Heaven. I wondered why the thought occurred to me that such beauty could prove a mixed blessing and was puzzled that something about her seemed familiar. I noted with surprise that she was in the middle phase of pregnancy.

'This is my beloved Araminta,' the marquise said, leading her forward. 'She tells me you have encountered her before.'

'In Bordeaux, Doctor Somers. You were kind.'

The light voice had acquired a more cultivated accent but it was recognisable.

'Minette!' I battled with my amazement as I bowed. 'I'm delighted to see you well.'

'They called me that at home but my name is Araminta. It was my mother's choice. You did not expect to find me here. Probably you thought me dead. You wouldn't have known my uncle placed me under the marquise's protection after that distressing incident in Bordeaux. I left Aquitaine with her household. Five years ago, that was. She has given me everything.'

'Forgive me. I'm astonished. I had no idea. Your uncle...Andy Armstrong?'

'He has been always good to me. He was my father's good friend.'

'He never told me you were safe. Indeed he let me search for you at the farm after...after Madame Coustances was killed.'

'He could hardly tell you he had dealings with an agent of the French king in the weeks before the battle of Castillon!' The marquise was laughing. 'We'd have had no objection if he informed you subsequently but he is instinctively secretive. I expect he assumed you'd forgotten Araminta existed.'

This invited gallantry and clumsily I obliged. 'No one could forget Mademoiselle Coustances.'

The marquise fixed her gaze on me. 'I heard long ago you were matchless for courtesy.'

I felt myself flush, reluctant to follow where that opening might lead, glad that the marquise reverted to the subject of her companion. 'When Araminta joined my household I could tell she had been running wild but I could also discern her potential to blossom as a cultivated attendant. I took my role as her patron seriously. It was not until some two years later, when the pain of losing Mathilde had eased, that I came to appreciate how the captivating young lady I was nurturing meant far more to me than a mere attendant. It is an unimaginable blessing that she returns my affection.'

Araminta looked down demurely. 'Doctor Somers saw something of the life I led: the men who mistreated me and gave me paltry baubles. The marquise took me from purgatory and brought me to paradise.'

This display of emotion embarrassed me so I snatched at a straw to change the subject. 'Have you remained in contact with your uncle?'

The marquise answered for Minette. 'Indeed. He visits us from time to time when he's in Flanders or France. He comes by land or sea: he is so talented, possessed of such versatility. We are indebted to him for protecting us against the danger we face. You may have noticed the manor is well defended against attack.'

'Who would attack you? Surely not the English?'

'Not England's king, but there are rogue elements among his subjects. You may remember the officer who murdered Mathilde and brought me immeasurable grief.'

'Jasper Coote?' It seemed beyond belief.

'He blames me for much that happened in the past and has traced where we live. He is intent on revenge. He came in person before we knew of the danger but most fortunately Master Armstrong was with us at the time and drove the intruder away. He has not returned but hired villains are plentiful, for him to employ, so we put in place our defences to thwart them. Coote hates you too, Doctor Somers. Is that why you have come to Calais?'

'It's one of several reasons.'

Her voice deepened. 'We heard from Master Armstrong of the gross trickery practised on you. We were appalled. But you love your daughter and care for her. That is admirable. You are fortunate to have her. We too are to be blessed, if all goes well and God wills it, as you may have observed. We never imagined such a thing but we are exultant and shall love our child devotedly.'

I nodded and smiled, not wishing to be prurient but all the time wondering ignobly who the father might be. It occurred to me that René might have obliged in fulfilling an unorthodox but perhaps not disagreeable duty. Did they invite him to do so?

The marquise fluttered her hands but otherwise maintained her equable manner. 'We had not envisaged the possibility but when fate intervened we rejoiced. Indeed we are greatly honoured. When Duke Philip was at his castle of Hesdin some six months ago he graciously bade us attend him. It is no distance from here.'

The implication was clear and needed no elaboration. Duke Philip might be around sixty years of age but he was reputed still to be an attractive man and of his potency there was no doubt. For her part, the beautiful Araminta Coustances was undeniably devoted to the marquise but advantageous exceptions could be made.

*****

After this initial conversation, the ladies avoided delicate topics and proved considerate hostesses. I was relieved that they obviously knew nothing of Gregory Bateby's death. They made much of Alys. The marquise played childish games with her, concentrating fiercely as she balanced wooden blocks on each other and tossed balls at a target. It was a pleasant period of relaxation for me and I was sorry when it was time to take to the saddle for our return journey. Only as we prepared to leave did Bonne de la Baule corner me when I was alone and address the matter I most feared.

'Robert de Beaune informed you of my friend's altered circumstances. I do not think you have profited from the situation.'

'I don't think it appropriate to try to recapture the past. So much will have changed.'

'Are you sure? Or is it only yourself you are speaking of? Shouldn't you investigate? I understood investigation was your pastime.'

'Not in anything so personal. Perhaps I'm a coward. I don't want to shatter the memory I carry in my heart.'

'Hmm. You are honest at any rate. It's unusual for a man to be so sentimental. I suggest you reconsider your self-imposed prohibition. I have learned not to despair even when all joy seems lost. I shall pray for you.'

'That's gracious of you. Like any man I'm burdened with guilt for so much in my life. I'm in need of all your prayers.'

'Yet you may hope to be touched by the seraph's coal on your lips. Remember that.'

I vaguely recollected lying injured, after Jasper Coote had tried to kill me outside Saint Edmundsbury, when Father Wilfred had spoken of the seraph's coal. It promised the purging of sin, I thought, but any deeper significance was lost on me. It seemed improbable that the marquise de la Baule would be acquainted with this abstruse symbol of forgiveness.

Chapter 30

Calais was abuzz with news when we returned to the town. On the last Sunday in May, on the Feast of the Blessed Trinity, Warwick's fleet had engaged in a ferocious battle with more than two dozen Spanish ships which sported great forecastles towering above the smaller English vessels. Despite this disadvantage, men from Calais succeeded in boarding several of the galleons and fighting persisted for six hours until the Spaniards were allowed to draw off, damaged and plundered. More than two hundred of their men were killed. Warwick's losses were said to be far less but he was still prowling the Narrow Sea, set to intercept ships of the Hanseatic traders bringing salt from the Bay of Biscay. There was little definite information about those from the Calais garrison who were not aboard the handful of craft which had returned to port for repairs.

Rendell was one of those unaccounted for although the vessel on which he served came limping into harbour with a broken mast. He could still be with the rampaging fleet aboard another ship but he might have been lost in the fighting. I questioned every mariner and soldier I encountered but could not establish with certainty what had happened to him until a master at arms who knew him told me Rendell had been injured. There were no details. Judith abandoned all pretence of disinterest and made her own enquiries, not trusting me to tell her the unvarnished truth. She was pale and drawn with worry. I wished she could be spared this extra pain but I too was troubled for my friend who had played so significant a part in my life's story.

I was in no mood to indulge in witty repartee with Robert de Beaune, who arrived in Calais without prior notice declaring he would remain there until Warwick landed. He was full of admiration for the Earl's buccaneering exploits and, when I could not continue to avoid his company without gross discourtesy, he told me how Duke Philip of Burgundy was following Warwick's fortunes with fascination.

'The Duke is a connoisseur of quality in any sphere. He gathers artists, craftsmen, philosophers and men of action about him, as I told you once before. So Warwick's success at sea delights him. But it is not just Earl Richard who has caught his attention. You, Doctor Somers, have captured his imagination. He would like to meet you.'

'How can he possibly know anything of me?'

'Why, I have told him, of course. But your reputation has also reached him from other sources. You are credited with achieving your King Henry's recovery from a most grievous malady. Sickness of the mind is a fearsome prospect and few are known to recover. A physician who has brought relief to one afflicted with incapacity of the mind is to be revered. Duke Philip will remain in Brussels for much of the summer and he expresses the hope that you will visit him there. I strongly recommend you to oblige the Duke – for your own advancement and enjoyment. His court is the nonpareil of civilisation – although it is at its most superb when in Dijon.'

I was flabbergasted and found it difficult to reply coherently. 'I've only recently returned to Calais. It's difficult to leave here again. I'm honoured. I'm amazed. I will consider...consult the Earl when he returns. Forgive me: I'm so taken by surprise.'

Robert spread his hands on his knees and beamed at me. 'You are too modest, Doctor Somers. You do not appreciate your worth. I am glad you have paid your long overdue visit to Abbeville but I counsel you not to neglect Duke Philip in the cavalier way you ignored the marquise de la Baule for so long.'

I had not mentioned visiting the marquise but accepted it as inevitable that Robert would already know I had done so. Whether he was working with her or spying on her I could not guess. I resolved that, if he was to learn the details of my conversations with that lady and her companion, it would not be from me. A needless resolution, I recognised: he had doubtless obtained a verbatim report of everything we said.

*****

The triumphant English fleet entered the harbour with pennants streaming and drums beating, to be greeted by half the population of the town lining the quayside. When Warwick disembarked at the head of his officers the cheers echoed from the walls of the castle with such force that I wondered whether they might be heard on the other side of the Narrow Sea. This was a fanciful idea but there was no question that Warwick's personal renown would be boosted on England's shores. He championed England's trade and burnished England's reputation. Conversely, the prospects of any man aspiring to rival him as York's foremost supporter would be seriously jeopardised by the success of this new warrior-hero. Gilbert Iffley would not be pleased.

As soon as the Earl's party came ashore I started to enquire for Rendell and was directed to a small ship moored separately from the others. This was where the more severely wounded had been placed in the care of an elderly surgeon and his assistant. I watched with increasing anxiety as a procession of grievously injured men were helped or carried onto land. Many were near death. Then I gave an audible gasp of relief as I saw him, white-faced and leaning on another man's shoulder, hobbling badly but otherwise apparently whole. I hurried forward, declaring I would take charge of his treatment, but soon realised he needed support on both sides to get up the incline to the castle.

He was clearly in pain and needed all his limited strength to keep moving. There could be no conversation until he had rested so I installed him on a pallet in the small anteroom where I could accommodate two or three patients requiring regular attention. Later I returned to examine him and was glad to see a little colour in his cheeks.

'You've been injured in more than one place, I can see. Tell me.'

'Some bastard managed to stab me below the shoulder-blade on the first ship we rammed: blind-sided me, sod him. It bled a lot but I kept fighting and the old leech patched it up a bit. It was still pretty sore and kept opening up again. I reckon it should have been sewn but they were too busy for that.'

I inspected the jagged gash which was oozing colourless liquid. 'You're right. It needs sewing. Luckily it's not fetid. It won't be as good as if it had been stitched at once but I'll do it when I've finished examining you. What happened to your leg?'

Rendell grimaced. 'The mast came down when the Spaniards tried a counter-attack. Me mates quickly drove them off but I was lying on the deck by then. A spar off the mast crashed onto me leg. Something broke. I heard the crack. I weren't no good to fight after that. The surgeon's dogsbody said he was a bonesetter. He tried to fix a splint but it don't feel right.'

I removed the binding and strip of wood which had been inexpertly strapped above the ankle and, as gently as I could, felt along the bone. Rendell read my face.

'Not good, is it?'

'I'm afraid not. Your leg's broken in more than one place. I can do a better job of splinting it than the other fellow and you'll get about again on your own two feet in a few months' time, maybe with a stick, but...'

'But I won't never be able to fight again! A one-eyed soldier with a smashed up leg ain't no bloody use to anyone.'

'It's harsh but it's best you know. You'll have to rest while the leg mends and you must think things through. You will be limited so far as fighting's concerned but there'll be other possibilities. I'm sure Warwick will assist. You won't be bed-bound or helpless; just a bit lame.'

'Like you and Johnny Tate?'

I nodded. I did not say that the consequences of Rendell's injury were likely to be more disabling than my limp or Johnny's handicap. He had enough to come to terms with for the present. I gave him a potion to dull his senses and set to work on his leg and shoulder.

I reported to Judith honestly about Rendell's condition and she understood at once the misery he would experience. She also appreciated that if he was told she would like to visit him, he would forbid it. Accordingly, a few days later, she marched boldly to his bedside and would brook no refusal by him to talk to her. As their voices rose I crept away. Judith's intervention might as easily devastate Rendell as assist his recovery but this was not a situation in which a physician was bound to intervene. I was not an instrument of divine will and must accept my limitations.

*****

Warwick sent for me in due course after he had dealt with all the business awaiting his return from sea. I knew he had already seen Robert de Beaune so he would be aware of Duke Philip's invitation and that spared me the awkwardness of raising the subject myself. Sure enough he gave me a questioning grin as he pushed a glass of fine Burgundian wine in my direction.

'I may be in danger of losing my estimable physician, I'm told. The good Duke Philip has his eye on you.'

'He's heard some nonsense about me curing King Henry. He'd like me to visit him in Brussels. That's all.'

'We'll see. He'd be a fine patron. You should cultivate him.'

'I'm not anxious to be away from Calais...'

'Nonsense: you must certainly go to meet him. I'd be delighted. It's most convenient. You can convey my messages to him without the need of an intermediary. Who better, Harry? We'll get Robert de Beaune to arrange it during the summer.'

I mumbled thanks, unsure whether or not I really wished to go. Then the Earl gave me the opening I hoped for.

'I'm grateful to you for helping to treat the injured in our enterprise against the Spanish ships. We didn't suffer too badly but the surgeon was overburdened at the time. Your friend, Sergeant Tonks, was among the wounded, I understand. How is he?'

'Progressing quite well. He's strong bodied. But his soldiering days are over, I'm afraid. He'll have a pronounced limp. I wanted to ask you if you could find a post for him where he could feel useful.'

'I'd be pleased to. Poor fellow.' Warwick thought for a moment. 'Can he read?'

'Only a little. He'd never make a clerk and he'd hate to be trapped indoors all the time.'

'Leave it with me. I'll consult the marshal and his officers. What bad luck! An active chap, like that.'

Within a week, Warwick summoned me again. I was to travel to Brussels in the month of August and I was free to determine how long I stayed. Specially designated messengers would provide a link between Calais and Brussels while I was there. I was commissioned to give the Duke an undertaking confirming the Earl's goodwill towards him. Warwick had even consulted his wife and assured me the Countess would treat Alys as one of her own daughters while I was absent. No loophole had been left for my objections.

In fact I regarded myself as in Warwick's debt because he had been true to his word. Rendell was to be offered the post of deputy gatekeeper at the castle and asked to assist with the training of new recruits to the garrison. It was a generous response to my appeal and I said so in thanking the Earl.

'I value good faith in dealings between men, Harry,' he said. 'For me it's fundamental. You and Tonks have

391

both served with dedication in your different spheres and both deserve recognition. I trust Tonks will find satisfaction in his new duties and not dwell on his disabilities. As for you, I hope you'll return to Calais and act as my physician and adviser for many years to come but I don't delude myself that you'll remain in my household indefinitely. Remember you are free, Doctor Somers.'

I was puzzled by his words although I recognised they were well intended. I had no ambition to leave the service of a considerate lord, nor to quit territory held by England's King. Even so, I was attracted by the prospect of meeting Philip, Duke of Burgundy, Count of Flanders and the holder of half a dozen other auspicious titles. More immediately, I knew I would have to placate an angry little girl annoyed that she could not accompany me to Brussels. That enterprise put other obligations into a healthy perspective.

*****

I went to Brussels with the full accoutrements of an official embassy and was received in the splendid Coudenberg Palace with all the ceremony an embassy merited. Duke Philip gave me an effusive welcome in front of his court gathered in the huge state room he had added to the old building. From my first sight of him I was impressed by his elegance and athletic build. At sixty-two years of age he was upright and slim, strong in the arm, with a weather-beaten face and a high forehead. He wore a black velvet doublet and matching hat, with the Order of the Golden Fleece, which he had created, gleaming about his neck. His appearance indicated wealth, good taste, lack of excessive ostentation and supreme self-assurance. Despite the formality of the occasion I caught a twinkle in his eye.

In this public encounter I conveyed Warwick's messages and the Duke invited me to join the daily discussions between eminent visitors and members of his entourage. I readily accepted. These robust and witty exchanges reminded me of similar debates which my first patron, Humphrey of Gloucester, held in his palace at Greenwich when he encouraged writers, philosophers, artists and physicians to attend him. I felt instantly at home in these Burgundian gatherings and was gratified by the respect with which I was treated by men revered in their fields for knowledge and wisdom. Everything Robert de Beaune had told me about the splendour and erudition of Duke Philip's court was manifested to me.

It was several days before I was granted a private meeting with the Duke. By then I had learned of the unusual hours he kept, staying up each night until nearly dawn and then sleeping late into the morning. He had even received a dispensation to hear Mass in the afternoon to suit his habits. I was not surprised to be called to wait on him around midnight but hoped I would not appear unduly sleepy. I felt honoured when I saw he was accompanied only by his personal body-servant and quickly gave him Warwick's verbal messages of friendship.

'Thank you, Doctor Somers,' he said. 'I reciprocate the Earl's warm feelings and hope to arrange a meeting with him before too long. I shall ask you to carry letters to him on your return to Calais. Meanwhile I am delighted you are enhancing the quality of discourse among my distinguished guests at court. My reason for asking you to come this evening, however, is to draw on your professional expertise. Are you willing to advise me on medical matters?'

'Why, of course, your Grace. I'm honoured.' I hid my amazement. 'Have you particular symptoms which concern you?'

'To be frank, I'm not certain. I have talked to my own physicians but they are noncommittal. Two months ago I suffered a fever after a lively game of tennis and was laid low for a day and a half but I then recovered quickly. What troubles me more is an earlier incident which may denote some weakening of my mind. Hence my interest in consulting you, with your experience of strange ailments affecting one's mental state.'

I could not imagine anyone less like the fragile-minded English King but was immediately intrigued. 'If you are agreeable, your Grace, I should like to examine your physical condition before we discuss curiosities of the mind and spirit.'

Duke Philip smiled and beckoned his servant to unrobe him while I conducted an inspection of joints and ribcage, felt his pulse, listened to his breathing and peered into his mouth. 'You Grace,' I said at the conclusion of my impertinent activities, 'I find you to be in excellent physical health. Many a man twenty years younger would be proud to possess your fitness. I know no reason why the fever you suffered should recur but it may be wise to moderate your more forceful exertions a little. A small concession to advancing years may be judicious.'

'Admirable, Doctor Somers. I admire your perception. Instinct tells me you are right. And you never even sought to prepare a horoscope.'

'I learned at the University of Padua to place confidence in assessing a patient's whole person, rather than looking to the stars for answers on specific symptoms. How is it you are concerned about your mind?'

The servant helped the Duke to dress and was then dismissed while his master poured wine and gave me mine in a superb goblet of Venetian glass. He set down his own on the table.

'One night last winter I rode out alone into the Forest of Soignes. It was damp and foggy and I had no mantle. I became lost but found shelter in the cottage of a charcoal burner where I was given food. I broke the bread with my own hands, with no trencherman to serve me. I hardly knew what I was doing that night and it has disturbed me since then that my mind was absent from my body during this misadventure. I have consulted my physicians but they can offer no explanation other than the deterioration of age – which does not please me. I would be glad of your opinion.'

I sipped the exquisite Burgundian wine. 'Your Grace, forgive me for my intrusiveness but may I ask whether something had distressed you before you went riding? Did you perhaps dash from the castle in a tumult of emotions? Is it your habit to take midnight rides unaccompanied?' I nearly added "without a mantle" but bit my tongue.

The Duke's dark eyes opened wide. 'No one has asked me such questions. In fact I had been in a fury with the Count of Charolais, my son and lawful heir, who had grown fractious and refused to obey my wishes. He is twenty-five and I sometimes think he is impatient for my demise. God forgive me, he is not the heir I would have chosen. Do you consider this relevant to the aberration I endured that night?'

'Not merely relevant, your Grace: I fancy it explains a good deal. Your mind was burdened by an unpleasant experience and you were filled with conflicting emotions. That's enough to make any man distracted and resort to physical activity in an attempt to drive away the horror of what had happened. It does not signify a weakening of the mind. It's quite unlike other mental afflictions I've tried to treat. There's a logical reason for your distress. Is it perhaps that your Grace is quick to anger? If so: as with my advice on extreme physical activity, I humbly suggest you should try to control the extremity of your passions.'

I felt myself flush as I counselled the overlord of the most glorious court in Europe but Duke Philip beamed at me. 'You read your patient with accuracy. Those Paduan academics taught you well. You have removed a burden from my mind, Doctor Somers. I cannot promise to control my vehemence but I will remember your advice and try to heed it.'

The Duke proceeded to tell me more about the many lands he ruled and in particular his native Burgundy. I detected a note of regret because the pressing business of governing Flanders and Brabant, with their important commercial markets, detained him in his northern territories. His wealth depended on the tax base of these states but his heart lay in the city of Dijon where he was born.

'You have spoken to Robert de Beaune,' he said, 'and must know of the fine hospice founded in the town he comes from to care for the poor and sick. I hope you will venture there to view it one day.'

'It would be an honour to do so.' I murmured the courteous platitude without any serious thought that I would ever be in a position to venture there.

'Doctor Somers, I know you must shortly return to Calais and the Earl of Warwick's service but I ask you to bear in mind what I say now. I should be proud to have a man of your calibre and experience resident in my lands. If in the future you feel it appropriate to make a move from your present position, for whatever reason, I beg you will consider this. Robert de Beaune will make any necessary arrangements, should the occasion arise. I do not offer you a post as one of my personal physicians, although if you were at hand I would certainly consult you when necessary. I judge you would be happier and better employed in treating a miscellany of patients, not merely a collection of ageing nobility. Am I right?'

'Your Grace, you read this physician with accuracy and I'm overwhelmed by your offer.'

The Duke laughed as I echoed his words and he tossed back the rest of his wine. 'I must ask you to excuse me now as there are lawyers waiting to bend my ear in preparation for cases to be brought before me tomorrow: widows seeking confirmation of their rights, wardships to be determined and so on. We will meet again before you leave Brussels. I am sincerely gratified to have had this conversation.'

'As am I, your Grace,' I said with absolute honesty. 'I'm honoured and overjoyed by your kindness.'

*****

The following afternoon one of the Duke's attendants showed me round parts of the palace I had not previously seen, particularly the new wings which had been built when the state room was added. I was delighted to be shown the ducal library of fine manuscripts and I listened to the singers of the court chapel practising motets by Guillaume Dufay, whose delicate melodies were harmonised in the Italian fashion. I was entranced and after my tour I wandered back alone along a corridor towards the guest chamber where I was accommodated, my mind abuzz with music and artistry.

Ahead of me, the door to an anteroom was opened by a servant and a lady holding the hand of a little girl of seven or eight emerged. I stood back as they turned to pass me and then began to shake so violently I needed to steady myself against the wall. The lady's lips parted and she gripped her daughter's hand more tightly. In that moment of recognition it was as if all that had happened in the last eleven years had vanished into unreality. I bowed.

'Yol...Madame la comtesse, forgive me. I had no idea. I'm overcome. The surprise is so great.'

She was, as always, in control of her reactions but she was very pale. 'I have the advantage over you, Doctor Somers. I had heard you were here but did not expect to encounter the Earl of Warwick's emissary. We are staying in the town and leave for home tomorrow. I am in Brussels as a humble petitioner craving the Duke's favour to confirm my late husband's settlement providing for our future maintenance. This is my daughter, Guigone.'

I bowed again, trying to gather my shattered wits, and the child gave me a solemn curtsey. I remembered my duty. 'I was sorry to hear of the Count's death.'

'You too have suffered much sadness, I understand, since...since...I left England.' For the first time her voice trembled and a trace of colour came into her cheeks.

I inclined my head. 'But I too have a daughter, Alys, who is my treasure. She is not yet four.'

'I'm glad. Robert de Beaune has brought news but it is mainly through the marquise de la Baule that I have heard of your achievements and griefs. I surmise you have heard something of my fortunes from her. It was remarkable that you should meet her, one of my oldest friends.'

'I met her in Aquitaine where I accompanied the English army five years ago. At the time I didn't expect to keep contact with the marquise. She has been very gracious to me.'

The comtesse de Saint Etienne gave one of her rare but radiant smiles which I remembered so well and my breathing quickened. 'Bonne has been a great support to me although I have seldom seen her in recent years.'

'I didn't know you were living in Duke Philip's domains. The Count, your husband, held lands there?'

'Indeed: hence our need for the Duke's endorsement. We moved to my husband's small Burgundian estate when he retired from service at the French court. His main estate is now vested in the son of his first marriage but he provided that the land in Burgundy be held in trust for my use and for Guigone until she marries when it will pass to her husband. It is not so far from Dijon. I am grateful for his thoughtfulness but we need the Duke's consent as our overlord and ruler.'

I understood what she did not say. It freed her from dependence on her brother who had insisted on her making a suitable remarriage when her first husband died. It would be inappropriate to refer to this. I was struggling to pluck up courage to say something more personal when an attendant appeared through the anteroom door and addressed her.

'Madame la comtesse de Saint Etienne, the Duke invites you and your daughter to return to his presence chamber.'

'Of course.' She looked at me before lowering her eyes. 'It seems we are to learn our fate forthwith. Excuse me. I am pleased to have seen you, Doctor. Truly. God bless and keep you.'

I lingered in the corridor for a long time until I learned from a serving-man that the comtesse and her daughter had been shown out of another door after their reception by Duke Philip. Further enquiries elicited from the Duke's secretary that Yolande's petition had been granted and her occupation of the Burgundian estate was confirmed. I was happy for her but I regretted our encounter had been so transitory, our conversation so formal. I had been too startled to think what I should say. I longed to renew our meeting, to find her again, to hear the cadences of her voice and gaze at that beautiful smile.

Despite my efforts to find out how I might contact her, it was not until the following day that I obtained definite information about where she had been staying. By then she and Guigone had left Brussels in a party travelling to Dijon escorted, I noted with irrational disquiet, by Robert de Beaune. I had been unaware Robert was in the city and it seemed significant that he had not sought me out. It seemed significant also that Yolande was journeying under his protection. It was not my business, could never be my business, but my mind was whirling, my heart pounding, my innermost spirit in turmoil. I spent the remainder of the day walking alone in the palace gardens until I sank down on a secluded bench and sobbed. It was useless to think one could recapture what had been lost forever eleven years earlier, useless to indulge in fantasies. My course was set.

Next morning I departed from Duke Philip's magnificent palace, set out for the prosaic realities of Calais and left behind that fleeting, tantalising illusion of what was destined never to be.

Chapter 31

The tapestry doll from Brussels helped the errant father make his peace with a sulky small daughter but she exacted a promise from him that, if at all possible, he would take her with him when he made another expedition away from Calais. I had no expectation of being called on to honour that conditional commitment but I spent the next two months, while autumn darkened the sky and churned up the sea, feeling as restless as the weather. I was discontented, liable to be short-tempered, not knowing whether I wanted company or solitude, only wishing to forget what had occurred in Brussels, the memories of pain and ecstasy it evoked.

I was pleased with the progress Rendell was making, hobbling at impressive speed with the aid of a stick, but I found it difficult to maintain patience with him. He was understandably peeved because the Countess's second seamstress had decided she did not wish to be bound to a crippled husband and was looking elsewhere for a beau. Judith, by contrast, was attentive to him without seeking any recognition and he gave none. Sometimes I would overhear them arguing with droll incisiveness, as in earlier days, which heartened me, but then Rendell would regress into sullen discourtesy. I did not dare to counsel him, for fear it would provoke an adverse response, but it saddened me to think he might throw away what should be precious to him. I was so bitterly conscious of what I had lost, I hated to see him gratuitously scorn the admirable woman who was inexplicably devoted to him – and whom, I believed, he loved as he had loved no other.

In the middle of October messengers came from England to speak with the Earl and shortly after they had reported to him he called me to his study. His expression was solemn but not disgruntled. He held out the customary goblet of wine he offered at our discussions.

'I'm bidden to attend another meeting of the Great Council in Westminster. In three weeks' time. It's incumbent on me to attend. I'm summoned to account for my actions in attacking the Easterlings' salt fleet. The merchants of the Hanse have complained to King Henry but the City of London authorities will raise their voices loudly in my defence. I'm popular with those whose trade had benefitted from my peccadillos at sea.' He laughed and drank wine. 'Moreover, my uncle of York has sent a note hoping to meet me. I'd welcome the chance to converse with him, to make sure there're no differences between us, given the mischief some of his acolytes seem intent on fostering.'

'You'll go well defended, as in the spring?'

'Certainly: I'm not troubled by the summons. But there's more – in a separate missive I'm asked to ensure that you accompany me.'

'Me? I have no wish...'

'See here: the request comes from Queen Margaret who wishes to acknowledge publicly what you've done to strengthen the king's health. I suspect she feared you'd be unwilling to return across the Narrow Sea: hence the direction is given to me as a means of ensuring you comply. Don't worry. We'll only be there for a few days and you need only go to Westminster on the one occasion. We'll lodge in the City and you can stay there in obscurity while I'm at the Council. I can't compound my alleged misdemeanours by flouting the Queen's decree.'

'I see that, my Lord.' I sighed, recognising there was no escape. 'The Queen's favour cannot be snubbed but it's damned inconvenient.'

My most challenging task over the next few days was to persuade Alys that a royal command to present myself at Westminster had to rank as meriting exclusion from my promise to take her with me on my next journey. Whenever she saw me she became fractious and naughty, screaming her anger and throwing toys across the room.

Fortunately Judith calmly soothed her and counselled me not to distress myself.

'All little ones throw tantrums when they think themselves aggrieved. They know no other way to handle their annoyance. It'll pass.' She looked at me with a roguish grin. 'Grown men's sullenness is more aggravating. It needs calling out perhaps by assertive action.'

I did not register her meaning but when I saw her walking in the courtyard with Master Wat Weedon, principal pantryman, I concluded she had decided to wait no longer for Rendell to come to his senses and accept where his best hope for happiness lay. Next day I put to sea with Warwick, accompanied by the vessels conveying his vast entourage, regretting my young friend's foolish recalcitrance. I was confident that whatever decision Judith made it would be a wise one.

*****

Warwick's journey through Kent and his entry into the City of London had the character of a triumphal progress, so many turned out to cheer and shower him with flowers. There was ample evidence of his popularity. After this excitement, I regretted that we were lodged at Grey Friars, uncomfortably near Newgate and my old home. I resolved to stay within the precincts of the friary except when required to go to Westminster and in order to visit Thomas and Bess. The morning after our arrival when the Earl had left for the palace I sent a message to the Chopes asking if I could call on them the following day. Then I retired to sit quietly in the cloister until I was advised that a man was asking to see me at the gatehouse and had been shown into an anteroom. I was surprised but thought Thomas must have come at once in person to welcome me to the City so I hastened to greet him.

It was not Thomas. A slighter figure shrouded in a friar's robe sprang forward to hug me, his ginger hair peeping from beneath his hood. In the two years since I

402

last saw him he had not lost his taste for disguises. Instinctively I recoiled but Andy Armstrong was not abashed.

'Dear God, Doctor Somers, why have you come to London? What possessed you to leave Calais? You're running a foolhardy risk.'

Taken aback by his vehemence, I was also amused that he did not know I was to be honoured by the royal lady he served. 'Warwick was instructed to bring me to London at Queen Margaret's request. Apparently she wants to give me thanks in public for my physician's services to the King.'

Armstrong's face creased with alarm and horror. 'Did Warwick tell you that?'

'I saw the scribe's letter. It came with the summons for the Earl to attend the Great Council.'

'Christ! This is serious. I can tell you the Queen has no such intention. She valued your past services but the time for recognition has passed. Since you joined Warwick's service she views you as disloyal to the King. Are you saying this false invitation had been inserted with the summons for the Earl to attend the Council?'

'Yes. No. Wait. Warwick had a packet of correspondence delivered to him in Calais. There was a personal letter from Richard of York as well.'

'Ah! That explains it. I was afraid someone close to the Queen was up to mischief.'

'You imply someone in York's entourage must have inserted the letter purporting to come from the Queen? That's possible. Gilbert Iffley may be up to his tricks again. He'd relish my humiliation when I realised I'd come on a fool's errand.'

'It could be worse than that. They may have set a trap in order to kill you. Jasper Coote is in the City and in the past he's blabbed about cutting your throat.'

I shrugged. 'He always was a loud-mouth. I fancy he's after more significant prey than me.'

Armstrong eyed me and gnawed his lip. 'You don't trust me, Doctor Somers, do you? What is it that's made you suspicious of me? We helped each other in Aquitaine, didn't we?'

I decided to be honest. 'We've had different loyalties since then. You've been known to deceive me, to undermine me. You move in a dangerous murky world as a confidential agent. I look for a simpler life.'

'My allegiance is simple enough. I've always served King Henry and, more particularly, Queen Margaret.'

I was irked by his self-righteous tone. 'I serve Warwick now. You've sought to undermine him.'

'Part of the game.' The flippant reply increased my irritation.

'A game that includes murder? You warn me about Jasper Coote. You weren't so squeamish about cracking open Norbert's head last year when he wouldn't divulge what you wanted to know.'

'What the hell are you talking about?' Armstrong's eyes flashed with anger.

'Norbert was Warwick's servant. His body was dumped in the sea off Calais just at the time *The Silver Lady* put into the harbour. The ship you were using...'

'Dear God! I should have remembered what an assiduous investigator you are. But I'll swear on the Host I know nothing about this fellow's death and no body was pitched into the sea from *The Silver Lady*. I wasn't happy but the ship's master insisted we put into Calais to mend the rigging. We were bound for Abbeville and then for Weymouth.' He fixed me with a defiant glare. 'I was going to see Minette.'

I took a deep breath. 'Where had you come from?'

Armstrong's mouth fell open as he thought back. 'Christ! I'd been in Bruges and just as I embarked on *The Silver Lady,* another ship was setting sail. That bastard Coote was on the deck and when he caught sight of me he ducked into the cabin. Later he tried to force an entry into the marquise's house at Abbeville, not expecting me to be there and I drove him off. I thought he'd crossed the Narrow Sea to harm her but he might have had two birds to kill in his little expedition.'

Was it a clever ploy to switch attention away from himself to a known villain who might wish harm to Warwick? Maybe, but Armstrong would not be aware of Rendell's suspicion that Coote had intruded into the garden of Warwick's lodgings with malicious intent only six months previously. I decided to give him the benefit of the doubt.

'Coote is working with Gilbert Iffley and there's some evidence that they're trying to undermine Warwick's position with Richard of York.'

Armstong whistled. 'Now that is news worth having. So we've got a common enemy, you and me and Warwick! Bear that in mind. I'll never act against you, Doctor Somers, not after all you did for Marie and Minette in Aquitaine. I confess I did deceive you over the girl, pretending she might be at the farm outside Bordeaux when I knew she was safe with the marquise. But you'd have asked too many questions if I'd told you the truth.'

'True enough.' I laughed, beguiled by Armstrong's engaging attempt at frank disclosure. 'Are you serious in warning me about Jasper Coote?'

'Completely. I reckon you and the Earl are both in danger while you're here. Warwick's got a host of bodyguards but you need your own. Johnny's outside and he's to keep an eye on you until you leave. That's my order. Remember my advice: wherever you go, watch your surroundings and don't leave yourself without an escape route.'

I was still uncertain whether I could exonerate Armstrong wholly from my earlier suspicions but I readily clasped his hand. The more I ran through in my head what he had suggested, the more consistent with Coote's nature and Iffley's deviousness it appeared. Even so, I grossly underestimated what they were capable of devising.

It was good to see Johnny Tate once more. I trusted him as I would never fully trust Armstrong and he seemed pleased to be appointed my bodyguard while I was in London. He was worried that the friary might be under observation by potential enemies. While he loitered at the stalls selling apples across the road, he had noticed a succession of men similarly idling their time, with an eye on the friary gatehouse, one arriving as another left.

'Old trick to mask what they were up to,' he said. 'Of course, whether it was the Earl or you they were looking out for, I couldn't say.'

'I only intend to leave the friary twice before we return to Calais. In two days' time Warwick may want me to go to Westminster with him and he'll have a full guard all the way. My only private expedition will be to see my friends tomorrow, in their house near the Tower. At least I hope to see them. I haven't heard back yet that it's convenient. I'd welcome your company for that visit. It'll give me confidence crossing the City having a man at arms beside me – just in case the danger's real.'

'Best to ride,' Johnny said with an air of authority. 'More difficult to attack riders in the crowded streets. I'll arrange horses and report back later.'

I watched him set off on his task, smiling at his punctilious manner. He was clearly enjoying his role as Armstrong's assistant.

An hour or so after he had gone I was summoned back to the gatehouse and expected to find a messenger from Thomas but it was a more notable and wholly unanticipated visitor who greeted me. I gasped with surprise.

'Lord Fitzvaughan, an unexpected pleasure. I'm honoured.' I bowed and escorted Gaston de la Tour into the antechamber. 'Are you in the City on business?'

'Disagreeable business but I'm glad of the opportunity to meet you, Doctor Somers. It's fortuitous.

406

I've been to Harrow on the Hill to see my wife's mother. You may have heard of her husband's untimely death?'

'I was very sorry. Sir Nicholas – Baron Chamberlayne – was a valued friend.'

'Indeed: a talented and congenial companion. His death leaves Lady Maud a widow for the second time and Eleanor has suggested her mother might move back into the dower-house at Hartham. I'm not enthusiastic. When she lived alongside us before, the atmosphere was not cordial.'

I tried not to grin, appreciating Gaston's discomfort at the prospect of Maud's return to his estate. 'Won't her stepson, the new Baron Chamberlayne, offer her a home?' I made a mental apology to Nicky for even suggesting the possibility.

'He's a bright young fellow. I've been to see him. He's under no illusions about his stepmother's wayward nature. She's genuinely in mourning now but I don't doubt she'll resume her old contrariness before long.'

'You're probably right.'

'It's a marvel that you're in London. Nicky and I were only speaking of you when I saw him. We agreed we'd both be entirely happy if you chose to resolve the situation. You're a distinguished physician these days, served Dukes and Earls, not to mention the King. It'd be her third nuptials and she's past her prime – although she manages to keep her incredible looks. I mean, she's a mature woman, it would be reasonable to let her express an opinion if it pleases her. She's always favoured you. So if you were of a mind to ask for her, we wouldn't object: Nicky and I. We'd wish you well...'

My mouth had fallen open as his meaning became clear. I could imagine rascally Nicky containing his mirth while conniving in this outrageous plan but Gaston was utterly serious.

'It's only six months since Maud was widowed, isn't it? Surely it's too soon to consider her remarriage?' It

407

sounded lame but I needed to proceed with care. I wanted neither to offend, nor become trapped.

'Oh, I don't propose a precipitate marriage. Next year would be appropriate. You could take her to Calais. She'd be happy to have her own household there, hobnobbing with the Countess of Warwick, receiving the eminent visitors who call at the port. It'd be a feather in your cap too, Harry: wedding a titled lady. I don't mean you're not worthy, quite the contrary, but appearances count.'

I was incapable of responding immediately and Gaston hurried on with his desperate, persuasive arguments. 'I know I frowned on your liaison with her in the past, when she was still married to her first husband and after she was widowed when Walter died. But circumstances change. She obviously attracts you and she's always had a fancy for you, until she met Sir Nicholas – and you were married by then of course. The wheel of fortune turns and this is your chance, Harry.'

I rallied my senses and forced my vocal chords to emit measured tones. 'I'm astonished, my Lord, quite dumbfounded. It's most gracious of you and Nicky to think of me in these terms. I never considered the possibility. I will do so now but I must stress my hesitancy. If I were to follow your advice I'd be reassured to learn that Lady Maud would be willing to receive addresses from me. I don't mean the idea should be put to her straightaway, not before I've considered the matter, perhaps next spring. I'd let you know when I've pondered. You must understand how unbelievable this seems.'

Gaston de la Tour, Lord Fitzvaughan, beamed at me, completely taken in by my delaying tactics and obfuscation. 'Dear Harry, you are too modest, lacking in the self-esteem you should possess. I beg you to consider very carefully what advantages and delight this match could offer. You will win the lifelong gratitude of Nicky Chamberlayne and mine. I owe you much already, my good friend. This close relationship will seal our bond.'

I did not remind him how once he sought my death. In truth, more than fifteen years had passed since then and, as Gaston said, circumstances change. He clasped me to him as he left the friary.

'It would not be improper if you were to call at the Chamberlayne manor in Harrow before you return to Calais,' he said. 'You could give your condolences to the lady in person and Nicky would be jubilant to see you. Perhaps you can go after the Great Council meeting. Warwick won't set sail for a few days, surely?'

I hugged myself in a frenzy of mirth after he had gone. I was tempted by the thought of meeting that young scamp, Nicky, whose ingenuity was clearly at work in the scheme put to me; but that would mean encountering Lady Maud and I was not ready for that. Would I be ready at some point in the future, when I had considered the extraordinary idea further? I honestly did not know.

*****

The bell was tolling for Vespers when the message came from Thomas inviting me to dine with his family the following day at noon. The delay had occurred because they were no longer living at the house I knew near the Tower of London. That building was now merely the Chope business premises with the workshops and accommodation for a gaggle of apprentices. My letter had been taken from there to the residence Thomas and Bess now occupied, with their combined families, in a prestigious area near the eastern end of Cheapside, an easy walk from Grey Friars. Even the diligent Johnny Tate agreed we could venture there on foot.

It was a joyful occasion. Thomas and Bess were visibly happy in their second marriages, as both had been in their first, and the combined tribe of children seemed noisily content. I rejoiced for them. No one deserved good fortune more than them, after the grief of their earlier bereavements. The grand half-timbered house with its gabled upper floors projecting over the street was furnished with unostentatious good taste. The master carpenter I had known as a scruffy lad had become wealthy and Bess had learned from the ladies of distinction she served, how to order her home with grace and efficiency. Yet I could not help pondering whether they both possessed a rare talent for finding happiness. Their serene natures seemed able to prevail over adversity in a way I struggled to emulate.

After the meal we sat quaffing our wine and gossiping long into the afternoon. We exchanged news and anecdotes and I heard much of Thomas's guild and the affairs of the City Corporation. My hosts were sensitive to my own position and did not delve too deeply into my personal life, though in fact there was little to tell, and I was glad to remain reticent. On safer ground, we joined in regretting Rendell's misfortunes and bemoaning his intransigence over Judith and her son. I did not tell them of Gaston de la Tour's proposition or my response to it, because I was in confusion regarding both.

I became aware that Johnny was growing twitchy and understood he would wish to see me safely back to the friary before darkness fell on that dismal November afternoon. I had already been shown the designs and woodwork produced by the Chope boys and was amused that nine year old Rob Willoughby seemed as likely as his step-brothers to enter Thomas's trade. It was equitable to praise the achievements of their sisters so we lingered a little longer while young Anne Willoughby showed me her immaculate needlework. Margery Chope was a year older than Anne but could not match the neat stitching Bess's daughter produced. Margery had a pretty voice, however, and she sang most pleasingly while plucking the lute strings to play simple melodies.

In due course we rose to depart and as I made my way downstairs I realised the quantity of wine I had drunk was affecting the stability of my legs. I grasped the balustrade to control my wobbliness, concentrating to hide my weakness when I bade an emotional farewell to my dear friends. I was sad to leave but I did not contemplate the possibility that I might never see them again.

Across the road a gaggle of lads whooped loudly, causing my head to throb. They ran off in different directions. Johnny took my arm and steered me slowly towards Cheapside while I filled my lungs with air hoping it would clear the ache behind my brow.

Ahead of us the narrow side road joined Cheapside and as we approached we could see something had happened which caused a blockage at the junction. People were milling about and there was aggressive, angry shouting. A horse was neighing and dogs barking.

'A cart's overturned,' Johnny said. 'They're arguing about who's responsible. We'd do best to avoid getting caught up in it. There's a lane on the right which cuts round behind gardens and comes out a little further along Cheapside.'

I let him guide me onto the track skirting the backs of properties which fronted the main thoroughfare. Piles of detritus and broken earthenware impeded our progress but we wove our way through the obstacles until we were beside the garden wall of the last house adjoining the lane. Despite the stench of rotting food and ordure, I was breathing deeply and beginning to steady myself more successfully.

I heard loud voices beyond the garden wall and as we drew near a gate flew open and a maidservant ran out in the direction of Cheapside.

'Help, a physician, help!' she cried and a man's voice inside the garden echoed the call 'A physician, for mercy's sake, fetch a physician!'

Without a second thought I hurried forward, shouting. 'I'm a physician. What is it?'

Johnny reached out to restrain me but I was already at the gate. The maid turned back and the man, a respectably dressed tradesman, advanced to grasp my arm. 'Merciful heaven,' he said. 'God has sent you to our aid. Come quickly. The woman is in dire pain.'

I followed him into the house and up two flights of stairs, stumbling and panting as I went. Inside the building I could hear the sounds of a woman moaning and sometimes shrieking. I guessed she was in labour. I had no instruments with me but perhaps I could give some assistance. I called to Johnny bidding him wait for me downstairs but he may not have heard me as our footsteps thumped the treads. I did not detect a reply.

The man flung open a door on the second floor and held it while I entered. The room was dimly lit but I could distinguish the outline of a woman, clearly pregnant, flopped in a high-backed chair against the light of the window opposite. She was sobbing. I was surprised to realise there were also half a dozen men standing around the walls and another hidden in the shadows of a niche by the fireplace. This figure moved forward, pulling his gown across his chest, lifting its furred lapels.

'Come in, Doctor Somers, come in. You are very welcome.'

Gilbert Iffley's honeyed tones froze my blood as I heard the key turn in the lock of the door. I could now discern the glint of steel in the hands of the bystanders and understood I was trapped. I did not speak but peered with half-closed eyes at the wretched woman whimpering in the chair. Inevitably, I knew her.

Chapter 32

Ursula Bateby dragged herself to her feet. Her face was pale and blotched. I judged her pregnancy to be of some six or seven months' duration. She tossed her head assertively and stared at me with hostility, no longer sobbing.

Iffley held up his hand. 'No need to say anything now, my dear.' He moved away from her as she subsided onto her chair and advanced towards me.

'You're in no physical danger, Doctor Somers. We intend no violent assault against your person. We needed to compel you into our presence merely so that you can be served with this legal writ and brought to appreciate the reality of your position. It seemed more convenient to inveigle you into a friendly house rather than trouble you at the Earl of Warwick's lodgings. Come forward, Master Sutcliffe, and perform your office. Master Sutcliffe is an officer of the court, Harry. The writ he holds bears the signatures of the City justices. I'm afraid it's time you made reparations for your transgressions.'

A short, stout fellow emerged from the shadows. He wore the attire of a justice's clerk emblazoned with the City of London's coat of arms and he had an air of self-importance. Although I was well aware of Iffley's pernicious contrivances I did not doubt Master Sutcliffe was a genuine official from the Guildhall. While he cleared his throat I wondered if, despite all that had happened since, I was to be accused of causing Stephen Boice's death six years previously. It would account for Ursula'a presence.

'You are Doctor Harry Somers, physician, currently serving the Earl of Warwick?' The high-pitched voice rang out with jarring shrillness. I acknowledged that I was.

'It is my duty to serve on you this writ requiring your compliance with the order of the court within one month, under pain of imprisonment and forfeiture of your possessions if you fail to obey. These men are witnesses to the execution of my function. I am also asked to inform you that the writ carries validity throughout King Henry's realm including his lands beyond the Narrow Sea. The Earl of Warwick will receive a direction of the court to ensure you do not seek to flee from justice but comply with the court's order.'

The pompous fellow bowed and thrust the parchment roll into my hand.

'What do you mean? What am I required to do? What offence have I committed? What allegations are laid against me?'

Men gripped my arms as I grew more agitated. The official gave me a supercilious look. 'Read the writ, Doctor Somers. It tells you all you need to know. Good day.'

He bustled to the door which was opened for him. I heard his feet pattering down the stairs. The key was quickly turned in the lock again and Gilbert Iffley let out a guffaw.

'Take a moment, Harry, to study what is specified in the writ. Then we can discuss practicalities. Don't look so nervous. It's nothing like the accusations we could have laid against you. It could have been a halter round your neck on the gallows. Of course, if you decided to disobey the court, that penalty could still be exacted but I'm confident your good sense will preserve you. Here, take this stool while you read.'

I scarcely took in his words as I unrolled the parchment and sat down stiffly. I forced myself to read and reread the unspeakable terms of the court order, concentrating on the import of each phrase, comprehending what the message conveyed but bewildered by its justification. What court on earth could lawfully demand what this purported to decree? Some heinous plot lay behind it, undoubtedly devised by Baron Glasbury, but the enormity of its machinations defied credibility. My mind was working too slowly.

The document was clearly addressed to me and recited my professional qualifications and achievements with scrupulous courtesy. There could be no mistake as to the designated recipient. Then it went on, with all the force of alleged legality, to charge me with abduction of a child and to put upon me the peremptory claim which tore at the foundations of the life I had rebuilt since Ursula left me. On or before the Feast of St. Nicholas I was required to deliver the child I called my daughter, *Alys, known as Alys Somers*, to the court in London where she would *be taken into wardship pending her return to her rightful parents*.

I gazed unseeing as the words danced before my eyes. 'What nonsense is this? What possible justification is there for it? Ursula, what does it mean?'

She said not a word but her answering stare was defiant.

'Come now, Harry, it should be perfectly clear.' Baron Glasbury intervened. 'You took this child with you to Calais and she must now be returned. Of course if you challenge the rights of the plaintiffs, the lawful parents, the court will decide the matter. Don't worry: the child will be safe during any proceedings. I have volunteered to act for the court and have been granted the wardship. She will be under my tutelage until any disputed paternity is decided.'

I erupted in impotent rage. 'What do you mean? What disputed paternity? Ursula will tell you: she and I are Alys's parents. You were present, Baron, when she agreed I should care for Alys, when she returned to Gregory Bateby. When she was compelled to return to her husband who wanted nothing to do with our child.'

The ability to reason was returning with increasing sobriety but I felt a black void in the pit of my stomach sucking me down towards obliteration. 'Ursula, are you saying that now you are widowed, you want to take Alys? I would understand that even if it would tear at my heart to lose her. Why is this contemptible suggestion of disputed parentage being made?'

One of the featureless armed men by the wall moved forward, smirking. 'You will remember me, Doctor Somers. I have long despised you, even before you stole

415

the child who should rightfully be mine. Now I claim restitution.'

Jasper Coote strode to Ursula's side and lifted her chin, stroking her cheek. 'Tell him, my love, how you were less than chaste during that naughty winter after we all returned from Aquitaine and our pious King was locked away at Windsor. I had you then and so did Somers, isn't that so? But you know, don't you, which of us fathered the brat?'

Ursula lowered her eyes and breathed a sigh. 'Alas!'

'It's a pack of lies!'

I felt nauseous but I clung to the knowledge that Ursula had sworn to me on the cross she had no other lover at the time Alys was conceived. Perhaps it was foolish to place weight on her words but that oath was sacred and, surely, once we had truly cherished each other?

'If you believed you had a right, why didn't you claim the child when you and the Baron brought Gregory Bateby to my house?'

'You can answer that yourself. It's obvious. Bateby was the lady's lawful husband and I did not wish to compound his misfortunes by disclosing the full extent of his sweet wife's harlotry. I had more respect for a man who had been greatly wronged. Now everything is different and I yearn to bring my daughter into my home.'

He was smooth and insinuating and I hated him. 'What barbarity have you practised on Ursula since Gregory died to make her complicit with your lies?'

Coote gave a sneering laugh and raised Ursula to her feet, slipping one arm round her waist and placing the other hand on her swollen belly. 'She carries my spawn once more and I assure you I had no cause to force myself on her. We are lawfully man and wife – lawfully, you note, Somers, although I admit we did not delay long after Bateby's obsequies before making our vows. She is mine at bed and board, with the blessing of Holy Church, and she bends herself to my will as easily as she opens herself to my fucking. Don't you, my frisky precious? Our joyful

416

family will be complete when our elder child comes to join us and if you have any decency you will relinquish the girl at once and not compel us to squabble in the courts.'

While he was taunting.me I felt faint and clutched my knees, leaning forward. The scroll dropped to the floor and Coote picked it up, brandishing it above his head while still grasping Ursula's hand. 'See his derision for the courts of law! – hurling their order underfoot. Come, my angel, this is no place for you in company with a godless reprobate. You must rest.'

He led his wife to the door but Iffley held his arm to whisper something I could not hear. I dragged myself upright and looked directly at Ursula 'How can you treat me like this? We loved each other and were happy...'

She gave a snort of derision. 'Oh yes, for a good four weeks you pined for me, didn't you? Then you had Judith in your bed and I was forgotten. So much for your devotion!'

'That isn't true. Judith came to care for Alys, nothing more. I was devastated at losing you.'

'Whatever you say, you nit-picking bastard! You may have lived chastely under one roof for a short while. But then you married her!'

'Who told you that? I've neither married nor slept with Judith. There was salacious gossip while we were in the City but it was all lies.'

I saw the tremor pass through her body and she clutched her stomach. 'At Ludlow they told me...Gregory made fun of me...he said my fancy man had deserted me...found comfort elsewhere...'

'And you believed him? That's why you wanted to hurt me? You're prepared to perjure yourself to take Alys from me and please this vicious lout you've married? Why, in God's name, did you marry him?'

Coote drew Ursula into his arms and fondled her breasts before kissing her, to the lip-smacking enjoyment of the onlookers. 'Because I please her, Somers, and I have no other entanglement. Come, my love, you need not see

417

this relic of the past again. You've signed your deposition for the court. The child will be with us by Yuletide.'

She was shaking as she turned to me but her voice gained in truculence. 'You should not have sent for Judith. It was inevitable there would be gossip. It was inevitable people had the wrong idea – if you're to be believed. You looked out for yourself but I can see you blame me for doing the same thing. I was supposed to submit and play the victim. That was never my method, you fool. Make no mistake, Jasper and I are gloriously happy. I'm delighted to oblige him.'

'By dishonouring your daughter's birth? Tarnishing her name..?' As I stepped towards her men seized my arms again. 'How can you demean Alys by pretending she is this scum's child?'

Coote's fist thudded against my chin and the men holding me staggered with the force of the blow. For a moment my head span but I was conscious that he and his lawful wife swept from the room, laughing. I remained under restraint.

Gilbert Iffley ran his hand over his fur collar and removed an infinitesimal spot of fluff. He leered at me and chuckled. For all my hatred of Coote, I was not deluded. He was the man of violence, the hothead, the boaster, but it was the Baron who calmly schemed. Glasbury controlled the development of the plot which threatened to enmesh us all in its artfulness.

'A deeply unpleasant scene, Harry, I think we can agree. It seems the lascivious Mistress Coote was under the erroneous impression that you had hastened into matrimony soon after your sham marriage with her had been exposed. Dear me, I may have failed to enlighten her. Remiss of me. I crave your forgiveness.'

'I shall fight Coote's claim every inch of the way, to the foot of the throne if necessary.'

'That is your right, dear fellow, but first you must surrender the child by the Feast of St. Nicholas. Don't forget that. I will come in person to Calais if you wish or I'll be happy to receive you wherever you designate in England. Above all remember that if you defy the law you'll be in grave trouble and Alys will be made a ward of the court whatever happens. Do think about this seriously, Harry. It saddens me that so promising a physician as yourself should run such risks and face such ignominy. Dear me, it is a shame!'

My arms were still gripped by his minions but I was tempted to spit in his face. He was willing me to lose control and for that reason I strove to appear impassive.

At last I was led downstairs and reunited with a furious Johnny who had been gagged and locked in an outhouse for the duration of my encounter inside the building. He threatened to call the City guard and make complaint to the authorities but, in quiet desperation, I dissuaded him from action which would be both provocative and futile. Such was my abasement.

****

The Earl of Warwick listened with increasing disbelief as I described the confrontation with Gilbert Iffley and Jasper Coote. I also told him of Armstrong's contention that Coote could have killed Norbert after encountering him in Bruges. He sat with a look of concentration, obviously mulling over how to interpret the various pieces of information and the dreadful events I had experienced.

'There's a wider significance to all this, Harry. You are Iffley's immediate prey: no doubt of that. He's a fiend who likes tormenting you and, because you've stood up to him, he wants to crush your spirit totally. By comparison, Coote is just a bully-boy but no less dangerous for that. Nevertheless I suspect the Baron's aims are more complicated.'

I did not distract his thought processes when he paused and he gave an ironical smile. 'I'm to be served with a direction of the court to ensure you comply with the

419

writ and don't escape justice. That sounds very like a device to trap me as well as you. They know I have a high regard for you and will want to thwart their vicious scheme. But Iffley has been trying to usurp my place as Richard of York's closest ally so if I were to scorn the court's direction, it would suit him very well to discredit me. Maybe Norbert was tortured and killed in an attempt to extract information for the same purpose.'

The Earl shook his head as if trying to dispel the idea. He lowered his voice.

'Uncle Richard is not always as forceful in asserting himself as I would wish and that plays into Glasbury's hands. Besides, my uncle firmly upholds law and order, making the distinction between his integrity and the untrustworthiness of the King's other advisers. Although he esteems me, he wouldn't tolerate highhanded action on my part, spurning a legal order; especially when I'm already charged with breaking the law by attacking those Hanseatic ships. It's a neat contrivance.'

'I don't ask you to take any action on my behalf which would jeopardise your own position.'

'I know that, Harry, but I'm not going to throw you and little Alys to the wolves. Yet, forgive me: are you confident, about Alys I mean? Is it possible you were deceived as Coote alleges? If you have doubts, can you still bear to...?'

He faltered, awkwardness causing him to blush.

'My heart tells me Alys is mine by conception but in any case she is mine now by the bonds of love.' I feared it sounded pretentious but Warwick simply nodded and cleared his throat.

'I'll consider how best to proceed,' he said. 'As I say, it's a clever trap for me as well as you. With the Queen seeking my punishment for harassing ships on the Narrow Sea, I can ill afford York's disfavour. You say this Armstrong fellow told you the Queen has no plan to acknowledge your work as a physician before the assembled nobles?'

420

'It must have been another of Iffley's ploys – to draw me back to England. Thank God I didn't bring Alys with me.'

'Amen to that. I think you should still accompany me to Westminster tomorrow. The Baron's bound to be there and it'll show him you have my support. There's another reason too. I'll have my full entourage with me in case there's any attempt by the Queen to have me arrested. If you were to remain at Grey Friars, the friary would be poorly defended and you could be in danger. I wouldn't rule out an assault on you by Coote and his thugs, whatever Iffley intends. Coote's impetuous by all accounts and he may find the Baron's machinations too uncertain for his liking. Am I right?'

'You've got his measure exactly, my Lord. I'm grateful for your thoughtfulness.'

So it was arranged. I was not enthusiastic about visiting Westminster but Warwick's reasoning was indisputable. On our return to the friary I had given Johnny Tate a detailed explanation of the ultimatum put to me by Iffley and during the evening he slipped out to meet Andy Armstrong. I had no objection to Armstrong knowing of my predicament although I recalled he had once questioned Alys's paternity. If he, as a loyal supporter of the Queen, found it of interest to learn of the tension between Warwick and the Baron, I did not care. In the nest of vipers England's rulers inhabited, my allegiance to any of them was severely strained.

I scarcely slept that night, tormented by horrors about Alys's safety and my own, wondering if my long struggle of attrition with Iffley was finally to end with my utter defeat. If I believed Ursula genuinely longed for her daughter's return, I would be bound to seek compromise arrangements but she had given no indication that love for Alys governed her extraordinary behaviour. She had been deluded by false information regarding Judith, which accounted for her animosity towards me, but in more than two years she had never enquired as to our daughter's wellbeing. Ursula was no man's mere chattel. She had given herself to Coote willingly and she was part of the conspiracy to destroy me.

*****

Weary and lacklustre, I travelled to Westminster Palace in Warwick's barge and on arrival sought a corner in which to shelter while the Great Council conducted its business. I decided to avoid the great hall which was crowded with retainers in different liveries glaring at each other. Already, scarlet clad members of the Earl's escort were voicing bravado and contempt for his foes, matched by thinly veiled reciprocal disdain from the followers of rival nobles and the royal household. It was a tense atmosphere which would do nothing to soothe the turbulence in my mind. Johnny Tate, who had accompanied me, took up a position in the hall alongside Warwick's men but I hurried on to look for a quieter spot.

For two or three hours I sat in a corridor some distance from the great hall and the chamber in which the Council was meeting. Even there I could not escape throngs of attendants crowding onto the benches along the wall, and knots of men conversing in huddles in the middle of the passageway. The hubbub of the palace went on around us but I felt isolated and disaffected. I paid no heed to the comings and goings, locked in my misery, concluding that after a miscellany of misfortunes in my life, I had reached my nadir. Whatever had been my achievements as a physician and as a man, they seemed worthless. The obstacles I had overcome proved of no avail. If I could not now protect Alys, nothing else was of value.

Unbidden, the image of Yolande came to my mind's eye with a surge of despair. She had been my truest love but it had been ludicrous to aspire to her hand. We both reaped the inevitable consequences of our presumption and time after time thereafter I had to force aside the regrets in my heart. Nevertheless I had been granted a new and cherished love with Kate – notwithstanding the pain of her mental distress – but she was taken from me in the cruellest manner. Then, as I rebuilt my life after the horrors of Aquitaine, I sought contentment with Ursula – a situation, I now recognised, designed to ruin me.

In an effort to cast aside my hopelessness I reminded myself that friends were currently urging me to pay court to Maud Chamberlayne, once my occasional mistress, always provocative, exciting, never a probable spouse – and yet.... I managed a rueful smile. I had promised Lord Fitzvaughan that I would visit her in the next few days but this was before my encounter with Iffley and Coote. Now I wanted only to return to Calais, to hold my daughter in my arms and take her to a place of safety.

A figure in the Queen's livery stopped beside me and bent forward to whisper in my ear, breaking through my self-absorption.

'I can't linger, Doctor Somers, but if there's any trouble, get out as quickly as you can by the door at the far end of the corridor. Don't go back towards the great hall. Warwick's barge is waiting at the quay. Johnny will join you there.'

As stealthily as he had arrived, my informant was gone. He was not now masquerading as Master Andreas, Father Ambrose or André Chartier. Andy Armstrong was himself, Queen Margaret's agent, proudly flaunting his allegiance before the assembly. His message was disturbing but wholly in character. 'Don't leave yourself without an escape route', he had always advised me. Whether he expected trouble was unclear. I trusted it was simply precautionary guidance.

I think that I must have dropped into a snooze and jerked awake when I sensed movement around me. Men had shot to their feet and were pointing back along the corridor but I could not at first discern why. Then a door opened in the distance with a clatter and there was shouting. Some of the bystanders began to run towards the noise and, disregarding Armstrong's wisdom for the moment, I drew myself up and took a few steps in the same direction to find out what was happening. The commotion grew louder and must be coming from near the great hall.

I stepped to the side when I heard footsteps pounding behind me and was shocked to see menial retainers from the royal household pushing their way through the crowd. Scullions, cooks and pantrymen were distinguished by their garb and each one brandished a knife, cleaver or mallet. Whatever had occasioned this rallying of infuriated retainers, it was co-ordinated, pre-arranged. The door into an anteroom was flung open and I was appalled to identify the alarm cry issuing from within.

'A Warwick! A Warwick!'

The Earl's men were under attack. The rallying cry signalled danger and was designed to summon help. Johnny who was in attendance because of me could be caught up in the violence. My mournful self-pity was dispelled and I let myself be swept forward in the surge of men making for the scene of the disturbance. In my physician's gown I was not identifiable as part of any man's retinue and no one obstructed me.

Red-clad followers of Warwick were pouring from the great hall to join their comrades embroiled with members of the royal household and the corridor ahead of me became filled with a swirling mass of hand to hand fighters. Skilled swordsmen were pitched against hatchets, spits and gimlets as well as daggers and poniards but the disparity of weapons was not always an advantage in the mêlée. Unorthodox equipment could sometimes penetrate a man's guard with unexpected moves and no one was wearing full armour inside the palace. For the second time the cry, 'A Warwick! A Warwick!' resounded and I was aware that the din had spread to adjoining rooms.

I flattened myself against the wall, regretting that I had not taken to my heels, as Andy Armstrong advised. There was small chance of distinguishing Johnny in the whirling conflict and nothing I could do to help him. Further along the corridor a howl of derision rang out and I realised with trepidation that Earl Richard himself had answered the cry from his followers and was now beset by half a dozen attackers. His officers attempted to form a protective buffer around him but they found it difficult to hold their positions with more and more royal retainers joining the fray. The Earl and his men alike were fighting for their lives, backing along the passage.

Despite the unruly combat, Warwick and his officers gradually gained ground, passing the place where I was cowering, and I surmised they were making for the door at the far end of the corridor which Andy had pointed out to me. It must lead directly to the courtyard beside the river where the Earl's barge was waiting at the jetty. Then, to my consternation, a small group of men burst from a side room behind the Earl and hurled themselves to attack from his rear. These were no kitchen menials but trained warriors and at their head was a man I hated with a depth of hatred which frightened me. Was it possible to believe my eyes? Could adherents of the Duke of York really intend to assist the aggression of the royal servants against his nephew?

Two of Warwick's guards clearly thought so. They turned to deflect a new onslaught and all I could see was a confusion of flailing bodies, some dressed in red, others in royal livery. Jasper Coote and his men wore no badges or jerkins of common pattern and for a moment I wondered if they were trying to create a diversion, allowing Warwick to escape. It was wishful thinking. Their intervention was ambivalent in purpose, adding to the chaos, and Coote did not hesitate to wield his blade against anyone who sought to frustrate his progress.

I joined the throng moving in the wake of the battle and as a space cleared around them I saw Coote engaged in fierce swordplay with an outclassed opponent. With a gasp of dismay I recognised Johnny Tate, helmet askew and face already bloodied, staggering to remain in contention.

'No, no!' I screamed uselessly. Then, in the flash of a hateful cutting edge, I saw my friend's head cleft in two.

I rushed to where he had fallen but I knew already there was nothing I could do, nor even the possibility of offering the comfort which a priest might rightfully bring. Johnny was dead and his killer was pounding on down the corridor splattering its wooden flooring with other men's lifeblood. Stumbling, slipping, buffeted by thrashing arms and jutting feet, I hurtled in pursuit and, in a gesture of ineffectual, insane audacity I drew the little knife from my belt.

The doorway was jammed with men and I had to wait to squeeze through, pressed against a swarm of bodies. Warwick and his companions had reached the other side of the courtyard, nearing his barge, but they were still compelled to fight for every yard of ground. By contrast, Coote had withdrawn his contingent from the brawl now it was in the open. He was leaning nonchalantly against the low parapet of the river wall, smirking as he wiped his blade on a kerchief. With mad exuberance, knowing the inevitable outcome, I flung myself towards him.

He had me at his mercy in seconds. His grip crushed my wrist while my fingers still vainly clutched the knife and he forced me to the ground. The point of his sword was at my throat.

'Oh no, Somers,' he said with sardonic pleasure, 'that would be most unwise. To kill the man who has brought a court case against you – to kill him all unprovoked – how would the justices judge that transgression? Besides, I could crush you as easily as I would snap a woodlouse between my fingers. But Baron Glasbury doesn't want you ripped in two or even swinging from the gallows – at least not before he's enjoyed your utter humiliation. There's nothing I'd like better than to slit your gullet but I promised I wouldn't. He's probably watching us now from an upper window so I have to be a good boy. You must go with the Earl of Warwick back to Calais, so you can deliver my sweet little daughter into Iffley's hands. Remember?'

He directed his boot into my stomach, winding me, before he hauled me to my feet. He lowered his sword from my throat but kept it unsheathed while his other hand maintained its grip on my right wrist. My hand was becoming numb. It amused him to see how determined I was not to drop the knife which I clung on to as if it was a meaningful mark of defiance to hold it. We moved towards the steps to the jetty where Warwick and his men were mounting their final defence as they retreated on board his barge. I understood I was being offered escape but my heart was seething with hatred and my one desperate thought was to destroy.

At the top of the wooden steps the wall and the parapet ended. Beneath us was a narrow strip of water between the barge and the jetty. Lower down the steps, men were leaping the gap to gain the deck of the vessel and the ropes making it fast were already being released. I was on the riverward side and as we turned onto the descent I made myself stumble on the wet planks and my left hand instinctively reached out across my chest to clutch Coote's arm. So it must have appeared to him. He was still holding my wrist with his left hand and his sword with his right but he bent his elbow for me to grasp it and steady myself. More by fluke than skill on my part, he was off balance as I grabbed him and leaned backwards with all my strength to heave us both off the steps and into the water six feet below.

'You fool!' His furious shout resounded as he lost his footing and his sword scraped against the jetty. Perhaps it was torn from his hand.

It was the impulse of a moment but I knew what I was doing, what I intended. As we fell together and he released his hold on my wrist, I drove my knife into his belly. We splashed into the widening band of water linked by my hand upon the little weapon lodged in its odious target. He seized my shoulders, a look of astonishment on his face, and as we were sucked down his fingers clenched around my throat. It was too late for him to kill me. His strength was gone and I pushed him away. The river would complete his task. My heavy gown would drag me down as I sank and I would not resist.

Chapter 33

When I was heaved onto the deck I was half conscious. The tussle with Coote had been observed by those on board Warwick's barge as it moved away from the jetty and two oarsmen were deputed to rescue me. They were strong swimmers and although I had no wish to be saved, I was too weak to repulse their efforts. They hauled me over the gunwales and deposited me face down, pounding my back to make me expel water I had swallowed. I have a hazy recollection of the Earl kneeling by my side, speaking earnestly, but I do not know what he said.

The barge took us to the Tower of London where, I am told, we spent the night before embarking at dawn on the seagoing vessel which bore us directly to Calais. I have scant remembrance of the journey. By the time we were crossing the Narrow Sea I lay in a fever and the Earl despaired of my recovery. Flashes of consciousness came and went but my mind was obsessed with only one thought: I am a physician, committed to healing, but I have killed, gratuitously and in anger. Once in the past, I had killed in self-defence and, at his behest, I had put Stephen Boice out of his misery when his clothes were ablaze. Coote's death was different. I was a murderer.

I have no memory of arriving in Calais and being conveyed to the castle. I know I lay there impassively for several days but then slowly regained my wits and became aware of my surroundings. Judith was caring for me but at first I was too feeble to acknowledge her. I tried to shut out the external world, willing myself to lose consciousness again and this time permanently. But it was not to be. A childish command rallied my senses and brought a stream of tears pouring from my eyes.

'Da-Da, get better. Must get better. You hear?' Alys thumped the pillow by my ear.

How could I have thought of abandoning her by inviting my own death? How could I be so negligent of my duty and the claims of paternal love? Whatever retribution

I had earned, I must provide for her safety. As I wept I gave a shaky smile and she threw her arms around me.

Rendell came to see me frequently as I grew stronger and I noticed that he and Judith were no longer avoiding each other. They exchanged jocular insults and sometimes laughed together. Perversely I wondered whether this denoted that I was on my deathbed and they were humouring me but they continued affable during my recovery. Young Roger was often with his mother when she brought Alys to see me and it was from him I learned that Judith had treated me with some of my own potions.

'I told her where they were,' he said with pride 'and Rendy opened the lock on the cabinet. He's clever. Mama knew what to do with the 'gredients.'

'Your mother's a skilful nurse.'

'I'll be a doctor like you. You see.'

'I hope you will, Ro-Ro.'

Overcome with shame for disgracing my profession's integrity, I could not say more.

As soon as I was well enough to sit in a chair beside my bed I appreciated that I must confront the reality of my situation and when the Earl of Warwick visited me, I knew the moment of reckoning had come.

'The saints be praised,' he said as he assessed my condition. 'I thought we'd lost you. Can you bear to talk about what happened?' He sat on the stool beside me.

I closed my eyes. 'I know I have to.'

'You and I are in the same predicament to some degree. Warrants have been issued to arrest us both although on rather different charges.'

I opened my eyes but did not speak.

'The Queen orders my arrest on a charge of disturbing the peace at Westminster. She was miles from the palace but she accepts the mendacious account she's been given in which I was wholly to blame for the skirmish and the death and injury of several of my men. I'm also commanded to hand over the Captaincy of Calais to the youthful Duke of Somerset who's wholly inexperienced.'

'You won't?'

'Correct! I shall bide my time, build up my resources and await events in England, where Uncle Richard is edging towards decisive action. Unfortunately this is where my prospects conflict with yours, Harry.'

'The warrant for my arrest charges me with murder?'

The Earl nodded. 'I gather Baron Glasbury alleges he witnessed it all. He's convinced my uncle of York that I'm shielding a dangerous felon who must be delivered up to face justice. Duke Richard is sometimes too credulous and hesitant for my liking. If he'd had the gumption he needs, he'd be sitting on pathetic Henry's throne by now, not depending on evil-minded toadies to wheedle him into doing what they want.'

'I won't embarrass you. In a few days I'll be strong enough to travel. I'll take the next ship to England and surrender to the court. But I refuse to hand over Alys.'

'Of course not!'

'I've been thinking what to do. I shall write to the marquise de la Baule. She might agree to care for my daughter and spare you the awkwardness of Alys remaining in Calais in defiance of the court.'

The Earl stood up shaking his head. 'Oh, Harry, how can you be so obtuse? You would receive a travesty of justice if you submitted to the court. You must never go to England while this hangs over you. It's true it would help me if you moved on from Calais but you and Alys could find refuge in Duke Philip's lands. He offers you sanctuary and will welcome you as an honoured physician, just as he is harbouring the Dauphin of France from the wrath of King Charles.'

I managed a weak laugh 'The circumstances are not comparable. He won't wish to harbour a murderer.'

'You don't listen to my words. Philip knows the truth, as I do. We have both received sworn statements concerning the outrageous threat made against you in London and the events at Westminster.'

I stared at him blankly.

'Your friends have protected your interest, Harry. That poor fellow, Tate, who came to Grey Friars as your guard, signed a statement about the assault made on you in the City which he left with one Master Andrew Armstrong, servant to her Grace, Queen Margaret. Furthermore this same Master Armstrong vouches for the violence perpetrated by Jasper Coote at Westminster, not least against Tate, and the threats he uttered against your person. Believe me: Duke Philip is most anxious to claim your services for his domain.'

'I...if...can it be true?'

'While you've been languishing Robert de Beaune has been hastening back and forth to Brussels and writing to a dozen acquaintances on your behalf. The marquise de la Baule would most certainly offer a home to both Alys and yourself but your career would flourish better under the auspices of the Duke, don't you think?'

'I'm stunned. When what I've done deserves punishment... when I see myself as guilty...'

'Nonsense! By the way, my lady Countess will berate me for this but if you wish to take that comely woman with you, who cares for the children, you could do worse than make her your wife. How's that for completing the circle?'

I smiled but I did not tell him Judith was never meant for me. She had made her choice long ago.

*****

A week later our preparations were almost complete. Alys was sad to be leaving Ro-Ro and her other friends but, as always, excited by the prospect of a journey. I was slowly accustoming myself to the reprieve I had not sought and did not believe I merited, but I was content to repay Fortune's bounty by dedicating the rest of my life to serving as a physician wherever I could. I wrote letters to my friends in England: to Thomas Chope, Gaston de la

432

Tour, Nicky Chamberlayne and even to Lady Maud Chamberlayne whom I had been unable to visit. I wrote also to my steward, Perkin, at Worthwaite, and signed papers putting the manor in trust for Alys. Circumstances compelled me to cut ties with my native land and to embark on a new and uncertain future. So be it.

But Fate had not yet finished with me. In the last few days before our departure, three extraordinary occurrences took place, each one enough to make my head reel. Taken together, a priest might deem them tokens of God's mercy, of forgiveness for an unworthy sinner, the cauterisation and healing which Father Wilfred had mentioned years before. I lacked his faithful certainty but nonetheless gave thanks for undeserved blessings.

The first cause of joy was news I had longed to hear. Judith seemed almost coy when she told me the Countess of Warwick had given her permission to accompany Alys and leave Calais. I had hesitated to ask her and started to protest but Judith shook her head.

'There's one condition I make, Doctor Somers, a quite unreasonable condition in my opinion.'

'Of course you'll bring Ro-Ro,' I said, trying to anticipate what concerned her.

She gave a most un-Judith-like skittish grin. 'Not just Ro-Ro,' she said. 'This fellow wants to travel with us and settle where you do. And I...well, we...'

Rendell stuck his head round the door, from where he had obviously been eavesdropping. 'What the tongue-tied woman means is I might find something more worthwhile to do wherever you go, not just being a deputy gatekeeper at the castle here. I fancy running a hostelry. I reckon I could do that. And if I was settled, perhaps in Brussels, she and I might... maybe... life's too short to throw away...you nearly died...'

'Who's tongue-tied now?

Judith put on a superior tone of voice but her next words were smothered as I embraced them both.

The following morning a ship came in from Sandwich and it brought me the first of the two letters I received that week. I stared at the writing in terror, tempted to burn it without breaking the seal, but in the end I prised it apart with trembling fingers. I read and reread its message with humility.

What devilish fate brought us together, Harry Somers, to cause each other so much pain? Our liaison was cursed and now you have made me a widow. I have left Ludlow and am once more in service with Duchess Cecily who is kind. In time I may learn to forgive you and I pray that you will forgive me for the harm I did to you. One deception I do regret. It was Jasper's jealous whim which drove me to it. Alys is yours, without any doubt. Love her well. Your erstwhile paramour, Ursula Coote.

A court of law might still choose to probe the matter with prurient precision but she had moderated the threat to Alys's safety. More especially, she had removed the possibility of doubts invading my mind on some future occasion, during the dark hours of the night when sleep will not come and wayward fancies are most dangerous. She had given me an inestimable gift and I was grateful.

The second letter was earth-shaking in its effect. On the very morning we left for Brussels it was brought to me and I shook uncontrollably when I saw the crest and the superscription in that elegant curving script. It was brief but it contained a multitude of meanings. I felt dizzy, the implausible words dancing in front of my eyes, but the message was unambiguous.

I have heard of your cruel misfortunes. They have broken open the false barriers we erected between us. If you still share the devotion which I have nurtured through all the vicissitudes of my constrained life, as I believe you do, I bid you come. All necessary arrangements for your journey from Brussels can be made with Duke Philip's consent. I claim the right, at last, to become your wife.

434

Epilogue 1464

Nothing is constant in the world of great men and their rivalries. During the six years since I left Calais, both France and England have new sovereign lords. The former Dauphin Louis acceded on the death of the father he detested and he seems likely to prove himself a shrewder and more ruthless ruler than King Charles. Certainly he shows no gratitude to Philip of Burgundy, who generously sheltered him from paternal wrath for several years. Philip himself is ageing and often at odds with his heir, the Count of Charolais, an altogether more headstrong fellow than his wise and cultured father. One cannot look for stability anywhere in the affairs of men.

Across the Narrow Sea there have been half a dozen bloody battles and, as I long feared, the throne was taken by force from pious, feeble Henry, who now lodges under guard inside the Tower of London. Queen Margaret has sought military help from the Scots and French but these interventions have failed. She and her son are currently impoverished dependents of her grudging kinsman, King Louis, maintaining the pretence of an exiled court beside the River Meuse. Yet the English crown does not adorn the head of Henry's long-term antagonist, Richard of York. The Duke died in battle even as the fortunes of his faction began to change. Young Edward, his eldest son, was crowned three years ago and is by all accounts an engaging and popular monarch – albeit self-willed in personal matters, no man's puppet.

The fortunes of the Earl of Warwick have soared, at least until recently. Victories on the battlefield and in diplomatic dealings brought him a position of pre-eminence in England. I am honoured to retain his friendship and receive occasional letters from him although we have not met since he visited Duke Philip in Brussels some months after I fled there. Sadly, I detect in his latest missive a hint of truculence which may signal new troubles to come. He naturally assumed the role of principal adviser to King Edward and was charged with arranging a marriage between the English King and French Louis's sister-in-law, Bona of Savoy. Only later did he discover that Edward had secretly married an English widow, a lady of worthy but not royal lineage. Warwick always valued integrity and he will not have taken kindly to this deceitfulness. I fear he will view Edward's action as a slight to his own honour and that could be dangerous.

Behind the scenes in the royal entourage a malevolent influence continues to hold sway. Acting for his own advantage and perverse amusement, Gilbert Iffley, Baron Glasbury, manoeuvres his way through shifting alliances, exerting his evil power over those unfortunates who cross him. I have escaped but others doubtless suffer his inventive spitefulness and controlling villainy. He has the young King's ear and prospers. There is no sign he will receive his just deserts in a court of law. If he is ever to incur the reckoning he deserves, it will not be on this earth.

I bless Heaven that I was saved from humiliation and death at Iffley's contrivance: and for a great deal more than that. When I left Calais it was not merely to escape horrors but to enter a new and rewarding life which I had never dared envisage. I have lost much that I valued and melancholy still sweeps over me when I contemplate those losses but what I have gained is of incalculable worth. I am free to pursue my profession as a physician and I have a treasured home and family in the place I regard as my sanctuary, the little town of Tournus beside the River Saône in the southern reaches of the Duchy of Burgundy.

Ever since those early days of exile spent in Brussels, I have been called on to attend Duke Philip from time to time. This involves a long journey from where I now live but only once has it proved a matter of urgency involving an exhausting and furious ride. On that occasion the Duke was seriously ill and doctors were summoned from far and wide, scurrying from all directions to treat him. I was distressed to see how weak he had become and feared the frequent bleeding which other physicians prescribed was worsening his condition. When the Duke of Milan's personal physician, who happened to be visiting Brussels, expressed the same opinion we were able to prevail over our medical brethren and curtail the bloodletting. Within days our patient rose from his sickbed. Doctor Luca Alessandro nodded sagely when he learned that I had studied at the University of Padua, saying it accounted for my enlightened views, which coincided with his.

I am summoned, when needed, to the ducal palace in Dijon to attend leading members of the Duke's Burgundian Council and other prominent citizens. More regularly, every fortnight, I make the shorter journey to the remarkable hospice of the Hôtel-Dieu at Beaune, where I am consulted by the nuns of the nursing order who care for the sick and impoverished folk residing there. Robert de Beaune is rightly proud of the hospital in the town of his birth and it delights me to assist its work. He travels less than he did and I see him often, an esteemed friend who has done so much for me.

Most of my old friends are across the Narrow Sea, far away, and I hear their news only intermittently. I miss them. So far as I know all are well. One irrepressible visitor does appear at our gate sometimes, usually without warning. Andy Armstrong continues to be involved in clandestine diplomacy of infinite complexity involving relations between rulers and their rivals in England, Scotland, France, Brittany and Burgundy. I do not enquire into his operations but welcome his company and the information he brings. I no longer share the confidences of great men but Andy's gossip about their deviousness is always of interest.

To my great joy my closest friends are resident in Dijon and their incessant witty bickering is evidence of their happiness. Somehow the miseries I suffered on that final visit to London and my subsequent near brush with death impelled Rendell to recognise the precariousness of this life in a way his own adversities had not. While I was still in Brussels he took Judith to wife and adopted Roger of Ravensmoor as his son. Later they came in my tracks to Burgundy and set up a fine and bustling hostelry in Dijon, where Rendell relishes his role as innkeeper. I fancy it is Judith who keeps the books and manages their supplies but she also assists the midwives in the town and is widely respected. They have produced two infants of their own and Rendell is proving an excessively proud father. Next year, when he will be twelve years of age, Roger, or Ro-Ro as we still call him, will join my household to begin the training which I hope will lead him to become a dedicated physician. His consistency of purpose is unusual in a young lad and it is a marvel that he shows none of his monstrous birth-father's characteristics.

I can allow myself a moment to celebrate completion of the task I embraced when I came to Tournus. In spare hours between consultations, travelling and family activities, I have finalised six volumes which record the events of my life in the preceding years. During those years I encountered leading figures at King Henry's court and tangled with affairs of state but my experiences brought me anguish as well as pleasure. They are behind me, together with the investigations I was asked to conduct which often caused me heartache. That life has ended. The world of my recuperated heart is unshakeably anchored here.

From my study I look out across the majestic River Saône which rises and falls dramatically with the changing seasons. When walking in our grounds, if I turn my head, I can see the distant bell-tower of the Abbey of Saint-Philibert, gleaming white and pink in the dying sunlight. Tournus is renowned for the Abbey which houses men of learned distinction, including the Infirmarian, a skilled herbalist who has become my close friend. The town beyond the Abbey, a buoyant small community, houses a hotchpotch of trades. It is home to moneyed merchants and humble fishermen, stonemasons, vintners, butchers and draymen. It boasts a clutch of churches, elegant timbered houses and noisome tanneries which discharge colourful effluent into a small watercourse. It is my privilege to offer physic to all degrees of men and women living here and it gratifies me that I have won their esteem in my own right, not simply as *'le mari de la comtesse'*.

Seventeen years ago I rashly aspired to become the husband of a widowed French countess but it could not be and we were compelled to part. Nothing less than a miracle of fortune gave us a second chance, in middle age, and five years have now passed since Duke Philip witnessed and saluted our union in Brussels. We have twelve lost years for which to compensate but together we look to the future.

Our beloved daughters eyed each other with suspicion when they first met but soon became devoted companions. Guigone is reserved and ladylike and I trust will be a good influence on my flamboyant little hoyden, Alys, but their joint mischief suggests the effect may be otherwise. They are a delight to a doting father.

Heaven has bestowed a further immense but unlooked-for blessing on us, for we had supposed Yolande was past child-bearing. Yet within a year of our marriage she was delivered of our sturdy rascal of a son, now four years old. We named him Jean-Pierre in honour of the two friends I lost to violent deaths at Westminster and Bordeaux. I should like him to develop Piers Ford's humanity and gentleness but when I watch him brandishing a toy sword and spearing a beetle with a pin, I fear he may possess more of Johnny's martial spirit than a philosopher's cast of mind.

Time resolves many things and little stays the same. There will be changes to come, challenges to be faced, griefs and happiness to be experienced. Now, however, I know there is one constant in my life. Its power endured despite the years in which I drove away remembrance of its unparalleled glory, believing its promise could never be fulfilled. I know now that our mutual passion will sustain us through good and ill, for in its late-achieved maturity it blossoms anew. Beauty and learning, common sense and imagination: it is a combination to which I respond with a depth of emotion unequalled in my lifetime. I have found the only destiny I crave but which I cannot believe I deserve. A tinge of shame and remorse remains with me, for failing to uphold the principles of my profession that bitter day at Westminster. Yet the benison of love I have received since then convinces me that my guilt must have been assuaged by the touch of the seraph's coal.

I turn the illuminated pages of the exquisite manuscript we are studying together and my fingers quiver as they brush against hers. She looks up, smooths the parchment, pauses in reading the Latin words aloud, and smiles at me: my countess, my wife, my inspiration, my enduring love, my teasing companion, my reason for sustaining hope – Yolande.

Historical Note

Most characters in *The Seraph's Coal* are fictional but recorded historical events provide the background to the story. These events include: Lord Talbot's military expedition to Aquitaine, culminating in the disastrous battle of Castillon; the mysterious but devastating illness of King Henry which confounded his physicians; the antagonism between Richard, Duke of York and Edmund, Duke of Somerset leading to the battle of St. Albans in 1455; and the growing importance of Richard Neville, Earl of Warwick, together with his activities at sea as Captain of Calais and the violence at Westminster when he attended a meeting of the Great Council in November1458. Also recorded are the glories of the court of Philip, Duke of Burgundy, known subsequently as Philip the Good.

As indicated in the Epilogue significant changes had occurred in both England and France by 1464, the point at which the Harry Somers series comes to an end. More changes were to come. In England the later phases of what later became known as *The Wars of the Roses* found the Earl of Warwick taking up arms against King Edward. Across the Narrow Sea the heirs of King Charles of France and Duke Philip of Burgundy proved to be very different men from their fathers and the relative stability previously established did not continue.

Many characters (both factual and fictional) in *The Seraph's Coal* appear in the earlier Harry Somers Books which are: *The Devil's Stain, The Angel's Wing, The Cherub's Smile, The Martyr's Scorn* and *The Prophet's Grief.*

The author

Pamela Gordon Hoad read history at Oxford University, and the subject has remained of abiding interest to her. She has also always loved the drama and romance of characters and plot in historical fiction. She tried her hand at such creative writing over the years but, due to the exigencies of her career, she mainly wrote committee reports, policy papers and occasional articles for publication. After working for the Greater London Council, she held the positions of Chief Executive of the London Borough of Hackney and then Chief Executive of the City of Sheffield. Later she held public appointments, including that of Electoral Commissioner when the Electoral Commission was established.

Since 'retiring', Pamela has lived in the Scottish Borders and been active in the voluntary sector. For three years she chaired the national board of Relationships Scotland and she continues her involvement with several voluntary sector organisations. Importantly, during the last few years, she has also been able to pursue her aim of writing historical fiction. *The Seraph's Coal* is the sixth and final book in the series about the young physician and investigator, Harry Somers. She intends to continue writing historical fiction but her immediate plans concern different protagonists and will be set in a different period.

Pamela has also published short stories with historical backgrounds in anthologies published by the Borders Writers Forum (which she chaired for three years). On behalf of the Dorothy Dunnett Society, she has acted as a judge in the annual historical short story competition which the Society runs in conjunction with the Historical Writers Association.

Books in the Harry Somers series of mystery-thrillers by Pamela Gordon Hoad

The Devil's Stain: From humble beginnings, Harry Somers becomes a physician but he is led into rash entanglements and troubling affairs of state including a treasonable plot. '*A tense fifteenth century English murder mystery, full of twists and turns*'.
ISBN 978-1-909411-46-3

The Angel's Wing: Harry seeks refuge in the northern Italian states. He studies at the University of Padua but his investigative skills are called on and they involve him in dangerous intrigue. '*The action and drama of the first book continue in this compelling sequel as Harry gains a reputation for his medical skills whilst becoming embroiled in the politics of fifteenth century Italy...*'
ISBN 978-1-909411-49-4

The Cherub's Smile: Harry returns from exile and takes service with the Duke of Suffolk who is negotiating a truce between England and France. He soon finds he must juggle his own allegiances. '*I felt I was there, caught up in the turmoil of fifteenth century England, and the characters were totally "real" – as well as intrigue, there is friendship, passion and disappointment... and pathos.*'
ISBN 978-1-909411-52-4

The Martyr's Scorn: Harry faces personal distress and is menaced by old enemies as rivalries between nobles at the English court intensify. '*A thrilling read. I could not put the book down. With so many strong characters, a real sense of the period and twists and turns that almost take your breath away, the writer has truly excelled herself with this latest addition to the Harry Somers series. Outstandingly good.*'
ISBN 978-1-912513-61-1

The Prophet's Grief: Harry becomes involved in Jack Cade's uprising against corruption and injustice but his conflicting loyalties are difficult to reconcile as violence erupts. *'It plunges the reader into a medieval world of rivalry and conflict, remarkably brought to life by a truly gifted writer and packed with giddying twists and turns...'*
ISBN 978-1-912513–62-8

Silver Quill Publishing

Silver Quill is an exciting new publishing group producing fabulous books for children, teens, young adults – and not so young adults. Take a look at our website, meet our authorsand browse through the titles we have to offer. Every book is a thrill with Silver Quill.

www.silverquillpublishing.com

Lightning Source UK Ltd.
Milton Keynes UK
UKHW021616040322
399574UK00008B/1923